THE MOTIVATED ANTICS SERIES

TANGLED SPLINTERS

T. L. HILL

Copyright © 2025 by T. L. Hill

ISBNs: 979-8-9990475-1-9 (paperback)
        979-8-9990475-0-2 (hardback)
        979-8-9990475-2-6 (ebook)

All rights reserved.

No part of this publication may be reproduced, distributed, or transmitted in any form or by any means, including photocopying, recording, or other electronic or mechanical methods, without the prior written permission of the publisher, except as permitted by U.S. copyright law. For permission requests, contact t.l.hillauthor@gmail.com.

The story, all names, characters, and incidents portrayed in this production are fictitious. No identification with actual persons (living or deceased), places, buildings, and products is intended or should be inferred.

Cover design by cheriefox.com
Editing by Cindy Draughon and Taylor Golden
Formatting by BookLayoutPro.com

"To those who had others believe in them before they believed in themselves.

Oh yeah—

And to those who love a killer story."

CONTENTS

Preface vii
Trigger Warnings viii
Acknowledgments ix
Prologue 1
The Luck of the Draw 4
Ask Stupid Questions, Get Stupid Answers 9
Spunky Is As Spunky Does 17
Gather the Team 24
Lack of Sleep Leads to Exhaustion 29
Chaos Ensues 35
On Edge 41
Play With Fire, Get Burned 49
Don't Wear Big Shoes If They Don't Fit 55
Trust is a Thin Paper 59
Waffles and Warnings 63
Grill Talk 66
Copy Cat? 69
Class Dismissed, Permanently? 73
Projected Truths 82
Ashes and Unanswered Questions 92
Sick Shade of Red 97
Friction and Fire 99
Burning Clues 104
Shattered Remnants 111
Still Waters, Hidden Tides 115
Crumbs of Control 119
Memories and Mayhem 126
Dead Wrong 134
Splintered Logic 140
Racing Silence 143
Fatal Whisper 145
Playback & Payback 148

Secrets, Syrup, and Suspicion	152
Headlights and Hindsight	157
Damn Woman	163
Prey and Play	169
The Heat is On	172
Cooked Up Shenanigans	177
A Recipe for Disaster	182
Karma's Trigger	186
Grease Stains and Grief	187
Law and Disorder	193
Do Not Cross	201
Fractured Composure	205
The Road Less Traveled, Literally	211
Sliced By Betrayal	214
Ink and Scars	220
Badged and Cornered	225
The Game Unfolds	228
Grave Consequences	233
Vile Thoughts	236
Threads of Fate	238
Triggering Tension	243
A Life in His Grip	247
Quiet After the Storm	249
Comatose Confessions	252
A Father's Measure	254
Caught in the Crossfire	257
Alcohol and Very Bad Decisions	260
Checkmate?	263
Shooting Blanks	266
The Final Dose	268
Finger-Snapping Moments	271
Breaking Point	273
It Takes Two to Tango	276
Jackassery at Its Finest	279
Paranoia Persona	282
Vested Interest	287
Riddle Me Stone	289
Where the Pages Lead	294
Brushed by Madness	297
Red Head's Silent Fury	299
Swerving Destiny	303
Fragile Calm	305
Rosa, Oh, Rosa	308
About the Author	311

PREFACE

Every crime leaves behind splinters—fragments of truth buried beneath lies, scattered pieces waiting to be uncovered. Some are easy to find, sharp enough to draw blood with a single touch on a piece of bark. Others are tangled in shadows, hidden in the spaces between right and wrong.

Tangled Splinters is more than just a crime thriller—it's a story of pursuit, of justice blurred by personal demons, and of a team trying to hold together while everything around them threatens to break apart. It's about the weight of the past and how it shapes the choices we make.

At its heart, this book is an exploration of trust—who we trust, why we trust, and what happens when that trust is tested. As Rosa and her team are pulled deeper into the web of crime surrounding The Wood Riddle Killer, the answers they seek may come at a cost they're not ready to pay. And lurking in the background is someone who knows exactly how to play the game.

This journey has been filled with late nights, relentless rewrites, and a love for storytelling that refuses to let go. If you enjoy investigations, tangled relationships, and the kind of suspense that keeps you second-guessing, then welcome—you're exactly where you need to be.

Because the truth is rarely simple. And in *Tangled Splinters*, it's never safe.

TRIGGER WARNINGS

This book contains themes and content that some readers may find distressing, including:

- Violence, murder, and crime-related content
- Discussions of death, trauma, and grief
- Childhood trauma and its psychological impact
- Mentions of abuse and psychological manipulation
- Strong language
- Depictions of drug use and drug-related investigations
- Gun violence
- Sexual content
- Alcohol use
- Suicide and suicidal thoughts
- Depictions of car accidents and related injuries

This is meant for readers aged 18 and over. Reader discretion is advised.

ACKNOWLEDGMENTS

To those who always believed in me—long before I even believed in myself—thank you. Your faith has been my anchor, especially in the moments when I doubted everything. You reminded me that dreams were worth pursuing, no matter how distant they seemed.

To my love—you have never once stood in the way of my dreams. Instead, you have been my biggest cheerleader, patiently supporting me through every challenge. Your quiet belief in me, even when I faltered, has made all the difference. You have shown me what true partnership looks like, and I am endlessly grateful for your encouragement.

To my family, who has been my foundation through every chapter of my life—thank you for always being there, whether near or far. Your love and support have shaped who I am, and I couldn't have made it this far without you.

Mama, thank you for never letting me throw away a single childhood notebook filled with scribbles, abandoned plots, and dreams I thought were failures. You saw something in me before I knew how to see it myself, and your constant belief in my potential gave me the strength to keep going when I felt lost.

Daddy and Tracey, thank you for always encouraging me to travel, to chase after the impossible, and to turn my dreams into something real. Your willingness to share your wisdom, life experiences, and guidance have paved the way for me to follow my heart, even when the path wasn't clear.

To my sisters, for loving me, no matter how many times I disappeared into a book or a story of my own making. Your unwavering support, even when you didn't fully understand my obsession with words, has meant the world. You are my safe place, my reminder that family is always there to catch me when I fall.

To my friends, for listening—endlessly, patiently—as I rambled on about books, characters, and plots that wouldn't let me go. You let me be obsessive, and for that, I owe you. Whether it was late-night phone calls or spontaneous brainstorming sessions, you made me feel heard, and that alone is a gift beyond measure.

To my incredible Bookstagram and BookTok community—you are my people. The endless book discussions, the shared excitement over characters, the late-night reading sprints, and the unwavering support mean more than I can say. Thank you for making the book world feel like home. You inspire me daily, and your enthusiasm keeps me going through the tough writing days.

Finally, to my young fans—my students—your energy, your excitement, and your belief in me remind me every day why I do this. You are the future of stories, and I hope you never stop believing in your own narratives, no matter how impossible they may seem. You are my motivation to keep writing and dreaming.

This book exists because of all of you. Thank you for being my support, my motivation, and my inspiration.

PROLOGUE

IN A QUIET, overlooked corner of a small forgotten national park, far from the buzz of the modern world, a young couple made their way up a winding mountain trail, their steps crunching softly against the dirt and leaves. The area was famous for its untouched, breathtaking waterfalls. During the hiking season, visitors often veered off the marked paths, chasing the promise of hidden beauty.

The park rangers were usually vigilant, quick to redirect wandering hikers, but today, they were too engrossed in an animated debate over the best local barbecue joint. Between bites of their sandwiches and playful arguments about smoky flavors versus tangy sauces, they didn't notice the couple stepping off the trail.

"Do you really think we'll find a waterfall out here?" she asked, her voice carrying a mix of curiosity and doubt. She laced her fingers through his. Their hands fit together easily after a year of familiarity.

"We might! The best views aren't always on the main trail." He grinned and nudged her playfully. "Besides, you always say you want more adventure."

She smiled, bumping her shoulder against his. "Yeah, but I meant, like, wine tasting in the city. Not wandering into a horror movie."

As they walked, the forest thickened, the sunlight filtering through the canopy in golden fragments. The damp air clung to her skin, carrying the scent of moss and rich earth. It was peaceful, but something about the area made her stomach tighten. Her gaze flicked to the shadows between the trees. A shape stirred high in the branches—an owl, she thought. Its wide, unblinking eyes tracked them in silence.

She swallowed, her grip on his hand tightening. "Maybe we should turn back," she murmured, more to herself than to him. But he was already leading the way, flashing her a teasing smile over his shoulder.

"Relax. What's the worst that could happen?"

She rolled her eyes but followed, the distant sound of rushing water pulling them deeper into the woods. The air felt heavier now, the quiet pressing in around them. She stopped abruptly as the unease in her chest grew stronger.

He felt a tug at his hand and chuckled. "Aw, come on, babe, don't start the ghost stuff on me again." He wrapped an arm around her waist, pulling her close. "Last time, we bailed, but this time, I say we go for the full experience." His hands slid lower, fingers grazing her backside. "Ever had sex out in the woods? In broad daylight?"

She snorted and shook her head, but stepped closer and pressed a slow kiss to the side of his jaw. Then, with a smirk, she let her focus dip lower before meeting his eyes again. "I bet we can get away with it… if you're as fast as you usually are."

He groaned. She laughed as he pulled her even closer. "Wow, just stab me right in the heart, why don't you?" he said, clutching his chest and staggering back in mock pain before sinking into a dramatic crouch. But as he did, his eyes caught something a little ways off. His expression shifted—playfulness fading into confusion, then a wary focus.

"Stay back!" he commanded, his voice suddenly firm.

His fingers trembled as he pulled out his phone and dialed, then backed them both away while keeping his eyes locked on what was on the ground. His breath hitched when something crept to the edge of his vision. A shadow? A trick of the light? Or was someone out here?

His chest tightened as he strained to make sense of it. "Stay back," he said again as she shifted closer to him. She froze in response to the unease in his voice.

There was something—he just couldn't tell what. He inched a little closer. Then a chill crept up his spine and his stomach lurched when he realized what he was looking at. The naked and dismembered remains of a man spread neatly on a black blanket, each part arranged with grim precision to replicate a human figure.

The air suddenly carried a faint, sour musk—a blend of sweat, decay, and an overwhelming bitterness of pine that churned his stomach even more. The man's face was beyond recognition, deep gashes running down his cheeks and across the empty socket where his left eye had been. The skin around it appeared bloated and discolored, as if the torment had ended only recently.

The longer he stared, the more his imagination turned against him. The severed fingers looked almost poised to move—frozen in a grim stillness that made his skin crawl. The only thing on the body was a piece of tree bark lodged against the man's chest like a cruel, unnatural ornament. Its edges were jagged, as if freshly stripped away, its grooves etched in fine detail. On its surface was a message written in blood, the letters twisted and uneven—deliberate, yet oddly contorted. The message was as chilling as it was cryptic, the bark itself a disturbing signature.

But worse than that, was the sheer, gut-wrenching horror of seeing a huge, mangey scavenger—something between a possum and a wild rodent—gnawing away at the decomposing flesh.

THE LUCK OF THE DRAW

THE OWL CLOCK'S blood-red eyes glared at her—unblinking, unsettling—as Rosa Ryker bolted for the front door. Her boots thudded against the wooden floor, the sound echoing through the too-quiet house. She was late—of course she was—but something about this morning felt off. Maybe it was the way the clock seemed to watch her. Or the faint creak of the staircase *after* she'd already come down.

One thing was certain: it was her first day as a detective, and she was running late.

A promotion at thirty wasn't exactly what her dad had pictured for her. He was proud, of course—happy, even—but maybe not thrilled about the job itself. Still, Rosa couldn't shake the feeling that this was the freedom she needed—the kind that might finally push her toward better opportunities.

And deep down, she couldn't ignore the sense that this was her calling. Even if not everyone believed she deserved it.

The department had been buzzing after her promotion, and not in a good way. Some of the older detectives barely concealed their irritation, side-eyeing her during briefings or making offhand comments about how "kids these days" were getting handed promotions too fast. Others were more direct—she'd overheard enough muttered remarks about how she hadn't earned her stripes yet.

It didn't matter that she'd cracked the smaller cases they had ignored. To them, she was still just a patrol officer playing detective. And then there were the nastier whispers—the ones suggesting she must have connections, or slept her way up the ranks. Her? A small-town woman with average looks?

They could be brutal—but more than anything, they were lazy. Most were content to let real cases slip through the cracks if it meant staying put in this small town. Rosa wasn't like them.

And the worst part?

There were moments when she wondered if they were right about getting the promotion handed to her.

"Get it together, Rosa," she muttered, snatching her keys from the table. Her heart pounded, but not just from rushing. She wasn't sure if it was anxiety, or just the weight of the title finally catching up with her, but she had an uncomfortable feeling crawling up her spine.

On the way to the front door, her boot caught the edge of the rug and sent her sprawling forward until her forehead smacked against the glass door with a resounding thud.

She groaned, lying there for a moment, the cold glass pressed against her cheek. Her chubby gray and white tabby settled down beside her looking amused, his tail flicking back and forth, teasing her with every movement as if silently mocking her.

"Perfect. Great start to the day."

She opened her eyes and casually glanced out the glass door to see if anyone had witnessed the unfortunate catastrophe, though she knew no one would—she lived in the middle of nowhere. After confirming that no one was watching her crisis, she lay there for a moment to decompress, then let out a long sigh.

"Are you planning on taking a nap there, or are you actually going to work?" a familiar voice teased.

Rosa's head jerked up to see her father standing on the porch, arms crossed, a smirk tugging at his lips. He wore his usual baseball cap and an old shirt covered in paint stains, dressed for a day of working around the house. Before standing up to greet her father, she gave the cat a pat on the head. He responded with a loving swat.

"Oh, come on, in the most embarrassing situations you just happen to appear. Seriously? Don't you have anything better to do, Dad? I have my own house now and although it needs some tender love and care, that doesn't mean you need to come over and fix everything all at once."

She managed to stand up, reaching for the handle of the door to let herself out. She stood next to him. "Anyway, I am so late, and this won't look good on the first day."

"No, it won't. But you didn't exactly plan ahead, did you? Reading through the Code of Ethics a third time the night before your first day on the job?" He shook his head with a playful grin. "Get moving. You bought a house that needs work, so I'll fix it for you—because obviously, I'm a good dad." He patted her shoulder, his voice light but with a hint of finality.

"Okay, okay, yeah, yeah, just make sure to lock up before you leave. Last time, you left the house unlocked and open. Sir Louie almost ran out." When she looked at the clock, her heart beat a little faster. "Don't forget, and hurry up, okay?" She rolled her eyes but was already hurrying down the porch steps, cutting across the corner of the flower bed to get to her truck faster.

The road to the Chattingsburg Police Department was a winding, backcountry stretch that most city folk avoided. Too rural. Too slow. Too many cows. They preferred to take the highway and bypass it entirely.

Rosa, on the other hand, always took the scenic route.

Living on the outskirts of town hadn't been her first choice. The house had felt too far removed from the pulse of Chattingsburg, but it was still better than the tiny town of barely 5,000 people, where everyone knew everyone else's secrets. The drive from her house to Chattingsburg took forty-five minutes each way. Nobody would ever mistake the area for suburbia. No big city energy here, but it suited her well enough.

Driving here felt grounding, even when it meant winding through unpaved roads that ran parallel to dusty fields and dark woods. It wasn't just about getting from point A to point B. It was her therapy.

Especially when she had the right playlist.

This morning, an upbeat, motivational rhythm pulsed through her speakers, giving her energy to take on whatever the day had in store. But still, as the trees blurred past her, the gnawing sense of doubt remained in the back of her mind.

How had she managed to land the only detective position after just two years as a patrol officer? Was it luck? Or something more?

A book, its pages dog-eared from countless readings, slid off the passenger seat and landed on the floor amongst the empty water bottles bouncing around with each pothole she hit.

The thoughts still nagged at her. What if she messed up? What if they were right, and she'd just gotten lucky? What if she really wasn't meant for this role?

The doubts clung to her, no matter how fast she drove. It was almost like the faster she went, the louder they became.

***

When Rosa arrived, she slid into the only empty parking space. She spotted Chief of Police Reese Chadford outside, admiring the new sign with a pride that seemed far too enthusiastic. Recent budget upgrades had funded renovations to the old department, and the chief was in an unusually giddy mood. Rosa figured it might work in her favor—but she wasn't about to test her luck.

With his broad shoulders, square jaw, and dark eyes that rarely gave away his thoughts, Chadford was a commanding presence, even when he was silent. A born leader. His salt-and-pepper hair made him seem more seasoned than his forty-six years on the job.

Some said he was unreadable, but Rosa had worked under him long enough to know that wasn't entirely true. He simply spoke only when it mattered—and when he did, people listened. He was tough, but fair, and Rosa knew for sure he didn't believe in cutting corners.

She tried not to slam the car door too loudly, but it still echoed across the lot. The piercing sound caught the chief's attention immediately—there was no one else around to distract him.

"I take it your morning hasn't been a grand one?" Chadford's skeptical gaze followed her as she approached.

"Actually, I tripped—it was a whole thing. But I'm good to go, Chief. Apologies—it won't happen again," she said, grimacing slightly.

Chadford gave her a once-over, a small smirk tugging at the corner of his lips. "You've worked here long enough to know that first impressions don't mean much in this building. It's what you do after them that counts."

Rosa nodded, shifting on her feet as she tried to gauge his tone. It wasn't warm, but she hadn't been expecting praise. Still, there was something about the way Chadford looked at her—measured, almost suspicious—that made her stomach tighten. She couldn't tell if he was questioning her readiness or just caught off guard by how quickly things had moved. Either way, she knew better than to expect favoritism.

She'd applied for the position fair and square, but she also knew respect wasn't handed over with a new badge. Some officers still saw her as just a patrol cop. Even with the title, she'd have to prove herself every damn day—whether she liked it or not.

"Unfortunately, you'll be stuck with paperwork for the next few days. It'll help you adjust to your new role—and serve as a slight punishment," Chadford said with a sigh, shaking his head in mock disappointment.

Rosa nodded, keeping her expression neutral. The first day in her new role as a detective had already started off on the wrong foot, but she couldn't afford to let that set the tone for the rest of her career.

"Understood, sir. Desk duty it is," she replied, forcing a smile.

Chadford gave a curt nod, still eyeing the sign. "I expect you to keep that in mind, Detective Ryker. Your performance reflects the department as a whole."

Rosa's lips tightened at the reminder. He wasn't wrong, but she knew that proving herself wasn't just about doing the job—it was about navigating a department where not everyone was ready to see her in this new role. Not yet, anyway. Still, she liked the way detective sounded next to her name, so she walked in with her head high and her confidence intact.

ASK STUPID QUESTIONS, GET STUPID ANSWERS

SURROUNDING THE GHASTLY scene, many officers kept their distance, hesitant to get too close. A rookie turned pale and vomited, his hands trembling, much like the man who discovered the scene. He stood farther from the crime now, his breath hitching as he whispered details of the horrifying find to an officer asking him questions. The woman beside him gripped his hand, offering much-needed comfort, her fingers pressed tightly against his skin as if grounding him to reality.

At the sound of footsteps, officers straightened up, adjusted their uniforms, and snapped their focus toward the noise. FBI Special Agent Simon Pikes retrieved a pack of cigarettes and leaned against a tree. He slipped one between his lips and lit it, shielding the flame with his hand, which made the soft light illuminate his stern expression. He took a long drag, the smoke curling upward as he exhaled slowly, his eyes scanning the chaos before him.

The woods were a mess—officers scurried to secure the scene, their boots crunching on twigs and leaves, while forensics meticulously dusted for fingerprints. Simon stood still, comfortably letting his instincts settle into place. What grated on him, though, was the nervous energy. They were a group of amateurs—too terrified to speak up and more concerned with impressing their superior than doing the job right. Once again, it fell on him to take charge. He couldn't help but question why he had to work with anyone at all. In that moment, his demeanor spoke volumes—he didn't want anyone talking to him, consumed by the thoughts of the case before him.

His gut told him this was the next murder in the more than ten-year trail he'd been following. Cold and calculated, he moved forward with a precision honed through years of experience. The blood and gore didn't faze him—he'd grown immune long ago, and the weight of emotion had been stripped away, leaving only a laser focus. Professionalism radiated from every movement, his steps steady, his expression unreadable. The stakes were higher than ever now, and beneath the surface, tension thrummed like a live wire. Every detail mattered, every clue just as important as the next. For him, the case wasn't just about justice—it was personal, and the price of failure was more than just another forgotten case.

As he walked toward the scene, lost in thought, something caught his attention—a piece of bark, with a cryptic riddle scrawled in the victim's blood. Another familiar puzzle, another enigma in a seemingly endless search. Steeling himself, he stepped closer, determined to uncover its meaning.

"Sir, Special Agent Pikes, uh..., welcome." The nervous rookie stammered, stepping forward to shake his hand.

Simon barely glanced at him as he walked straight past, leaving the rookie flushed with embarrassment. He didn't have time for his fan club to bother him at the moment. Nearby, a couple of other rookies snickered quietly, their eyes flicking toward the mortified rookie.

Ignoring the glances, Simon slipped on a pair of nitrile gloves and crouched beside the victim, his focus fixed on the riddle written in blood. With measured precision, he removed the pin fastening the bark to the torso and stood, holding the piece in his gloved hands. It took only a moment for the heavy, unsettling words to register.

"I watch from above, where the wise often dwell,
A place of learning still, where stories they tell.

The keeper of secrets, where lives are bought and sold,

Unveil its truth, or the next will unfold."

His eyes narrowed as he studied the words. They seemed straightforward, almost too deliberate, which made him instinctively doubt their surface meaning. "Above" could mean a physical vantage point—a tree, a tower—or something metaphorical, like a higher authority or knowledge.

"Any ideas?" the forensic specialist asked, wrapping up the futile task of dusting for fingerprints. "Not that it's a surprise—there's never anything to find. But you already know that." He straightened up, giving Simon a pointed look. "This body's been preserved for a couple of years, too. Same M.O." His tone carried grim certainty. "I'd bet my job it's him again."

Simon took a moment to absorb the scene, his attention sweeping over the body. It was carefully arranged, the positioning almost ritualistic—and the signature piece of bark, as always, had been meticulously staged. Even the victim's hands, clenched into tight fists, looked unnaturally posed, as if the killer had intentionally left his mark. "Betting anything at this point seems pointless," Simon muttered, removing one of his gloves and pulling out his phone. His thumb hovered over the image of the riddle from two years ago—the one etched into the bark on the last victim. He studied the photo again, as though it might finally reveal a deeper truth.

"I dwell where silence and thought intertwine,

A haven for minds, where the opinionated dine.

Seek the keeper who guards what's unknown,

A clue to the next is by wisdom alone."

Simon's jaw tightened as he compared the riddles. The forensic specialist walked over to the body, taking initial measurements, a necessary step before the medical examiner arrived. Simon noted how the victim's dismembered body appeared unnervingly preserved, suggesting the killer's methodical approach to maintaining the body's condition. There was no blood pooling around the victim—only on the piece of bark where the riddle was scrawled, a stark contrast to the careful arrangement of the remains. Even the absence of blood always seemed deliberate. Simon's eyes briefly flicked to the specialist's scuff-free boots, and he wondered how many other cases had left them both standing in scenes like this, filled with just as much coldness.

"Again with the ideology of wisdom," Simon muttered, his voice laced with frustration. "He thinks he's wiser than everyone else—as most killers do—but it's all a game to taunt us because he knows we don't have shit to go on. It's not just the riddle," Simon said aloud, pacing. "The timing, the location—everything about this feels calculated. It's like he's leading us to something bigger. The trafficking case in D.C. was the same: encrypted messages, calculated moves. This killer's not working alone, and this isn't just murder."

He paced around the area where the victim was found, his eyes scanning for any overlooked evidence—a footprint, a broken branch, anything. The overhead lights from the FBI's mobile forensic unit cast long shadows over the scene, and Simon's eyes fell on the tire tracks leading out from the woods. They were too clean. The narrow grooves and precise treads suggested a motorcycle or bike, yet there was no sign of skidding, no erratic patterns—just a smooth exit. It was as if the killer had ensured nothing was left behind to trace the make or model.

Simon's voice sharpened. "That last riddle—'where the opinionated dine'—at first, I thought it might be symbolic. But now?" He glanced toward where the rangers stood. "I think it was a dig—a jab at the park rangers running their mouths instead of watching the grounds. 'Opinionated dine'? That's exactly what I saw—three guys arguing over damn barbecue sauce while the killer probably walked right by."

He shot a pointed glare toward the rangers, who shifted uncomfortably under the weight of his words. Simon didn't tolerate negligence—not because he was a rule-follower, but because this mattered. Because this was personal.

The rangers exchanged uneasy glances, defeat across their faces.

Simon's attention returned to the riddle.

"'The keeper who guards what's unknown'..." he murmured, pacing. "Could be a name, a title, or just metaphor. Park name, museum, librarian, hell—even a professor. The wording's too vague, and that's what pisses me off the most."

He held up the bark again, fingers tightening around the blood-streaked wood. "But this new line—'a place of learning'—that has to mean something. School, university... He's giving us something to follow. If we can figure it out."

The forensic specialist, a lanky man with red hair and a somber tone, spoke up cautiously. "He always brings up secrets in his riddles. Maybe this one's tied to something in his past? Still, that's just a guess."

Simon didn't respond. He was already two steps ahead, mind spinning, trying to pull something concrete from metaphor and blood.

He turned abruptly, his voice sharp. "What's the closest city to this park?"

The park rangers flinched at the sound, one of them already fumbling for an answer.

As Simon approached them, the rangers grew nervous, fidgeting, eyes flicking between his face and the ground, unable to hold his piercing glare. The female ranger's eyes lingered a moment too long, her expression shifting as she noticed the jagged scar running from the left side of his jaw down to his neck—a wound from a past mistake long since closed, but never fully healed. It was an ugly reminder of the cost of doing his job.

Simon caught her staring and smirked, leaning toward her. "Something on my face?" he teased, giving her a quick wink.

Her cheeks flushed a deep red and she quickly glanced away, her nervousness palpable. The shift in atmosphere was immediate—her discomfort, his light teasing, and the momentary break in tension. But the undercurrent of serious business never wavered. There was still work to be done.

"Let me look it up," the male ranger said, pulling out his phone. The action drew an irritated tut from Simon, causing the ranger to flinch. "Um… Chattingsburg," the ranger stammered. "It's about an hour northeast."

Simon removed his nitrile gloves, sealing the evidence in a plastic bag and handing it off to the forensic specialist trailing him. "Small town? Real tucked away?"

"Yes, I believe so," the ranger confirmed with a quick nod.

The forensic specialist chuckled, nudging Simon lightly in the side. "I don't even want to know how you already know that. It's not like you're from this neck of the woods."

Simon ignored the attempt at humor, his focus unwavering. Letting out a short breath, he said, "I need to make a call." He stepped away, giving the riddle one last glance. "Finish processing the scene, but this could tie into Kershaw's drug trafficking case back in D.C. Get Chattingsburg's UC involved immediately. The answer to this isn't here anyway—it's always in the riddle."

"Um, Special Agent, sir, we were wondering if we could tag along," two rookies stammered, sidling up to Simon with an anxious look. They couldn't have been older than twenty, their youthful faces alight with almost childlike awe.

Simon didn't need to look at them to know the type—they practically oozed hero worship. The way their wide-eyed gazes lingered on him made his skin crawl. Like he was the police force's divine savior. He hated these kinds of cops the most: the doting ones who revered him like some untouchable legend instead of focusing on their damn jobs.

"What could you bring to the table by tagging along?" Simon's voice was cutting, almost dismissive, his attention fixed elsewhere as if their presence barely registered.

The rookies froze, clearly taken aback by Simon's cutthroat response. They'd heard rumors of his solitary work style, but also stories of him mentoring new recruits. The reality didn't quite match the whispers—maybe they'd caught him on a bad day. Or not.

"Here," Simon said abruptly, pulling the evidence bag from the forensic specialist's hand beside him. "Take a look at this riddle. Got any ideas? You've got two minutes of my time before I call it wasted."

He held the plastic bag out, the blood-stained bark taunting them with its cryptic words. The rookies hesitated, then leaned in to read, their brows furrowed in concentration. Silence hung thick with uncertainty.

After an agonizing pause they exchanged glances and wordlessly handed the bag back to Simon. Their downcast expressions might have earned sympathy from someone else, but Simon didn't feel generous.

Noticing the irritation building on his face, the rookies exchanged a brief, sheepish glance before retreating, careful not to provoke him further, until they disappeared from view.

"You are the reason many rookies quit. You do realize that, don't you?" the forensic specialist said, taking the bag from Simon's grip. His tone was firm but not unkind. "You can't do this alone, even if you think you can. If you could, you'd have caught him by now."

He gave Simon's shoulder a soft pat—an unspoken gesture of encouragement—before heading toward the van holding the remains of the eighteenth victim.

Simon walked back toward his car after leaving the woods, the path leading him past the park entrance and toward the gravel parking lot off the road near the entrance cabin. As he neared the cabin, he startled the female park ranger who was heading inside. Her eyes flicked to the scar running down his jaw, and a flicker of unease crossed her face. Simon couldn't resist a sly grin but didn't linger on her discomfort. Reaching the hood of his car, he leaned against it, pulling out a cigarette and lighting it with practiced ease.

He exhaled a plume of smoke, his thoughts churning as he stared into the distance. A "place of learning" could mean anything—a library, a school, a university, or even a bookstore. Without more leads, he was grasping at straws. One thing was clear: this killer was always ahead of them, and the window to catch him before the next murder was closing fast.

The victim they'd just found appeared to have been preserved for two years—at least, according to early forensic estimates—which aligned gruesomely with the killer's timeline. And now, the eighteenth victim loomed like a shadow, a promise of more to come. The pattern was as clear as it had been from the beginning, and Simon clung to the hope they wouldn't have to wait another two years to find the next body. This time, he had to get ahead of it.

The killer had to have left breadcrumbs—more to follow than what met the eye. Somewhere nearby was the next step in the twisted game.

After a few puffs of his cigarette, rumors from D.C. about a high-profile drug or human trafficking ring came to Simon's mind. Clues pointed to a nearby suburban city—a place possibly tied both to the riddle and to another tangled web of crimes. He felt drawn to go there—not just for the case, but for a friend he could always count on, another special agent who might just need his help.

Simon slipped through the car door, tossing his pack of cigarettes and lighter onto the passenger seat. He pressed down on the gas pedal, adjusting the radio to his liking before speeding off toward his next destination.

SPUNKY IS AS SPUNKY DOES

ROSA BALANCED AN armful of coffees and a couple of café boxes, the strain making her shoulders ache. She was strong—she had to be—but this felt excessive. All because she'd shown up late to work.

"First it was paperwork, and now this," she muttered under her breath, throwing in a few choice obscenities she figured no one would hear.

"Well, maybe that colorful language of yours is part of the problem," a voice drawled, followed by a low chuckle.

Startled, Rosa froze and her eyes widened as she realized she wasn't alone. A man leaned casually against a Chevrolet Bel Air, its body painted a rich, dark turquoise—the exact shade she secretly loved. Her view of him was partly obscured by the precarious load in her arms, but she caught a glimpse of his boots: scuffed leather, sturdy, and well-worn. The coffee cups in her arms wobbled clumsily, and she gritted her teeth, adjusting her stance to steady them. *Great. Now I have an audience for my misery.*

"And what's it to you?" she snapped, tilting her head just enough to glare at the boots, the kind someone who lived on their feet would wear.

The man chuckled again, a low, warm sound that somehow managed to irritate her even more. "Just an observation. Didn't mean to offend."

"You didn't," she retorted, taking a step forward.

He straightened up, and as he did, Rosa caught a glimpse of his face. Distinct features, dark stubble along his jaw, and a smirk that could have been charming if she weren't already so annoyed. His jet-black hair was disheveled but somehow looked intentional, and a pair of aviators rested in the pocket of his leather jacket. She couldn't take her eyes off the jagged scar running along the left side of his jaw. It was raw, demanding her attention in a way she didn't fully understand. Realizing she had been staring too long, she shifted her gaze to the warm tan of his skin, stretched taut over a lean, muscular frame.

"Noted," he said, raising his hands in mock surrender, disregarding the stare she gave him. "You need a hand with all that, or do you prefer juggling acts?"

"I've got it," Rosa snapped, though her arms were already screaming in protest. She pushed past him, determined to ignore the way his laughter followed her as she made her way to the Chevrolet Silverado parked in front of his car.

Just as she was reaching for the handle of the truck with an elbow, she heard his voice again. "You know, I didn't mean to upset you. I just couldn't help but notice someone carrying half the contents of a cafe. Figured you had a story."

Rosa hesitated, turning just enough to meet his gaze. His eyes were a piercing brown that matched her favorite sweet tea, and despite herself, she softened—just a little.

"Yeah," she said, her tone losing some of its edge. "The story is: I was late to work, and this is my boss's idea of a consequence."

He smiled, not unkindly. "Fair enough. For what it's worth, you're handling it like a pro. No spills yet."

"Yet," she muttered, finally getting the truck door open. She put the contents down in the passenger seat and glanced back to see him watching her with that same easy smile—though there seemed to be a faint glare there for no apparent reason. He didn't appear to be as warm hearted as he let on.

She shut the door, then made her way to the driver's side, wondering why the encounter stayed in her mind longer than it should.

Then it hit her—she'd been given a time limit to get back to the office, and she was over it. Of course she was.

***

"Yeah, Kershaw, meet me at the address I texted you," Simon said into the phone, standing in front of a house and surveying it with a critical eye. He ended the call and glanced around.

It was one of those classic Southern homes, the kind that looked like it had stood there for over a century—weathered but proud. A wide wraparound porch stretched along the front, its white railings chipped and sun-bleached. Wind chimes tinkled lazily in the breeze, swaying near a hanging fern that had seen better days. The lawn was unkempt but not wild, like someone had once cared but hadn't kept up. Towering oaks lined the property, their thick branches casting patchy shadows across the yard, and between the dense trees, you could barely glimpse the neighboring houses. The whole place felt isolated—quiet in a way that was foreign to Simon after years of city noise.

It was almost too quiet.

Simon adjusted the cuffs of his sleeves and scanned the street again. The neighborhood felt still, almost paused in time. He'd overheard Kershaw—the agent in charge of the drug trafficking case—mention the town mayor, Thompson, and planned to question him. Maybe it was nothing more than a lead connected to the drug investigation. Still, Simon wasn't in the business of ignoring possibilities—especially not out here, where everyone seemed to know each other and secrets had more room to grow. With the killer sending mixed signals, he couldn't afford to overlook anything.

With his mind made up—he was used to doing things alone—he stepped up onto the creaking wooden porch, knocked firmly on the red door, and pressed the old-fashioned doorbell. A faint chime echoed from somewhere deep inside the house. Simon took a step back, waiting, scanning again.

A voice called out instead—from across the street.

"Oh, hello there! Mayor Thompson won't be in for another month," said a man pushing a wheelchair down the sloped driveway of the house opposite. "He's off campaigning… something or another. I don't much care for politics, though."

Simon turned to see him clearly. The man was younger, mid-thirties maybe, with short black hair slightly tousled by the breeze. His frame was lean, casual in a faded gray t-shirt and jeans, a slight limp to his left leg as he walked. He paused what he was doing to call over, one hand still resting on the back of the wheelchair, which had rolled gently toward the open door of his car.

There was a quiet warmth to him, something inviting without trying. Not the nosey type—just the kind who'd speak up if something seemed out of place. A small gesture, but enough for Simon to take note.

"Name's Ropa," the man said with a polite nod. "Been here a long time. It's usually pretty quiet—so it's always a little surprising when someone new shows up." He gave a friendly chuckle, adjusting the wheelchair beside him. "You just passing through, or looking for someone?"

Simon offered a tight nod, eyes still flicking between the porch and the street. "Just checking on something."

Ropa shrugged. "Alright then. Let me know if you need anything."

He turned back to his task, steadying the wheelchair and gently folding it into the backseat of his car with practiced care.

Simon lingered a moment longer, watching as the man opened the car door for an elderly woman. She moved slowly, unsteady on her feet, but the man seemed genuinely happy to help. There weren't many people like that in the world.

As the van began pulling out of the driveway, the man rolled down the window and gave Simon a friendly wave.

"Quick question," Simon called out. "Which direction is the police station?"

"You *do* have that officer aura," Ropa chuckled again. "Just head down to the downtown area—it'll be just to the left of the church."

"Thanks," Simon said simply, offering a slight nod as Ropa grinned and drove off.

***

Rosa stood just outside the police station's front door, arms overloaded with two drink trays, a pastry box stacked on top, and several paper bags balanced precariously between her fingers. She had insisted she could handle it all, but now the weight was starting to drag.

Behind her, voices drifted through the morning air. She recognized the sharp, familiar tone of the man from the café—calm but edged with irritation—as well as a second voice, lighter but tense.

"You can't just leave that there," the second voice said.

The first voice snapped back, "With all the trash you've seen in your line of work, I'd think you'd be less uptight."

There was a brief silence, then the first voice muttered, "One day the world's going to collapse under its own filth, and you'll regret adding to it."

Rosa swallowed hard and focused on the door handle just ahead. Almost there.

Her toe caught on the edge of the concrete step.

The world tipped.

The trays wobbled.

Coffee spilled. Pastries scattered. Bags tumbled free.

Rosa stumbled forward, crashing face-first through the door and into the station lobby.

She froze for a moment, stunned by the fall and the heat of coffee soaking her shirt.

Then laughter erupted around her.

"Hey, you okay?" a voice asked.

Rosa turned her head, wincing as she pushed herself up. A man with curly red hair knelt beside her, rubber gloves stretched over his hands. Kind eyes met hers — he looked more like someone who worked in a lab than a police station, but there was warmth there.

"Now this is a crime scene," came a dry, familiar voice behind her.

Rosa's eyes darted toward the sound—the same voice from the café, steady and sarcastic, stepping through the mess.

She couldn't see the man's face clearly, but the sharp boots and the way he moved were unmistakable.

Her shirt was drenched in coffee, her hair plastered to her face. Despite herself, the dimple in her left cheek surfaced in a sheepish smile.

"Clumsy Detective strikes again," one of the older officers called out.

"Clean-up on aisle three!" another added, laughter rippling through the room.

Rosa's jaw tightened. The bitterness in the room was obvious—they resented that she'd been promoted over them.

"Detective, what the hell is all this noise?" Chief Chadford's voice boomed.

Rosa's pulse quickened as she took the offered hand and stood, trying to brush off the worst of the mess.

"Do you know who this is?" Chadford hissed, nodding toward the man with the familiar voice.

Rosa blinked. She didn't.

"We sent Detective Rosa to bring breakfast," Chadford said stiffly. "Wasn't expecting you all so early."

"One of our guys is on his way," the man answered flatly.

"That's him! That's the—" one officer began, but a sharp elbow stopped him.

"Everyone, this is FBI Supervisory Special Agent Simon Pikes and FBI Forensic Examiner William Gilbert," Chadford announced firmly. "They're here to assist with a drug trafficking case potentially connected to a serial murder."

Whispers filled the room.

Rosa's heart pounded.

"Detective, your appearance isn't exactly acceptable," Chadford muttered lowly.

Grateful he hadn't said it louder, she nodded and made for the locker room.

She found a baggy black T-shirt in the lost-and-found and pulled it over her head.

The door swung open.

"Hey, you're the talk of the station—I can't get over it!"

Rosa spun.

"Raya!"

They embraced tightly.

"Slow down, tiger."

"Three months undercover? Are you okay?" Rosa asked, scanning Raya's bruises and stitches.

"Nothing I can't handle," Raya shrugged.

Then she smirked. "But did you see that guy out there? Those jeans were doing him justice."

Rosa groaned. "Of course you noticed that first."

"What can I say? I'm definitely an ass woman—so sue me." Raya stuck her tongue out, and the two of them burst into laughter, the tension easing for a moment.

Rosa had known Raya since they were three years old. They had been neighbors for years until Raya's family moved to the next town over. While Rosa had spent the last few years picking up the pieces of her life after losing her mother as a teenager, Raya had been training to become an undercover cop, finally achieving her dream. Rosa couldn't be prouder of her. Through the toughest moments in her life, Raya had been a constant presence—one of the few people Rosa could always count on.

As Rosa eyed the freshly braided twists in Raya's hair—dyed a deep purple that was subtle enough to slip past the chief's strict protocol while still maintaining her signature color—she caught something else. A far-off look in her best friend's eyes, as if her thoughts were miles away.

Before Rosa could ask, the locker room door creaked open again.

"I don't mean to cut this reunion short, but Chadford needs you both in the meeting room."

GATHER THE TEAM

"WHERE IS THE tech guy when you need him?" Chadford projected his nervous energy as a joke, but the FBI agent leaning against the office table didn't look pleased. The room was tense, especially with Simon's piercing glare. He definitely took his job seriously.

As Simon drilled holes into the back of Chadford's head, he noticed Rosa entering with a woman at her side. She seemed more composed than before, likely because of her companion. They seemed to radiate a different energy from the rest of the room. Simon clicked his tongue, breaking the anxious silence just as the chief misplugged a cable, delaying the monitor setup.

Simon took another look at Rosa. She had changed into a baggy men's T-shirt, attempting to cinch it with a hair tie. The oversized fit swallowed her frame, but her confidence remained. He forced himself to shift focus.

"Yes!" Chadford muttered as the screen flickered on. "I'd like to disclose that we weren't exactly sure when you'd be making an appearance, Agent Pikes…" His words were tinged with an attempt to salvage his own image. He was right, though—no word had been given, but Simon had kept it that way for a reason. If anyone here was involved in the drug-related incidents, he needed to keep them on edge.

He eyed the people in the room, mentally noting their strengths, flaws, and tells—already forming judgments he wouldn't speak aloud.

"Welcome back, UC Raya!" Several of them stood to greet her warmly.

"Now, now, let's settle down," Chadford cut in. "There are a few tests you'll all need to pass before joining the task force. Apparently, they do things differently up there in D.C."

Simon could sense the irritation simmering beneath the chief's forced politeness—small-town police chiefs had a tendency to feel threatened by sudden visits from federal agents. But Simon didn't care; this was his operation, his task force. He had the backing of the higher-ups, and that gave him the authority to do things his way. He knew he needed the right people, and while the whole process felt slightly off, he was willing to give everyone a fair shot. Still, his attention had already settled on two of the female detectives in particular. He just needed to see how they handled the pressure.

As the officers took their seats—only twelve of them—Simon remained standing. "Before we get into the details of the case, I've got a riddle for you. Solve it, and you're in. Fail, and you're out. No room for amateurs." He glanced at William, who nervously adjusted his rubber gloves.

"I'm not sure why we have to go through this," an officer muttered, clearly irritated.

"Just humor him," another one nudged. "He's one of the best." She batted her eyelashes at Simon, but he didn't even glance in her direction, making her shrink back into her seat, embarrassed.

"There hasn't been this much excitement since the incident fifteen years ago," one of the older officers said loudly, his tone almost boasting. But another shot him a nudge in the ribs, signaling him to shut up. Both officers glanced at Rosa, their gazes lingering a moment too long. Rosa pretended not to notice, showing no reaction to their comment.

Simon caught the glance between the officers and the subtle tension in their voices, but he didn't recognize the incident they were talking about. Apparently, it had once made national headlines—buzzing across news tickers and flooding front pages—but whatever it was, the case had long since gone cold. The culprit was never caught. In a town this small, the whole thing had probably faded from memory, buried beneath time and everyday life.

"Agent Gilbert, why don't you give them the riddle?" Chief Chadford interjected, clearly uncomfortable with the side comments.

William cleared his throat, a little awkward. "Uh… 'I show you who did it, but you can't touch or see me directly. What am I?'"

Confusion spread across the room. Rosa and Raya exchanged glances before quickly scribbling their answers—a shadow or a reflection. One by one, the people in the room called out their guesses aloud: "Ghost," "Shadow," "Reflection," "Spirit," "Mirror."

William listened carefully, then nodded toward Simon. "Alright. Those who answered 'shadow' or 'reflection,' stay. Everyone else, please leave the room."

Simon's tone was curt and final, making the rejection sting. A handful of officers gathered their things and filed out. Rosa and Raya exchanged a quick high-five under the table, relief in their eyes.

"Don't get too excited. There's another." Simon projected a new riddle onto the monitor, written on a piece of bark. The smeared red lettering made Rosa shiver.

William read aloud, "I dwell where silence and thought intertwine, A haven for minds, where the opinionated dine. Seek the keeper who guards what's unknown, A clue to the next is by wisdom alone."

Raya frowned. Simon figured it was probably because riddles weren't her thing—Rosa was probably the one who thrived under this kind of pressure.

He glanced at her now, watching closely to see how she'd piece it together.

Rosa leaned forward, her tone slow and deliberate as she addressed the group.

"'Dwell where silence and thought intertwine…' That suggests a quiet place, meant for reflection and focus."

She paused, considering. "'A haven for minds, where the opinionated dine.' Not food—but ideas. Somewhere people go to feed their minds, maybe even debate. A place where strong views are shared, shaped, or challenged."

"'Seek the keeper who guards what's unknown.' That sounds like someone who oversees knowledge—probably a librarian."

She nodded slightly, her voice steady now. "Altogether, the riddle points to a library. A quiet place of reflection and learning, where people come with questions, beliefs, and opinions—hungry for understanding."

A beat of silence passed before a few heads nodded, clearly impressed.

Simon noted the shift—the officers who had been skeptical before now gave Rosa a bit more respect. He could see some grudging acknowledgment in their eyes, though a few still whispered doubts.

Rosa glanced at Simon, her expression steady. She had spoken clearly, with confidence, and the room had listened.

"There were only seven of you who guessed the first one correctly, and only Rosa seemed to piece together the second," William whispered.

Before Simon could dismiss the other officers who hadn't solved the second riddle, a booming voice shattered the tension. "What did I miss?!"

Several officers jumped. A newcomer laughed, clearly pleased with the reaction. Simon took in his tall, muscular frame. He looked like he'd stepped out of a fitness magazine—neatly shaved afro, strong jawline, and dark skin that accentuated his sharp features. His broad chest and well-defined arms were visible even through his shirt.

Raya sucked in a breath. Rosa nudged her a little too hard, making her fall out of her chair. Scrambling back up, Raya turned away, flustered.

"You can ogle all you want, ladies, I don't mind," he teased, winking before greeting Simon with a firm handshake and a quick hug.

"Wow, Agent Kershaw Blackwood, what an entrance!" William grinned.

Chadford remained stiff, clearly unimpressed by the interruption. Simon could see the discomfort in the man's posture—uneasy with outsiders. Oddly enough, Simon found he didn't mind it. Maybe he even enjoyed it a little.

"You may leave," Simon said, addressing the other officers in the room. "Rosa, Raya, stay. Raya, you have information on this drug case that may be connected to our investigation, and Rosa, you answered the riddles."

The officers leaving the room continued to eye the agents invading their police station with a mix of curiosity and disdain.

"Looks like we have our team," said Kershaw, the tall guy, as he scanned the group. "If he hasn't kicked you out, you're in. Welcome." He extended a hand to the closest person standing near the door. Rosa shook it firmly, but when he reached Raya, she held on a little too long.

"I get why Raya's here—her undercover work's been invaluable," Chadford said, his eyes shifting. "But Rosa? She's barely gotten her detective badge. Talented with riddles, sure—but green."

Simon noticed the heat rising to Rosa's face, though she said nothing, her jaw tight. The insult stung—more than she let on—but she kept it carefully hidden. He knew she wasn't here to impress Chadford. She was here to prove herself to him... and maybe even more so, to herself.

Simon didn't miss the tension. He arched a brow, almost amused, like he was waiting for her to snap.

"I'll be the judge of that," he said coolly. Then, without looking at Chadford, he added, "We'll need the room for a preliminary briefing. Just the candidates for now."

Chadford exhaled roughly and left, closing the door with a heavy thud behind him. Rosa let a small smile slip—her dimple showing.

LACK OF SLEEP LEADS TO EXHAUSTION

WHEN SHE GOT home, Rosa tossed the keys toward the side table near the door, but they slid across the surface and hit the ground with a loud thud. The gray and white tabby scurried away, sensing she wasn't in the mood to pay him any attention.

She headed to the kitchen, where the new marble countertops her dad must have installed today gleamed under the dim light. Normally, she would have stopped to admire them, but tonight her focus was elsewhere.

Opening the pantry cabinet near the fridge, she grabbed the bag of Meow Mix dry food. "Must be nice being a cat. Everything's always handed to you," Rosa muttered, pouring food into the bowl.

Sir Louie, weaving between her legs, darted straight to the now-filled dish. Rosa gave him a quick pat on the head before turning away, the events of the day replaying in her mind.

The images of the victims wouldn't leave Rosa's mind. Every time a new detail came up, it dragged those faces back to the surface. They'd spent four exhausting hours listening and dissecting the case, and still, she couldn't wrap her head around it all.

Simon had kept things from them—important things. She hadn't missed the way only the men who'd arrived with him seemed fully in the loop, their shared history pulling a quiet wall between them and everyone else. It was hard to ignore, harder not to take personally.

The rest of the team showed their usual quirks, subtle glances and unspoken tensions circling the room. Rosa stayed quiet. So did

Raya. Neither of them voiced what they were thinking. Not there. Not yet.

A serial killer's backyard stretched across the entire country, making it nearly impossible to pin him down. Rosa set her glass of water on the table with a loud thud, startling her chomping feline. Sir Louie shot her a glare, clearly irritated by the interruption to his dinner. She grabbed her work-issued laptop and muttered,

"These murders started years ago, and still no one has caught him?"

She shook her head in disgust. The thought of so many victims' families never finding closure made her stomach churn. The men had been killed violently—dismembered in ways she couldn't even begin to understand. The women, though... theirs seemed slower, strangled to death with deliberate force. Rosa didn't know which was worse. Both felt like different versions of the same nightmare.

And then there was the bark—smeared with blood, a cruel riddle left behind like a signature.

It seemed so unreal. After over thirty years, he was still free. It didn't make sense. But what was even more disturbing was the control he must have had—planning each murder so precisely, spacing them out with just enough time between each to make it feel like the case had almost faded from memory. It gave him the freedom to keep planning. He saved the bodies for that long? She couldn't fathom how he managed to maintain that level of control, the patience required to let time work in his favor. Was it all part of his strategy—to throw off the agents chasing him, to make it seem like they were dealing with something beyond their understanding? She flipped through the case notes again, her eyes glued to the details of how he had kept the bodies for two years—preserving them in ways that seemed to defy logic.

Simon's voice echoed in her mind from their earlier briefing. He'd been the one to point out how the gaps between the murders seemed to follow a predictable pattern—every two years. It was almost like clockwork, but then, Simon added, "It's a strategy. The killer is making sure everyone has forgotten about him. Time works for him. We've had cold cases, disappearances, dead ends... but not a single lead that ties it all together. We're still running blind, but his patience is a huge part of his game. It's psychological warfare."

Rosa's eyes scanned the pages, the dim light of the kitchen casting long shadows over the computer screen. She could almost smell the sterile, biting scent of chemicals as she read the details. The notes were disturbingly precise. He had perfected the process of preservation—injecting the bodies with a mix of formaldehyde and other fluids to halt decomposition. The skin, once pale and lifeless, now retained a sickly, almost unnatural hue, the kind of color that stood still between death and life. She could almost feel the stiffness that would have settled into the bones.

The killer's method was disturbingly precise—each body carefully wrapped in plastic, sealed to keep any trace of air away from the lifeless flesh. Rosa's stomach tightened as she imagined the bodies, stored in some hidden, dark room, each one kept in a state of eerie perfection. It was as if he wanted them to remain frozen in time, to maintain that moment of stillness, so the case never fully faded from memory. The killer's control over his grisly trophies was unnerving, his patience extending far beyond what any normal person could comprehend.

She scrolled down the page, her stomach kept tightening with each word. As she read the details of how carefully the bodies had been kept, she imagined him checking on them regularly—making sure the chemicals hadn't begun to wear off. She could almost hear the soft, unsettling sound of him adjusting the wrapping, the faint crackle of plastic as he inspected each embalmed corpse, like a collector scrutinizing rare artifacts. The bodies weren't just victims—they were his personal testament, frozen in a grotesque display. A twisted reminder of his power over life and death.

Simon had added, "It's not just about the kills for him. He's collecting. Each body is a marker, a part of his legacy. That's why we have so little to go on. He's making sure we never catch up."

And it seemed these agents were also branching out to Chattingsburg on a drug trafficking case. Unlikely as it was that the two were connected, Rosa's first day ended with a headache she couldn't shake. What troubled her the most, though, was the fact that the lead on the case would be none other than the workaholic Special Agent Simon Pikes. Without realizing it, she opened a private browser and searched his name. The accolades that appeared made it seem like he was much older than thirty-four. *What's your story?*

She shook her head, then pulled up the private files from the investigation again, focusing on an image of a victim. The victim's name was Lisa Carter, the first known victim of the "Wood Riddle Killer"—the name the police force had given him.

There was evidence of sexual abuse, but it didn't align with this specific killer's methods. The DNA matched that of a man who would later become the killer's second victim. Lisa Carter had blonde hair and was a well-known prostitute in the area. The tear stains on her cheeks, captured by the forensic photographer's lens, revealed a painful reality, while the bruises around her neck told a grim story of struggle—her attempt to fight for survival even after the first brutal attack. The poor woman.

Rosa shifted uncomfortably on the bar stool she fidgeted on, her gaze locked on the investigative photographs and evidence. As she stared at the very first riddle the Wood Riddle Killer left behind, a chill ran down her back.

> *"Two faces I wear, though one is unseen.*
> *In shadow, I linger, where wisdom convenes.*
> *Name me, the one who knows all that has been.*
> *A keeper of truths, both whispered and keen."*

She read the riddle aloud to herself, unable to shake the feeling that it was too profound for a first clue. But this was the only known victim at the time, and the case had been a shock three decades ago in a suburb of New York. It had sparked turmoil and civil unrest across the country—even before Rosa was born.

For a moment, she considered calling her father, wondering if he had any insights from that time, since the case had hit the nation hard. But then she glanced at the clock and hesitated—it was close to midnight. He had been working on repairs all day. And he probably had another wild, high-profile vet conference to prepare for. She settled for sending him a simple thank-you text and left it at that.

As she stood, the riddle replayed in her mind like an echo: *Two faces I wear, though one is unseen...* It stuck with her—the idea of something watching, knowing, hiding. Something old. *"Where wisdom convenes,"* she murmured. Then it fell into place again, like the riddle before. "Library," she whispered. That had to be it.

Before she walked up the stairs, she caught sight of the family heirloom clock staring at her from the wall. She'd always thought it was an ugly thing, with those beady owl eyes, but her mom had adored it—said it reminded her of Rosa's father and the long hours he used to keep. *I never had the heart to tell her how creepy it looked.* The way the eyes seemed to follow her was just... *wrong*. She shook her head.

"Come on, you mean cat, let's go to sleep," she muttered, reaching down to scoop up the feline beside her. But the mischievous creature darted away, staying just out of reach as he followed her up the stairs.

Her final thought before bed was unwelcome: it was only her first day on the job, and she'd already been pulled into the shadow of an unsolved case—one that could potentially tarnish her record for good.

***

The cheap motel wasn't what he wanted, but right now he didn't really care. The lack of sleep blurred his thoughts, leaving him unable to think clearly most days. Focus was his only goal—there was nothing else to do. After reading the riddles over and over, he threw the photos across the room in anger.

He took another sip of bourbon and appreciated how it soothed his throat on the way down. Running a hand through his disheveled hair, he sat on the corner of the bed. Something about being in this small town dredged up memories he had tried to push aside, memories he wanted to keep buried. But there was no time for reflection—ten years had passed since that event, and his obsessive nature wasn't going to let him stop now. There was a reason he had ended up here, and he was determined to get to the truth.

He grabbed the suspect list and began tracking down any leads he might have overlooked, especially Rosa's earlier mention of a library. Her focus on the library—even before the latest victim was identified—struck him as odd. How she zeroed in on it so quickly was either incredibly impressive or a gut feeling told him there was more to it than that.

While shuffling through the suspect list, his cell phone vibrated—Kershaw. That could only mean one thing. He sprang to his feet, grabbed the tactical vest, and secured his weapon in the side holster in one smooth movement.

By the time he pressed the answer button, he was already slamming the motel room door shut behind him.

CHAOS ENSUES

ROSA THUMBED A quick message into her phone as she tossed the covers aside, startling Sir Louie, who hissed as she leapt from the bed and grabbed her clothes.

Happy birthday, Dad! It's midnight. I was finally drifting off to sleep when I got a call. Something about a new case. Let's celebrate a different day instead. Sorry.

She'd nearly forgotten it was her father's birthday. Technically, it had only just started—but the date flashing across her phone when the call came in snapped her memory into place. It wasn't like her to forget something like that, even for a moment. She made a mental note to pick up a cake later—maybe something from that overpriced bakery her dad pretended not to like.

But for now, she had to move.

Raya had been brief, her voice low and urgent. *"We got a situation. Simon wants everyone on-site. Something bad happened, Rosa. I don't know all the details yet, but you need to get here as soon as you can."*

There hadn't been time for questions—just the address, and a pause heavy enough to make Rosa's skin prickle. If Simon was calling the entire team in at midnight, it wasn't for a routine update.

She shoved her legs into jeans, her mind already racing. A murder? A new lead? The fact that Raya hadn't seen the scene yet only added to the unease creeping in. Whatever it was, it had rattled someone enough to escalate it fast.

Being forty-five minutes away didn't exactly help her feel competent—or punctual.

As she grabbed her badge and keys, the guilt over the birthday message faded beneath something sharper: the sense that whatever waited at that scene wasn't just going to change her night—but the whole case.

***

Rosa pulled the massive truck up beside the Bel Air and hopped out. The thing was oversized, a beast on wheels—but practical. Still, it dwarfed her, and she imagined it probably turned heads, especially in a small town like this. As she swung the door shut, a chill swept across her arms. She slipped into her snug blue sweater, rubbing her sleeves as she scanned the scene ahead.

Her friend, Raya, was already approaching—her stride quick, her face unreadable. Rosa braced herself.

Raya leaned in close, voice low. "They think it's tied to the drug trafficking ring, not the serial murders."

Rosa's breath caught. "Who was it?" she asked, her voice barely above a whisper.

"It was Mr. Ropa," Raya said.

Rosa's stomach dropped. "Mr. Ropa?"

"I think he saw something he wasn't supposed to," Raya said, her tone grim. "They put a bullet right through his forehead—and all parts of him." Her face went pale. "He was the most harmless person in the world."

"Gosh," Rosa murmured. "Did someone inform his wife?"

"Someone's been sent to the house already," Chadford's voice cut in, authoritative and crisp.

As they moved toward the group gathered near the front entrance of the community center, Rosa instinctively straightened at the sharp tone of the chief of police. But her gaze quickly shifted to the man standing just off to the side—Simon. Half-hidden in the dim shadows, he exhaled a slow plume of smoke before deliberately crushing the cigarette beneath his boot. Detached, almost removed from everything around him. That didn't seem unusual for Simon, but tonight there was something different—an edge she hadn't seen before in the earlier briefing, like he was holding something back.

Most people saw Simon as cold, bitter, and too quiet for his own good. But Rosa had learned to read beneath the surface. The subtle signs—the tightness in his shoulders, the slight clench of his jaw—told her he wasn't merely observing; he was calculating. And maybe this night, even more than usual.

They continued walking along the side of the building, the uneven gravel crunching beneath their boots as they rounded from the front to the back of the community center. The scene ahead suddenly pulled Rosa from her thoughts.

Harsh white floodlights lit up the area, casting long, stark shadows across the back wall and bathing the scene in an unforgiving glow. The light caught on the blood—splattered across the weathered exterior walls, now glistening in streaks against the cracked, faded wood.

The air hung heavy with the metallic tang of fresh blood and the sharp sting of gunpowder, both scents still thick in the cool evening air. Rosa blinked, swallowing hard. This had happened recently—too recently.

She forced herself to walk closer. Mr. Ropa's body was barely recognizable. A shotgun blast had obliterated his face. Two more shots had torn through his torso—one in the stomach, another in the chest—before the final, devastating blow. This wasn't a kill. It was rage.

Rosa's stomach flipped as she looked down at his contorted form, his limbs bent unnaturally, shirt soaked through in patches of dark red. His hands were curled slightly, palms up—almost like he'd tried to fight back.

She studied the direction of his body—angled away from the woods.

He was running.

The thought landed like a rock in her gut. Someone had chased him out of those woods—and whoever it was, caught him here.

Two crime scene investigators moved carefully, their yellow tents dotting the ground. Rosa watched as one crouched and aimed a trajectory kit near the blood spatter. Another snapped photo after photo of the body.

"Time of death?" Simon's voice carried from nearby.

Rosa barely turned. William was already checking the skin with his gloved hand. "Three to four hours ago," he answered. "I'll confirm during autopsy."

She nodded to herself, letting the detail file away mentally. But her focus had shifted—scanning, reading the scene like a puzzle.

She reached into her coat pocket and pulled out a small flashlight, clicking it on. The beam cut through the darkness, casting narrow cones of light across the ground as she moved slowly, methodically.

Something caught her eye—a phone, shattered, half-buried in the grass. Its screen was spiderwebbed, shards scattered like glitter across the dirt. She crouched down, angling the light just right.

The sole of a boot had stamped the back.

Another forensic analyst stepped in, carefully bagging the item. "We'll send it to digital for analysis. If the SIM card's intact, we might be able to pull some clues."

The Chattingsburg PD team led the processing—by protocol—but Rosa stayed close. She watched William working with precision, his attention narrowed on possible links to the serial killer's patterns.

Farther out, search teams combed through brush with flashlights, planting small evidence flags in the dirt. Off to the side, a local officer interviewed witnesses, scribbling notes between nods.

Rosa noticed the eagerness in their eyes. For many of them, this was probably their first brush with something this brutal. It showed. She wasn't impressed by the enthusiasm. She was too busy trying to figure out what kind of killer could do this to someone like Mr. Ropa.

She scanned the group, noting Simon talking to a few of the officers. They were discussing the tree line—how it was common for people to walk the path by the woods, even at night. No unusual reports. Still, it didn't sit right with her.

Her breath hitched as she glanced back at the body. This wasn't just about shutting someone up. The sheer brutality—it was excessive. Furious.

He must've seen something.

Mr. Ropa, the former postman. The helpful neighbor. The kind-eyed volunteer. He wasn't reckless. So whatever it was, it came to *him*—or found him by chance.

Her thoughts tangled as questions rose. *Connected to the drugs, maybe. But why this level of violence?*

She shifted her focus to a faint trail in the grass—flattened blades leading toward the woods.

"Can we get a closer look here?" Rosa asked, signaling one of the crime scene techs.

Kershaw stepped up beside her with another flashlight. "Someone came through here fast—running away, most likely."

Her eyes narrowed. She followed the trail to a large tree, heart pounding. There—on the bark—something dark caught the light.

Blood. And more than that.

She inched closer.

Written into the bark were smeared, unmistakable letters. Red. Fresh.

Rosa's breath froze.

This wasn't just blood. It was a message.

The words hadn't faded. The edges were sharp. *Intentional.*

This was a signature—*his* signature. The same serial killer. And now, his taunt had appeared here, at Mr. Ropa's scene.

Simon stepped up beside her. She didn't need to look to know he was there—his presence always felt like a shadow at her back.

"Whoever did this," he said, low and firm, "wasn't him. He always leaves it on the body. This isn't his kill. But the riddle—what does it say?"

Rosa didn't flinch.

She gestured to the techs instead of reaching. "Bag and tag this."

"Glad you didn't touch it," Simon muttered dryly.

She ignored the comment.

William arrived swiftly with gloves and an evidence kit. As he collected the bark fragment, faint lines emerged under the forensic light. A riddle—drawn in blood.

"And now it starts, the clock's slow chime.

Two years asleep, the wise see time."

Kershaw read it aloud. "It's him?"

William frowned. "He never left a clue away from the body. Are you sure it's his?"

Kershaw nodded. "Same handwriting, from the looks of it. Same method."

"But why leave it now?" William asked. "What's changed?"

Raya crossed her arms. "He's never done this before. What is he trying to say? You two know him better than we do."

"He thinks he's smarter than all of us," Rosa said, though her voice held less certainty this time. Her jaw tightened as she glanced back at the note. "But... I don't know. Something about this doesn't feel the same. It's like he wants us to think it's him—but what if it's not?"

She caught Chadford watching nearby but let it go. Too many thoughts were racing through her head to pay him much attention.

"This feels like last time," Kershaw muttered. "When you got close—and what led to Mary—"

Simon's glare cut him off mid-sentence. The tension snapped so hard Rosa felt it in her chest.

Kershaw backed off. Rosa didn't respond.

But she recognized that kind of stillness—the kind born from buried memories and threats too deep to name.

She knew that feeling far too well.

ON EDGE

A FEW DAYS had passed, and the message carved into the bark had left pressure among the newly formed task force. Simon could feel it in every sideways glance, every clipped conversation. But it was more than discomfort. It was distrust—some subtle crack in their cohesion that deepened every hour they spent under one roof.

Chief Chadford didn't help. From the moment the team assembled, the man inserted himself into every briefing like he was still in charge, undercutting Simon's strategy with the tone of someone desperate to reclaim authority. It was clear Chadford now saw this as *his* case, ever since Ropa's body was found.

Simon had tolerated it for as long as he could.

"Does he always act like this, or is it just this case getting to him?" Kershaw muttered low, leaning toward Simon as Chadford overruled another plan mid-sentence.

Simon didn't answer.

Then it happened.

Another interruption. Another smug correction from Chadford about what *should* be done next, how *his town* needed proper policing—not some out-of-town specialists running the show.

Simon stood.

"Sir," he said sharply, his voice edged with restraint, "I understand your experience, and out of respect, I'm going to ask you to kindly leave the room."

The room fell quiet.

"There's a reason I put this team together. Right now, you're not helping. You're getting in the way. Please. Leave."

His voice rose slightly at the end. Every word sliced with precision. He didn't shout. He didn't have to.

Chadford's jaw tensed. His face flushed with indignation. And for a second, Simon wondered if the man would throw a punch. But instead, the chief turned on his heel and stormed out, slamming the door so hard that the glass rattled.

Simon let out a slow breath. He didn't regret it.

Rosa sat nearby, saying nothing, her brow drawn tight as she stared at the wall. If she had thoughts about what just happened, she kept them locked behind that guarded expression she always wore.

Kershaw broke the silence. "You think the killer came to this town on purpose?"

Simon didn't respond. He didn't know. And that's what unsettled him.

The hours that followed were slow. Dragging. The case sat heavily on Simon's shoulders, grinding down his focus. They'd already revisited the crime scene that morning, combing over every detail one last time—again. Forensics had finished sweeping the area the night before, but Simon still felt like something had been missed. He, Kershaw, and Raya had canvassed the surrounding buildings, even questioned the pastor at the small church just down the street. No security cameras, no new leads.

And the witnesses? Sparse. One woman reported hearing the shots around eleven that night but didn't call it in—she assumed it was someone hunting illegally again, out in the woods past the tree line. A few others mentioned seeing Ropa near the community center earlier that evening, laughing with a friend as he loaded a box of supplies from his car. Just hours before he died.

Simon remembered talking to one of those witnesses—a teenager who worked at the gas station two blocks over. Kid couldn't have been older than sixteen, but his voice had cracked when he spoke about Mr. Ropa.

"He always came in every Saturday," the kid had said, eyes red-rimmed. "Bought a candy bar for me and told me to keep studying so I didn't end up pumping gas forever. Said he used to get Cs in school, too."

It stuck with Simon—how even in a small, forgettable town like this, a man could leave ripples behind.

Now, hours later, he noticed the sluggish way the others moved—Kershaw rubbing his temples, Raya shifting in her seat—but no one complained. No one had to. Simon knew the team was running on fumes. He was too.

He sifted through crime scene photos, cross-referenced reports, and tracked every name linked to the drug trafficking routes that ran near the town's outskirts. Still, nothing tied back to Ropa cleanly. Nothing stuck.

"Perhaps we could do a stakeout on some of the local drug dealers who frequent this area," Raya said softly.

Simon's hands froze mid-turn of a page.

He looked up at her, then slammed his palm onto the table. Hard.

The sound cracked through the room.

He didn't even know why that suggestion had pushed him over the edge. Maybe it was how tired he was. Maybe it was how little progress they were making. Or maybe it was the idea that anyone could still treat this like a straightforward case—when it wasn't.

"Dude, chill out," Kershaw muttered, reaching out to place a hand on Simon's shoulder.

Simon shoved it off without thinking. Kershaw stumbled backward, his elbow knocking into Rosa, who let out a sharp yelp as she hit the edge of the desk. Simon flinched but didn't move to help.

Rosa straightened, glaring at him.

"That's it," she snapped. "You're doing too much, sir!"

Simon blinked.

"Go take a walk and cool your head before you hurt someone worse than you already have—with your words or your hands!"

He didn't answer.

"You dragged us together for three straight days with no breaks, no sleep, and expect miracles. But we're human, not machines. You're being a fucking ass!"

She slammed her hand on the table.

"I'm going home. I'm taking a shower. You want this team to actually work? Then stop driving everyone into the ground."

The silence that followed felt dense. Rosa's anger echoed in his head longer than he wanted it to.

Simon stared at her. He didn't speak. Not because he didn't have words—but because the ones he wanted to say weren't helpful.

She turned to Raya. "Come on. I'll drive you home."

Without sparing Simon a glance, Rosa left.

Raya hesitated for a beat longer. "She gets a little heated when she's tired," she said awkwardly, her voice pitched between apology and self-preservation.

Simon said nothing. He didn't look at her.

She turned to leave, brushing past Kershaw, who stood frozen between laughter and discomfort.

Kershaw cleared his throat. "What's next, boss?" he asked. "What do we do now?"

Simon didn't answer immediately. He glanced down at the open file, then at the board on the wall where Ropa's name was pinned.

He didn't have a next step. Not yet.

And he hated that more than anything.

***

"Girl, you went off!" Raya laughed from the passenger seat, but her amusement dimmed when she noticed Rosa's white-knuckled grip on the steering wheel. The dim dashboard lights painted her friend's face in sharp relief—jaw tight, eyes locked on the road like it might fight back.

"Well, he's only been here a few days and has already pushed everyone to the brink—maybe even over it," Rosa muttered. Her voice wavered more than she wanted it to. The second those words had left her mouth back in the station, she'd felt them hit harder than intended—but not wrong. Just... raw. "I couldn't help myself. Do you think he's going to kick me off the team?"

Raya snorted. "No way. You think he wants someone different now that all of this has happened so fast? Doubt it." Then, grinning, she added, "Besides, he totally didn't see that coming. Took him a full minute to reboot—props for knocking the robot offline."

Rosa gave a weak laugh, letting her grip loosen slightly. "Great," she murmured. "Now how am I going to sleep tonight?"

The mood shifted. Neither of them said it, but it hung between them—the last few days, the pressure building in that station, and the gnawing question they were all too afraid to name aloud: What if they couldn't stop this killer? Or what if it wasn't even the killer at all?

Raya cleared her throat softly. "So… what do you make of Mr. Ropa's murder? That riddle carved in the bark—it feels different. Like he's trying to say something, but I can't quite figure out what."

Rosa's eyes drifted to the road, her voice barely above a whisper. "It feels like bait. Something meant to send us chasing shadows while the real killer slips away. The drugs, the murder—they're tangled, but I can't tell if this is a scare tactic or a misdirection."

"Yeah," Raya nodded, "and if it's a warning—who's it for? The cops? The dealers? Someone else entirely?"

Rosa shook her head slowly. "I'm not sure. But this isn't just about Ropa. It's bigger than that. And I'm not waiting around to find out what exactly."

The road ahead stretched long and dark. The trees on either side loomed like sentries, casting jagged shadows across the asphalt. Rosa kept glancing at the rearview mirror, half-expecting to see headlights following—or worse, nothing at all.

When they finally reached Raya's apartment complex, a few of the overhead floodlights buzzed to life, casting a pale glow across the cracked pavement and weather-worn steps. A flicker of normalcy in a week that had been anything but.

"Text me if you can't sleep," Raya said as she grabbed her bag and stepped out. Then she added, "Or if Supervisory Special Agent Simon Pikes shows up to haunt you."

"Thanks for that image," Rosa said, forcing a small smile as Raya closed the door behind her. The truck suddenly felt too quiet.

The drive back to her own place felt longer. Her limbs were heavy, but her thoughts moved too fast, circling the memory of Simon's voice—the way he'd slammed his hand on the table, barked orders, shut down every suggestion like they were beneath him.

But worse than his anger had been the stillness that followed her outburst.

Rosa's fingers tightened around the wheel again. The desk edge had left a bruise along her side, the throbbing a dull reminder of how far things had spiraled. Not just with the case—but with herself.

She pulled over near a gas station that had already gone dark, the neon OPEN sign switched off. The emptiness around her carried more force than any engine's hum.

Had she gone too far?

She had never lost it like that on the job. Not in the academy. Not in field training. She'd seen leaders crack under pressure, but she'd always prided herself on staying grounded. And yet—tonight—something inside her had snapped. And it wasn't just because of Simon's tone.

It was the bark.

It was the damn bark with that riddle carved in blood. That signature. That proof.

The killer wasn't just killing—he was toying with them. With her.

Rosa let out a shaky breath and leaned her head back against the seat. Maybe Simon wasn't handling this well. Maybe she wasn't either. But something about the way he'd reacted at the scene, at the table… it didn't feel like ego or power-tripping. It felt like panic. Like a man whose past had just caught up to him and didn't know how to outrun it.

And maybe that's what unnerved her most. She didn't want to admit that she recognized it.

With a quiet sigh, she put the truck back in drive and eased onto the road again. The trees had stopped swaying. Everything was still. But Rosa's mind whirred.

There's more to this case, she thought. *There has to be.*

She pulled into her driveway, sat in the truck for a moment longer, then climbed out, flipping off the headlights. The night seemed to inch forward the second she stepped out, but she didn't look back.

Tomorrow, she'd face whatever fallout was coming. For now, she just needed a shower, some lousy sleep, and time to think.

***

Simon stood beside the turquoise Bel Air outside the motel, the cold air biting through his coat. Kershaw leaned against the car, the faint click of his lighter breaking the quiet as he lit the cigarette Simon had handed him. A smirk tugged at Kershaw's lips, his shoulders shaking with quiet amusement.

"Would you give it a rest?" Simon muttered, pushing his hands deeper into his pockets and narrowing his eyes against the chill.

The sharp autumn air smelled faintly of wood smoke drifting from nearby chimneys. It wasn't winter yet, but these small towns always felt colder, quieter—almost too quiet for Simon's liking. The neon motel sign hummed softly overhead, its flickering light casting long silhouettes that stretched toward the dark tree line looming just beyond the gravel lot.

Kershaw exhaled a thin stream of smoke. "Alright, alright. But damn, she really laid into you back there." His grin grew wider, eyes bright with teasing. "Someone finally stood up to you. Props."

Simon grunted, his lips twitching in a reluctant half-smile before tightening again.

Kershaw took another drag, flicking ash onto the ground. "You might want to apologize for shoving me into her, though. She hit that desk hard." His voice dropped a notch, serious but still laced with a wry edge. "If you keep snapping like that, people will start to wonder if you're fit to lead. I know it's personal, but you've got to hold it together."

Simon didn't answer right away. His gaze drifted toward the darkened woods, still and hushed, the rustle of leaves barely audible. That familiar prickling sensation crept up his spine—the feeling of eyes watching him from the dark. He pushed it aside, unwilling to give it power.

"What if it wasn't the real killer?" Simon said quietly, his voice low. "That riddle—someone else planted it. It was meant to look like him, but it's not his work."

Kershaw blew out smoke slowly, eyes narrowing. "You really think some copycat's trying to fool us? That the serial killer's not back?"

Simon's jaw tightened. "I'm sure. This feels different—like a distraction. Someone wants us chasing shadows while the real killer stays hidden."

Kershaw's brows pinched. "So the drug angle's just a smokescreen?"

"Maybe," Simon said. "Or it's the cover this copycat is using."

Kershaw stubbed out the cigarette on the car's worn paint, the scrape sharp in the night. "If that's true, then we're behind. Again."

Simon didn't respond. Just stared at the woods like they might spit out an answer. The pressure of it all wrapped around him tight, refusing to let go.

Kershaw jerked a thumb toward the motel's peeling siding and flickering porch light. "This place? Nightmare fuel. But I'll try to get some sleep. You should, too. Before your brain breaks open under all that overthinking."

Simon gave a low grunt in reply, his expression unreadable.

Kershaw disappeared inside, the door creaking shut behind him. Simon stayed by the car a moment longer, the cold settling deep in his bones. His eyes slid back to the woods. They looked darker now, more ominous. The pull was there again, like a whisper only he could hear.

He exhaled slowly and finally turned toward the motel, the neon sign continuing to hum its eerie lullaby as he headed to his room.

PLAY WITH FIRE, GET BURNED

HER THIN, FRAIL body lay sprawled on the cracked pavement, the icy chill clinging to her pale, lifeless skin. So fragile in life, she seemed even smaller now, curled unnaturally, limbs askew. Brown eyes—once warm, quick to laugh— stared upward, glassy and fixed, accusing him in their stillness. In that frozen stare was the truth Simon could never shake: he had failed her in the seconds that mattered most.

Her black hair, usually straightened to perfection the way she liked it, now tangled and soaked with blood, fanned out around her head like a dark, broken halo. The crimson had dried in jagged rivulets along her neck, tracing the thin slit carved clean across her throat—precise, practiced, deliberate.

Simon stood in the nightmare, unable to move. He had watched this scene a thousand times—awake and asleep. Could still taste the metallic sting, smell the iron, the damp ground. Could still feel the faint warmth of her hand when he'd reached her too late.

She hadn't been collateral damage. She had been the warning.

The killer had known who she was—*what* she was to him. Her murder hadn't been about loose ends or accidental sightings. It had been personal. A calculated blow designed to break him in the cruelest way possible.

And it had.

His twin sister. His best friend. The only person who had ever truly seen him.

He used to lie to himself, tell others she must've gotten too close to something. But Simon knew better now. The killer had taken her *because* of him—because Simon had come too close to unraveling the game.

Back then, there had been a lead. A pattern no one else had noticed—a timeline, hidden in plain sight, mapping out every kill over three decades. Simon had tracked the locations, narrowed the search to six counties. He'd even cross-referenced victims' professions, looking for what connected them outside the obvious. And it was working. He'd found an overlap in service records—court clerks, bailiffs, a retired judge.

And then... she died. The trail went cold. The game changed.

The killer didn't just want to keep his identity hidden then. He wanted Simon to suffer every day he failed to see the truth he'd once been inches from. And Simon had let him.

The guilt pulsed in his chest, raw and consuming.

He jolted awake, drenched in sweat. His breath came in shallow pulls, and for a second, the dark motel room felt like it was collapsing in on itself. He grabbed the water bottle from the nightstand and drained it in seconds, but it did nothing to stop the shaking.

The clock glowed red in the corner. Still too early. Still too dark.

He checked his phone—no messages. Not from the team. Not from anyone.

Simon dragged a hand through his damp hair and sat up slowly. Sleep was useless. The nightmare always came back.

He needed to get out. Move. Think. Obsess. *Control* something.

There was the Waffle House, probably open. The thought of greasy food was a faint comfort—something solid in the middle of the fog he lived in. Maybe a coffee, maybe another deep dive into the case files, or into the folder only he had—the one with his sister's name on it.

He pulled on his black leather jacket and paused. The killer hadn't needed to make it personal.

But he had.

And Simon had every intention of returning the favor.

***

"I still don't get why you drag me out every time it's my birthday," her father said with a chuckle, lifting his sweet tea for a sip. "But I'll admit, these little outings aren't half bad."

"It's the only place open, and you're the one who picked a last-minute wildlife conference across the state and called me so early," Rosa replied, smirking. "Plans changed, remember? You're the one with a fan club."

Her father—famous in the world of conservation—shrugged. Revered for his ability to read and rehabilitate even the most dangerous species, he had built a life out of preserving what others gave up on. He never chased recognition, but it always found him. Rosa admired him deeply. He had rebuilt his life from the ground up after her mother passed—and she'd watched it happen, step by step. He even had an owl tattoo across his inner arm, which matched her mother's, because his love for animals was on a whole other level.

He set his glass down. "Well, I've got a two-hour drive to the airport. I know you haven't been sleeping much, so let's eat quick so you can get some rest."

"Sleep? Not likely," Rosa muttered. "Yelling at a federal agent doesn't exactly lead to a relaxing evening."

Her father raised a brow. "Maybe not your best move."

She pulled a small box from her bag and pushed it toward him. "I still managed to grab cake. The market was closed, but Mr. Jay opens the storage early, so he let me slide by. You're welcome."

He cracked a grin. "Chocolate. My favorite."

It was their tradition—Waffle House on his birthday. Her mother's favorite place. Simple. Familiar. It grounded them both.

"Your mother was a terrible baker, you know," he said between bites, grinning. "I can still taste that brick of a cornbread cake she tried to make."

Rosa laughed. "She had many talents. Baking just wasn't one of them."

The door chimed.

Her eyes flicked to the entrance—and she stiffened.

Gruff-looking Simon Pikes.

He looked like he'd barely slept. His shoulders hunched forward as he moved toward the bar, jacket creased, face unreadable. The harsh diner lights only made his weariness more visible. He dropped onto a stool near the line cooks without scanning the room, his attention seemingly turned inward.

"Shh—don't look," Rosa hissed under her breath as her father turned to glance.

He blinked. "What? Is that the agent you've been working with?"

Rosa didn't answer. She kept her gaze fixed on the napkin dispenser, willing herself invisible.

Her father leaned in slightly. "What's he doing here?"

"Eating, I assume." But even as she said it, a knot formed in her gut. *Why here? Why now?*

He stood, brushing his hands on a napkin. "Well, I've got to grab my bag. You going to be alright?"

Rosa gave him a thumbs-up. He left a few bills on the table, gave her shoulder a squeeze, and walked out without another word.

She stared down at her half-eaten plate, trying to mentally reset—until arms appeared, slinging over the back of the booth.

She flinched.

Then looked up.

Simon.

Her breath caught. She'd barely processed the sight of him when her hand knocked over her tea. It spilled fast, sliding across the table and down the booth seat. She lunged for napkins, her movements jerky, frustrated.

Simon didn't speak. He just helped her clean it.

"Uh—sir," she began, avoiding his gaze. "Good morning. Didn't expect to see you here."

He sat across from her, calm, inscrutable. "Didn't expect to see you either."

She finally looked at him. "Why are you at my booth?"

"I wanted your thoughts," he said simply. "On the case. You've been quick with the riddles. I want to know how your mind works."

She blinked. "If you're accusing me of something, just say it."

"I'm not," he replied. "But I am trying to understand what you see that others don't."

Rosa's guard went up. "I've always been good with language. Riddles. Wordplay. I don't know what else to tell you."

Simon tilted his head slightly, as if that answer only half-satisfied him.

Then, without warning: "Why did you join the force two years ago?"

That caught her off guard.

She narrowed her eyes. "That's oddly specific. I don't remember telling you that."

He said nothing.

A jolt of unease hit her. "You've looked into me."

"I look into everyone on my team."

There it was.

"I don't like being watched," she said quietly.

"I don't like surprises," he replied.

For a beat, they just stared.

The noise of the diner faded into the background. Somewhere behind the counter, a spatula clanged against a griddle. Plates clinked. But at this table, it felt like they were hovering just above something unspoken—a quiet unease neither of them had yet named aloud.

Rosa leaned forward slightly. "You've been acting like we're chasing a ghost. But I think you know more than you're letting on. Every time something happens, it's like you already expected it. You get quiet. Calculated."

Simon didn't flinch. "You think I'm hiding something?"

"I think you're afraid to say what you already know, or admit whatever truth you have buried."

Simon exhaled slowly, gaze never breaking from hers. "Do you think I'd be here if I knew how to stop him?"

She didn't answer.

But something in his tone—flat, low, empty—told her everything she needed to know. He had been close once. Close enough that it cost him something. And now he was chasing that mistake like a ghost in the woods.

He stood.

"I brought you onto this case because your mind works differently. Because you might see what I can't anymore. But if you're not careful, Rosa, this case will consume you the way it's consumed everyone else."

"Then maybe we should stop being so secretive and actually start talking about what we know," she shot back.

He offered a dry nod. "Maybe."

Then he walked away, vanishing into the fluorescent buzz of the diner.

Rosa sat alone, heart pounding. He wasn't just chasing a killer.

He was chasing something he'd already lost.

DON'T WEAR BIG SHOES
IF THEY DON'T FIT

"I THINK HE leaves traces behind in important and personal areas, but so far, we haven't been able to pick up on many of them. Maybe this place is one of those spots? We need to locate these hideouts if we want to make progress. Given all the riddles we've got, is there anything we should focus on while we're here? This town's small—maybe only 5,000 people, at most," Kershaw said, biting his thumb as though even thinking was a struggle.

Rosa listened quietly as the others spoke, her mind sifting through the fragments of the case. She could feel the pressure in the room, the decades-old failure pressing down.

"We still need to check out the schools—elementary, middle, and high," William muttered, eyes scanning the cluttered table. "Between Rosa's thoughts on a possible library connection and Simon's theory that a school is a 'place of learning,' it seems tied together somehow. The question is, is it this particular school, or are there others across the country with similar significance?"

The table was covered with photos—victims' faces, pieces of bark with riddles carved in, crime scenes from years ago. Thirty years of hunting this killer had passed through different hands, each generation grasping at threads, only to lose them again.

Rosa's gaze landed on the photo of the serial killer's second victim—George Fisher. She knew who he was: a man with a dark past, a predator. Whether he deserved what happened didn't matter. A small voice inside her wondered if that made her cold, but she quickly shoved the thought aside. This was a case—her first real case. She couldn't afford to let emotions cloud her judgment.

George's victim, Lisa Carter, had been assaulted before the killer finished the job. The murder was called a mercy killing, necessary because she was too weak to fight back. The fact that the killer had targeted George hinted at a motive deeper than random violence—a psychological drive behind the killings.

The murders showed a chilling pattern: men were dismembered with precision, while women were killed swiftly but cleanly—always with bark left behind as a clue. The killer switched victims' gender every two years without fail.

Simon believed the killer was male, based on the pattern of overpowering victims and leaving no struggle with female victims.

Rosa's frustration built as she thought about how little they had to go on. After all these years, the key piece was still missing.

Her thoughts shifted back to the early days of the investigation, long before this task force.

She picked up a photo of a detective—*Lee Hepple*.

"Hepple was the lead detective on the case for many years," Rosa said softly. "The case existed before him, but he was the one who pushed it further than anyone else. He connected the dots and even dubbed the killer—the Wood Riddle Killer."

Her fingers traced the edge of Hepple's photo, lingering near the jagged scar on his right hand where his pointer finger was missing. The wound was a grim souvenir—a testament to how close he'd come to the killer's deadly grasp.

"He found the first known hideout? Which probably took the killer by surprise?" Rosa asked calmly.

She eyed the photos spread across the table, her breath catching as the images pulled her in.

Though she wasn't there, Rosa could almost picture the basement beneath the old pharmacy in Chicago—a nightmare trapped in stone and shadow. In one image, a rusted, dented trashcan sat shoved near the back alley door, and behind it, barely visible, a narrow trapdoor. The kind most people wouldn't notice unless they were looking. Another photo showed the floor below: cracked, grimy tiles littered with fragments of broken glass and shattered drug bottles.

Even through the pictures, Rosa imagined the air—stale with rot, the scent of mold thick and suffocating, mingling with the coppery tang of dried blood. A flickering bulb hung in the center of the room, captured mid-swing like a pendulum, casting uneven light across dark stains smeared on the walls—old blood congealed into grisly patterns.

In the corners of one of the photos, she spotted discarded syringes, torn scraps of paper—and what appeared to be sharp instruments, likely used to dismember the men. They were grim reminders of the horrors that had unfolded down there.

Simon was the first to uncover these photos, safely locked away in Hepple's cluttered office—a stark window into the basement's horrors and the killer's handiwork. It was one step closer to the truth, but the price Hepple paid for that knowledge was carved into his very flesh.

"You said he found the pharmacy above a bustling city in Chicago? That was one of the first hideouts?" Raya asked, cutting into Rosa's thoughts.

"Yes," William said, his voice low. He wasn't one for many words, but the force behind them settled over the room, unspoken but impossible to ignore.

"The pharmacy was covered in blood—not exactly left to be found," Kershaw said, glancing briefly at Simon before spreading out other photos from a new folder on the table. Raya had to look away, unable to stomach the images: faint outlines of shattered glass, smeared blood trails, and the dark, empty corners of that basement—witnesses to the violence that had taken place there.

"And then, he was shot?" Rosa asked.

Kershaw nodded grimly. "Yeah. Hepple was shot while working a different case. We always suspected it wasn't random, especially considering the missing finger."

Rosa's eyes narrowed. "Because he was too close?"

"Exactly," Kershaw said, handing her the file again. "Too close for the killer's comfort. After that, the investigation went cold."

She felt the weight of the case's tangled history settle over her. This wasn't just a murder investigation—it was a legacy of silence, suspicion, and maybe betrayal.

Raya's voice broke through, a little sharper than before. "If Hepple's death wasn't an accident, then it was foul play—no question."

Rosa nodded slowly, gripping the file tighter. "It makes sense. He wanted to stop him from uncovering the truth."

Kershaw sighed, the sound heavy with memories. "We never fully ruled out foul play, but we couldn't find enough evidence to reopen the case."

Rosa's gaze flicked to Simon across the room. He sat still, eyes watching their every move, lips curled in something like a smirk—cold, almost unreadable.

She realized then what Simon wanted—not just for them to uncover the truth, but to feel the unease, the doubt that came with suspecting someone powerful was keeping the case buried.

TRUST IS A THIN PAPER

"AND YOU THOUGHT it was okay to keep this from us after we signed on to be part of this team?" Rosa's voice cut through the hum of the fluorescent lights, sharp as a blade. The harsh glow reflected off the wooden table between them.

She slammed her palm down, rattling a half-empty coffee cup near Simon's elbow. The sound echoed in the sterile room. She caught Raya's eyes flick to her, the subtle shake of her head warning her to hold back.

"At least tell us beforehand so we can make the damn decision," Rosa said, chest rising and falling in quick, shallow breaths. "Walking in blind like this doesn't sit right. And just because Simon keeps everything to himself doesn't mean we all have trust issues."

Her fingers curled into fists before she shoved Simon—just enough to make him rock back a step. The heat of her anger crackled between them.

"This is bullshit."

"Calm down, Rosa," Raya said quietly but firmly, reaching out to tighten her grip on Rosa's sleeve. It was a gentle anchor, trying to keep her from tipping over in her fury.

"This is literally my first week on the job, and already decisions are being made for me?" Rosa's voice was sharp and clipped, barely containing the heat beneath.

Simon chuckled, lips curling into a smirk as he leaned back slightly, hands loose at his sides. The glint in his eyes wasn't amusement—it was something colder. Entertainment. He was enjoying the show.

That only fanned Rosa's fire.

She swung fast and impulsive, but Simon was quicker, blocking the strike with ease. The smirk didn't fade; it grew. Rosa felt the burn of frustration coil tighter.

She switched tactics.

She drove her knee up toward his stomach—maybe a little lower—but Simon caught her mid-motion. His grip was firm, yanking her off balance as he twisted her arm behind her back and locked it in place.

"You do realize I'm a foot taller than you, right?" His voice was smooth, casual, almost amused. He leaned close enough for Rosa to feel the weight of his words at her ear. "And you're causing a scene. Those nosy people out there, watching?" He nodded toward the glass window, where Rosa saw a few heads turned in their direction. "They're likely about to talk. If you have a problem, you're free to walk away now—no reprimands."

For a moment, Rosa stilled. Simon might have thought he'd won.

Then, with a swift twist, she slipped free from his grasp, spinning out of his hold with precision that made him step back again.

She met his intense eyes head-on, steady fire burning in her own.

"No one said I wanted out," she said coolly. "But a team only works if all the cards are on the table. And I know you like doing everything alone, but that's not how this works. Especially when this guy hasn't been caught in over thirty years."

Before Simon could answer, Kershaw's voice cut through.

"We didn't tell you because we needed you to figure it out yourselves." His tone was steady, edged with something measured. He stepped forward and flicked the blinds closed, casting the room in shadow. "We had to be sure you were smart enough to read between the lines."

William spoke next, hesitant but clear. He fidgeted with his sleeve; the faint crinkle of his rubber gloves filled the quiet. "I told them we should be upfront. But... they thought this way was better."

All eyes turned to him. The charged air dropped into heavy silence—like the calm before a storm.

Rosa softened a little at William's words, sensing the weight behind them. Simon arched an eyebrow, unreadable, calculating.

Kershaw stayed impassive, his glare steady, authority filling the room.

William swallowed and shifted. The rubber gloves squeaked faintly as he clenched his fingers.

The unspoken truth settled over the room: this wasn't just a case. They were being tested—pushed to prove themselves. Maybe even manipulated. But by whom? The killer? Or someone higher up, someone with power who wanted to keep this buried? The thought sent a cold spike down Rosa's spine, a chill worse than any fear of the killer—because this was something rotten within their own ranks.

"Alright, alright, the tension is too much," Raya said, exhaling as she ran a hand through her hair. "We're part of this team, but next time, a little truth needs to be had. And trust should be there if we're supposed to work together." Her tone was firm but not unkind.

She shot Simon a pointed look before placing a steadying hand on Rosa's shoulder. Rosa was still bristling, but she didn't push again.

Rosa glanced around and realized how much everyone was carrying. This wasn't just about solving a crime. It was about holding the team together.

"Trust is earned," Simon said evenly, his voice tight—an admission wrapped in a challenge.

Rosa scoffed and rolled her eyes. "Well, you sure started it off on the right foot, then," she muttered under her breath.

Before Simon could react, Raya's hand clamped over Rosa's mouth, muffling the words. Rosa's eyes widened briefly, catching a faint smirk at the corner of Raya's lips.

Kershaw raised his hands in mock surrender. His tone was light, but his eyes carried a seriousness that didn't waver. "But the next meeting has to be outside this building—because of the truth that was just revealed. We were still unsure if we could even trust you two."

Rosa frowned — the killer might be higher up than they'd ever imagined, or someone connected to them was pulling strings behind the scenes. The case wasn't just about the murders anymore. It was about exposing a web that stretched far beyond the crimes.

Raya crossed her arms and exhaled softly. Her voice dropped, almost to herself. "I still want to know who killed Mr. Ropa…" The sadness in her words softened the room's edge, the unanswered questions settling heavily.

Rosa noticed the shift. The focus was no longer just on their conflict — it was on the case, on what they were really up against. And she was now more determined than ever.

"We'll find out who did this and why," Rosa said firmly, wrapping an arm around Raya's shoulders. Her grip was steady, offering comfort her friend hadn't asked for but clearly needed.

Mr. Ropa wasn't family, but in a town like theirs, that hardly mattered. Everyone knew each other—had grown up together, shared stories, crossed paths too many times to count. His loss wasn't just another crime; it was a crack in their foundation.

Raya's gaze lingered on the door as she spoke softly, "I'm going back to the scene tomorrow morning. Double-checking everything. We might have missed something."

The words hung with the dread of what might be waiting.

Rosa nodded, understanding. "I'll go with you."

They had to find out the truth. Before it got worse.

And they all knew it would get worse before it got better.

WAFFLES AND WARNINGS

"CAN WE STOP at Waffle House?" Rosa flicked the blinker on, fingers drumming against the steering wheel as she waited for the light to change. Exhaustion settled deep in her bones, the kind that sleep wouldn't fix. They still weren't sure where the next meet-up would be—whether the motel or somewhere else.

Raya glanced up from her phone. "You always end up there when your head's got too much rattling around."

Rosa let out a breath. "It feels wrong, Raya. Thinking about the station—about Chadford—maybe the killer isn't working alone. Maybe the person higher up is connected to Chadford. Or what if he is pulling strings?"

Raya frowned. "You don't think Chadford could be involved, do you?"

"I don't know," Rosa said, eyes on the road. "But we need to figure out who else has power here—who might be covering things up."

"Like Mayor Thompson?" Raya suggested. "Or that millionaire—Miller? The one who won half the land up the street in that shady auction?"

Rosa nodded. "Exactly. And Chadford, of course. He's head of police, and from the way things are going, he's not exactly on our side."

Raya smirked. "Sounds like a conspiracy waiting to happen."

Rosa pulled a small notepad from the glove compartment. "Let's list them. Mayor Thompson. Chadford. Miller. Anyone else who might be connected."

Raya flipped open her own paper pad and grabbed a pen from her pocket.

They started jotting down names, filling the silence with theories and half-formed questions. Once they finished, Rosa started driving again.

Pulling into the Waffle House parking lot, Rosa's chest tightened with exhaustion and a numbness she couldn't shake. The truck rumbled to a stop, but she didn't move right away. What was the point? It was too late to go questioning people—they'd have to wait until morning.

They climbed out of the truck, and Rosa reached for her phone. Her thumb hovered over the screen as she unlocked it.

The message was already there—stark, impersonal. Words blinking back at her:

You should quit.

Her breath caught, pulse quickening as she tapped to open it.

The next message leapt off the screen, direct and accusatory:

You don't know anything. You're too weak to be a detective.

The words terrified her as if the sender knew her every insecurity and had crafted the message to expose them. She scanned the parking lot through the windshield, half-expecting to find someone standing there, watching. But there was nothing—just the usual quiet at this hour. The Waffle House sign pulsed in the distance, the night pressing in around her, but her mind clung to the message.

Her gaze snapped to the dumpster by the entrance. She scanned for any sign of movement—anybody hiding, ready to jump out.

No sign.

She tucked the phone back in her pocket, jaw tight. "Raya, I need to show you this."

Raya's eyes narrowed as Rosa read the messages aloud.

"This... this isn't just a threat. Someone related to the case could be involved."

"I won't ignore it. But I don't know if it's about the case," Rosa said.

Raya nodded. "We'll figure out who's behind it. But you need to stay sharp—and not let this shake you."

Rosa forced a smile. "Yeah. Because I'm definitely not weak."

They stepped into the warm glow of the restaurant. The scent of syrup and coffee wrapped around her like a familiar embrace, but the unease clung to her—persistent, unwelcome, and hard to shake.

Rosa followed Raya's gaze to the high-top bar table.

There he was.

Their new boss.

The one she had just managed to piss off. Again.

Great. Just great.

Raya shot her a look, half-amused, half-you've really done it now.

Rosa exhaled slowly, bracing herself.

This night just kept getting better.

GRILL TALK

"FOR ONCE, LET'S just not talk about work outside of the job," Kershaw said, his tone almost pleading as he leaned on the bar table.

Simon watched from his seat, taking in the scene. William smirked. "I'm surprised the health nut picked this place."

William took a big swig of sweet tea, then immediately coughed, eyes wide. "Wow! That is sweet! How do these Southerners drink this stuff?"

An older waitress nearby laughed—a warm, hearty sound. She was a broad, full-figured woman with light brown skin, soft with age but still carrying a glow of warmth. Her round cheeks lifted as she beamed, short curls tucked neatly beneath a headband. Simon caught her setting a glass of unsweetened tea in front of William, teasing, "Northerners are always so fun to watch."

As she glanced up and spotted two women approaching the far side of the counter—Rosa and Raya—she lit up and walked over, pulling them into a hug.

It wasn't until one of them said her name aloud that Simon realized who she was—Miss May. He didn't know her personally, but clearly, they did.

Miss May's voice carried softly but clearly. "You know, when he's away, your daddy always tells me to check in on you."

Simon caught the mention of Rosa's father but kept his gaze elsewhere. He wasn't sure if Rosa appreciated the familiarity. Her smile was small, strained.

Miss May's concern was obvious. "How's your new detective job been, honey? I know it ain't easy—especially with what happened to Mr. Ropa."

Simon's eyes flicked to Rosa, noting the strain etched into her features—born from the case and the gossip swirling through the town.

Kershaw glanced toward them. "This the only place open this late?"

Raya called back, "It's after midnight."

Rosa hesitated, staring out the window.

Raya moved over to sit next to William at the bar table, leaving Rosa to join Simon.

She sat down, careful to keep distance. The vinyl stool squeaked under her.

"You might just fall out of your seat, Detective Rosa," Simon muttered, eyes on her.

Rosa didn't reply.

Kershaw tried to lighten things. "Relax, we're not talking about work."

Rosa nodded, ordering her usual—a cheesesteak sandwich with hash browns.

Simon watched her pick at the food, her appetite off.

He noticed her eyes flick to her phone, the tension beneath the surface.

Why did she seem so unsettled?

He wondered if she'd bring up whatever was bothering her—he hadn't seen the text she'd looked at, but he could sense it gnawing at her.

"I know an overthinker when I see one," Simon said quietly.

She nearly spilled her tea, startled.

"I think twice in a week spilling something is bad luck," he added with a smirk.

She muttered "clumsy," but Simon could tell her mind was elsewhere.

After a pause, she checked the time on her phone. "I think I'll head home. It's a long drive."

Simon nodded as she stood, waving to Raya, who was caught up in conversation.

Simon muttered to Kershaw, "I'll grab a smoke from the car," then stepped outside.

He lit a cigarette, watching Rosa near her truck.

The vehicle was loud, oversized—a shield, maybe.

"Why are you so good at riddles?" he asked softly.

She hesitated. "It was a game I picked up. Used to love reading them."

Simon caught the faint olive branch in her tone.

"This case is personal to you, isn't it?" she asked.

Simon didn't answer, exhaling smoke, staring into the night.

She pressed on. "You've been chasing him nearly ten years, right? Most people would've moved on."

He said nothing.

She turned away, climbed into her truck, and drove off with the music blasting.

Simon watched her go.

The case was all that mattered.

COPY CAT?

THE MORNING SUN streamed through the bay window in Rosa's bedroom, casting golden streaks across her sheets. She stirred and rolled onto her side, squinting as the brightness pulled her from the last remnants of sleep. The familiar purr of Sir Louie's engine-like breath rumbled beside her, and a small smile tugged at her lips.

She thought back to the day she got him, six years ago—her little meanie, full of attitude. But he had always known when she needed him. Whenever she was sad or crying, he would jump onto the bed and curl up against her, his warmth grounding her. And then, in true Sir Louie fashion, the next moment he'd sink his teeth into her hand as if to remind her he wasn't soft. She loved him anyway. She couldn't imagine coming home to an empty house without him.

But the moment of warmth was fleeting. The case slammed back into her thoughts like a freight train, and a wave of nausea made its way up. Somewhere out there, a man had been hiding in plain sight for decades. How could someone be so sick as to do this? It made no sense. Psychology might explain that their brains were wired differently, but no justification in the world could ever make hurting another human being acceptable.

She muttered the latest riddle aloud as she pulled herself out of bed and started getting ready for work.

"And now it starts, the clock's slow chime,

Two years asleep, the wise see time."

The words took a permanent place in her mind. What did it mean? She reached for her mascara, but her hands were clumsy with distraction, and the container tumbled into the sink. Her brows furrowed.

The killer never left direct messages—never openly, at least. The riddles had always been different. Cryptic. Purposeful. But never lazy. They usually *led* somewhere—a new location, a new victim, a twisted breadcrumb trail left for the team to follow.

But this one?

It didn't feel like that.

Well, Kershaw had tried to say something earlier but got cut off by Simon. She wasn't trying to blame them, but were they still holding things back? If they didn't trust her or Raya, how were they supposed to do their jobs properly? It felt misleading. Like they were always a step behind—because someone wanted it that way.

Her thoughts snapped back to the riddle.

The only other time the killer had broken his two-year silence was after the death of Simon's former boss. Rosa wasn't sure of the full story, but she could tell it haunted him. And the unanswered questions from the higher-ups back then? Too convenient. Someone had buried the truth—Rosa was sure of it. What she wasn't sure of was whether this new riddle fit that pattern at all.

The Wood Riddle's work was always meticulous. Precision, sterile crime scenes, not a single forensic thread to pull. Always a body. Always a riddle. It was ritualistic. Obsessive. Neat.

But Mr. Ropa's scene? The riddle didn't feel like a clue. It didn't lead anywhere. It sat there—almost like an afterthought, like someone had dropped it in the middle of chaos and called it a pattern. No follow-up. No direction.

She couldn't shake the feeling that it wasn't real. That someone wanted it to *look* like the killer's work... but hadn't understood what made it his.

Was it a warning? A setup? A redirection to throw them into the drug case?

Or was someone baiting Simon?

What if it wasn't the real killer at all?

Her thoughts spiraled faster now. The riddle carved into the bark had been shorter than usual. Sloppier. Not the usual four-to-six-line structure that defined the Wood Riddle's pattern. It was too simple. Off rhythm. Off tone. Something about it made her skin crawl.

He never strayed without reason—and when he did, it was always tied to someone specific. Someone he'd been watching. But this… this wasn't targeted. It felt clumsy. Like an impersonation.

Her heart slammed against her ribs as realization struck.

She hit the counter, eyes wide.

"A copycat."

Snatching her phone, she dialed Simon's number. The moment he picked up, she blurted it out.

"There's no way he would've done this. I think it's a copycat. Or someone who was given instructions by the real killer. Where was that last victim found again?"

"In a national park an hour or so away."

His voice was rough with sleep, and for a moment, Rosa hesitated. Something about the way it sounded—raw, unfiltered—caught her off guard. A rare crack in his usual control.

She shook it off and pressed forward.

"I really think…" she paused, her mind scrambling to keep up, "the riddle on that piece of bark—it might've been staged. Like someone copied the one from the national park case and planted it by Mr. Ropa's body. Maybe to throw us off. To shift the focus—from the drug case to the Wood Riddle murders. It would make sense."

She rubbed her temple. "But then… the real killer—he still has to be tied into this somehow. He's connected. To Chattingsburg. To all of it. I just can't piece together how—unless he was planning something, and someone else disrupted it?"

Her thoughts reeled, grabbing at fragments that wouldn't settle.

"The riddle at the national park—it led you here, right? And one of the only schools nearby is Owl Creek High."

She took a breath. "Do you want Raya and me to check it out? There's a week off for fall break, so the place will be empty. William and Kershaw can check out that old shed behind the community center, deeper in the woods—two or three miles back. I heard William mention it, like it was overlooked in the initial sweep. And the high school has a bigger library—actually a well-known one, better than the public library, especially for a town this small."

She hesitated, then added, "And... that library—it *was* in the riddle from the national park, wasn't it? That's what might have led you here in the first place. So maybe there's something there—something that connects everything, or at least gives us a new lead."

There was a beat before Simon responded.

"Get ready and meet me there in an hour."

The line went dead.

Rosa sighed. She would've preferred to handle this with Raya, but this was Simon's case. Somehow. And she worried—being so close to it might cloud his judgment.

She rushed to get ready. There was barely time to brush her hair, but she still paused to mix Sir Louie's soft and hard food, drop ice cubes in his water bowl, and scratch behind his ears. He blinked at her with those big, knowing eyes, and she smiled.

"Sorry, buddy. Gotta run."

Just as she reached for the door, her laptop chimed—a new email. No subject. No reply address. A fake account.

Her heart pounded. She clicked it open.

It's better to quit while you can. A useless detective like you.

Her jaw clenched. This time, the message didn't rattle her.

It pissed her off.

Frustration flared hot through her. She slammed the laptop shut, the force sending a tremor across the desk. The audacity.

She grabbed her keys, hands trembling with impatience.

CLASS DISMISSED, PERMANENTLY?

KERSHAW STUCK HIS head out of his motel room, his voice cutting through the quiet. "Where are you going this early?"

Simon's door clicked shut behind him. "Checking something out," he muttered, reaching for a cigarette but not lighting it. "Get some rest, man."

Kershaw sighed, running a hand over his face. "If the case doesn't kill you, that thing in your hand, will. And it's five in the damn morning. You told everyone eight since we were up half the night. Now you're already up and heading out?" He squinted at Simon. "Need backup?"

"I already asked Rosa to meet me at the high school nearby—we're following up on a lead," Simon said, tucking the cigarette behind his ear. "We'll handle that.

"Once you hear from Raya—and once William finally drags himself out of hibernation—you and Raya head to the woods near the community center, where that old shed turned up. Conduct a secondary sweep. It doesn't look like the initial team processed it thoroughly. It could be a stash site. Bring backup—we still can't rule out compromised personnel.

He opened the door to his car.

"I also sent William instructions to run an analysis on the handwriting found on the bark. It's nearly identical to the killer's signature—close enough that most would miss the difference—but it's not a confirmed match. That opens up other possibilities. We'll need to canvas the other local schools too, but that shed might be the key. No detail gets overlooked. Reassess everything."

Kershaw nodded, confusion in his eyes as he stretched his arms overhead. "Don't worry, you've got the best of the best." He grinned, pressing a kiss to his own bicep, trying to lighten the mood before the storm of a new day hit.

Simon smirked, shaking his head as he climbed into his car. He adjusted the rearview mirror, flicking on the radio. A popular '90s track crackled through the speakers as he pulled out, the early morning fog still clinging to the pavement.

***

Rosa rushed to the truck, yanked the door open, and slid in. As the engine roared to life, she connected her phone to Bluetooth and hit call. The screen lit up: *Dad*.

"Hey, can't talk long," she said, throwing the truck into reverse. "Just wanted to check in. How's the vet trip?"

"We saved a few more wild tigers," her father's voice came through, proud but strained. "Can you believe people still buy them just for show, then sell them off like collectibles? The local police had to get involved—some kind of illegal trafficking ring. It's a mess."

Sirens wailed faintly in the background, muffled by the hum of the freeway as Rosa sped up. She could picture it all—her dad knee-deep in the commotion, sleeves rolled up, refusing to walk away. Always the same. Always putting himself in the middle of it.

"Aren't you in California?" she asked, checking the time. "It's the middle of the night over there. Already knee-deep in emergencies?"

He gave a tired laugh. "Yeah. Got called in last-minute after the conference. We managed to get the cats into a secure sanctuary, but it's far from over. Deep-rooted operation—people making real money off these animals. We're trying to shut it down for good."

Rosa switched lanes, eyes flicking between the road and the clock. She needed to be at the school in under twenty minutes.

"That's awful," she muttered. "But I'm glad you're there. They're lucky to have you."

She could still remember those childhood trips to wildlife sanctuaries, her small hand wrapped in his, learning about endangered species and ecosystems most people ignored. It was the first time she'd felt something like purpose. That same anger she felt when people hurt animals—that had only grown with time.

"We do what we can," he said, then added more softly, "You'd never believe the things we see out here. But we're trying."

Her grip on the wheel tightened. "You always do. I'm proud of you, Dad."

He hesitated, voice softening. "And I'm proud of you, too. Still chasing those leads?"

Rosa's jaw clenched. Her foot pressed harder on the gas.

"Yeah… still chasing," she said. "Trying to stay ahead of it."

"Just take care of yourself. You've got people watching out for you—especially your old man."

"I know." She exhaled. "Thanks. I'll call you later, okay?"

"Be safe."

The line disconnected, but his words lingered. She didn't have time to dwell. Not now.

Rosa turned onto the main road, the school just minutes out. Time to get back to the case—and whatever puzzle waited next.

Her dad had always felt larger than life—always in motion, always chasing the next rescue. He'd raised her on his own, the steady presence in her life. But sometimes Rosa wondered if all that movement was just a way to outrun the past. To avoid *that* conversation neither of them had ever dared bring up.

She wasn't sure she could bring it up even now.

Still, one day… she knew she'd have to. He'd never dated after her mother died—never even hinted at trying. And though he never said he was lonely, she could feel it. She hated that part. Hated knowing and not knowing what to do with it.

Her eyes flicked to the clock on the dash—crap. Simon was probably already at the school, and she was still ten minutes out.

She pressed her foot down harder, speeding up just enough to make up time. The urge to flip on the sirens hit her. Just a tap of a button and she could fly down the backroads without worry.

Her lips tugged into a half-smirk. The sirens were still new—part of the unmarked truck built for undercover work. It wasn't technically illegal to use them. But still…

She sighed and left them off.

Not yet.

***

Simon knew Rosa would take a while—she still had at least ten minutes to get across town—so he didn't wait. He stepped out of his truck and walked toward the front entrance of Owl Creek High School, the only public high school in a town of five thousand. The building looked like it hadn't seen a major update in decades. Red brick, aging and chipped along the foundation, clashed with the fresh coat of pale blue paint that had been slapped across the office windows and main entrance. A freshly planted flower bed flanked the front steps, a clear attempt at charm. But charm didn't fool Simon. Not in this job.

Inside, the scent of lemon floor cleaner clung to the air—too strong, as if someone was overcompensating for something. The front office had a cheap modern renovation: laminate flooring, off-white counters, and a reception desk that looked like it had been bought from a liquidation sale. The school clearly wanted to make a good impression at first glance.

But once he stepped past the front area and glanced down the main hallway, the illusion cracked.

Faded linoleum tiles lined the floor, stained in places with age or possibly water damage. Rows of beige lockers stretched along both sides of the corridor, dented and chipped from years of use. The lighting was dimmer in the halls—older fluorescent bulbs flickered overhead, humming faintly in the distance. Posters from school events, long since passed, curled at the edges. No students, of course—it was fall break—but even if they had been here, Simon guessed the school rarely felt lively. It had that heavy, stagnant feel—the kind of place that kept its secrets tucked away in storage closets and forgotten faculty rooms.

Renovate the front, leave the rest behind. Typical.

Simon clocked it all without stopping. Public education in small towns worked more like a business than people liked to admit. Shine up the parts people see. Leave the rest to rot. Still, none of that mattered unless it tied back to the riddle left in the bark at Mr. Ropa's murder scene. Rosa had suggested the library might hold a clue—based on the national park riddle's reference. But where to start? And more importantly, what was *real* here?

A sharp cough broke the stillness.

Simon turned his head as a heavyset man emerged from a nearby office, startled to find anyone else in the building. Late-fifties, balding, pale skin flushed across the cheeks, sweat darkening the collar of his short-sleeved button-down. He blinked at Simon with glassy eyes, a half-step delayed.

Simon recognized him instantly from the preliminary search: Mr. Ronald Adams, principal of Owl Creek High School. He hadn't expected to see staff during the break. This felt more like someone caught on accident—unprepared, possibly in the wrong state of mind.

"How can I help you? I'm Mr. Ronald Adams, principal here," the man said with forced cheer, voice too loud for the abandoned halls. His hand fluttered toward Simon in greeting, but Simon noticed the faint tremble, the uneven stance. The man reeked of something off—whether it was nerves, guilt, or alcohol, Simon couldn't tell yet.

He offered his hand anyway. "Special Agent Simon Pikes, FBI."

The handshake was quick, but the moment Simon's grip met the man's, something shifted. Adams stiffened—subtly—but Simon noticed. The man's posture drew inward. His smile dropped half an inch. There was guilt in there. About what, Simon wasn't sure. Drinking on school grounds? Something worse?

He could address it later—it wasn't related to the case.

Simon didn't need to get sidetracked. Not now. Not when there was a real chance the national park riddle was pointing them here—to this school. And more specifically, to this school's library.

"I'm here to follow up on an active federal investigation," Simon continued, voice clipped, professional. "I'll be conducting a walk-through of the library and a few other locations on campus. I assume you're the one with access?"

Adams swallowed, then nodded, brushing a sweaty palm down the side of his khakis. "Of course, yes, yes—anything you need. I, uh... didn't know anyone was coming today. Thought we were shut down for break."

"You thought wrong."

Simon's tone left no room for negotiation.

Adams gestured toward the west hall. "Library's this way."

Simon followed, already analyzing more than he was being shown.

***

Inside Owl Creek High smelled like old books, lemon cleaner, and dust caught in vents that hadn't been serviced since last spring. Rosa's boots echoed against the linoleum as she moved down the hall, weaving through a faint haze of memories. The walls were a mismatched patchwork—new paint slapped over years of grime, trying and failing to mask how aged the place really was.

She remembered the same paint job from fifteen years ago—when she'd walked through these halls as a nervous freshman, clutching a schedule she barely understood. The school had bragged about a renovation then too, but all they'd really done was roll on a fresh coat of beige to cover up the peeling pastel underneath. It had smelled the same then, too—sterile, like something trying too hard to be clean.

She found Simon in the library, already scanning the space with narrowed eyes. He didn't say anything when she stepped in, but she felt his attention shift to her. The moment was brief.

Mr. Adams hovered too close behind them, practically breathing down their necks as they stepped deeper into the room. Rosa clocked the way Simon's posture shifted—tense, coiled. He clearly didn't appreciate being followed, and his voice sharpened just enough when he finally spoke to the principal.

"Sir, we need space to work."

That was Simon's polite version of a warning. Rosa stepped in quickly, offering a tight smile.

"Mr. Adams," she said, drawing him a few steps away, "maybe give us a little room. You know how this goes—paperwork and reports. We'll keep you updated if we find anything."

He hesitated, red-faced and sweaty, but eventually mumbled something about needing to "get back to grading" and disappeared down the hall. Rosa let out a breath once he was gone.

"He doesn't like people," she muttered under her breath to Simon. "Thinks the town's his to manage. Especially this school."

Simon didn't comment.

The library was cooler than the rest of the building, with light filtering in through tall windows that cast stripes across the floor. Shelves lined the walls—some newer, some clearly left over from decades past. Her eyes drifted to one of the large windows. She stepped closer, running her fingers over the windowsill.

Her and Raya's initials were still there.

Carved deep into the wood, right where they used to sit. A small piece of the past, untouched by time.

"Off topic," she said aloud, half to herself, "but aside from the food being awful, we actually had some good memories here. One time, there was a school-wide food fight. Mr. Adams lost his mind." She let out a low laugh, shaking her head. "Even the quiet moments spent in this library would never fade for me. It really was a 'safe haven.'" She scoffed at herself. "I hate agreeing with a riddle from a serial killer."

Simon, as usual, didn't respond. He was wandering through the aisles like he was searching for something he couldn't name.

Rosa moved toward the shelves lining the side wall. They looked oddly misplaced, like someone had tried to organize them and gave up halfway. She ran her fingers along the edges, her eyes catching on a dusty stack of *Huckleberry Finn* and *Tom Sawyer* books.

"Book choice needs updating," she muttered, then paused as she scanned the room again.

Freshman year. The year her mother died.

Her grip tightened around the nearest book—too tight. She knew what was coming before it hit: the crash of memory, the rush to the accident, the coldness that followed. Her breath caught.

"What did that book do to you?"

Simon's voice pulled her out of it. She flinched.

She hadn't noticed him come up beside her. He was watching her, eyes looking to her white-knuckled grip. She looked down and quickly released the book, clearing her throat.

"Nothing," she said, turning—

—straight into an unstable shelf.

It teetered, wobbled—

—and crashed.

A chain reaction. Every shelf next to it followed suit.

Rosa stood frozen for a second, staring at the wreckage.

"Oh, good God," she muttered, her attempt to stop it utterly useless.

Behind her, Simon let out a slow exhale, a near-silent huff of amusement. When she turned, she caught the signs of a smirk tugging at his mouth—barely there, but definitely real.

"I'm still wondering how the hell you passed the PT part of the test," he said dryly.

Rosa's cheeks burned. "Shut up." But she couldn't stop the faint smile that crept in. She never thought she'd see even a glint of humor from him—especially not here, in a library that smelled like her childhood, dust, and forgotten time.

Before she could say more, a familiar, irritated voice boomed across the room.

"What on earth happened here?"

Mr. Adams came rushing in, face flushed red, buttons on his shirt pulled dangerously tight over his round stomach. He looked like an angry Santa Claus, and that's what sent Rosa over the edge. She ended up trying to contain her laughter by covering her mouth.

But as she tried to remain professional, something caught her eye. The shift made her pause, her mirth fading. That's when she saw it.

One of the tiles had come loose in the chaos. As she cautiously knelt to pry it free, she glanced beneath—and any hint of laughter vanished instantly.

Beneath it was something—a toy. One every kid in this town had played with: a wooden stick with a small bucket at the end, used to catch a red ball attached to a string.

But her focus wasn't on the toy.

Next to it was a finger.

A man's finger, carefully wrapped in a piece of tissue. It looked cold. Flesh pale as wax. Bruised from the tip all the way down to the knuckle. The nails, cracked and broken, seemed to press against the ground as if still holding onto something—or someone. The chill of the flesh seemed to seep into her fingertips as her hand hovered just inches from it. She fought the urge to recoil, the heaviness of it sinking in.

And beside it, an all-too-familiar piece of bark.

Rosa's breath faltered, her stomach tightening as the chill of realization crept through her. The laughter that had almost filled her lungs just moments ago evaporated into a feeling close to suffocation.

Her fingers twitched slightly, but she forced herself to stay still, to not recoil—even as her pulse pounded in her ears.

The riddle was scrawled in blood on the piece of bark, just like the others before it.

The room, the absurdity of the fallen shelves—it all disappeared.

Something about Simon's expression told her he understood the full significance of the discovery—that the Wood Riddle Killer had left his mark here. His jaw tightened, his entire posture went rigid, as if bracing for the storm this would bring.

And just like that, the case had taken a sharp, dangerous turn.

One call was all it took to turn the school into a crime scene.

PROJECTED TRUTHS

LEANING AGAINST THE wall across from the fresh crime scene, Rosa replayed the riddle in her mind over and over.

"It watches quiet, never speaks,
a hidden clue the darkness keeps.
Once it pointed, now it's gone,
a severed truth, a life withdrawn.
A hunter felled, a case reborn."

Something about the final line stuck with her. *A hunter felled.* Not just a metaphor. A direct message.

She opened the folder again, her eyes scanning Hepple's old case file like she had a dozen times that week. Hepple—the lead detective who had come the closest to putting a face to the killer. The same man Simon and Kershaw mentioned in low voices, as if saying his name aloud might invite bad luck. Hepple had been shot multiple times while working a case the higher-ups still insisted wasn't connected.

But Rosa had noticed something when going through the photos. One detail no one ever really explained.

His right hand had been partially hidden in the crime scene photos—angled awkwardly, blurred in one or two shots. In the autopsy notes, the damage had been attributed to the gunfire, but no specifics were ever listed.

And now, here it was.

That same finger. A clean sever, wrapped in tissue. Left beneath a tile at her old high school.

She knew exactly who it belonged to.

This wasn't just a discovery. It was a message. A resurrection. A dare.

The truth hadn't stayed buried. It had been placed here, like bait.

They were getting a step closer.

Or they were being lured in.

Simon's demeanor had changed over the last half hour—more clipped, focused, but volatile. His fuse was shorter. His silence sharper. Rosa noted it the way any trained detective would, cataloging it as part of the larger pattern. Stress also did that. Especially when something didn't fit.

She hadn't told him about the threats. Not yet. The anonymous text messages—random, menacing—had trickled in over the past week. Someone was watching. She didn't need to run a full trace to know they weren't random. Her instincts told her to keep them to herself for now. Sharing too soon risked noise. Distraction. Or worse—panic.

Still, the connection that could be there buzzed at the edge of her thoughts like static.

The finger.

She kept circling back to it. Why would the killer hold onto a severed finger for over a decade? And why leave it here, in this specific place, now? It was too deliberate to be random. Too theatrical. If it was the real killer, he was staking a claim—showing the world that whoever had tried to mimic his style had done it poorly. Rosa didn't miss the subtext: *You'll know when it's really me.*

Mr. Ropa's death… it didn't line up. Wrong energy. Sloppy execution. A planted riddle, too short, too vague. The details were off. Someone else was using his name to cause a distraction.

She wished Raya were here. They balanced each other out— where Rosa spiraled, Raya filtered. And vice versa. But with Raya knee-deep in the drug angle with Kershaw, Rosa was on her own.

For now.

She heard the footsteps before she saw him—Chief Chadford. He approached with that measured gait of someone who'd spent years pretending not to limp. He stopped beside her, laying a hand on her shoulder. Firm. A reminder she wasn't invisible anymore.

"Looks to me like you got yourself tangled in one hell of a case right off the bat," he muttered, voice low.

Rosa didn't flinch. She kept her gaze on the hallway ahead, processing the crime scene, the riddle, the timeline.

"Maybe," she replied. "Or maybe it's been tangled a lot longer than we realized."

Chadford didn't respond, but Rosa could still feel his stare on her. Heavy. She couldn't tell if he doubted her or was slowly beginning to trust her instincts. Maybe both. Either way, she didn't have time to dwell on it.

The case had shifted. And if they weren't careful, it wouldn't just bury the facts—it would bury them too.

The library changed everything. If she hadn't already suspected something was hidden there, they might've missed it entirely. And if not for her clumsy mistake with the shelves, they wouldn't have had the breakthrough. She didn't want credit—but she couldn't shake the question. Would anyone else have found it? Or had the killer wanted someone like her to?

That finger... preserved all this time. It wasn't just gruesome—it was intentional. Methodical.

The riddles, no matter how cryptic, always carried a sliver of truth. But this one—this wasn't a breadcrumb leading them somewhere new.

It was a statement.

Had the killer expected a copycat? Was this his way of reclaiming power? Of drawing a boundary? One more step, and Simon would be next. Rosa didn't need Simon to say it—she could see it on his face. Whatever this stirred up in him, it wasn't the first time something had hit this close.

There was more to Simon's past. She knew that much. And whatever it was, it wasn't just private—it was dangerous.

Still, maybe this was the clue they needed to start pulling the threads tighter.

"Ryker, you need to draw up the paperwork," Chadford said, handing her a clipboard. His tone was even, but she caught the hesitation in his eyes. "Doesn't matter who you're with—FBI or local—someone's gotta file the damn thing."

She nodded, grabbing the clipboard without a word. She wasn't in the mood to explain anything. Not with the riddle still burning in her mind.

It wasn't just a taunt or clue. It had to be a threat. Directed at someone. At them. Or the impostor. Or both.

Rosa repeated the line to herself again.

"It watches quiet, never speaks, a hidden clue the darkness keeps…"

Her fingertips brushed the old windowsill, right where her initials were carved beside Raya's—faded but still clinging to memory. A relic of another time. A simpler one. Before the case. Before the killings.

Her gaze drifted to the spot where the finger had been found, her mind circling it again.

"Why leave the finger now?" she murmured. "Why here? Is it what he's watching… or what he's hiding in plain sight?"

She tapped the end of her pen against her lip, scanning the room again. Every shelf, every tile felt suspect now—as if any crack could give way to another buried truth. Her thoughts spun fast, too fast, fragments forming patterns she couldn't quite pin down.

And then Simon's voice cut through the haze.

"Thoughts?"

She didn't look at him right away. "What happened in the past?" she asked, sharper than she intended. "This message—this whole setup—it was meant for the imposter, but also you. We both know it. So what are we missing? If he's targeting you, why now? What did you do to set him off?"

She paused, trying to collect herself. The signs had all started pointing in one direction, and she hated the conclusion it led her to.

"You—"

"No," Simon cut her off. His tone was clipped. Final. "This conversation isn't happening here. It might not happen at all."

He turned slightly toward her. Not confrontational. Just closed off. Defensive.

"This was your school," he added, his voice low. "You sure there's no one from back then who'd be capable of something like this?"

Rosa let out a quiet breath, her fingers tightening around the clipboard.

"Even if there were, it was a dark time. People change. Some disappear. Some pretend nothing ever happened. Like you, I'm not in the habit of digging up what's already been buried."

Something about saying it out loud left a sour taste in her mouth. She didn't know why it stung—maybe it was the way this place, her past, had been dragged into the orbit of a killer who thrived on memory and misdirection. The school had always been a symbol of routine, of resilience. Now it was part of the nightmare.

And the longer this dragged on, the more inevitable it felt.

Another victim was coming.

Carefully staged. Unmistakably his.

A woman, she knew.

She just didn't know who.

That was the only pattern. Every two years, a different gender. No connections between victims—no shared blood type, no similar appearances, nothing to connect them.

"This finger is years old," the examiner from Chattingsburg's police station announced, carefully holding the evidence. "We'll take it back to the lab, but judging by the preservation, the DNA might still be intact. Whoever did this wanted it found exactly like this."

Rosa's jaw tightened. He was stating the obvious.

"It watches quiet, never speaks, a hidden clue the darkness keeps…"

Rosa's eyes traced the edges of the room, pausing on the shadows where light dared not reach. Darkness. The word pulsed through her thoughts like a warning. The riddle had said it was something that "watches quiet"—it wasn't a living thing, not a person. But what could it be? Her mind raced, cycling through every possibility.

Her thoughts kept spinning around that key phrase: "the darkness keeps." The clue had to be something hidden in the periphery—something that only revealed itself when the absence of light allowed it to come into focus. A clue meant to be seen only when darkness cloaked it.

A basement? A storage closet? An attic? Of course the school had them—but where exactly? She tried to picture the layout, but the memories blurred together. Everything from that time felt hazy now, like pieces of a dream she couldn't quite hold onto.

Rosa approached Mr. Adams, pressing him with her questions. He fumbled, clearly uncomfortable, fidgeting in a way she noticed. She studied his unease, wondering what he might be hiding.

Mr. Adams mentioned a forgotten basement—barely in use, mostly for electrical boxes. People were only sent there in the event of a power outage, but no one cleaned it. Over time, it had become a storage space for random, forgotten items the school didn't know what to do with.

She nodded, trusting her instincts about what the darkness could be—or perhaps what it probably was. Simon seemed too absorbed in reading the riddle, trying to solve it on his own, leaving her to follow her own lead. He sure as hell wasn't much of a partner to be working with. She didn't wait for him.

She yanked the door open, realizing there was no working light source. The basement was stale, thick with the scent of old, muddy water and damp mold. The dim light from the hallway barely stretched past the doorway, casting long, murky blotches over the cluttered space. Discarded science lab equipment, rusting desk legs, and brittle stacks of outdated textbooks were haphazardly shoved into corners, forgotten like the room itself.

Rosa wrinkled her nose and pushed an overturned chair aside. The space was larger than she'd expected.

Her fingers skimmed over a splintered wooden desk, her breath slowing as she took in the details—cobwebs clinging to the legs, deep scratches in the surface, initials carved into the corner. It felt…

wrong. Like something was buried beneath years of neglect, waiting to be noticed.

A creak behind her made her freeze.

Simon leaned against the doorframe, arms crossed, his eyes locked on her with intensity. The soft light cut across his face, sharpening the angles of his features.

"You find something, or are you just playing scavenger hunt?" His voice was low, measured, but there was something else beneath it—suspicion or maybe just impatience; she couldn't quite tell.

Rosa exhaled slowly through her nose, steadying herself. "Just thinking," she said, her fingers tracing the dust on the desk without really feeling it. She pulled out the flashlight issued to her and swept its beam over every corner and inch of the room.

Her fingers hovered over the dust-coated desk, her breath steady but her pulse anything but. She looked past the scattered debris, past the broken chairs stacked haphazardly against the wall, settling on something at the back of the room.

"I think I guessed the riddle," she murmured, more to herself.

Simon didn't move. He stood just inside the doorway, arms crossed, eyes locked onto her—not on the room, not on the mess, but on her. There was something in his expression, something quiet and reserved, and for the first time, Rosa felt a restlessness that had nothing to do with the crime scene itself.

It wasn't just the case he was piecing together. It was her.

And then she saw it.

Something half-buried under years of grime and neglect, tucked away beneath a layer of age and disuse. She almost missed it, but there it was—a forgotten object resting where the darkness pooled.

Her heart skipped a beat.

A projector.

"Look!" she exclaimed, her voice rising with realization. "It 'watches quiet, never speaks' because it hasn't been used in years—covered in dirt and cobwebs. And 'the hidden clue the darkness keeps' could mean there's something recorded or a slide left inside—something you can only see when the room is dark."

Rosa rushed over, her fingers brushing the worn, faded edges of the machine. It was one of those old video projectors—the kind long since phased out in favor of newer tech. Its bulky frame and yellowed plastic were stark reminders of classrooms from years ago. The lens was caked in more dust, and the reels looked like they hadn't spun in ages. Someone had tampered with it, but there were likely no fingerprints left behind—just the passage of time.

She grabbed the projector, rushing past Simon in her eagerness to find a working outlet. She hurried up the stairs, lugging it with her, her breath quickening with anticipation. Once inside the nearest classroom, she wasted no time. With a swift motion, she thrust the plug into the socket and adjusted the projector's angle toward the nearest blank wall.

As she powered it on, the projector's beam buzzed to life, casting grainy footage across the wall. But what played wasn't anything they expected.

The video showed Mr. Ropa—panicked, desperate—stumbling backward inside a dimly lit shed. Across from him stood a very overweight Mr. Adams, his bulk barely contained in a stiff suit, motioning toward a third figure cloaked in shadows. "Make the call," Adams ordered, his voice calm, as if arranging a simple errand.

The camera, though shaky, captured more than just the exchange—it revealed crates of drugs lining the walls. It was the same shed Kershaw and Raya were infiltrating at that very moment. The same shed they'd initially dismissed, thinking it wasn't relevant—or had someone suggested they avoid it? The same shed Mr. Ropa had fled from, running through the woods toward the town's community building in a desperate bid to find safety and call for help.

But something else came into view.

On one of the crates, barely visible in the corner of the frame, was something that made Rosa's breath catch.

A bomb. Handmade—wires coiled, taped, a crude timer blinking faintly. The camera zoomed in as if someone had set it to record the entire operation in secret.

Simon's phone was out before she could speak. "Kershaw, get out of there. Now," he snapped once Kershaw answered, his voice sharp and clipped with urgency.

Rosa's stomach dropped.

This wasn't live… it couldn't be live.

But if this was filmed recently—and if Kershaw and Raya were headed to that same shed—

No.

Her head turned sharply toward Simon, just in time to see the blood drain from his face.

Then—silence.

And in that moment, through the phone's speaker, they heard it.

The explosion.

Simon's posture locked. His jaw clenched, his breath hitched for a second too long, then he was already moving—fingers dialing, mind working. Trying to assess. Trying to gain control.

But Rosa could only stare at the screen.

The video kept playing. The camera—hidden, perhaps by someone who had wanted to catch Adams in the act—remained trained on the shed.

And there he was again.

Mr. Ropa. Alive in the footage. Desperate. Trying to back away. But they grabbed him.

She couldn't make out the other two faces. Just figures, just outlines. Just a struggle.

Two shots fired—one to the chest. One to the side.

He didn't fall right away. He ran out the shed door, clutching his side—faster than they probably thought he would.

Rosa's throat tightened as she watched him stagger out of the shed, bleeding, just before the camera glitched.

Then, as the screen flickered a few moments longer, a final image came into focus.

A figure—unidentified, face obscured—walked in front of the camera, leaving the shed, spinning something small in their hand.

That toy. The wooden one with the string and the red ball.

With a flick, they landed the ball in its cup and tucked it into their jacket.

An obvious message.

They were all being played.

Every one of them.

Rosa's heart pounded. The explosion, the setup, the finger, the toy—all of it connected. And it wasn't just symbolic.

It was a trap. A calculated misdirection.

Someone—the real killer—had planted the bomb, knowing investigators would follow the drugs. It wasn't just murder anymore.

It was war.

And they were already behind.

ASHES AND UNANSWERED QUESTIONS

THE SHED LOOKED like it had been forgotten by time—its wooden frame slumped inward, warped and silvered by years of rain, rot, and loss. Rust clawed at the hinges of a door hanging lopsided, swaying slightly in the breeze like it was exhaling. Mildew and wet soil tainted the air before they even stepped inside, laced with a sour, organic decay. Ivy wormed through every crack, creeping up the walls like it had claimed the place for itself.

Raya stepped cautiously inside, boots creaking against the warped boards. The smell hit her immediately—dense, wet, with the sharp sting of something chemical beneath the mold and gasoline. Her stomach turned.

To her left, Kershaw let out a low whistle. "Shit, would you look at that?"

She followed his gaze. Along the back wall, bricks of narcotics were stacked like warped books on a shelf. Vacuum-sealed. Tagged with colored tape. Organized. Intentional.

Her brain stalled for a second. She blinked, trying to catch up with what her eyes had already confirmed. This couldn't just be coincidence.

"These are the missing drugs from your report? From when you were in Atlanta?" Kershaw asked.

"Yes," she said, voice barely audible. Her pulse was picking up now, each beat pressing against her ribs. "But the amount..." She trailed off, taking another slow step forward. "The sheer amount—it doesn't make sense."

She didn't dare touch anything. Even breathing too hard felt like a risk. Everything about the scene screamed preserve it—don't contaminate, don't disrupt.

She reached into her coat pocket and pulled out her phone, raising it slowly. Snap. Snap. Snap. Angles, corners, every identifiable marker. They'd need this evidence preserved. Chadford had to be looped in immediately. Technically, this was still his jurisdiction.

Her eyes scanned the shed again. No one hid this much product out here without reason. Not in a place this remote. The location wasn't just a hideaway—it had meaning. Or a link.

She bit the inside of her cheek. Could this be connected to the killer? Or was someone else trying to use the commotion left behind to profit? The copycat, maybe? Someone trying to make their own name?

The space seemed to tighten. Off.

Then Kershaw's phone buzzed.

She couldn't hear the voice on the other end, but she saw the change in his face—sudden, instant. Alarm bleeding into every line.

Before she could even ask, his hand clamped down on her arm. "Move."

They barely made it through the door before the world exploded.

The blast erupted behind them with a deafening roar. Light and heat surged outward—blinding, searing—as the shockwave hurled them forward. Raya flew hard. Her shoulder slammed the ground. Wood cracked behind them. The shed was gone. Just smoke, fire, and the sound of her own heartbeat pounding in her ears.

***

"Give me your keys!" Simon's tone was urgent and clipped. His outstretched hand trembled slightly, though Rosa couldn't tell if it was adrenaline or fear.

The words barely registered before she shoved the keys into his palm. The explosion still ringing in her head—the sudden, guttural roar crackling through the phone, followed by a deadened lull that pressed against her ears like a warning. Her mind raced, tangled between what they had just heard and the unknown fate of their friends. Had they escaped in time? Had the call come too late?

Simon clenched the keys, his jaw tightening. Rosa noticed how his gaze flicked to her for a split second—shaken but focused. He didn't need to speak for her to see it: his mind was running just as fast, thinking about outcomes, bracing for worst-case scenarios.

Raya. Kershaw.

Were they okay? Were they even alive?

Her fingers twitched against her thigh, her whole body tense.

"Your truck isn't much faster," Simon muttered, already moving, "but it's faster than mine."

Without hesitation, they sprinted out of the school, boots pounding against the pavement. Rosa veered to the passenger side—a rare occurrence—as Simon launched himself into the driver's seat. The engine roared to life. Sirens screamed in the distance as the truck peeled away from the school.

Simon grabbed the radio, already switching gears.

"This is Special Agent Simon Pikes, en route to the explosion site—woods behind the town community center. Possible casualties, possible active crime scene. Request immediate perimeter lockdown. Notify local authorities we're taking jurisdiction."

The radio crackled with a brisk reply. Rosa, moving on instinct, popped open the glove box and yanked out their credentials. Local cops would be all over the scene soon. They needed control—fast.

Not a word was spoken in the truck. No conversation. No reassurance. Just the blare of the sirens and the tense rumble of the tires eating up the road.

Then came the smoke.

It bled into the horizon like ink in water, curling upward in long, black tendrils. The closer they got, the more it thickened, the stench of burning chemicals seeping through the truck's vents. Rosa's throat tightened against the acrid bite.

Then—fire.

Orange flames licked at what remained of the shed, dancing like twisted fingers reaching for anything left to consume. Firefighters worked in chaotic rhythm, their silhouettes sharp against the wreckage.

Ash clouded the sky, spinning in frantic spirals. But something finer floated through it too—white flakes, drifting like snow.

Rosa's stomach turned. Cocaine. The explosion had ignited the stash.

Simon slammed the truck into park and was out before the engine stopped growling. Rosa followed close behind.

He flashed his badge at a nearby officer. "FBI. This is a federal case now. Has the scene been secured?"

The officer hesitated. "Perimeter's set, but we're still checking for secondary devices. We had to hold off evidence collection until the fire was controlled."

Rosa stepped up beside him, raising her own badge. "Who was first on scene?"

"UC Raya Thestle and Special Agent Kershaw Blackwood. They're over by the ambulances."

Her eyes snapped to the flashing lights. For a second, everything blurred—until she saw movement.

Raya.

Relief slammed into Rosa like a punch to the gut. There she was, slouched on the edge of the ambulance, face smeared with ash but alive. Kershaw stood nearby, also smoke-covered and shaken. But breathing.

Rosa exhaled sharply, only now realizing how long she'd been holding her breath. But the relief wasn't pure. It had a bitter edge. This was no victory.

They'd lost this round.

"Dude, how did you know?" Kershaw clapped Simon on the shoulder, pulling him into a hug.

Rosa stayed a step back, watching. There was stiffness in Kershaw's grip, a weight in the way he moved. They were both coated in soot—clothes, skin, hair. The smell of fire clung to them—sweat, chemicals, and traces of blood from visible cuts.

"If Rosa hadn't found the evidence at the school," Simon said, his voice tight, "you might not have made it out of that shed."

Kershaw let out a dry laugh. "Yeah, well, she saved our asses big time. We were just finishing up inside when the call came through. A few more seconds, and we'd have been toast."

Rosa's insides flipped. Five minutes—that was the margin. That's all it took to shift everything.

Her voice came out tighter than she expected. "What's happening?" She looked at Raya now, unable to ignore the sting in her eyes or the ache building behind her ribs.

Raya finally raised her head, her gaze locking with Rosa's.

"Trap," she said hoarsely. "We walked straight into it."

The word hit like a blunt object.

Rosa glanced at the wreckage—the charred remains of what was once a shed. The embers hissed, wood still curling inward, the structure collapsing on itself in slow motion.

She turned toward Simon. His face was unreadable, but his eyes said everything. He was already running calculations, already mapping connections. So was she.

Why here? Why now?

As Rosa filled them in—explaining what led them to the school, to the evidence, to the riddle—her voice became automatic. But the more she talked, the more tangled everything became. The case wasn't coming undone—it was binding tighter, growing more complex by the second.

A tense stillness settled around them until Raya spoke again, her voice breaking through with calm certainty.

"One thing's certain," she said, her tone grim. "The drug case and the Wood Riddle Killer are connected."

Rosa didn't speak. She didn't have to.

Because deep down, she already knew that to be true.

SICK SHADE OF RED

"IF I'M GOING down for this, so are you." Mr. Adams rifled through the glove compartment, pressing the phone hard against his shoulder as it rang and rang, then went to voicemail. Frustration tightened his jaw as he tossed the phone aside.

A voice, cold and calm, slipped out of the shadows behind him. "You won't find what you're looking for."

Mr. Adams spun around, eyes wide, but before he could react, the voice cut in again.

"You'd think they'd be foolish enough to believe that riddle was mine," it sneered, the words heavy in the stale air. "I had it all set up—perfectly staged for the detectives. And yet you had to interfere. Trying to leave your own mark. Handwriting close enough to fool most, but not me. Did you really think you could get away with it?"

The moment stretched, dense with menace.

"This isn't how I usually handle things," the voice said, low and steady. "But you—you blocked the path forward. You stalled the chase, delayed the trail leading to the next location. You became a problem. So you had to be stopped. To send a message."

Before Mr. Adams could process the words, a shotgun blast shattered through the night. Blood sprayed, splattering the inside of the car a sick shade of red.

"Copycat?" the voice whispered, a hint of amusement cutting through the cold tone. "No, those detectives are smarter than that. Because of you, my grand reveal will have to wait. Thirty years hidden, patient in the background. But now… my time is coming. They will see me. They will know me."

***

Simon moved steadily along the tree line behind the school, the late afternoon sun filtering through the bare branches and casting fractured outlines over the cool ground. The strong scent of pine and wet soil lingering there—but underneath, a sharper, metallic tang hit his nostrils. Fresh blood.

Ahead, a rusted van sat half-hidden beneath the canopy. It hadn't been there during his last sweep. Now, its side panel was splattered with a vivid, glistening crimson—fresh enough that it still caught the light.

Simon's pulse quickened as his gaze dropped downward. There, slumped beside the van, lay the broken form of Mr. Adams. A shotgun blast had left a brutal, savage wound; the body was still warm and soaked in blood. The scene was merciless—clear and gruesome.

He crouched, drawing his service pistol with the calm precision drilled into him, eyes scanning every inch of the scene and the darkening perimeter.

The blood splattered wildly across the metal. But the savagery wasn't random. It was a deliberate retaliation—an unmistakable statement that no one messes with the Wood Riddle's work.

A snap of a twig in the underbrush drew Simon's gaze. His jaw clenched tight.

"You fucker!" he shouted into the trees, voice low but raw with frustration. "I'm coming for you. Show yourself!"

His muscles tensed, every fiber alert.

No pretenses. No riddles this time.

This was the Wood Riddle's wrath.

He reached for his radio with steady authority. "FBI to dispatch: body discovered east perimeter near abandoned van. Cause of death—shotgun blast. Scene is fresh. Secure the area and send evidence team immediately."

Simon exhaled slowly, his eyes locked on the blood-streaked van. The case shifted once again—but now, the killer was here, in this town.

FRICTION AND FIRE

SIMON HAD GIVEN them two days off—well-earned, but rest never came easily, not with a case that clung to the back of someone's mind even in sleep. The explosion had left more than scorch marks in the woods; it had splintered something in all of them. And now, word of Mr. Adams's murder swept in like a cold wind, confirming the killer was nearby.

Raya, of course, refused to sit still. She didn't want to be alone, and she wasn't subtle about it either. What started as her casually crashing at Rosa's for the night had morphed into a full team gathering.

"This is your fault," Rosa muttered, darting around her living room, tossing clutter into a basket. "You invited the damn team, and I haven't even started cleaning."

"You haven't had a single visitor since your dad helped you buy this place," Raya countered, vacuum in hand like she was ready to fight crime with it. "Don't forget—he co-signed, too. You're just gonna let this house collect dust?"

Rosa rolled her eyes. "It's not collecting dust. I live here."

"Exactly my point."

Sir Louie, her overly dramatic tabby, bolted under the couch at the vacuum's first growl. Rosa sighed and reached to straighten the nearest stack of books—again.

"You even invited the boss."

"Simon's not a 'boss.' He's just…" Raya shrugged. "Someone who could use dinner and a break."

The truth was, Rosa's house—tucked outside the town limits, hidden behind pines—had become their quiet escape. The inside told stories of someone who read more than she spoke. Floor-to-ceiling bookshelves ran along nearly every wall, some shelves organized with obsessive care, others a chaotic mess of bookmarks, folded pages, and worn spines. A rolling ladder rested against one side, unused but very necessary. The scent of old paper, polished wood, and vanilla candles lingered in the air. It was the kind of place that felt still, even when people were talking.

By the time Rosa was done straightening everything that didn't need straightening, she was wiped out. A hot shower helped melt away the tension in her shoulders. She pulled on a navy hoodie and oversized gray sweatpants, hair still damp and tied back messily. Sir Louie followed her downstairs, rubbing against her legs as if congratulating her on surviving another day.

In the kitchen, Raya had somehow transformed the space. The smell of garlic, rosemary, and slow-cooked meat floated through the home. A freshly baked loaf of bread rested on the cutting board, next to a picture-perfect charcuterie spread.

Rosa leaned against the counter, blinking. "I'm not saying this looks better than sex, but—"

Raya tossed her a slice of cheddar. "That's because I actually know how to cook. Unlike someone who once set pasta on fire."

Rosa popped the cheese in her mouth. "One time."

"The grilled cheese?"

"Okay, three times."

"Water."

"That pot was defective."

They were still laughing when the doorbell rang.

Kershaw stepped in first, followed by Simon, then William a few seconds later. His eyes lit up the moment he took in the homey interior—the books, the soft glow of candles. "Rosa, this is insane. Are you secretly eighty?"

"She's been collecting books since kindergarten," Raya explained. "If she had more shelves, there'd be more books."

Simon said nothing at first, but Rosa could feel him taking in everything around them. He didn't belong here—too taut, too shadowed—but somehow, he looked less hollow than he had all week.

"I'm going back out for a smoke," Simon muttered, already moving toward the front door, but Rosa interrupted him.

"I'll show you the backyard. This way." She walked down the hallway and was just about to open the back door when Sir Louie stepped into Simon's path, making her pause and turn her head slightly to look back.

Simon stopped and bent down to scratch behind the cat's ears. A thunderous purr rumbled through the house.

Raya smirked nearby. "Congratulations, you passed. He doesn't let anyone touch him usually."

Rosa stepped out onto the porch, letting Simon shut the door behind him, then went straight to gathering firewood in her arms as the crisp night air settled around her. Simon followed, leaning against the back porch railing. Her backyard stretched wide and fenced in, string lights swaying gently in the breeze, while a half-built koi pond caught flickering reflections. She moved around the firepit, stacking logs with careful ease.

Simon's voice floated from the porch. "Need help?"

She didn't even look up. "Nope."

The quiet—no, the space between them—lasted until Raya called for dinner.

As Rosa headed back up the steps, her foot caught the edge. She stumbled forward—but Simon was already there, catching her by the elbow before she could hit the deck.

Her cheeks burned. "You didn't see that."

"I see everything," he muttered.

Inside, the night unfolded in warm tones—banter, shared plates, Kershaw's bear-like laughter. Rosa even smiled when William compared her shelves to the Library of Congress.

But that warmth shattered the moment her laptop pinged in the corner.

She walked over and tapped it open, expecting junk mail.

Instead, she froze.

It was a photo.

Of her.

Taken just minutes ago, outside. Hauling firewood.

"What the hell?" Her voice cracked, louder than she expected.

Simon was at her side before she could shut it.

"What the fuck is that?" he asked, his voice sharp.

Rosa flinched as he snatched the laptop.

"You've been getting messages like this?"

"Simon—"

"This isn't the first time, is it?"

She crossed her arms but said nothing.

His voice dropped into something darker. "You didn't think I needed to know? You're out here alone, getting surveilled, and you say nothing?"

"Lower your voice," she hissed. "Everyone's trying to enjoy themselves."

"They shouldn't be. Not if you're a possible target."

She tried to take the laptop back, but he pulled it away.

"Simon, seriously."

He stepped closer, crowding her against the hallway wall, one hand pressed above her head. "Would you be able to fight someone off like this?" he asked, his tone a quiet, burning fury. "You think a killer like this gives second chances?"

Rosa stared up at him, pulse rising—but not from fear. From frustration. And something else she didn't want to name.

His jaw clenched.

"Message received," she said. "But don't act like you're the only one allowed to carry secrets. Raya knows, so it's not like I didn't tell anyone."

He said nothing.

"I've got cameras installed. We'll check them—but not right now."

Her voice was calm and even, but something in her eyes told him to back off.

For once, he did.

As laughter drifted in from outside, Rosa remained still, her heart pounding. Someone had been close. Watching. And Simon knew it, too.

But for now, the fire was lit. The wine was poured. And the killer hadn't made their next move—yet.

BURNING CLUES

"WHY'S HE BROODING?" Raya whispered a couple of hours later, her voice nearly swallowed by the soft crackle of the fire. The light danced across their faces, casting flickering shapes that stretched along the grass and fence line.

Rosa followed her gaze to Simon. He sat apart from the others, flicking his lighter open and closed, the flame never staying lit. His eyes were fixed on the treeline, not the fire, not the people. Kershaw was mid-story beside him—something about a drug bust gone wrong—but Simon wasn't listening. He was watching. Waiting.

Rosa knew that look. He had started thinking about the case—probably never letting himself forget it, never allowing himself a good time.

Earlier, when she slipped away to grab a charger from the kitchen, she hadn't expected to find Simon standing over her laptop again. Somehow, another threat had come in—this one vague, but with just enough venom to raise alarm. Raya had seen it, too, and for the first time, the humor in her expression faded into something uncertain. Concern, real and quiet, appeared behind her eyes, even though she had already been told about it. They were preoccupied, thinking it wasn't connected. She didn't think much of it.

Rosa had waved it off. "We'll check the cameras once everyone heads in," she said, brushing it away like lint. The truth was, she already had a feeling nothing would turn up. Whoever was behind the messages was careless and just wanted to make a stupid joke.

And she didn't think it was the Wood Riddle Killer anymore.

No… this felt different. Like someone holding a grudge. Maybe it was connected, maybe it wasn't—but the timing didn't feel calculated. Just random. Still, it was close enough to blend in with the chaos already unfolding around the case, so others might see it as related. Rosa didn't dwell on it, even if it made her a little uneasy.

She refused to let it spoil the night. Even if they were detectives, they had every right to have a life outside the job.

"He does that a lot, doesn't he? Brood." she murmured now, her breath fogging in the cold air. She tried for a smile, but it didn't quite stick.

"Should we play truth or dare?" Kershaw suddenly blurted, rising like he was on a mission.

"No, thank you," came the unified chorus of four exhausted voices.

He looked around, clearly offended. "You guys are no fun. I'm getting more mac and cheese." And with that, he stomped inside like a disappointed camp counselor.

"I'm kind of hungry again too," Raya said, already standing and stretching. William rose at the same time, their movements almost identical. They shared a quick laugh as they headed in together.

And just like that, Rosa was alone with Simon.

She rubbed her palms together, then pressed them to the fire, the heat biting into the cold that had sunk deep in her skin. Sparks cracked and popped, and for a second, she was back in her father's backyard, barefoot on the porch, holding cocoa in both hands while the fire pit burned low. Simple. Safe.

She missed that feeling.

From the corner of her eye, she saw Simon shift in his seat. "Ignore it for now," he said quietly, like an afterthought. "Two detectives. Three agents. No one's stupid enough to make a move with this many people staying the night."

His words struck a chord. Something in the way he said *ignore it*—like that would somehow make it go away. She swallowed, nodding even though her mind was jumbled.

"Okay," she muttered.

Then the full meaning hit her. She turned. "Wait... you don't mean you're—"

"Raya extended the invitation. We should accept—for the sake of Southern hospitality," he cut in, deadpan. "And she's right. This place is remote. If someone's circling, it's better we're here than scattered in separate rooms across town."

He glanced toward the house. "When they come back out, I'll check again. For cameras. Or movement."

"I already checked earlier," Rosa replied, arms crossed. "But be my guest."

Simon rose, rolling his shoulders with a slow, practiced motion. "Besides," he said, fishing for another cigarette, "anything's better than a motel bed."

Rosa followed him toward the house. She didn't reply, because deep down, he wasn't wrong.

The moment they crossed the threshold, a loud pop echoed through the space.

Rosa flinched instinctively, heart in her throat, every muscle locking. Her hand shot out, gripping Simon's arm as she ducked slightly behind him. Pulse racing. Eyes scanning.

Then—laughter.

A cheer.

It was champagne. Not a gunshot.

Her lungs gave out a long, trembling breath. She stepped away from Simon quickly, avoiding his gaze as embarrassment flared hot beneath her skin.

"Idiot," she whispered to herself. But her smile returned, practiced and quick. She grabbed an empty glass and slid seamlessly back into the fold of the party, even raising it with a mock toast as someone reached to pour for her.

She declined with a polite shake of her head and filled it with soda instead, all while the laughter buzzed around her like static.

But even as the warmth of the night returned and the fire crackled outside, Rosa's gaze flicked toward the dark beyond the windows. Someone had been close. Close enough to watch her. Close enough to take a photo without her noticing.

Simon knew it, too.

And while they'd check the cameras, Rosa knew they wouldn't find anything.

Because this wasn't about the case.

Not exactly.

This was probably a past mistake catching up to her.

***

The rest of the night drifted by in a blur—card games, childhood stories, half-spilled secrets, and bursts of genuine laughter. It was exactly the kind of night a team like theirs needed, even if none of them could fully detach. Simon stayed on the edge of it all, present but even more detached, his mind constantly crawling back to the case, to the van, to the blood.

When the energy in the room finally dipped, the clock on the wall read 1:32 a.m.

William stretched with a yawn that practically cracked his spine. "Guess it's time to crash."

"I'll show you to the rooms," Raya said, smiling at him and Kershaw. "Y'all look like you could use a real bed. That motel you picked isn't even the best option." She gestured toward the hallway. "Four bedrooms—two upstairs, two down. The ones upstairs have private bathrooms. Rosa, Simon, and I are up there. Downstairs has one room that used to be a garage and another that's basically an office with a daybed. Kershaw and William will have to share a bathroom."

Then she turned to Simon. "You get the one upstairs at the end of the hall. One of the master bedrooms."

Her tone was playful, teasing. "Boss perks."

He didn't bother answering. Just gave her a short nod. When she walked off with the others, he felt Rosa watching him from the corner of the room.

"I'll show you yours," she said finally, and started for the stairs.

He followed her without a word, his legs aching with each step, his muscles stiff and slow with fatigue. But it was more than tiredness—it was a gnawing, crawling agitation that hadn't left him since the moment he found Adams.

The killer was nearby.

Still circling.

He shouldn't be lingering this close to the case, not now. Not this openly. Simon had spent a decade chasing this man—the man who lurked in the background, sure. But he never stayed where he might get caught. He didn't loiter.

Unless he wanted to be seen.

Or unless he was unravelling.

He clenched his jaw, gripping the railing briefly as he followed Rosa down the upstairs hallway. She stopped halfway down, clearly distracted for a second, then caught herself and moved to a door on the left.

"This is it," she said, opening the door and stepping aside.

Simon scanned the room as he entered. It was cluttered, but not messy—just lived-in. Shelves packed with books lined the walls, some in neat rows, others stacked in lazy piles, like someone who meant to organize them eventually but never quite got around to it. The scent of paper and cedarwood in the air, warm and oddly comforting.

Suddenly, a blur of gray and white fur shot between them.

Sir Louie.

The cat launched himself across the room and into a round bed tucked beside the bookshelf, circling twice before plopping down like a small king reclaiming his throne.

"Sir Louie loves this room," Rosa said, leaning against the doorframe. "That's his favorite bed. If it's a bother, you can shut the door."

Simon barely reacted. "I'll leave it open."

The cat had settled already, breath slow and steady. No point in kicking him out now.

Rosa hesitated. "Sorry for the clutter. My room's worse, or I would've offered that instead."

He didn't care about the clutter. Didn't care about the books. None of it mattered.

"Towels are in the bathroom, extras too. I always over-prepare—comes with the anxiety, I guess," she added with a half-smile, reaching to flip the bathroom light on. Warm light glowed across the wooden floorboards. "Anyway. Good night, boss man." She gave a lazy salute and gently closed the door, but not all the way.

He didn't move.

From beyond the thin walls, he heard Raya call out, "Rosa! I'll shower since you already did earlier!"

Rosa's muffled response: "Okay, be quiet! You know the walls are thin."

He stood there, unmoving, listening without meaning to.

There was a brief mention—Raya saying something about how tonight felt like the old days, when Rosa's mother was alive. Then nothing but soft footfalls and the creak of pipes.

Stillness. Not peace. Just quiet enough for his mind to start up again.

The case.

The killer.

The body in the van. Still warm.

The splatter on the car's interior hadn't been a signature. It had been punishment. Vicious. Fast. Brutal. Not to warn Adams—but to retaliate.

Simon ran a hand down his face, letting it drop with a tired sigh.

Who was Adams trying to impress with that fake riddle? He'd inserted himself into something far too complex. And the killer hadn't appreciated it.

Simon could feel it in his bones. That scene hadn't been about misdirection. It was about vengeance. A personal line had been crossed.

But why here? Why now?

He turned slowly in the room, letting his eyes drag across the walls, the books, the corners. He didn't know what he was looking for—something off. A sound. A detail. A presence. But there was nothing.

Still... he couldn't shake it.

The killer was still nearby. The thought repeated, over and over again.

But he shouldn't still be poking around town—not this long after a hit. Not unless he wanted to be seen. But why now? Why did he want to be seen now?

Simon wanted to leave, to search every inch of this godforsaken town, but he couldn't chase ghosts tonight. His body was betraying him—too tired to keep moving, too drained to think straight. His thoughts blurred. His shoulders slumped.

He sat on the edge of the bed and exhaled slowly, letting the stiffness win for once. Somewhere down the hallway, laughter still resounded faintly. Something clinked in the kitchen.

It could all go to hell in the morning.

But tonight, he was out of moves.

And eventually, without meaning to, Simon passed out—fully clothed, boots still on, the day dragging him into sleep like quicksand.

SHATTERED REMNANTS

THE BLAST SHATTERED *the morning stillness, a deafening roar that swallowed the world in fire and carnage. The mailbox, once an ordinary fixture at the end of their driveway, was now a twisted heap of shrapnel and smoking debris. And where her mother had stood just seconds before—smiling, sifting through envelopes, unaware—there was nothing but scattered remnants of flesh and bone.*

The explosion had torn her apart.

Rosa ran, legs burning, breath coming in frantic, choking gasps. The stench of charred flesh hit her first—thick, metallic, nauseating. Smoke curled into the sky, curling around the jagged remains of what had once been their front yard.

Then she saw it.

A leg—severed at the knee, the skin shredded and blackened, tossed like a discarded doll's limb beside the shattered mailbox. Strips of clothing clung to it, blood soaking into the dirt, pooling, steaming. A hand lay further away, fingers curled as if still grasping the letters her mother had been opening.

The bile rose in Rosa's throat before she could stop it. She doubled over, heaving onto the pavement, her entire body trembling with a sickness she had never known.

There was nothing left of her mother that could be whole. Only pieces. Fragments. A red smear where she had once stood.

She didn't hear her father's truck at first, didn't register the screech of tires until the sound of his scream tore through. A raw, guttural cry—one that rattled through the trees, through the hollowed-out remains of what had been a piece of their home, through her very bones.

He collapsed to his knees in the wreckage, his hands digging into the blood-soaked dirt, clawing as if he could put her back together. As if he could hold her one last time.

But there was nothing left to hold.

The officers had arrived after the incident, too stunned themselves to fully process the horror that had unfolded. Rosa could hear them calling for backup, for paramedics, for something—anything—but no one spoke to her.

No one could.

Because how do you tell a girl that her mother died in pieces?

How do you tell a man that his wife's remains have to be scraped off the pavement?

The casket had to stay closed. There was nothing left for a final goodbye. But her father resisted the reality, raging against the truth as if his fury alone could undo what had happened.

And Rosa... she simply stared. Stared at the place where her mother had been. Stared at the blood drying against her own hands. Stared at the empty sky, swallowing her screams.

"Rosa!"

Raya's voice was soft but urgent as she gently shook her awake, pulling her from the nightmare's suffocating grip.

Rosa's breath came in shallow gasps, her pulse hammering against her ribs. The explosion still clung to her mind—the searing heat, the scent of burnt flesh, the sickening crunch of bone. Even after all these years, it found its way back to her.

She pressed her palms against her face, willing the images to fade, but they never truly left. Every time she closed her eyes, she saw the fragments—the leg by the mailbox, her father's broken sobs, the blood staining her hands. She had scrubbed them raw that day, but no amount of washing could erase what was burned into her memory. Some nightmares never ended. They just lay dormant, waiting for the right moment to claw their way back.

Simon appeared in the doorway, his hair disheveled, eyes heavy with sleep, yet still sharp with concern. He looked half-dead, wrenched from what was probably his first decent rest in weeks, maybe even years.

"Everything alright?" His voice was rough, edged with the instinctive wariness that never seemed to leave him.

"It's fine," Raya answered for Rosa, though the grief in her expression said otherwise. "Go back to sleep, Rosa. It's only been two hours."

But Rosa didn't move. Couldn't. The past was an invisible force holding her down.

***

Raya sighed and climbed out of bed, grabbing a jacket and slipping it on. She shot one last glance at Rosa before motioning Simon to follow her. The door clicked softly shut behind them as they descended the stairs.

At the bottom, Raya leaned against the wall, arms crossed against the clinging chill. She stared into the dark, as if searching for something in the shadows.

"We all have our ghosts, don't we?" she murmured. Her voice held a quiet understanding, one born from experience. "Your eyes are just like hers. Both of you have seen death. Lived with it. It's not my story to tell, but… I guess the police are out there chasing justice in a world that doesn't always care. And God—" She let out a bitter, hollow chuckle. "Sometimes I think He watches the pain He allows, like some twisted spectator."

"Someone sent her threats," Simon said, running a hand through his hair. "This case is bigger than either of you realize. We're dealing with a killer who's been on a rampage for more than three decades. There was never a chance he wouldn't notice who got involved. Keep an eye on her."

Simon's eyes stayed fixed on the banister. Raya glanced at him, then lowered her voice.

"I know this isn't my story to tell," she said, "but you've been around long enough to know—we all have a past. It's part of why we're here."

She clicked her tongue, confirming the gut feeling she'd been struggling to name. "I knew about them—sorry for not disclosing it earlier—but I don't think those messages are from the killer. It wouldn't make sense," she muttered.

"Look, we didn't become detectives for nothing. I'm honestly surprised she didn't join us sooner. Someone did something horrible to her mother—brutal—and still got away with it. She still doesn't know who killed her. To this day."

She paused, gaze growing distant.

"But now… after everything, she's found the courage. I've never seen her so determined." Another pause. Her voice softened.

"And as much as I get mad at God… He's got His reasons for how everything comes together. Guess we're too far in to back out now, huh?"

Simon didn't respond right away. His jaw was tight, his fingers curled into fists.

"We need another lead," he finally said, voice with restrained fury. "Something triggered this." The cruelty in his tone was impossible to miss, and for the first time, Raya wondered—what had broken this man so thoroughly? What had left him so angry, so aggressive, so obsessed?

She studied him for a moment, then shook her head. "Obsession might get you killed," she murmured, turning toward the stairs.

Simon didn't stop her.

He was too lost in his own storm.

STILL WATERS, HIDDEN TIDES

SINCE THE EARLY afternoon had already turned cold, Raya started the bonfire early, stacking firewood until the flames danced higher. Rosa stepped outside, wrapped in the same hoodie from the night before. The smoky scent drifted through the crisp air as she crossed the yard to help, her breath visible in the chill.

"How foolish do you think I looked after that little episode?" she asked, grabbing a piece of firewood and hoisting it onto her shoulder.

Raya didn't look up. "You don't have to handle everything on your own anymore. We're a team now—we'll figure it out together."

Rosa stretched her arms overhead, agreeing as she tried to ease the tension deep in her muscles. "Apparently, this is our new headquarters. Chadford gave the okay. He didn't love the idea but didn't fight it either. You know how he is."

She turned toward Raya, a faint smirk tugging at her lips. "So today, I plan to enjoy it before we get back to it. Starting with your chocolate chip pancakes."

Raya rolled her eyes just as Rosa slung an arm around her shoulder.

"Oh, you wanna bring up my pancakes?" Raya warned, and lunged, fingers finding Rosa's sides.

Rosa shrieked, laughing as they collapsed to the ground in a tangle, rolling like they were back in college again.

"This feels like a night in undergrad," Kershaw's voice called out behind them. He lobbed a pinecone in their direction, pretending to aim. "Can we build a fort next?"

"Oh, you're asking for it," Rosa grinned, scrambling to her feet and grabbing her own pinecone. Raya mirrored her, and together they mock-charged.

Kershaw threw his hands up, dramatically falling to his knees. "Man, screw this. I'm getting too old for this."

Their laughter bounced off the fence in the yard—loud, carefree, and brief.

William emerged from the house in his overcoat and gloves, giving them all a judgmental look. "Why are grown adults rolling on the ground?"

That only made them laugh harder.

"You're the weirdest of us all and you know it," Kershaw said, clapping him on the back. "But you're still one of us."

"I think that's my cue to cook," Raya said. "Did anyone wake boss man?"

"I'm not doing it," Kershaw replied. "Last time I tried, I nearly got shot in the face."

Rosa laughed again, but it quickly faded. She hadn't forgotten the way Simon reacted to being startled. None of them had. Raya didn't comment further, just walked back toward the house.

Rosa followed her inside but veered toward the foyer. The laptop sat where she'd left it, and she had already checked the cameras earlier that morning—watched every angle of her yard from the night before. Not a single person had come close. No signs of anyone entering her property. Nothing was out of place.

And yet, someone had taken that photo. Someone had been close enough to see her.

They hadn't caught a damn thing.

"I don't think this is the serial killer," she had whispered to Raya earlier. "It doesn't feel like him. It feels like something else."

She hadn't disagreed.

Now, as she sat down again and refreshed the feed, there were still no new alerts. No more messages. No more threats—for now.

A flicker of relief moved through her, but it didn't last.

Her phone rang.

Her dad's name lit up the screen.

"Well, I guess those tigers really did get saved," Rosa said with a smirk as she answered. "I read the article. You're famous again."

"Yeah, yeah," he muttered, but she heard the smile in his voice. "How's the new headquarters treating you? Saw your text."

"We're basically camping in the middle of nowhere," Rosa replied, rolling her eyes. "But I'll admit, the place looks good. You did a better job fixing it up than I gave you credit for."

"Of course I did great," he said. Then, a pause. "I'm actually going on a date tonight."

She choked. "Wait—what?"

He chuckled. "It's just casual. I called for advice, but then again, your dating life hasn't exactly been solid since that Jacob guy."

"Ew. Goodbye." She hung up, making a disgusted face.

Raya, who had been eavesdropping from the kitchen, burst out laughing. "Your dad's going on a date? Finally! He deserves it."

"Shut up!" Rosa called, slapping the counter as she walked in. "Why does he call me for this stuff?"

"Because he misses you," Raya said, not missing a beat. "You do know how lucky you are, right?"

Rosa glanced down at her coffee. She did know. Even if she didn't always say it.

Raya had grown up under pressure—strict rules, never-ending expectations. Rosa had always been her escape, and over the years, they'd become inseparable. Raya had spent more holidays at the Ryker home than with her own family. It hadn't been perfect, but it had been real.

Her father was her anchor. After her mom died, he didn't fall apart—he dug in. He made sure Rosa stayed grounded, even when it felt like the whole world was trying to spin her out of control. Her love of animals wasn't just a passion. It had been a lifeline—one that kept her close to him during the worst moments.

So hearing that he was dating… it felt strange. Good, but strange.

And it made her think—maybe they were both trying to move forward, in their own quiet ways.

She tried to push the thought away, but it lingered, stubborn as ever.

"I don't want your help," Raya teased, breaking the quiet. "Last time, you almost blew up the kitchen."

"I didn't blow it up. I just... aggressively seared the bacon," Rosa muttered, settling on a barstool.

Outside, through the kitchen window, William was chasing Kershaw across the yard—probably trying to get his gloves back again. His coat flared behind him like a cape. Rosa couldn't help but smile.

"Everyone's weird in their own way," she murmured.

Then, her tone shifted.

"I know we said we wouldn't talk about it… but the threats brought something back. Memories. Not forgotten—just buried."

Raya turned from the stove, her eyes softening.

"I figured," she said quietly. "It's been a long while since you had a nightmare that bad."

She reached out, giving Rosa's hand a small squeeze.

The gesture said what words couldn't. They had survived a lot. Together.

Raya smirked again, trying to lift the mood. "Still—your first case? And it's a full-blown psychopath? That's just bad luck."

Rosa exhaled dryly. "The worst kind."

Though they joked, cooked, and carried on with their morning, that statement stayed in the back of Rosa's mind. Whoever this killer was, and whoever had taken the photo hadn't just trespassed.

They'd gotten close.

Too close.

And maybe he'd been one of the neighbors in town all along.

And they knew nothing about it.

CRUMBS OF CONTROL

TWO MORE WEEKS passed.

They knew the finger was Hepple's, and the toy—it was the same one from the projector video. Of course, no fingerprints had been found, not even a smudge, as if the culprit had scrubbed away every trace of themselves—obsessively meticulous, just like in the cases before. OCD freak. The riddle? That was the only thing they had to go off of.

Mr. Adams had already been shot and killed by the serial killer before he could say more—or even be questioned. Simon kept wondering: what exactly had Adams been thinking? Was he just trying to steer them away from the stash? Most likely. But would he have even talked? The killer got to him first, silencing him forever.

Adams had never even been a key player in the underground organization—barely more than an informant with limited intel. Just a small cog in a much larger machine. He'd seemed more preoccupied with his school job, fixated on who the next principal might be, convinced no one could possibly be better than him.

But Simon remembered the nervous fidgeting, the constant nail-biting at the scene with the finger, the sheen of sweat on his forehead. A man drowning in fear. Useless, maybe—but not without a clue.

He'd only managed to make one thing clear before shutting down completely: there was another partner—maybe even two. The video from the projector proved that much. Beyond that, he'd clammed up—mouth dry, boots scraping against the floor like he was trying to escape without moving. Guilt had radiated off him, dragging him deeper into whatever hole he was too scared to climb out of.

He hadn't noticed anything else from Adams.

And now? That witness was gone for good. And it pissed Simon off even more—especially today.

Chattingsburg was steeped in unease. Whispers rippled through the town like slow-moving poison, disbelief striking the air. An undercover drug cartel? Here? In their quaint little town? No one wanted to believe it, but the gruesome evidence spoke louder than doubt. Instead of answers, there were only more questions.

They had questioned multiple people, tossing out theories like stones thrown into a still pond. Maybe it was Mayor Thompson. He'd been gone for three weeks, vanished without a trace. They'd tried to call him, to locate him, but even the FBI agents stationed near his last known whereabouts couldn't find him. It was as if he didn't exist. Another strange loose thread tangled in the case.

Simon was still seething, a storm trapped beneath his skin. The main office in D.C. had already called, urging him to move on—maybe there wasn't anything left to find. Maybe this case had already given up all its ghosts. But Simon knew better. He felt it like a phantom itch in his bones, an unshakable certainty that something remained hidden. He just couldn't prove it. Not yet.

The lack of evidence, the riddles that led nowhere—it ate through his patience.

So he pushed harder. Harder than he should have. Ripping through case files. Scrutinizing every detail. Drilling his team with the same questions over and over until their patience wore thin. They were ready to wring his neck, and he knew it. Did he care? No. He wasn't here to be liked. He wasn't here to play nice.

He only wanted one thing. And he didn't care how he got it.

Even those hazel-brown eyes he had caught resting on him more than once—wouldn't distract him from that.

Especially not today.

Because today marked ten years.

Ten years since everything changed.

The thought burned in his chest but he refused to acknowledge it. Instead, he turned it into fuel, letting it stoke the fire already roaring inside him. He lashed out without meaning to—but even if he had, he wouldn't have stopped himself. Not today. Today, the past was breathing down his neck, and he needed something—anything—to tear apart.

A voice at the doorway. Cheerful. Warm. Too warm.

Then Rosa walked in, the warm, buttery aroma of freshly baked chocolate chip cookies from Raya filling the air. A bright, almost defiantly cheerful smile spread across her face as she held up the tray.

"Here, we need a small break, and—"

Something inside Simon snapped. Not today.

Before she could even finish, the tray was smacked from her hands. The metal clattered against the floor, sending the cookies scattering in a mess of broken crumbs.

The room stilled and her eyes widened in shock, fingers twitching as if they still held the weight of the tray. No one moved. No one spoke.

Simon was already on his feet, his chair scraping violently against the floor. His fury crackled through like static before a lightning strike, raw and unchecked.

"There's shit to get done, and you have nothing new to show!" His voice was serious. His hands curled into fists at his sides, his breathing heavy, his restraint obliterated.

The cookies lay forgotten between them, a stark contrast to the venom in his voice. The warmth she had tried to bring into the room had been stomped out in an instant.

"Simon!" Kershaw jolted off the couch, his delayed reaction finally kicking in. His brows furrowed as he took in the scene, the scattered cookies, the tension was enough to choke on. "Dude, don't be a dick."

But before anyone else could step in, Rosa grabbed the tin tray from the floor and shoved it hard against Simon's chest. The clang resounded through the room, the force of the blow pushing him a step backward. For a brief second, shock spread across his face, his anger momentarily stunned.

"Don't forget—you're in my house," she snapped, her voice trembling with barely contained fury. "Pick up the damn mess. And just so you know? Fuck you and your egotistical methods. There's something seriously wrong with you, you obsessive freak." Her breath hitched, but she didn't flinch. "I need a moment. I'm taking a break."

She spun on her heel, snatching up her keys with a rough jerk. As she stormed past, Sir Louie let out a low, warning growl, his green eyes fixed on Simon, a silent reprimand.

The front door slammed behind her, rattling the walls.

A second later, the roar of the truck's engine filled the air. Raya bolted toward the door, bursting outside just in time to see the taillights disappearing down the driveway.

"Rosa, wait!" she shouted, sprinting a few desperate steps forward. But the truck was already gone, swallowed by the night.

"It's already half past ten," Raya muttered, pulling out her phone. She tapped Rosa's number, pressing it to her ear—only to hear a familiar ringtone chirping from the couch. Her stomach sank. She left without her phone.

Raya exhaled tensely, her patience thinning. "I get that tensions are high, and yeah, we're all frustrated," she said, her voice tight with irritation. "But did you really have to do that?" Her piercing gaze flicked to Simon, but she didn't wait for an answer. She was too pissed off to hear whatever excuse he might come up with. "I'm stepping out for some air." She turned on her heel, heading toward the backyard, needing space before she said something she'd regret.

Simon didn't move.

William, however, let out a long, quiet breath, his jaw tightening. "You went too far this time." His voice was firm, but there was an underlying edge to it now, a crack in his usual control. His dark eyes locked onto Simon, searching him as though he could pull the truth from his face. "I know what today is," he said, softer now, "But they don't. How could they? We don't talk about it. We keep everything bottled up—act like it's just another day… until it isn't."

He paused, fidgeting with a loose button on his sleeve. He shook his head, as if he wanted to say more, but the words wouldn't come.

Something was building behind his eyes—something urgent—but he swallowed it down, leaving the stiffness between them filled with unsaid things.

The space between them felt taut, drawn thin like a bowstring, and yet, neither of them spoke.

Before Simon could respond, Kershaw let out a long, exasperated sigh, rubbing a hand over his face. "Come on, man. Let's go for a walk." He reached out, but Simon yanked back, the motion abrupt, like the last thread of patience had snapped.

Without a word, Simon grabbed his keys and stalked toward the front door. It all felt suffocating, closing in on him from all sides. He needed space—needed to get out before the pressure inside him cracked even more.

He was more disgusted with himself than anyone else. He knew he hadn't protected her—his twin, his identical fucking twin. She'd warned him that getting too close to cases would ruin him, but he hadn't listened. He thought he could save everyone from pain. And yet, here he was.

A few seconds later, the click of the front door cut through, followed by the low rumble of an engine turning over.

***

Minutes passed, the moment settling like a dense fog over the house.

Finally, Kershaw exhaled, running a hand down his face before stepping out onto the back porch with William. His voice was almost hesitant. "Hey… sorry for him."

Raya stood leaning against the railing, arms crossed tightly over her chest. The night was cool, but not enough to calm the resentment still burning beneath her skin. She glanced at them, exhaling through her nose. "What's his problem? We all have a past, but come on." Her voice was stern, but not completely unkind. She wasn't ignorant—just tired of walking on eggshells around Simon's outbursts.

Kershaw hesitated, his gaze dropping to the wooden boards beneath his feet. "It's not really something we like to talk about," he said carefully, rubbing the back of his neck. His usual lightheartedness was gone, replaced by something—something grief-stricken. After a long pause, he finally continued, "But I will tell you this—his twin sister was murdered by this serial killer. Because he got too close. Today marks the ten-year anniversary of her death."

Raya stilled, her heart skipping a beat.

Kershaw's voice had thinned at the edges, cracking slightly on the last few words. When she looked up at him, she noticed something raw in his expression—something not just about Simon.

Her focus shifted to William. He wasn't his usual stiff, judgmental self. His lips were pressed into a thin line, his arms crossed so tightly his knuckles were white. His eyes, unreadable, looked far away.

They weren't just telling her a story. They had lived it.

The realization settled. No wonder they were so close, no wonder Simon's obsession was all-consuming. This wasn't just about revenge—it was about a loss that had shattered him.

William said nothing. He didn't have to.

Kershaw cleared his throat, forcing out a humorless chuckle, but it didn't quite reach his eyes. "Simon may be a jackass, but today? He's barely holding it together."

Raya swallowed hard, her earlier words pressing against her chest. She hadn't known. And maybe she never truly would—not in the way they did. But now, at least, she understood.

A pause stretched between them, filled with the presence of a secret revealed. The wind rustled through the trees, carrying the distant chirp of crickets, but none of them moved, lost in their own thoughts.

After a long moment, Raya finally spoke, "Rosa won't get fired, will she?"

The tension shifted, replaced by something lighter as Kershaw let out a short chuckle. William followed with an amused exhale, the corners of his lips twitching upward.

"Hell no," Kershaw said, shaking his head. "But she's got balls. I haven't seen anyone go at him like that since… well, Marybeth. But damn."

William's breath hitched just slightly before he sighed, his expression turning wistful. "Yeah... she reminds me of her in a way. Stubborn as hell."

Raya glanced between them, catching just a hint of something behind their eyes—something raw. This wasn't just about Rosa's defiance. It was about someone else, someone who had stood up to Simon before... and wasn't here to do it again.

"She'll be fine," Kershaw murmured, rubbing the back of his neck as if shaking off the past. "Simon's pissed, but he knows she's a damn good detective. He'll cool off."

Raya nodded, though a knot of unease tightened in her stomach. "Still... I should try to reach her, but she left without her phone."

William met her gaze, his knowing smile tinged with something softer. "She'll turn up. Just... give her a minute."

Raya nodded but wasn't convinced.

MEMORIES AND MAYHEM

"I ENDED UP cussin' him out," Rosa vented into the phone, pacing the worn wooden floor.

"You never could hold your temper when someone's yelling, my darlin'," her father chuckled on the other end. His voice was warm, steady—like a lighthouse cutting through a storm. "But I really do think he went too far. It'll boil over. Your new team seems close overall. I think they're good for you."

The soothing familiarity of his voice helped ease some of the frustration tightening in her chest. She let out a long breath, slumping against the arm of the couch.

"I'm sorry for interrupting your date, though," she added, guilt creeping into her tone. "I just didn't know who else to call."

"No, never. I always have time for you, sweet pea."

She rolled her eyes at the nickname, but a small, tired smile tugged at her lips.

"Anyway, I feel fine, but I can't believe I drove all the way here." Her gaze drifted around the house—her childhood home. It had been years since she stepped foot inside, and yet, nothing had changed. The air carried the faint scent of cedar and aged books, the same as it always had.

"Probably because you forgot your phone," her father reminded her, amusement laced in his voice. "You mentioned that as soon as you called using the landline."

"You're the only one I know who still has a landline. Old man."

"Hey, it came in handy this time, didn't it?"

"Yeah, yeah," she murmured, shaking her head. "Thanks. Have fun."

She hung up, letting the quiet settle around her. It wasn't an empty kind of quiet—no, it was strong with history, with warmth that had outlasted time. The walls still carried the memories of laughter, of whispered bedtime stories, of long talks over late-night cups of milk.

Rosa made her way into the kitchen, running her fingers over the old, wooden countertop. It was dingy, but clean—just like always. Her father never cared much for new, shiny things; he preferred keeping what had meaning.

Her gaze landed on the painted red roses on the wall. They were uneven, the brushstrokes clumsy, the color slightly faded—but they were still there.

She could still hear the laughter.

She and her father had painted them when she was little, giggling as they smeared too much paint on the wall, her mother standing nearby, shaking her head but smiling all the same. *They're ugly,* she had told them, *but if they make you happy, I suppose they can stay.*

And they had.

No matter how many times the kitchen had been scrubbed down, how many things had changed, the roses remained. A part of the house. A part of her.

Her eyes drifted further, landing on a small section of the wall near the door—where a child's drawing was forever sketched into the paint. It was hers. A stick-figure family, drawn in bright crayon, preserved beneath a layer of varnish her father had added when she was five. *It's our home,* he had said. *And this is part of it now.*

She swallowed hard.

This house had always been filled with love, even after her mother passed. And yet, she had avoided it for so long, letting the memories sit untouched, afraid of what they would stir.

But tonight, standing here, she didn't feel grief clawing at her.

She just felt... home.

But it was still lonely.

Her father had never brought anyone here. He barely spent time in the house anymore, always rushing off for veterinary visits, always on the move. His work consumed him, and, over time, she found herself following in his footsteps. The past still whispered but now, the house felt frozen in time—waiting for someone to fill it again.

A creak from the old wooden porch outside made her stiffen.

She frowned, tilting her head slightly, listening.

Nothing.

Letting out a slow breath, Rosa wandered into the living room. The old couch, soft with age, welcomed her as she sank into it. The cushions still held the faint scent of her father's cologne, mixed with the warmth of old wood and coffee.

Her eyes landed on the small stack of books on the coffee table, exactly where they had always been. She reached for one—half-finished, the corner of a page folded down to mark where her father had left off.

Settling in, she flipped it open, letting the stillness wrap around her.

For tonight, she could sit here. She could pretend, just for a little while, that this place wasn't so empty.

Somewhere in the hushed comfort of the old house, Rosa drifted off. The scent of aged pages and faint traces of her father wrapped around her, lulling her into a dreamless sleep.

A noise.

Rosa's eyes popped open.

The house was bathed in darkness, the only light spilling in from the streetlamp outside.

She sat up slowly, rubbing her face. It was late—too late. Raya must've been worried sick.

But, as she awoke, something felt... off.

She exhaled softly, glancing around, but the house was still as she left it. Maybe it was just her own paranoia, creeping in after too many close calls lately.

With a gentle sigh, she folded the blanket neatly and placed it back where it belonged. The house felt colder now, the warmth of her presence fading as she moved through it. She turned off the last light, her footsteps soft against the worn wooden floors.

At the door, her fingers hovered over the lock.

Something pricked at her nerves.

She shook it off and twisted the key, the clicking sound loud in the stillness of the night.

Outside, the breeze was crisp, carrying the scent of cooling asphalt and wet leaves.

She didn't glance at the mailbox—not once. She refused.

Instead, she focused on the truck ahead, her boots crunching against the gravel.

Then—

A shift.

The whisper of movement behind her.

Her chest tightened.

She barely had time to react before—

A sudden, brutal force slammed into the back of her head.

Pain exploded through her skull.

A shaky gasp escaped her lips, a jarring hitch of sound that barely made it out. She staggered forward, fingers instinctively grasping at the truck for support. A hot, wet sensation trickled down her temple—blood.

The world around her spun.

Her vision blurred at the edges, shadows bleeding into one another. She tried to turn, to get a look at her attacker, but her body wasn't cooperating.

Her knees buckled.

And then—darkness.

***

"It's not like her," Raya muttered, pacing the front porch, running a hand through her hair. Agitation radiated off her in waves. "She usually gets angry and storms off, but she always comes back."

It was nearly one in the morning.

The moment Simon pulled up, he noticed the change—concern tightening their features, coiling in their stances.

"She hasn't come back yet," Kershaw said quietly, stepping closer. Raya's nerves were already showing.

Simon didn't hesitate. "Any place she'd go?"

"Only her childhood home," Raya answered, fidgeting. "At least forty minutes away. And with those threats—" Her voice rose. "I can't believe I let her go off alone."

"Don't jump to worst-case," William said, catching her arm, steadying her. "Relax. We'll figure it out."

Simon turned to Kershaw. "Let's head over. This could be an abduction if those threats are real. Coordinate with local PD on arrival." Then, to William: "Stay here with Raya. Send the directions to my phone. Don't leave her alone."

They moved fast, the flashing lights of their vehicle slicing through as they sped toward Rosa's childhood neighborhood.

Forty minutes later, Simon scanned the quiet streets with a grimace. "Why would she leave a place like this for where she is now? Country people... they're built different."

Kershaw's eyes locked on the road ahead, scanning. Then he stopped short.

Rosa's truck sat in the driveway. Driver's door wide open.

Simon's instincts snapped alive.

"Shit," he muttered, grabbing his radio. "Possible burglary. Checking it out now. Keep radios open. Stay alert."

He was out the car before the dispatcher responded, moving fast.

Near the truck, dread curled in his gut. Rosa slumped against the front wheel, one hand trembling against her head. A slow trickle of blood glistened on her temple under the porch light.

She was moving. Barely.

Simon crouched beside her, gun at his side but ready. His pulse thundered, eyes flicking toward the house.

Kershaw veered toward the open front door, gun raised. Every muscle coiled, senses alert. His heart pounded, adrenaline surging. Simon knew he entered cautiously and would clear the rooms with practiced precision.

Simon's voice was steady but urgent. "Rosa. Can you hear me?"

She let out a faint, breathless chuckle. "I seriously have the worst luck."

"Don't move," Simon warned, voice low but firm. His hands were steady as he assessed the wound, careful not to worsen it.

"You're bleeding pretty bad."

"No kidding," she murmured, managing a weak smirk.

Simon's fingers hovered over the injury, feeling the warmth of blood and pain beneath. His breath caught but his face stayed neutral—only her safety mattered now.

"Who did this?" he asked, voice level.

Rosa winced but smirked. "If I knew, I'd be a lot more pissed—maybe smack them with a tin foil tray."

Her humor barely touched the stress tightening Simon's jaw.

Flashing lights and sirens cut the night. Neighbors emerged, murmuring anxiously.

Rosa caught fragments of their voices.

"Now it's burglaries," a woman muttered. "What's next? Time to leave this town."

"I'm gonna need another day off, boss man," Rosa joked as Simon reached for her hand. She took it, leaning heavily against him despite herself.

He smirked softly. "Truce for today." His gaze flicked back to the house, scanning.

A voice shattered the moment. "Are you okay?!" Raya charged forward, shoving Simon aside as she reached Rosa.

"Feeling fine and dandy, honest," Rosa quipped, letting Raya help her toward the ambulance.

Simon watched them go, jaw tightening. He'd told Raya to stay with William at the other house. Clearly, no one listened.

He saw a medic check Rosa for concussion signs. No immediate danger. "Big bump later," the medic said, calm but professional. "Other than that, you're good."

Rosa nodded, relief and exhaustion mixing on her face. The medic's reassuring pat was the last contact before she steadied herself and headed back inside, where police swarmed the house.

***

Kershaw scanned the rooms. "Nothing missing?" His voice was low but edged with concern.

Rosa slowly looked around, fingers brushing familiar furniture edges as if to confirm normalcy. "No. Everything's here." Her words felt hollow.

Her eyes drifted to the door, the broken seal a grim reminder. The phone call to her father loomed.

Her stomach churned. She imagined the conversation she'd have with him later—his insistence on flying back. She couldn't blame him. "I'm fine," she would mutter, knowing it wouldn't matter. By tomorrow night, he'd probably be there.

"I still don't understand why they're targeting Rosa," William said.

Rosa and Raya exchanged cocked eyebrows.

"I have to ask," William said. "We need to piece this together."

"It has to be the drugs," Raya snapped, frustration sharp in her voice. "This drug case has the town on edge. It can't just be Mr. Adams. There's more. And coming after Rosa? Too random. We're missing something. Maybe it's an old grudge or something."

The conversation dragged on, suspicion filtered in. Inside Rosa's childhood home, their theories piled up, fragile as a house of cards—each more tangled than the last.

The truth was clear: they already knew something bigger was at play. The drug case? A distraction. Beneath it all, someone else pulled the strings.

Someone who didn't just want to sell drugs. Someone who wanted to tear everything apart.

And unspoken but obvious, if they didn't solve it soon, they might never get the chance.

The mastermind wasn't just playing the game. He was controlling it.

Rosa knew the drug case was just a smoke screen. The real puppet master was the Wood Riddle Killer—someone desperate for attention, always playing his twisted game. But Rosa getting hurt?

That didn't fit his style. This felt different. Something—or someone—else was involved.

Raya had her theory about old grudges, but even that didn't feel like enough motive to go this far. Unless something had been taken, and this was another cover-up. But Rosa was fiercely attached to her things, deeply emotional and memory-driven. That theory didn't sit right either.

Even if this wasn't the killer himself, it was a different demented message meant to make them hesitate.

But Rosa knew the truth.

They wouldn't back down.

The Wood Riddle Killer was watching regardless. Every move. Every word. Every second.

To acknowledge it—give him even the slightest satisfaction—would be to admit defeat.

DEAD WRONG

THE NEXT DAY, Kershaw and William spent hours combing through every inch of Rosa's newer home, searching for any sign her attacker may have slipped inside while they were at her childhood house. They moved like they expected danger to leap out at them.

Meanwhile, Rosa's father was in full-blown panic mode—as any father would be. He paced relentlessly, eyes darting between Rosa and the door, as if expecting another threat to appear at any moment. Every few minutes, he checked her over, his hands hovering near her shoulders, fingers twitching like he needed to physically confirm she was okay. His arms flailed wildly as he ranted, frustration and relief colliding in bursts of anxious energy. It took three exhausting hours for him to convince himself she was truly safe. Even then, before he left, he vowed to return every day to check on her.

"Your father is… unique," Kershaw chuckled, shaking his head.

"Tell me about it," Rosa muttered with a sigh.

"He really is," Raya added with a smirk. "Mr. Ryker's always been like that—even before, um… everything. Honestly? It's kind of cute. He's the dad everyone wanted."

"Yeah, yeah, heartwarming stuff," Rosa said, waving them off. "Can we focus on who did this? I checked the cameras at the other house and here—nothing. Unless they used one of those blackout connectors to jam the feed, but even then, there wasn't any static. Just… nothing."

William, who had been quietly processing everything, finally spoke. "To be honest, I don't think this is related to the Wood Riddle." His voice was hesitant at first, but as everyone turned to him, he went on. "It's a stretch to think he'd do this. He's done some wild things, sure, but he's always precise. This feels rushed. Desperate, not strategic."

Raya tilted her head, considering. "You might be right... Maybe someone in town got spooked when the FBI showed up?"

She glanced toward Simon, who was hunched over the footage, rewinding and replaying the same clips in slow motion, searching for something—anything—that shouldn't be there.

"We have to start suspecting everyone," Raya murmured, shaking her head. "I just... I don't think anyone in this town is capable of something like this. At least, not the people we *know*." She paused. "Then again, we never thought Mr. Adams could do that either. He was just a harmless principal who yelled too much—until he wasn't."

"People do a lot for money," Kershaw muttered, cynical. "And then they get greedy. So—who around here has financial problems?"

Rosa leaned back, thinking. "The Summers family, but that's because they have eight kids. I doubt they'd have time to sneak around, let alone pull something like this off." Her brow furrowed. "My guess? It's someone unmarried—someone with free time and a flexible schedule." Her voice dropped. "It could to be someone from the department."

It made sense. The department had access to case files, reports—everything tied to the drug operation. They could stay ahead of the investigation. Slip through unnoticed. Hide in plain sight.

But who?

"Whoever it is has to be smart, calculating... someone who wants to stay involved in the case without drawing attention," Rosa murmured, more to herself than to the others.

Her thoughts tumbled one after the other. Who had her phone number? Her email?

She was still relatively new to the office. Most of the team had grown up together. The newer transfers? She barely interacted with them.

Her brain rewound, scanning through crime scenes. Who was always there?

Her breath hitched.

Chadford.

The chief.

He had been at every single scene.

But still… Chadford had studied computer science, even dabbled in coding, though not very well. It didn't fit. He was overbearing, sure—intimidating even—but to throw away his badge for this?

No. He couldn't.

He had even given up his second love for his first—his job.

Rosa let out a sudden breath, a knot forming deep inside her.

It had to be someone else.

"You've had that same look on your face for an hour," Raya said, nudging her with a cold water bottle. "Drink something. Still no dizziness? No signs of a concussion?"

Rosa shook her head. But the truth was, she didn't feel as steady as she pretended.

"I want to go to the office."

She stood abruptly, but Simon spoke before she could take a step—his eyes never leaving the screen.

"Funny. You'd think if someone was hiding in plain sight, they'd pick a crowded place. Not a town this small."

His voice was casual, almost offhanded—but it struck a nerve.

Rosa froze.

Crowded place.

Her pulse spiked.

The library.

Her memory jolted—back to the riddle. Something about the phrasing. What if part of it had been added… or removed?

Her inhale hitched. The projector. The riddle that should've been there.

"I think—" Rosa's voice came out more abrupt than intended. She turned, eyes wide. "Someone took one of the riddles. The one that was supposed to be with the projector. Even if Adams interfered, the killer would've left a different riddle. Something. Especially now that he knows we're getting closer."

The room stilled. Even Simon looked up.

Raya frowned. "Wait—what do you mean… took it?"

Rosa's mind raced. "The riddle felt off because it was incomplete. The projector wasn't just there for show—it was supposed to lead us to something. But someone got there first. Someone removed it."

Her stomach knotted.

This wasn't just a game anymore. The serial killer had set the stage—but someone else had started rewriting the script again. Manipulating it. But why?

"Think about it," Rosa said, heart pounding. "The first clue—the finger—it pointed to the basement. That was his. But the second one? That's where it starts to unravel. There should've been another riddle. The Wood Riddle Killer doesn't make mistakes. He's too meticulous. Adams disrupted something. That's why it all started pointing to him. The riddle at the park already led us to the library, and if that changed, the killer would've adapted. Not erased it."

Everyone went quiet. The realization settling in.

Someone had tampered with the killer's riddle that was with the projector.

"But why?" Raya whispered.

"He's not done," Rosa breathed, the truth crashing in. "And if I were him, I'd be furious that someone stepped in—again—like Adams. Someone messing with his work. Which means…"

Her heart pounded harder.

"He has to stay here. In Chattingsburg. To fix it."

Her eyes widened. "He's still nearby—even after two weeks!"

She bolted to her feet, certainty hardening in her chest. "Let's go back to the school library. Now. Something has to be there."

Urgency ignited. Coats grabbed, boots stomped, the front door flung open.

A brisk gust rushed past as they ran out—but Rosa halted.

Simon had reached his car first and stood frozen.

The others nearly crashed into him as they followed his stare.

There—resting on the driver's seat—was a jagged piece of bark.

Dark streaks ran across its surface. Crimson, dried into the grooves.

Blood.

No one spoke.

Simon didn't move at first. Then he reached—paused. No contact. Not yet.

"Back up," he ordered, grabbing his phone. "No one touches anything."

They obeyed instinctively. Simon snapped a photo, keyed his radio.

"This is SSA Pikes. We have a direct message at the scene. Taunt from the Wood Riddle Killer. Dispatch forensic techs and CSU to my location. Full sweep—vehicle and perimeter."

Kershaw was already slipping on gloves. "I'll log for chain of custody."

"Good." Simon turned to him. "Coordinate with local PD. Get traffic cam footage from every possible exit within five miles. I want eyes everywhere."

Simon pulled out a fresh evidence bag, lifted the bark carefully. Dried edges crumbled slightly as he turned it.

Carved into the bark.

> *"The wise one watches, silent and still,*
> *A hunt in the dark, a shadow to kill.*
> *She never saw, she never knew,*
> *That wisdom fades when night is through."*

Rosa shivered. The words pierced.

Simon sealed the bag, passed it to William. "Fast-track it to the lab. Chemical analysis on the blood. Trace comparison. Anything."

Rosa swallowed hard. "It's a warning," she whispered.

Simon's jaw clenched. "No," he said, low and sure.

"It's a declaration."

Too late.

The killer had already been here.
And whoever "she" was... might already be gone.

SPLINTERED LOGIC

"I KNOW EVERYONE wants to give this right to the police, but maybe we should hold off," William said, his voice tight.

Outside, the occasional wail of sirens broke through the quiet as local units made their way. The delay stretched time thin.

"We were too late!"

Simon's palm slammed down on the coffee table. The crack bellowed, sharp and final, as a fresh fracture split across its cheap surface. The lamp beside it wobbled dangerously.

From the corner of his eye, he saw Rosa flinch. Her gaze flicked to the table, then to his face, reading every line of tension he couldn't hide. He didn't care. Frustration surged through him like fire licking up dry timber. His jaw locked so tight he swore his molars might crack. His fists clenched white at his sides, veins corded along his arms.

"Taking it out on the furniture isn't going to help you," Rosa snapped. The stale coffee smell mixed with anger kept everyone standing. "And William might be right—especially if there's a mole."

Simon didn't answer. The words grated, mostly because they weren't wrong. The room felt brittle, every creak of the old floorboards loud and accusatory, every breath drawn through clenched teeth.

Outside, car doors slammed. Kershaw moved to meet the arriving officers, leaving the rest of them.

Rosa dragged a hand through her hair, staring off like the riddle had burrowed into her skull. She looked like she was circling it in her mind, dissecting every word.

"But I'll be honest…" she said finally, voice slower now, more cautious. "This riddle doesn't necessarily mean she's dead—yet."

Simon's eyes snapped to her.

The air shifted. Everyone stayed frozen. It was like someone had sucked the oxygen out of the room. Even Simon had to blink, the absurdity of her words stalling his thoughts.

"What?" Raya whispered.

Rosa exhaled. "It says, 'That wisdom fades when night is through.' It sounds like a warning, not a confirmation. But it must've been changed since the basement. This couldn't have been the original riddle—we would have had more time if someone didn't tamper with it." She hesitated, then added, "And now, whoever did just pissed him off even more."

Simon narrowed his eyes, heat rising again under his skin. "You mean the victim could still be alive? That doesn't make sense. The only pattern we've seen is gender—nothing else." His voice came out taut, clipped, dangerously close to breaking. He hated this conversation. Hated the uncertainty. Hated being cornered by a riddle again.

"Look, I could be wrong," Rosa said, her words tumbling fast, "but riddles are about wordplay. You know that. I know that. He anticipated every step before we took them. The library was renovated last year, but that toy and riddle were planted long before—only the finger was added recently. That means he knew exactly how to time it. So tell me—after two years of silence, is it really that unlikely he set up his master plan right here? Or nearby? Or even miles away?"

She leaned forward, her intensity matching his. Her shoulders squared, her eyes unwavering.

"Maybe his MO is changing. Maybe he's getting older, messier—or evolving. If we don't figure out what's different since the last body, we're just reacting. Again. Who knows? But unless you have a better plan, standing here arguing won't get us anywhere."

Simon stared at her.

She didn't blink.

"So? Do you have a better idea?"

He didn't answer.

His nostrils flared, breath rough through his nose. His chest rose and fell in slow, measured drags as he worked to keep himself level. Every nerve in his body was screaming. She was making sense, and he hated that. Hated that she was pulling pieces together faster than he could. Hated that she was solving *his* case with half the experience and none of the scars.

A seed of doubt lodged itself in his chest.

How? How was she reading the killer this well? She saw through the noise, cut to the core of things in a way that made him uneasy. That kind of insight wasn't common—not even among seasoned agents.

His gaze flicked to her again. That intelligence in her mind… it was undeniable. But there were gaps too. She missed social cues. She responded with raw fear to the threats. That part was real.

And yet… it didn't add up.

Frustration twisted inside him. He wanted to point fingers, to assign blame, to find *someone* responsible for how far behind they were. For ten years of chasing smoke. Ten years of failure.

Ten years of guilt.

His jaw ached from clenching. A low hum settled in his ears—rage and futility colliding in the static.

And the worst part?

There wasn't a damn thing he could do about it.

RACING SILENCE

THE LINE CLICKED, followed by a slow, deliberate breath—calculated, cunning—bleeding through the static.

"They're closing in," the first voice murmured, low and gravelly, like crushed glass scraping against stone. "The woman's smarter than she looks."

A pause. Then a quiet, mirthless chuckle—dry and abrasive, like a blade dragged across leather. "The academy doesn't take fools."

"I beg to differ."

Quiet. Stifling. The faint tick of a clock sounded in the background, each second stretching like a noose tightening around a throat.

The second voice exhaled—a fractured hiss, frayed with irritation. "If you don't want to get caught, I suggest you lay low. Or better yet—keep your fucking mouth shut."

"Oh?" the first voice hummed, smug and knowing. "Funny, coming from the one who could've given us away—switching the riddles. You never should have gotten involved, and you decided to change the damn riddle. We can't afford to be fools if we want to catch him."

A harsh intake from the other end. The creak of a chair shifting. Then, nothing.

Seconds crawled by, danger hanging in the air like a predator poised to strike.

Finally came the last words, flat and laden with warning.

"He wouldn't be too pleased so he's probably coming after you," the first voice snapped, frustration clear.

The line went dead.

FATAL WHISPER

SIMON MOVED SLOWLY through the library, his steps cautious, the flashlight beam cutting across shelves and dust. It was their third time back, and the frustration in the air was almost palpable. Kershaw and William moved in opposite directions, circling the space like predators with no scent to follow.

"I mean, maybe he originally planned to do his business elsewhere," Kershaw muttered, crouching near a display cart. "But when someone tampered with the clues, he had to improvise. Maybe that's why he switched locations. Shifted focus to someone here."

William didn't respond right away. He stood near the librarian's desk, sifting through piles of paperwork that had already been searched twice. Then he shook his head. "Still feels like the drug stuff connects," he said, voice low. "Timing's tight, sure, but maybe not coincidental."

Simon remained quiet, eyes sweeping across the rows of bookshelves. His gaze briefly drifted toward Rosa—she stood at the far end, near the oversized reference table, flipping through a binder with the same distracted energy she'd had since the message appeared. She wasn't listening, not openly anyway, but she was close enough to catch what mattered. And he had no doubt she was paying attention.

The bark—the message—still sat sealed in the evidence bag near his feet. The carved lines in his mind.

Whoever tampered with the scene had stirred the hornet's nest.

And now, just like with Mr. Adams, they'd invited consequences.

Kershaw's voice dropped further. "Someone local did it. Has to be. Someone who thought they could get away with changing the narrative. But now?"

Simon didn't answer. He didn't need to. The reality had already settled over them like fog.

Whoever interfered... would be the next target.

Behind him, Rosa shifted slightly, rubbing her temple, her steps slower than usual. Simon didn't turn to her, but he caught the way her shoulders drooped, how her eyes seemed unfocused, like she was fighting off fatigue. She said nothing—just moved along the perimeter, pretending to search.

Raya stepped closer, lowering her voice. "She"—she nodded toward Rosa—"could mean anyone. But is there any chance these riddles are about her?"

Simon's jaw tightened. "I doubt it," he muttered, but even he could hear the hollowness in his own voice. "There'd be no reason."

"But the threats," Raya pressed, "the emails, the texts—we couldn't trace them. Everything's been rerouted, hidden. And it was sent directly to her."

"Relax," Kershaw said. "If it was about her, we'd know by now. Maybe someone just wanted to shake her up. Scare her. Test her. She's the newest detective on the team, right?"

He glanced toward Simon. "Could be internal. Does she have enemies?"

"With her mouth?" Raya said with a dry snort. "Plenty. Her ex for one—controlling, manipulative, the whole deal. That didn't end well. And some of the guys in the department didn't love that she got bumped up over them. She doesn't play politics. And she doesn't care."

Simon kept his eyes on the far shelves as Rosa moved slowly past them, her fingertips brushing the spines without really looking. She was still listening.

Kershaw's jaw ticked. "Should we talk to the ex?"

William finally spoke again. "Even if the threats aren't connected to the killer, they're still threats. And we need to rule them out."

Simon gave a slight nod, his stare now fixed on the wall behind them. "We'll pay him a visit in the morning."

A brief lull followed.

"She's barely sleeping," Raya added quietly, watching Rosa now. "Can't say I blame her."

Simon said nothing. He scanned the library once more, the sterile quiet now laced with subtle hesitation. They weren't any closer to answers—but they were getting closer to danger.

Somewhere in the darkness, something had shifted.

PLAYBACK & PAYBACK

JACOB LEVINE STOOD with his thumbs twiddling, a smirk refusing to fully fade as Kershaw pressed him with question after question. The guy radiated cockiness—something Simon and the others had no patience for. His casual stance, the unbothered look in his eyes, the way he seemed to shrug off the entire situation—it grated on Simon's nerves like sandpaper.

Kershaw and William kept the pressure on. Simon leaned lazily against the fence, arms crossed, cigarette balanced between his fingers, watching. He didn't need to say much—Jacob was already uncomfortable. Anyone could see it. But the guy refused to admit why.

Kershaw flipped open a small notepad, pen tapping against the page. "Where were you a few weeks ago between midnight and two in the morning? I'm sure you know what we're referring to." His voice was even, calm. But the question wasn't casual.

Jacob chuckled under his breath. "Oh, so we're doing the whole 'where were you on the night of' thing, huh?" He tried to sound amused, but Simon noticed the twitch in his fingers.

"No," William said flatly. "We're doing the 'make sure you weren't within five miles of a crime scene' thing." His tone was like ice. "So, go ahead. Tell us."

Jacob shifted his weight. "I was at a local bar. Ask anyone—bartender, regulars. They'll vouch."

Simon flicked ash to the ground. "That's convenient." He let the silence stretch for a few seconds, then added, "You pay cash, or card?"

Jacob blinked. "What?"

"Cash or card," Simon repeated, voice even. "If you used your card, there's a timestamp. If you paid cash, we'll need someone to place you there—on camera."

There was a pause. A subtle beat too long. "Cash," Jacob said finally. "But look, man, I wasn't exactly keeping track of the time. I was just—"

"Drinking?" Kershaw cut in.

Jacob scoffed. "No."

"Then you should have no problem recalling details," William said, flipping the page in his notepad. "Who was sitting to your left? What was the bartender wearing?" His eyes narrowed slightly. "Or were you too busy talking about Rosa?"

Jacob froze.

The cracks were small, but they were there. His smirk didn't quite disappear, but it faltered at the edges. His composure began to unravel in slow motion.

"Y'all seem awfully curious about Rosa," Jacob said suddenly, his tone forced. "How is she, by the way?" His lips curled into a smile that made Simon's knuckles tighten instinctively.

Kershaw crossed his arms, unmoving. "You seem like someone who knows that threats are illegal," he said evenly. "And those kinds of threats? They carry weight."

Jacob still didn't flinch, but discomfort had settled on him like sweat. He wasn't afraid yet—but he was getting there. Simon could see it. The guy wouldn't fold just because someone raised their voice. He was the type that needed to be cornered.

"Threats? Me?" Jacob scoffed, shifting on one foot. His smirk didn't reach his eyes. "Come on, guys. I haven't even kept track of where Rosa is or what she's doing."

Simon exhaled through his nose, slow and controlled. He pulled the cigarette from his lips, flicked it to the ground, and stepped on it. The quiet crunch beneath his boot was the only sound as he stood up to his full height.

"I've seen him before," Simon said, his voice low and edged in something dangerous. He walked over to the car, opened the door, and retrieved his laptop. A few quick clicks later, he spun the screen toward Jacob.

"First day we were in town. Coffee shop." Simon's tone had sharpened, slicing into the moment. "Guess who's there? Staring. Following her. Watching, without her even knowing."

Jacob's smirk twitched. A hesitation. Just a second.

"That doesn't mean anything," he muttered, eyes drifting away from the screen. But Simon caught the stiffness in his posture, the tightening of his shoulders. The guy was unraveling.

Simon didn't blink. He held Jacob in place with his stare alone.

"Okay, look," Jacob finally sighed, dragging a hand through his hair. "She embarrassed me, alright? Broke up with me in a way that made me look stupid. I just wanted some payback." He let out a dry laugh. "I sent a couple of texts and an email, followed y'all to her new house. That's all. Harmless. Not—" he scoffed, "sneaking up on her childhood home and attacking her. Come on. Her father could've been there."

Kershaw stepped closer. "Good god, man, get a grip. If a woman doesn't want you, you move on." His voice dropped, sharp with contempt. "This? This is illegal."

William shook his head. "Yeah, and it's not just 'not cool.' It's harassment. You'll be reported."

Jacob rolled his eyes, scoffing. "Oh, come on. A bitch doesn't deserve—"

He didn't finish.

Simon didn't lunge. He didn't yell. He didn't have to.

His presence shifted instantly—the atmosphere grew dense with raw electricity. The look in his eyes was lethal, frigid. It wasn't fury. It was something colder.

Jacob instinctively took a step back.

Simon's voice, when it came, was barely above a whisper. "You will turn yourself in." A pause. A breath. "Because if you don't… something far worse will come for you."

Jacob swallowed hard. His bravado fractured, his breathing uneven. He tried to posture again, tried to sound firm.

"Is that a threat?"

Simon didn't flinch.

"It's a promise."

The words dropped like a blade. The wind rustled through the trees, but even the sun couldn't warm the chill that settled around them.

For the first time since they'd arrived, Jacob looked afraid.

***

The drive back was quiet at first, the encounter still settling around them.

"I almost shit my pants," William admitted from the backseat, breaking the silence. "You weren't playing around."

"Does he look like someone who jokes?" Kershaw chuckled, reaching over to smack Simon's shoulder.

Simon barely reacted, eyes fixed on the road ahead.

"But seriously," Kershaw continued, his tone shifting, "that's a relief. At least it had nothing to do with the case. That's why it didn't make sense."

"Yeah," Simon said, his voice clipped, his posture still tight. "Just a distraction—an unnecessary one."

SECRETS, SYRUP, AND SUSPICION

A COUPLE OF hours passed and the sun dipped lower, streaking the sky with shades of burnt orange and dusky purple.

"I'll get out of your hair, but you look happy, even if this is such a dangerous time," Mr. Ryker said, wiping his sweaty hands on his pants before pulling Rosa into a quick, one-armed hug. His grip was firm, grounding. "Please be careful. I don't know what happened to your side table there, but I'll have to fix it up. I'll take it with me, too."

As he bent down to grab the damaged table, all eyes darted toward Simon—quick, fleeting glances, their faces carefully blank. Simon shifted uncomfortably, his stance rigid under their scrutiny-filled glances.

Mr. Ryker paused, narrowing his eyes. "Hmm."

"See you, Dad," Rosa cut in hastily, looking away before her expression could betray anything.

"It's going to be a cold one tonight, so bundle up, kids!" He hoisted the side table over his shoulder like it weighed nothing, then strode off, leaving them to their own devices.

The second the door shut, Kershaw groaned, kicked off his shoes, and flopped onto the couch like a felled tree.

"It's been a while since I did yard work," he muttered, stretching his long frame across the cushions.

"At least he didn't make us rake the whole hill," Raya quipped, running a hand through her hair. "Now, let's get cooking!"

"Or," Rosa interjected, "we could go out."

Raya arched a knowing brow. "You craving your hashbrown fix?"

"There are other restaurants besides that one," Rosa muttered, but the slight flush on her cheeks gave her away.

"And we could probably pick up some town gossip while we're at it," Raya said, immediately backing Rosa's idea—though, truthfully, she was craving her fix just as much. They hadn't been to Waffle House in what felt like forever, which was practically unheard of for them. It was a ritual—a weekly, sometimes twice-weekly, tradition—but they'd been trying to be good hosts and chase down a madman.

"I'm down," Kershaw, who had just moments ago seemed too exhausted to move, suddenly sprang to life. "Those waffles were on another level."

Even William looked eager. All eyes shifted to Simon. He gave a simple, swift nod.

"Me and Rosa will go separately," Raya announced, grabbing Rosa's arm in a way that made it clear she wanted to talk privately, away from prying ears.

Rosa headed upstairs to grab her hoodie. The moment she stepped into her room, a strange sensation prickled at the back of her neck—something felt... off.

She couldn't quite place it, but a strange pull tightened in her chest, like a whisper of something she had yet to notice. She opened her closet—and there was Sir Louie, peeking his little head out, ears twitching.

Her brows furrowed.

The door had been shut. Locked. Sir Louie meowed, stepping out as if complaining about his unexpected imprisonment.

Rosa blinked. She never closed the closet door—not ever. Maybe Raya had done it by accident? It wouldn't be the first time she'd shifted a few things around when she stayed over for long stretches. But even she knew about Sir Louie's usual spots.

A shiver skated down Rosa's spine, but then Raya's voice rang out from downstairs. "Rosa, let's go!" Rosa exhaled and shook it off. Probably just paranoia creeping in after everything that had been going on.

She gave Sir Louie a quick scratch behind the ears before heading downstairs.

***

"You know, we are always traveling, but we didn't even check this place out in D.C." Kershaw shoveled down two plates of waffles while everyone else stared in awe or disgust at him eating like his life depended on it.

"Slow down," William muttered, peeling his eyes from the scene in front of him, taking his bites slowly and actually enjoying the flavors on his tongue. Even Simon seemed to be content with the waffle in front of him. He added vanilla ice cream when Miss May forced him to do so saying he "wouldn't regret it." He didn't appear to regret it, and the older lady watching felt content.

It was usually crowded by this time, all the locals filing in one after another.

"Did you hear about Mr. Adams doing that to Mr. Ropa? Can't believe it! He is—or was—the biggest teddy bear, literally. I never would've guessed that."

One of the local gossipers spoke a bit too loudly, which worked perfectly in the team's favor.

"Yes, darlin'! How is that possible? You think you know a person for years and years, and sure, he wasn't as harmless as he appeared—but a drug lord? Nah, he wasn't smart enough. Someone else had to be pulling the strings." Another voice chimed in, more curt but no less eager to keep the conversation alive.

The group of older townsfolk giggled and carried on, yapping away like there was no tomorrow.

"I'm still worried about them burglaries happening," a third voice added.

"It used to just be some local teenagers playin' pranks, but it's getting out of hand."

"Miss Carissa down the road said she felt someone in her house, but nothin' was taken."

"Miss Carissa's got one foot in the grave," someone quipped, and the table erupted in laughter. But beneath the humor, there was something about how things had suddenly changed in town.

"Now, if you're talkin' about a mastermind behind an underground drug ring, I'd say old man Chadford would be a perfect fit."

Gasps of exaggerated shocks sounded around the table.

"Now don't you go blamin' a good man!"

"Just 'cause you fancy him, darlin', don't mean he's a good guy."

"What say you?"

"I saw him sneakin' into them woods a time or two, but I never thought much of it. But now?" The speaker trailed off meaningfully. "It's all gone to bits and pieces."

"Literally," someone added with a chuckle, setting off another round of laughter.

"Now, all y'all stop that ruckus!" Miss May, the diner's longtime owner, scolded from behind the counter. "You're gettin' too loud!"

Another man, a nosy neighbor who had been eavesdropping from his seat, turned around and added his own two cents. "I think it's more that new fella who came to town. He's strange."

"Oh yes, strange as can be! What was his name? Monroe? Jean?" The old man frowned, clearly frustrated he couldn't remember.

"You can't remember anything, old man," his friend teased, slapping the table.

"I'm pretty sure it was Dean."

"Dean! Yes, Dean."

"You mean that fine young man on the corner of West and Thumper?"

A few of the women exchanged knowing glances before one of them grinned.

"I wouldn't mind gettin' my hands on him," she said, sending another wave of giggles through the table.

One thing was certain—the team had a new suspect to look into. And another was just as clear: this town loved to talk.

As Rosa and Raya listened to the murmurs and half-truths, they made a pact—they wouldn't end up like those old ladies when they got older, sitting around gossiping about every little thing.

But the last, most unsettling truth? Someone in this town was still guilty.

The only question was—who? And how much time did they have left? Had they already run out of time before the next victim? They got nothing accomplished the day before, maybe there was more to the riddle and they were missing something.

Rosa sat there, stirring her drink absently, her appetite gone. The waffles were warm, the chatter around her familiar, but in the back of her mind a harsh reality took hold.

Simon's eyes bored into her as if sensing her confusion. Had they already fallen a step behind?

HEADLIGHTS AND HINDSIGHT

KERSHAW AND ROSA were sent to check out the new guy in town: Dean McAllen. He wasn't much older than them, but something about him seemed off. He had the look of someone always expecting the worst, eyes darting toward the windows as if the walls were closing in. As they approached the house they saw his lanky frame shifting behind the curtain, peeking out in quick, nervous bursts.

Before they could raise a fist to the door, it creaked open—just a hair. A single bloodshot eye peered out, wide and jittery. His pupils were dilated, and his skin had the waxy, unhealthy sheen of someone who hadn't seen daylight in far too long. He didn't say a word, just stared.

Did that mean they were supposed to enter?

When they hesitated a second too long, he twitched, then jerked his head in a quick nod before vanishing back inside.

The house was suffocating. The smell was laced with something musty, like unwashed clothes and the bitter tang of old sweat. The blinds were drawn, casting long, claw-like outlines across piles of junk—scraps of paper, empty fast-food containers, and broken electronics stacked haphazardly against the walls. It wasn't just messy. It was decayed, like he'd let life rot around him.

"You came because people are blaming me?" Dean's voice burst out of the dimness, piercing and too loud, as if he wasn't used to hearing himself speak. But the moment the words left his mouth, he recoiled like they had physically struck him, his whole body twitching in protest. His fingers drummed against his thighs, restless, unable to stay still.

Kershaw exchanged a wary glance with Rosa, his hand resting lightly on his holstered gun. He wasn't ready to draw—yet—but he was waiting for the right moment.

Dean let out a brittle, dry laugh, running a trembling hand through his greasy hair. "I'm a druggie, not a killer," he said, his teeth flashing in something that wasn't quite a smile. Then, without warning, he shot up from the couch so fast it sent a ripple of tension through the room.

Kershaw didn't hesitate. His gun was out in a blink, steady and locked onto Dean's chest.

Dean froze, eyes blown wide, hands shooting into the air. "Whoa! Whoa, man—I was just standing!" His voice cracked, raw with panic.

"My bad," Kershaw said, though his tone suggested he wasn't sorry at all. "But you're twitching like you drank five shots of espresso."

Dean swallowed hard and motioned weakly to the corner of the room. A sad little pile of plastic baggies, burnt spoons, and old syringes sat there like an altar to bad choices. "I buy drugs, yeah. But there's no way I could be runnin' anything." His hands shook as he gestured toward the mess. "I can't even run my own life."

It was clear—Dean was no mastermind. Just another lost soul spiraling down a pit he didn't know how to climb out of.

Kershaw's grip on his weapon eased, but Rosa took that as her cue to step in. She gently grabbed his arm, steering him back toward the door. "Thanks for your time," she said smoothly, already moving to leave.

Dean's head snapped up, eyes locking onto her like he'd just noticed something new. "You have a nice smile," he said suddenly, and before Rosa could react, he grabbed both of her hands in his clammy grip. "No woman has ever been in here before."

Her body stiffened. "Uh... thanks?" She tried stepping back, but his grip held firm.

Kershaw was on him in a heartbeat. "Aye, grabby hands," he warned, tone low and cutting. "Touch her again and we're gonna have a problem."

Dean shrank back instantly, his entire body curling inward like a scolded dog. He nodded jerkily and sat back down, folding his hands in his lap like a polite schoolboy.

As soon as they were outside, Rosa let out a long sigh, shaking her arms like she was trying to rid herself of the feeling.

"I need to take a shower now," she muttered, shuddering.

Kershaw chuckled at her comment. "Another suspect crossed off the list."

That only left Chadford. She wasn't sure what unsettled her more—the possibility that he was capable of it, or the guilt rising in her for even considering it. He had been a pillar of the town for years, a constant presence. Questioning him felt almost like betrayal. Still, the feeling stayed beneath her skin, crawling like a warning she couldn't shake.

***

"It's best if outsiders question him," William said. His tone was neutral, but Simon caught the subtle flicker of discomfort on both Raya and Rosa's faces. "Maybe we should leave scouting him out to someone else too?"

"I'm okay with that," Raya replied, her voice level, though a brief glint of something unreadable passed over her expression.

"I'd prefer to be part of the scouting," Rosa said, and Simon noted the shift in posture around the room—subtle, but not missed. "Look, we all know by now—it has to be someone from this town. We can't keep avoiding that fact. Whether it's him or not, the evidence will speak for itself. Plus, there are only five of us, and we have to be in pairs for safety. That means someone has to rotate shifts."

Her tone left no room for argument.

The first shift fell to William and Raya. They apparently took notes, but nothing significant happened—Chadford stayed holed up in his office all day, only leaving later in the evening. That's when

Kershaw and Simon took over, staking out his house from a parked car just down the street.

"This town has a way of getting under your skin—in a good way," Kershaw said after a while, tilting his head back against the seat.

Simon didn't even look at him. "Don't get too comfortable."

He could feel Kershaw glance his way. That was always Simon's answer—don't get comfortable, don't get attached. And he meant it. They never stayed in one place long enough for comfort to matter. Simon's work carried them across states, across lines others wouldn't cross. Technically, Kershaw dealt with drug-related crimes, while Simon operated on a broader level—tracking serial patterns, connecting the dots others missed. That latitude gave them both more freedom than most agents could dream of.

But Simon knew freedom came with a cost. The moment someone decided to tighten the leash, it would all vanish. And when that day came, Simon wouldn't take it well.

"Look, I know, man..." Kershaw's voice broke the quiet again, lighter this time. "But don't tell me you're not fond of Rosa."

Simon's jaw tightened. "There's no time for that."

He didn't care how blunt it sounded. It was easier that way. Easier to shut it down. If Kershaw noticed the sharpness in his tone, he didn't push it.

The conversation died there.

A few moments later, headlights suddenly washed over the interior of the car—too fast, too bright.

"What the—"

The rest was chaos.

Metal crunched with deafening force as another vehicle slammed into them from the side. The impact spun them sideways. Simon's body jolted against the seatbelt, the car lurching violently as the tires skidded. Screeching steel and shattering glass filled the air, then the thud—sickening and final—as they slammed into the enormous trunk of a tree.

Simon's head snapped forward, pain bursting across his skull. The airbag hadn't deployed. Smoke hissed from the crumpled hood, the stench of burning rubber creeping into his nose. His ears rang, and for a beat, he couldn't hear anything else—just that high-pitched buzz.

Somewhere nearby, he registered Kershaw groaning, shifting in the passenger seat.

An engine roared in the distance—another car pulling away.

Simon's vision snapped back into focus. His hands gripped the wheel hard, instinct taking over as he checked the rearview mirror. A pair of taillights blinked in the distance—fading fast.

The bastard was already gone.

Without hesitating, Simon slammed his foot on the gas. The tires screeched against the pavement, jerking the car forward. It rattled, barely holding together, but he didn't slow. Smoke coiled through the vents, stinging his eyes. The coppery taste of blood touched the back of his throat.

No one followed.

No second impact. No pursuit.

Just nothing—and the cold realization that whoever had hit them hadn't meant to finish the job.

Beside him, Kershaw hissed through his teeth, pressing a hand to his forehead. Blood trickled down the side of his face. "Damn it. Who the hell—"

Simon didn't answer. He kept his focus locked on the road, scanning the stretch of pavement ahead. No movement. Whoever it was, they were gone.

The only sound was the strained hum of the engine and their uneven breaths.

Simon's eyes kept shifting between the mirror and the road. There was nothing—no cars, no shadows. Just empty black ahead and the sense that something was watching.

If someone had wanted them dead, they would be dead.

They'd been warned several times, but this one took the cake.

He didn't see the cloaked figure standing in the tree line beyond the road. Didn't hear the whispered words into the phone. But he felt it. The intent.

His instincts screamed it.

Beside him, Kershaw let out a breath, tilting his head back against the seat. "Well," he muttered dryly, "message received."

Simon didn't speak at first. His grip flexed around the wheel.

His voice, when it came, was low. Cold.

"One thing's for sure," he said. "Chadford has something to do with it."

DAMN WOMAN

"SOMEONE KNEW WE were watching." Kershaw stood up, stretching his stiff limbs as they stepped out of the hospital. Raya had forced both of them to get checked out, and neither had the energy to argue. Rosa stood beside them, watching carefully.

"But how?" Raya's voice was taut with frustration. "It's only us on the case, and we're not about to start blaming each other."

"Maybe someone overheard?" William suggested.

Rosa glanced at him. The relief on William's face that his team was okay was obvious. She felt it too—that pulsing gratitude that Simon and Kershaw were still standing. But something about the way William reacted when the crash was first mentioned stuck with her. A subtle change, barely visible, but she knew him well enough to catch it. He had tensed, not with surprise, but like he'd been expecting something bad. It wasn't like him. It meant something—she just didn't know if she was overthinking it.

"Is the house tapped? Or one of our phones?" Rosa asked aloud, her mind already spinning through every possibility. "Either way, we have to be more discreet now." Her voice dropped, her words edged with resolve. "They won't know what hit them."

She saw it on their faces—the same fury boiling just beneath the surface. No one said it out loud, but they all felt it. The closer they got to the truth, the more dangerous this became.

With the stakeout escalating, they needed a plan that could last days. Rosa listened as they talked strategy—how to strengthen surveillance around Chadford, what angles to pursue. They already had hours of footage showing shady behavior: late-night comings and goings at the community center, suspicious deliveries, hushed conversations that didn't sound like normal business. The goal now was to dig through past security recordings and connect the dots. Drug trafficking? Money laundering? Something worse? They wouldn't know until they found a pattern.

And of course, Raya insisted that she, Kershaw, and William get groceries too. She was set on keeping everyone together, working from one central place. That 'place' was Rosa's house—small, cozy, and apparently now their war room. It made Raya feel useful, Rosa knew, especially since she didn't piece clues together as quickly. She saw herself more as the muscle than the mind—but Rosa never doubted her instincts.

When the others left, Rosa and Simon climbed into her truck. As soon as the doors shut, the absence of sound was almost tangible. Every breath, every shift in the seat seemed to heighten. Outside, the town moved along with its usual rhythm—streetlights blinking on, cars rolling through—but in this particular car, everything felt too still.

She kept her eyes on Simon as he pulled out his phone and called headquarters in D.C. His voice was low and clipped, professional. He briefed them efficiently, keeping the control in his hands, making it known that they didn't need backup—at least not yet. Rosa sat quietly beside him, absorbing every word.

She could see the frustration written all over his face. Simon didn't bother to hide it. Especially when he was angry.

She didn't need to hear the other end of the call to know how it was going. The higher-ups weren't thrilled. The case had dragged longer than expected, and patience was wearing thin. Still, the drug bust tied to Mr. Adams had been a big win—Rosa knew it. It could unravel a massive East Coast network, and D.C. wanted that takedown just as badly as Simon did.

Even so, she could feel it pressing in—the doubt, the pressure. The case was becoming more layered than even he anticipated.

***

Simon knew he'd been sitting there too long without speaking. Rosa was fidgeting with her hands, but his mind was racing through everything that had happened so far again. Just like many times before. Was this really their serial killer?

Serial killers had their own agendas, so getting tangled up in a drug ring felt off. But then Simon remembered something — a line from one of the riddles buried in the case file years ago, about one of the countless victims.

"A king must feed his court before he feeds his hunger."

At the time, it sounded like philosophical bullshit. But now? It read like a confession. He wasn't just tangled up in the drug operation. He was orchestrating it — feeding it to feed himself.

And if Simon knew anything about this one, it was that he had no leash. He was rabid. Yet somehow, he thrived in society, slipping through the cracks, blending in. But this changed everything. He didn't just want disorder — he wanted control. The cartel wasn't a means to an end. It was a small part of his kingdom.

Stupid fucking riddles.

Simon sat in the passenger seat, his head pounding—badly—but he wouldn't let Rosa see even a speck of discomfort. Pain was nothing new. Pain was manageable. He could feel her eyes boring into him.

"Are you okay?" Rosa asked, her voice softer than usual. Concern filled her as she noticed the rigid set of Simon's jaw.

"Just dandy," he muttered, his voice laced with biting sarcasm. It came out harsher than he intended, but he didn't bother correcting it.

"I'm sure," Rosa hummed, not believing him—not for one second. But she kept quiet, eyes on the road, fingers tapping lightly against the steering wheel.

Rosa could feel the tension radiating off him, like he was made of coiled steel, wound too tight for his own good. She had the distinct feeling that he didn't just dislike her—he resented her, and yet, even he didn't seem to know why.

"Why don't you trust people?" she asked suddenly, keeping her tone light, but her curiosity was genuine.

Simon exhaled, turning to the window, watching the town blur past in streaks of neon and streetlamp glow. "People have to earn trust," he said, his voice lower, rougher.

"And once they do?" Rosa pressed, tilting her head slightly. "Does that tough interior of yours change?"

A muscle in his jaw twitched. He let out a soft sigh, more air than sound—cold, detached, the same as always. But there was something restrained beneath it.

"You're allowed to have a life, you know," she said, echoing words Kershaw had thrown at him countless times before.

Simon's fingers curled his fists against his thighs. His lips parted, as if he might say something—something real—but then he shut it down. Just like always.

"Just drive, Rosa," he said curtly, his voice clipped, final.

And that was that. Conversation over. Or so he thought.

"Can you stop being such a hard-ass? You really want to be alone forever?" Rosa's voice cut through, frustration lacing every syllable.

Simon stiffened. Normally, people shut up when he shut them down. But not her. She kept pushing, prying. Why? What made her think she was different? Worse—why was she so damn annoying?

Before he could snap back, Rosa glanced at the rearview mirror. Her expression changed.

"I think we have a tail," she said, her voice suddenly steady, all frustration vanishing into something sharper.

Simon snapped upright, his eyes darting to the side mirrors.

"Keep driving at the same pace. Pretend you haven't caught on." His voice was low, controlled.

Rosa gave a small nod, gripping the wheel a little tighter, finally listening to orders instead of running her mouth. His headache was already drilling into his skull, and now, on top of that, they had a potential tail to worry about.

Then, without warning—without a single damn warning—Rosa jerked the wheel hard to the right.

"Shit—Rosa!"

The truck lurched violently, tires shrieking against the pavement. Simon's shoulder slammed into the door as momentum yanked him sideways, his vision blurring for a split second. The smell of burnt rubber filled the cab as Rosa stomped on the brakes, the force shoving them both forward against their seatbelts. The sudden halt sent the truck rocking on its axles.

Behind them, the tail car swerved, tires screeching as it struggled to keep up. The headlights cut wildly through the darkness as the driver lost control, skidding sideways before veering off the road, the dull crunch of metal against dirt.

Before Simon could even process the insanity of what she just did, Rosa was already throwing the truck into park and reaching for her gun.

Jesus Christ.

Simon barely had time to unholster his own weapon before she was out of the vehicle, charging forward with reckless determination. He had no choice but to cover her, his pulse spiking with adrenaline.

The driver—a scrawny, twitchy guy—sat frozen in his seat, knuckles white against the steering wheel. His pupils were blown wide, his face pale.

"I—I'm sorry! You were just so pretty!"

Simon blinked.

Rosa let out a biting, humorless laugh, lowering her weapon just a fraction as recognition clicked. Dean McAllen. Of course.

"You ran us off the road because you couldn't handle seeing a woman in the force? That's a new one." Her tone was dry, unimpressed. "What's next? Robbing a bank because the teller smiled at you?"

She stepped closer, boots crunching against the asphalt, her stance unwavering. "Let me make this real simple for you—if you ever want a woman's attention again, don't start with attempted vehicular manslaughter." Her voice was calm, but there was a keen edge to it, honed enough to cut. "Now, step out before I drag you out."

The guy obeyed, stumbling slightly. Rosa barely had to lean in to catch the stench of alcohol clinging to him like a bad decision. She cocked her head. "I could light a match right now, and you'd go up in flames. You been drinking or bathing in it?"

She didn't even need a breathalyzer—he was a walking DUI. As she put him through the standard field tests, he failed. Miserably.

Rosa sighed, shaking her head. "Congratulations, genius. You've managed to commit three crimes in under five minutes." She grabbed her radio and called it in, her expression justified. "We'll add 'reckless dumbassery' to the charges."

Simon's smirk remained, though his eyes were keenly perceptive as they took in the scene. He didn't comment—Rosa had it well under control. Once everything calmed down, Rosa shifted her focus and moved toward the truck with purpose.

She perched on the hood of her truck and watched the patrol car slowly pull away, Dean's slumped figure barely visible through the rear window. The flashing lights painted her face in harsh streaks of red and blue, her expression soft.

"Maybe this will save his life," she muttered, her voice low, almost a whisper. It was more to herself than to Simon, and the words carried an edge, like a promise she wasn't sure she could keep.

Simon just stared at her, still gripping his gun. His head pounding. His patience shot.

And this woman—this reckless, unpredictable, impossible woman—was going to drive him insane.

"Well, that was fun," she said lightly, jumping down in front of him, her boots scuffing against the pavement. "But you're not looking too good, so let's go home."

Home.

The word hit him harder than he liked. It wasn't hers to say—not to him. Not when he hadn't felt anything close to it in years.

This was becoming a larger migraine than he needed. He had to get answers. And then he had to leave.

As soon as possible.

PREY AND PLAY

"DID YOU KNOW owls are considered some of the wisest animals?" Raya mused, tossing a card onto the pile.

The deck showed signs of frequent use—softened edges and slightly worn corners from countless games of Bullshit. The cards slid smoothly against each other with a faint crinkle. The living room was cozy and inviting, with plush furniture and warm lighting casting gentle shadows across the space. A half-full bottle of water rested on the polished coffee table, and the faint aroma of freshly brewed coffee mingled with the scent of damp jackets hanging by the door. Maybe they played to keep their minds off things. Maybe, for a few minutes, it was just a real game.

William gave her a look, raising an eyebrow. "That is... completely random."

Raya shrugged, smirking. "Blame Rosa. She used to hit me with random animal facts all the time. Her dad's a famous vet, an expert in his field, you know. Owns an owl refuge."

"An owl refuge?" Kershaw repeated, skeptical.

"Yeah, like a sanctuary. He takes in injured owls, helps them heal, and gives them a place to live in the wild." She leaned back against the couch, absentmindedly twirling a card between her fingers, her elbow brushing against the armrest. The fabric of the couch was soft, worn, like it had been stretched too many times by people finding comfort in its imperfections. "It's about three hours from here. You wouldn't believe how big it is."

Before anyone could respond, the front door creaked open. Cool night air seeped in, carrying the faint scent of rain and earth—as if the storm that had passed was just a whisper away. The soft hum of streetlights outside mingled with the quiet buzz of conversation inside, briefly interrupted as Rosa and Simon stepped in, bringing with them a sense of something imminent.

Kershaw gave a mischievous grin. "Hey, did you know owls are some of the wisest animals?"

Simon shot him an odd look, but Rosa's face lit up.

"Yes! And did you know they swallow their prey whole and spit up the bones?" She practically vibrated with excitement, pulling out her phone to show him a video. The soft blue light from the screen illuminated her face in flashes, casting quick shadows over her features.

Kershaw's regret was immediate. "Yeah, nope. I'm good."

William, on the other hand, leaned in with interest. "Wait, so do the pellets always contain bones, or—?"

Rosa grinned, launching into a rapid-fire explanation.

Simon barely listened. His eyes swept over the room, taking in the small details. The way the others were gathered—comfortably, naturally—as if none of them had a care in the world. The hum of the refrigerator, the faint rustle of a windblown tree outside, the smell of something sweet and warm coming from the kitchen that made his insides knot. The space felt smaller somehow, the walls closing in with the weight of his thoughts.

He noticed the slight tension in William's posture, his gloved hands resting lightly on the table, like he was always ready for something to happen. Kershaw, sprawled back with his usual cocky grin, seemed to take up all the air in the room. Raya's eyes darted around, quick and alert, like she could vanish out of view at any moment.

And then there was Rosa.

Unpredictable, brilliant in ways that seemed almost impossible. She had a way of commanding attention, making everyone lean in when she spoke. As much as Simon hated to admit it, she was the one holding this crazy mess together.

This team had its flaws. Its cracks. Its personal hells.

But for the first time in years, Simon felt something inside him—something poignant, something endearing. He let out a slow breath, feeling his ribs constrict as his pulse quickened. The pain in his shoulder seemed to throb in time with his thoughts, a reminder of how much longer this pursuit had gone on. His fingers tightened against the worn armrest of the chair, the fabric digging into his skin.

Simon's fingers tightened against the worn armrest as he thought about the killer and how he must know they were closing in. He wanted the killer to shrivel under the pressure. He was certain they would catch him—and that the killer would crumble when that happened.

And that certainty? It settled in the pit of his stomach, a never ending hunger. His teeth ground together as a faint sweat beaded on the back of his neck. The pressure, the obsession—it was like a tickling, almost unbearable itch that made his skin crawl.

That certainty was as dangerous as the hunt itself. It was a hunger killers could smell a mile away.

THE HEAT IS ON

"I VOTE WE use some good old Southern hospitality," Raya said, her eyes sparkling with mischief as they flicked toward Rosa. The others exchanged curious looks, but Rosa caught the hint—something was brewing.

Before anyone could protest, the plan was set in motion—a massive cookout, with Rosa's father happily taking charge of the grill. She could almost hear his voice crackling with excitement over the phone, giddy like the sizzle of meat over an open flame. He didn't need to know the real reason behind the gathering—the subtle 'fishing for answers' game they were playing. Let him stay blissfully unaware. It was better that way.

Rosa and Raya both knew one thing for sure: this town adored a good cookout, no matter the season. Whether it was the crisp air of fall or the biting cold of winter, no one could resist the tempting scent of grilling meat wafting through the streets, drawing people out from their homes to gather around the warmth of the fire.

In this town, anything for gossip, and people would drive miles—sometimes even 45 minutes out of their way—just to be part of it. The plan was set: in exactly one week, guests would file in and out, spilling over the backyard, filling the space. There was plenty of room, but the thought of opening up her home to all these people—especially those she wasn't sure she could trust anymore—made Rosa's nerves tighten.

The day arrived after five days of planning, getting the word out that it would be the following weekend, and Mr. Ryker showing up with his massive charcoal grill—the kind that could feed an army. Simon and Kershaw helped him carry it through the backyard gate, a clear reminder that this cookout wasn't going to be as casual as she'd hoped.

"We're about to feed an army!" her father joked, grinning. "But don't worry, you're still guests, so I won't put you to work... much."

By the way he said "much," Rosa knew Simon and Kershaw were in for it soon enough, just like with the raking.

Rosa and Raya darted around, hauling trays of catered food from the truck bed. With so many people expected, the food and drinks seemed endless. William, with his lanky frame, was tasked with carrying the coolers. He managed one or two, but soon found himself struggling. Rosa grabbed a few herself, arms straining but determined.

By the time they finished, about ten coolers lined the porch. They'd rented tables and chairs to accommodate everyone and set up tents in case of rain, the plastic flaps swaying slightly in the breeze. Her father had brought over two unused firepit holders, and he'd asked a couple of friends to bring more once they arrived. It was going to be a full house. Just like they'd hoped.

Still, Rosa couldn't shake the strange feeling of her home becoming a makeshift mission. She never thought her house would be overrun like this, and she certainly never imagined so many people would show up for something she wasn't sure was a good idea anymore.

Hours passed, the air filled with chatter and gossip. A group of younger teenagers gathered in a corner, holding their own little party, careful not to be seen by the officers milling around. Chadford and some of his old coworkers joked about how he should've already retired, but when the topic came up, Rosa saw the slight annoyance flash across his face. His deep, hearty belly laugh was enough to put everyone at ease, but she watched him carefully.

Then, to her dismay, Jacob Levine made an unexpected appearance, accompanied by the town's most "infamous party girl," as the locals liked to call her. No one really cared, though; it was just another strange occurrence in a small town full of drama.

Raya glanced at Rosa and she felt the weight of her friend's eyes, seeing the tightness in Rosa's posture and the way her expression hardened for a moment before she pushed it aside. Rosa refused to let it shake her. Not now. They were all scanning the crowd, observing, looking for anything unusual, particularly keeping an eye on Chadford. He seemed oblivious to their attention, relaxed and unaffected.

But then, a quiet ripple of conversation began—a whispering game that William had no intention of stopping. She caught him letting something slip to one of the officers—a casual remark about there being leads and possible suspects. The comment was dropped on purpose, a spark thrown into the fire of town gossip, and as expected, the rumors began to spread.

It wasn't long before Chadford caught wind of it. Rosa noticed the annoyed looks officers exchanged whenever he passed by, the hushed tones that fell silent as he approached, and the subtle shift in the room's energy. For a split second, his eyes narrowed with panic as the pieces clicked into place—he was one of the suspects. But he quickly composed himself. He couldn't make a scene—not in front of everyone. No, he'd wait. There'd be a more private conversation later.

"Why are your nerves so bad?" Simon asked, his voice low as he leaned against the railing next to Rosa. She was staring out at the crowd, the hum of conversations drifting through the air, while Simon's gaze stayed on the house, focused.

He pulled out a cigarette, the tip glowing as he lit it. The faint smell of tobacco mixed with the cool evening air. Rosa hesitated, unsure how to answer. It threw her off that he even bothered to start a conversation. His presence always seemed to carry weight, making her feel even more on edge.

"Just feels wrong—bringing all the townsfolk here to watch and poke around," she admitted, her voice barely above a whisper. Her fingers twitched against the cold metal of the railing, the coolness a stark contrast to her discomfort.

"Seems right to me," Simon said, exhaling a cloud of smoke, his tone calm, detached.

"Of course you would," Rosa muttered under her breath, irritation creeping into her words. She didn't understand why he was so unbothered, so untrusting—like nothing could shake him, like everything was just another game to him. Very similar to the killer they were chasing.

"Before you get too hard in the heart, try this." Rosa pulled something from the cooler, shoving a sweet tea bottle into his hand.

"I don't drink on the job," Simon said, but he took it without hesitation.

"Take a sip and lighten up," she urged, frustration creeping into her voice.

He complied, taking a sip—and immediately his eyes widened. It wasn't alcohol. It was the sweetest tea he had ever tasted. He spat it out over the edge of the porch, his face scrunching in surprise.

Rosa tilted her head, watching him. "You're not even from the North! D.C. still has sweet tea, you know."

He paused, leaning his head against his hand, softening for a moment. It was a rare instance of vulnerability, one neither of them wanted—or did they?

Then, in an instant, a heavy shove from a drunk troublemaker sent Rosa's drink splashing across her, the sugary sweetness soaking through her shirt and into her skin. The scent of cheap alcohol hit her nostrils, mingled with the faint smell of sweat and body spray from the woman standing too close. Her clothes clung to her, the sticky liquid dripping down her arms, pooling at her feet in a fizzing, sugary mess.

Time seemed to stretch as Rosa's body tensed, fingers curling into fists, muscles coiling with the urge to strike back. When she looked up, the town's so-called party girl met her glare with ice-cold eyes, a sneer twisting her lips—a silent challenge. A hush rippled through the backyard, conversations faltering as Rosa's fury simmered beneath the surface.

But she knew better. The woman was too drunk to be reasoned with, and any reaction from Rosa would only turn the spotlight on her. This wasn't the time for distractions. They had a mission, and she couldn't afford to let it unravel over something so petty.

"Watch where you're going!" Rosa snapped but kept herself controlled. The words were more of a warning than a threat.

Before anything could escalate, Jacob appeared, stepping between Rosa and the woman. His posture was stiff, too perfect, a little too polished for someone trying to defuse a situation. He grabbed the woman's wrist, pulling her away from Rosa with almost too much force. His eyes flicked to Rosa, narrowing just for a split second, and in that moment, Rosa caught something dark flashing beneath the smooth surface of his expression.

"I'm sorry for her," Jacob said, voice low and silky, his apology crafted for effect—like it was more about controlling the scene than offering genuine remorse. He made sure to keep his body angled toward Rosa, positioning himself as the calm mediator.

Rosa never wavered, voice steady but biting. "I know your game, and I'm not playing."

She brushed past him, her damp shirt clinging to her skin, moving with the cool calculation of someone who had learned not to take the bait. Jacob's eyes followed her for just a beat longer, and as she moved past, she didn't miss the brief flash of anger—the subtle hostility brimming just beneath the surface.

COOKED UP SHENANIGANS

ROSA SAT ON the edge of her bed for a moment, gathering her thoughts. Jacob was a controlling bastard, but he was the least of her concerns tonight. She didn't much care about the past, but the constant social expectations had drained her already, and she just wanted to be done with the evening. They'd seen Chadford get worked up about the rumors circulating, a clear sign of a guilty conscience, so they had accomplished their goal, right?

But still, she found herself second-guessing everything. A bit of a guilty conscience surged through her, the faintest whisper of doubt nagging at her. Had she done enough? Was she missing something?

"You know, you're the host. You're being rude." The voice, laced with venom, sliced through the air.

Rosa's stomach twisted as she turned to see Jacob standing in the doorway, his presence as unwelcome as ever. She yanked a black T-shirt over her head, her skin still warm from the stress the night had put on her. The history of their relationship charged between them waiting to explode.

"Get out," she snapped.

"No. I want to know why you did me dirty like that—breaking up with me in public," he growled, stepping further into the room, his anger simmering just beneath the surface. She could feel it—his need to control, to be the center of everything. It wasn't just about the breakup; it was the power he thought he was entitled to. Rosa knew that all too well. He had tried to control everything—from her time to her emotions—and she'd let him for too long before deciding to become a police officer, now a detective. But tonight, she was done.

"You didn't take the hint." Rosa's voice was barely more than a low hiss, and she stepped toward him, her body coiling with frustration. "Now. Get. Out."

Before she could make it past him, Jacob's hand shot out, grabbing her wrist with an iron grip. His touch sent a spark of anger through her veins, a flash of heat that burned through her chest. Without thinking, she swung her fist, the punch landing square on his lip. A sickening crack echoed through the room as her knuckles collided with flesh, and his blood spurted from the cut, staining the floor beneath him.

Jacob stumbled back, spitting blood with a vile sneer, his expression darkening. But instead of backing down, his eyes narrowed, and the rage in him only grew. He was no longer just angry—he was furious. The control he craved was slipping through his fingers, and that made him dangerous.

Jacob's anger flared and his eyes narrowed as he wiped his lip, probably feeling the hot surge of humiliation. No woman—especially not Rosa—was going to make him feel small in front of others. The fact that she'd rejected him in public, that she thought she could push him away like this—it burned him. His pride was shattered in a single moment and his need to control turned into a consuming fury.

Rosa could feel it. The past was never truly gone. It just waited for the right moment to resurface.

She remembered how Kershaw had told her that Jacob admitted to sending those threatening texts and emails after she broke free—angry messages full of threats and warnings because she simply couldn't be controlled. Kershaw said Jacob told him to just block that number; he wouldn't use it again. Still, the memory of that bitterness lingered, a reminder of how dangerous Jacob could be. But Rosa was done with him controlling her, which was why she broke up with him in public years ago—the one place he couldn't do anything about it.

Rosa's heart pounded as she rushed out the door, but in the commotion, she made a mistake. She wasn't prepared for the force of Jacob's shove. It sent her stumbling, and she tumbled down the stairs, the impact piercing and jarring. Her arm twisted unnaturally, and a flare of pain shot up her wrist. The sting felt like fire, but there was no time to react as she scrambled to regain her balance.

"Not so tough now, are you?" Jacob's voice came from behind her, cold and mocking. His boots thudded heavily against the wooden steps as he descended, closing the distance between them. Before Rosa could turn, his hand tangled in her hair, yanking her head back with a razor pull.

"Say something now," he taunted, his breath hot against her ear.

Before she could react, a voice cut through the tense air—steady, calm, but commanding.

"Now, I don't like to tangle in young folks' business," her father said, his tone deceptively calm. "But I'm gonna need you to take your hand off my daughter."

Rosa looked up from the bottom of the staircase to find her father standing in the doorway of the living room. His grip was tight around the cold metal handle of a hamburger spatula. The easygoing man who had spent the evening flipping burgers was gone, replaced by someone incisive, more imposing. His eyes, usually warm, were now hard as steel—a fierce determination sparking in them, one Rosa had only seen a handful of times before.

Her stomach twisted. This wasn't just about protecting her anymore. It was about what he was willing to do to keep her safe. Jacob's controlling presence had pushed her father into this—an urgent reminder of just how far he'd go for his daughter. Rosa swallowed hard, the heaviness of it pressing down on her.

For a brief second, he hesitated—doubt in his expression, the moment pressing down heavier than he expected. She recognized that hesitation. It was the same look he had when stepping in to stop a schoolyard bully, the same look he wore when helping her with her lunch tray as a kid. This wasn't a childhood scuffle, but the protective instinct was there, fierce and unmistakable.

Then, before she could stop it, Jacob moved. His fist sliced through the air, connecting with her father's jaw in a sickening crack. The older man staggered back, eyes wide with shock. For a moment, everything froze—the sound of the blow hanging in the air—before the blood rushed hot to his face. Though stunned, he regained his composure with terrifying speed. The anger surged, erasing any signs of hesitation. His grip tightened on the spatula, turning it into a weaponized extension of his fury.

Rosa saw that raw force ignite in her father—pure protectiveness, not crossing any lines she could see. Memories drifted in her mind of him in the schoolyard, jaw clenched, lifting a bully by the shirt collar with no words, just a look. The same look he was giving Jacob now. Her pulse raced. She admired that fierce loyalty. But something about that unsettled her—the dangerous edge he carried—and Rosa knew this fight was far from over.

Suddenly, the hallway erupted with movement as Simon rushed toward the living room. Rosa's eyes locked on her father and the tight grip he had on the spatula. Her stomach clenched at the tension radiating from him—this wasn't just about her safety. It was about how far he was willing to go to protect her. There was something fierce in his stance, but beneath it, a desperate need to fix something long broken.

Before she could think, Simon grabbed her father's arm, pulling him back with surprising force. The older man was no longer young, but the strength in his grip told Rosa otherwise. There was a raw power there, dangerous and sharp, and Simon looked like he needed to stop it before it escalated.

"Dad!" Rosa's voice cracked, urgency bleeding through her words. "Cut it out before this gets more out of control!"

She shoved past Simon and stood firm, staring Jacob down. "Jacob, you're no longer welcome here. You're not blaming me for your mess. Get. Out."

With a brisk push, Rosa sent Jacob stumbling toward the door. The slam echoed through the house, slicing through the noise like a knife. She didn't care who saw. This wasn't about Jacob—it was about keeping their mission on track, making sure they stayed in control, not pulled into catastrophe. What if this was exactly what the killer wanted? Or Chadford?

"Cool down, will ya? I already got a punch in—I didn't need my dad to do it, either," Rosa shot back at her father, sarcasm dripping from her voice. She wasn't about to let anyone fight her battles for her. She could handle herself just fine. With that, she stormed up the stairs, putting distance between herself and the situation that just occurred below.

A moment passed by.

Simon turned to Rosa's father. "You good, Mr. Ryker?"

The older man exhaled slowly, his expression hardening for a moment before softening into something that almost looked like regret. "Yes... I just lose my cool with her sometimes. She's all I have left."

His voice carried a heaviness that Simon didn't quite know how to respond to, the mixture of sternness and sadness in the room. He was a father, and no matter how much strength he showed, that truth was undeniable. But Simon couldn't help but wonder—how much was he trying to control, even now?

Simon hesitated. He looked toward the stairs, to Rosa retreating, and then back to the older man standing in the room, a storm of emotion behind his eyes. There was an instinct to stay, to comfort the father, to help him make sense of his emotions, to help the family hold together after everything that had just happened. But no. Simon's pulse quickened.

He took a deep breath. The case. Always the case.

Without another word, Simon gave a tight nod and exited through the hallway door leading to the backyard. There was only space for the truth. His focus sharpened as he walked away, but he couldn't shake the thought: Would he ever be able to disentangle himself from the mess of personal ties? Not until the case was solved, he figured. But would he even have time for any of that?

A RECIPE FOR DISASTER

ROSA IGNORED HER dad for the rest of the night, though before he left, she promised she'd call him in the morning. She knew he meant well, and deep down, she understood his actions hadn't truly jeopardized everything they were trying to uncover. But in the heat of the moment, her anger got the better of her. The whole incident felt like a threat to all their hard work—even if, logically, she knew it wasn't.

This wasn't the time for a cookout. How foolish had they been, trying to blend in and have fun when people were being murdered? They didn't even know if the next victim was already gone. From the way things looked, they were either out of luck or running out of time.

She sat down heavily on the couch, the frustration twisting inside her. Her hand brushed against the phone on the table just as the screen lit up—an incoming call.

***

The night air was filled with the scent of frying oil and stale coffee as Miss May pulled the diner doors closed behind her. She had just finished the last of the cleanup, wiping down the counters and setting the chairs in their usual places, when she noticed the trash bag sitting by the back door—waiting to be taken out. She sighed, frustration bubbling up. The busboys had forgotten their end-of-shift duties again, and now it was up to her.

"Why is it always me?" she thought, wiping a stray hair out of her face. She was tired, bone-deep tired, but someone had to do it. She'd promised Rosa she'd come to the cookout tonight, but here she was—doing the work someone had left undone.

She hefted the bag onto her shoulder, and it weighed her down. Some days, she wondered if she were just a janitor, always cleaning up after others—whether it was the diner, everything in town, or Rosa's life.

She should have been there with them. Rosa was handling so much. Miss May could only imagine the burden of it all—what Rosa had to carry alone all these years. Her heart ached for her, but that ache felt different now. It was the kind of ache that made her feel guilty for not being more present. She used to check on Rosa and Mr. Ryker daily, making sure they were okay, but days turned into weeks, then months. The distance had grown, and now Miss May was realizing just how much she'd let slip away.

"I should have gone to that cookout. She needs me. This whole town needs someone who's not in their own head all the time."

As she trudged across the cracked asphalt, the trash bag seemed heavier with her guilt. She should have been there. Rosa had enough on her plate, and yet here she was, alone in the dark, shouldering this burden, trying to bury the pain of what happened fifteen years ago. A mother blown to pieces. How could anyone—especially a woman—carry that kind of trauma?

She was damn strong, Rosa was.

The smell of the trash was overpowering—a mixture of old grease and uneaten food—and Miss May grimaced as the bag swung with each step, jarring against her hip. Her legs ached, the exhaustion from the long shift beginning to sink in, but the sooner she got this done, the sooner she could go home.

She reached the dumpster and, with a grunt of effort, lifted the heavy bag high over her head, tossing it inside. As she turned to leave, the corner of her eye caught something strange. A flash of light pierced the gloom of the night.

What was that?

Confused, she shuffled toward it, her shoes scraping across the gravel. She bent down to pick it up, but as her fingers closed around the smooth plastic, a sticky sensation caught her attention.

Blood?

Her stomach lurched, nausea rising in waves. She yanked her hand back, her heart pounding like a war drum in her chest. The phone slipped from her grasp, clattering to the ground as she stumbled backward. This wasn't just a random mess. The texture, the smell—this was blood. Fresh. Someone had been dumped here. Left behind like trash.

Her lungs heaved in short, sharp gasps. The air felt thick. Too thick. What was this? She wasn't ready for this. She wasn't some seasoned investigator. She didn't know what to do in moments like this. None of this felt real.

Still trembling, she paused—but something inside her, raw and instinctive, pushed her forward. She crept around the dumpster, chest tight and pounding, barely breathing as she tried to make sense of what she was seeing.

The phone's flashlight—now lying on the ground where it had fallen—flickered weakly, casting jagged shadows across the asphalt. But what caught her eye was far worse.

A body. A woman's body.

Miss May's pulse quickened. Her blood ran cold. The woman was young, her features peaceful in death, almost as if she were sleeping. But the stillness was unnatural. The body was lifeless.

The woman had been arranged with unsettling care, as if someone had taken great pains to stage her. She lay on a white bedsheet, stark against the dark ground. Neatly placed on her dress was a piece of bark, pinned delicately but precisely. Red letters were sketched into the bark—crude, jagged markings that spelled something Miss May couldn't fully comprehend at first glance.

Her stomach twisted, and her throat tightened. This wasn't just a random death. This was too much. She'd seen people dead before—hell, she'd seen too much of it in her life—but this? This was different. She could feel it deep in her bones. A chill crept up her spine as she backed away slowly, every nerve screaming at her to run.

What if the killer was still around?

Panic set in.

This was different. Not just a dead body. She knew it had something to do with what was going on in this town.

Her head swung wildly from side to side, eyes searching the darkness. What if the killer is still here? Hiding just out of sight. Watching her?

The darkness felt suffocating. The pinpoint of light from her phone the only thing connecting her to the world. The only way to get help. She could still feel the blood on her fingers. Clinging. Seeping into the tissues, settling in her bones. She wiped her hands on her apron. Over and over.

All she could think of was Rosa. Rosa would help.

KARMA'S TRIGGER

ON THE OTHER side of town, Jacob slammed the door to his crummy apartment, anger boiling over. The sting of Rosa's punch still burned on his lip, and the humiliation twisted deeper with each step he took. He pulled the gun from the drawer, his hand steady despite the rage inside him. Maybe he should pay them all back—show them who he really was.

With a sneer, he raised the gun, his finger brushing the trigger.

A shot rang out—sharp, deafening.

For a heartbeat, everything stood still. The gun trembled. The stench of gunpowder appeared. His chest seized, heart hammering in his ears.

Then came the flash.

He staggered backward, eyes wide, as blood splattered across the floor—a grotesque spray against the concrete, too vivid to feel real. His own blood.

It happened too fast. His grip had slipped—or had someone else pulled the trigger? Had it ricocheted off something? The pain bloomed in his abdomen, sharp and searing, and the realization struck like a cold slap: he hadn't meant for this. Not like this. But here it was. His mistake. His reckoning.

He dropped to his knees, the weapon clattering beside him. Blood pooled around him, viscous and dark, crawling in every direction. The world spun, vision tunneling as the darkness crept in, choking out the edges of everything.

The stillness that followed spoke louder than any noise, a reminder of the price he had just paid.

GREASE STAINS AND GRIEF

AT THE CRIME scene, Rosa stood near the dumpster behind the dimly lit Waffle House. The body, a woman in her fifties, lay sprawled across a sheet on the cracked pavement. The stench of fresh grease and rusted metal hung in the air, mixing with something more grotesque—the unmistakable scent of death.

A soft breeze rolled through the alley, stirring rain-dampened leaves. Everything else was still. Her chest was tight. Her thoughts foggy. This woman from the riddle was gone.

Rosa wasn't thinking like a detective. Not really. She was just... watching. Frozen. Trying to make sense of a scene that would never truly make sense.

The officers worked around her, snapping photographs, collecting samples, muttering into radios. The forensic team was already cataloging evidence. Every piece carefully placed in bags. Every drop of blood traced. The woman's head injury had caused bleeding that left a stain on the white sheet beneath her, but Rosa could see the real cause of death—the bruising along the neck, deep and unforgiving. She had been strangled, just like the others. The blood was fresh, the skin still pale and soft. This one hadn't been preserved. She hadn't been stored.

She was fresh.

That fact alone meant a change.

Her eyes drifted. William moved methodically through the scene, scanning for prints near the dumpster. His hands were steady, respectful. Each movement said he understood the weight of this moment. Rosa admired that—his quiet care for the dead. Even here.

She reached up to rub her eyes, only to realize her hands were trembling. She was too exhausted to feel steady anymore.

A soft cough nearby startled her, and she turned to find Chief Chadford standing beside her. He looked as shaken as she felt. His posture was rigid, his face pale.

"I can't believe this happened here… in my town," he said, voice low.

Rosa didn't respond right away. She studied his face, unsure whether to speak or stay silent. She hadn't expected him to sound so… hollow.

She remembered what this town used to be. Before all of this. Before the riddles and the headlines and the mess. She had walked these alleys as a teenager, and now she was staring down at a woman who had died violently because they were too slow.

Chadford rubbed the back of his neck, his voice tight with restraint. "Before Rosa, the last murder we had was fifteen years ago. That mailbox explosion…" He paused, swallowing hard. "Everyone said it was a prank gone wrong. But no one ever came forward. No prints, no witnesses. The case just… died before it even began. And now, we have two back to back…"

Rosa glanced sideways at him. It was rare for him to speak about cold cases. Especially that one. The one that meant everything to her.

"It always felt wrong," he said quietly, almost reverently. "No answers. And now, no more answers? What the hell is really going on?"

Rosa said nothing.

He let out a breath. "Now this. Right here in plain sight." His gaze fell back to the body. "I know what people are saying. About me. About the department. That I've lost control. Maybe I have. But this? I didn't want this."

She could feel the heaviness in him. The guilt. Maybe not guilt for killing, but guilt for missing something. For being late. For being outmatched.

He looked at her. "I'm not the enemy, Rosa."

She didn't answer, not directly. But her eyes softened, just slightly. He wasn't the man she trusted—but in that moment, he didn't seem like the killer either. Just someone afraid of what it meant to be powerless.

Then she caught William's signal across the alley, calling her attention back to the body. She glanced once more at Chadford, then turned away.

She hadn't said a word to most of them since arriving. Hadn't had the energy. But the tears were creeping in again, pressing hot behind her eyes.

Raya noticed, stepping in front of her. "Rosa, don't do this. Please."

But it was already happening. Her breath hitched. A sob caught low in her throat. The pressure of the moment, of all the moments, cracked something open inside her.

The woman's lifeless body. Simon's distance. The old griefs she hadn't unpacked. The fear she might never figure this out.

It all spilled over.

She turned slightly, away from the others, wiping at her face. "Damn it," she whispered. The tears kept coming.

Raya stepped in front of her, trying to shield her from the others' view. It was instinctive, protective. It didn't work. Rosa knew people had noticed. She didn't care.

And then she saw him.

Simon.

He wasn't looking at her, not directly. But he had paused. His head had turned. His eyes had found her for just a second.

And then he looked away.

It was better that way, wasn't it?

Raya reached for her arm. "We've got work to do," she said gently.

Rosa nodded. Wiped her eyes. Took a breath.

The riddle was still in her hand. She looked down at it.

"Who sees in the dark, with eyes wide and wise,

Catching whispers the world denies.

Patience once ruled, but age takes its toll,

Now time is the prey, not the soul.

A man will follow, his fate now sealed,

In shadows he hides, where truth is concealed."

She glanced up at the team walking towards her. All eyes were trained on her, waiting for her to break the code. They had been watching her, but she hadn't spoken a word to them since she reached the scene. Raya, still uneasy about her emotional state, shifted on her feet, trying not to let the concern show, but Rosa could feel it—like an invisible thread tugging between them. Despite whatever was swirling inside her, she was determined to push through.

She wouldn't let this break her.

There was too much at stake.

She had a job to do.

***

A couple of hours later, the first light of dawn began creeping over the horizon. Rosa sat in her truck, still parked outside Waffle House, the door open to the morning chill while the others stood nearby.

She stared at the photo on her phone—the one she'd taken of the carved message on the tree bark. The words seemed to pulse with a life of their own, sinking into her mind at a slow pace. A cool breeze brushed against her face, grounding her with the faint scent of damp earth and the sweetness of the air freshener in her truck. The smells reminded her of mornings spent alone, waiting for something to click.

Rosa's brow furrowed as she stared, the riddle starting to pull her in. She leaned forward, her eyes tracing the text, and the tension in her shoulders deepened.

"The first line feels arrogant... 'Who sees in the dark, with eyes wide and wise.' He's referring to himself again. He thinks he's clever, thinking we're too blind to catch him. But the next part—" she chewed on the next line, her lips slightly parted as she worked through it. A frown tugged at her face as the words tightened around her thoughts.

"'Catching whispers the world denies.' That's the new part. It's not just about him now. This is someone else, pulling strings behind the scenes, working in the shadows. A puppet master. He's not alone in this anymore."

She saw Simon and Kershaw shoot a glance at each other; they didn't notice her watching, but she sure noticed that look they exchanged. She could feel their unreadable expressions, as though they were already jumping to conclusions before she had finished unraveling the mystery. Or worse, another secret.

That thought made her glance around carefully. Even without turning fully, she could sense Simon nearby—his presence like static. She caught the rhythmic tapping of his foot, the twitch of his fingers at his side, and though she didn't look directly at him, she could sense it. William wasn't listening; his focus was locked on the crime scene, eyes scanning every detail with mechanical precision. Kershaw and Raya stood a little too close, trying to keep up but clearly out of their element. Both looked at Rosa expectantly, as if she held the key they couldn't quite piece together.

"And then there's this: 'Patience once ruled, but age takes its toll.' It's different now. The killer's losing his patience for something. Or did he grow tired of waiting for something to happen that never did? So he made it happen. And he's definitely getting older... age takes its toll. He's losing control, but not really losing control. He's even showing off that he can kill faster—unless, because he's older, he needs something to be revealed now. Maybe that's why he's killing at a faster rate."

Rosa paused, the riddle slipping through her thoughts like water—elusive and hard to grasp. She felt Kershaw's skepticism—he was thinking too logically, dismissing what her gut told her. Could this really be a killer losing control? The idea felt foreign, but the clues were there.

Her mind slipped into overdrive. There's no way this murderer would lose control unless something medical happened to him—though even that seemed far-fetched. She couldn't shake the feeling that something else had triggered this change in the killer's behavior.

She felt Simon's frustration simmering. His jaw clenched and his eyes darkened, but she kept her focus steady on the screen, forcing herself through the mental fog.

The next lines felt like they were too strong. "'Now time is the prey, not the soul.' That's the kicker. His impatience is getting to him—it's making him more desperate. He needs to act faster. Time's his enemy now. He doesn't want to admit it, but he will age. So his task needs to be finished—soon. Whatever it is, whatever the cost. Winning the game? Damn, I don't know anymore."

Rosa's voice steadied, her pulse still thudding in her ears as the next realization crept up on her, curling in the back of her mind like a whispered warning. "A man will follow, his fate sealed. In shadows he hides, where truth is concealed."

She hesitated, her breath catching slightly in the brisk air before her voice softened, absorbing the gravity of the words. The chill in the atmosphere mirroring the frost creeping into her bones.

"This line—'In shadows he hides, where truth is concealed'—it's layered," she murmured. "At first, I thought it described the killer. But maybe it's not. Maybe that line is about the man who's going to die next. Someone who lives in the shadows of the truth... someone who hides or manipulates it for a living. A lawyer, maybe even a judge. Someone whose entire profession revolves around bending or revealing truth."

She looked up, her eyes fixed now. "Whoever it is, he's the next one. That's where we need to focus—the killer's chosen his next target."

LAW AND DISORDER

"THE VICTIM IS Louisa Franklin. Her husband is a well-known lawyer up north in Pennsylvania," William said swiftly after the first twenty-four hours passed.

"Kershaw, Raya, you two head north and talk to the husband," Simon ordered, already dialing a number as he strode away, his voice firm when someone picked up on the other end.

"Looks like we're in for another long night," Kershaw muttered, his gaze fixed on William with a tight edge. "Let's hope he has answers—maybe something that points us toward whoever the killer's after next. Maybe it's him." His tone wasn't panicked, just focused.

Rosa frowned. Everything felt like smoke—leads that drifted apart the closer they got. The riddles, the timing, the precision of the killer's pattern. None of it added up fast enough. And while everyone else stayed busy, chasing angles and doing their part, she felt they were missing something entirely.

The killer wasn't going to strike again immediately—his patterns were controlled. Calculated. But that didn't make it easier to sit with. This wasn't random. It was a quiet race against something invisible.

And decoding this new riddle? That was its own beast. Rosa wasn't ready to say it was meaningless—but it wasn't offering clarity, either. Each word felt like a maze. She hated this waiting game.

She kept the frustration to herself. Simon had looked more alive in the last twenty-four hours than he had in weeks, and she wasn't about to dull that energy. If there was something buried in all this noise—something they were meant to see—she'd find it. On her own terms.

"I know that look," Raya murmured, stepping closer. "Don't do anything reckless."

"I won't." Rosa waved off the warning, muttered a quick goodbye, and climbed into her truck. The station was her next stop—she needed to comb through the list of lawyers within a few miles of town. If the clue was pointing toward a man hiding behind some version of the truth, a legal profession still made the most sense.

"And there she goes," Raya muttered with a low whistle, shaking her head. "I swear, half the time I don't know what's running through that girl's mind."

Simon was already walking back toward them, brow furrowed as he watched Rosa's truck disappear down the road. Raya turned to him, her tone shifting. "But you, boss man," she said, pointing at him, "keep an eye on her. William'll be tied up with the autopsy, and if she's running around alone, that's not good for anyone. She had that look—the one where she's cooking up theories."

"Or maybe," Kershaw cut in, hands stuffed into his pockets, "she just needed to get away from the ice-cold air swarming around here." He nodded toward Simon. "Maybe she didn't want to have to yell again."

William and Raya stifled a laugh—quick, half-contained, but sharp enough to draw a warning glance. Simon didn't join in.

"I have my own theory to look into," he said, tone clipped as he addressed Kershaw. "They're letting you borrow a car, but it's probably best to fly—you'll get there faster. William will drive you to the airport and head back after. Keep me updated. I might be out of service for a couple of hours."

Kershaw and Raya exchanged a glance—uncertainty passing between them. Maybe they didn't agree with the plan. Maybe they didn't trust where Simon was going. But neither of them said it. Not out loud, anyway.

***

Simon returned to the national park—the same place where, just over a month ago, they had discovered the preserved body in the woods. It hadn't been that long, but the memory served as a stark reminder of the killer's pattern.

Before that, the last known murder had been two years earlier—a slow, methodical pace the killer had kept for years. But the recent killing, just the day before, shattered that pattern completely.

The DO NOT CROSS tape still fluttered in the breeze, the faded words CRIME SCENE INVESTIGATION stamped across the barrier. The faint scent of decay crept in, even as nature steadily reclaimed the space. Twigs snapped softly underfoot as Simon stepped carefully, eyes scanning for anything unusual—a disturbed patch of soil, a faint footprint, or broken branches hidden among the fallen leaves.

Something about this sudden escalation felt wrong. The killer was speeding up. The rules were changing.

Like someone knew all the details before they should have. Almost as if the scene had been tampered with.

Simon's mind immediately jumped to the insiders—the few people close enough to the investigation who might be feeding information or manipulating evidence. Was someone on the force playing a dangerous game? Or worse, was the killer closer than they realized, hiding in plain sight?

Trust was now the rarest commodity.

Simon had been chasing this guy for over ten years—there was no way he wouldn't recognize when something was wrong. The pattern was too familiar, the precision too calculated. This was his work. But this was also something else. Something new.

He exhaled, his breath visible in the crisp air as he scanned the tree line, eyes flicking to the twisted branches and patches of trampled grass near the creek bed. He crouched low, searching for anything that didn't belong—disturbed soil, torn fabric, the faintest print in the mud. The only sound around him was the dry crunch of leaves beneath his boots and a distant crow calling in the woods.

He knew this killer. Every habit. Every signature. The careful placement of clothing. The faint scent of that same cologne. The precise way the scenes were arranged—like a ritual. The Wood Riddle Killer didn't rush. He didn't leave things messy.

But the woman behind the dumpster? Her blouse sleeve had been pushed up, like someone had started tugging at it. Normally, the killer would've straightened every button, smoothed the fabric, made sure the clothes looked as untouched as possible. But not this time.

And over a month ago, it was the man in the national park. Dismembered. Left on a black blanket. The edge of the blanket had been flipped up slightly, like someone had knelt beside it, then hurried off. His clothes hadn't been folded nearby the way they usually were. They'd been scattered.

He hadn't said anything at the time. Maybe he hadn't wanted to believe it.

But now he was sure.

Someone had been there before them. At both scenes.

Someone was searching for something.

Simon's gut twisted. Whoever it was, they weren't just interrupting crime scenes—they were interfering with a killer who noticed everything.

He stood slowly, eyes narrowing as he scanned the area again. The killer was already dangerous, but this? This was going to escalate things.

And if Simon was right, it already had.

To cover their tracks, maybe?

What was he missing?

Was Wood Riddle really getting old and slipping up? That didn't seem likely. Riddle was too smart, too based in methodology. He'd been eluding them for too long for that to be true. But in the last two years, something had changed. Something crucial. But what? None of it made any fucking sense.

The only thing Simon knew for sure was that the killer wasn't done. More bodies this quickly meant the Wood Riddle wanted to play in full visibility this time.

And yet, deep down, Simon felt something disturbingly close to relief.

More kills meant getting closer to him. Closer to revenge. The thought burned like poison on his tongue, bitter and consuming, a necessary fire that kept him going, but also a wound that would never fully heal. He'd been chasing this man for so long, but it wasn't just about justice anymore. It was far too personal. His pursuit had become more than just the hunt—it had become an obsession, a way to fill the emptiness left behind when Marybeth had been taken.

The twisted irony of it all was that revenge had become both a reason to live and a reminder of everything he'd lost. And sometimes, in the quiet moments between the madness, he wondered: *What happens if I do catch him? If I finally make him pay—will it ever be enough?*

He rubbed a hand over his face, his fingers brushing over the scar that still felt fresh. He thought about his worst fear. *If I can't catch Riddle, if I can't end it… will it ever stop?*

Would he ever feel whole again?

The pain, the bitterness—they always led him back to her: Marybeth. His sister. The one who had sparked this entire pursuit on a deeper level. The one who had always tried to keep him grounded, reminding him there was more to life than this chase—case after case. But she was gone now… and it still felt like he had disappeared, too.

He wasn't the same man who started this chase over a decade ago. The man who believed in justice, who thought he could stop the darkness. That man was long gone. In his place was something else—something colder. The fixation had eaten away at him, changed him in ways he couldn't undo. It was a cancer, slowly consuming him, taking away parts of himself he didn't even realize he'd lost until it was too late.

Would he ever be able to escape it, or had the darkness that had consumed him all these years gone too deep to pull back from?

But he didn't care. He would do it. Even if it meant ripping his soul to hell. He would hunt Wood Riddle down, and he would make him pay, no matter the cost.

***

Rosa rustled through the paperwork on her desk—piles of it, stacked so high it felt like a personal attack. Chadford had dumped every minor case on her desk just to prove a point, and after they returned from the scene where they found the woman in the dumpster, her regular workload from when she first joined the task force was still waiting. She was behind, drowning in files.

Even so, her mind was elsewhere. A theory had been forming.

For hours, she sifted through reports, the dim glow of her desk lamp the only light left in the nearly empty station. At some point, the others had gone home, but she barely noticed. She could feel the case taking hold of her. The burden of time ticking away, the faces of the victims haunting her thoughts. If she didn't solve this, the next victim would die. *What if I'm wrong?* she wondered. *What if this leads nowhere?*

"Lawyers..." she murmured, skimming another page. Five different names popped up within a twenty-mile radius of the latest crime scene. She pulled their information onto her screen, filtering through cases involving anything from drugs to murder.

Then—

John Willington.

The name sent a jolt of something through her gut. The fifth lawyer's face filled her screen—a peculiar, almost forced expression, like a man trying to exude power but coming across as approachable. Those were always the dangerous ones. The ones who pretended to be harmless.

A familiar name appeared in his record. Mr. Adams. His lawyer for something about embezzling money years ago in Chicago.

It's too easy to overlook, Rosa thought, but the pieces were starting to fit too well, especially if someone was covering it all up. Her mind was working faster than she could keep up with, pulling threads she didn't fully understand yet.

Rosa's fingers moved quickly, pulling up old cases. Most of them were useless, minor offenses that had no connection to the case at hand. She was just about to scrap the theory altogether when—

"What are you looking into?"

The sudden voice behind her made her jump. Her heart slammed against her ribs as she spun in her chair, eyes wide.

William stood there, arms crossed, watching her.

"Still here?" he asked, amusement across his face.

"Jesus, Will, you scared me," Rosa exhaled, pressing a hand to her chest.

William grinned sheepishly. "Didn't mean to sneak up on you."

"Look at this," she said, waving him over, her focus snapping back to the screen. "The husband was too easy of a suspect—if he was ever a real target to begin with. But this guy..." She pointed at the name on the screen. "He's on Kershaw's list of suspected drug traffickers."

William leaned in, scanning the monitor.

"This guy also happened to be the lawyer for several high-profile community leaders—politicians, business moguls, and other influential figures," Rosa continued, her voice tightening with excitement. "And get this, he was the lawyer for every single one of the killer's victims in the last ten years. At some point, they were all connected to him. You'd think the investigators would have looked into this by now."

William's expression darkened. "So the killer's motive is targeted."

"Exactly. We've always known he gains something from these kills, but we never figured out what. Why these specific people? Why these specific cases?" Rosa's fingers drummed anxiously on the desk.

Her hands trembled for just a moment, doubt creeping in—doubt that maybe she wouldn't find the answers in time. But she shoved it aside. She had to stay focused.

"If this lawyer is the common thread, then he's hiding something. The truth is always concealed in the details." She met William's eyes, her mind racing with a thought. *If I don't solve this... if I don't stop this man, someone else will die.*

"Let's go to him now," Rosa said, locking eyes with William.

"Now? Shouldn't we loop Simon in first?"

"Not until we're sure it's something," she countered. "You've seen how obsessive he is—he'll take it too far."

William hesitated, but didn't argue. Rosa was right.

She grabbed her coat and keys, already moving toward the door. William followed, pulling on his own jacket.

"I'll drive," he said, his tone light but firm. "It's late for a woman to be out driving alone."

Rosa arched a brow, half-amused. "Chivalry, huh?"

"Something like that," he said with a smirk.

Truth be told, she was too exhausted to argue. Maybe letting him take the wheel wasn't such a bad idea.

DO NOT CROSS

SOMEONE WHO KNEW the crime scene. Someone who could cover their tracks—not just anyone, but someone close enough to move unseen. Simon had come back here because a nagging detail didn't sit right with him—a subtle clue he hadn't noticed before, something buried beneath the surface of the usual evidence. The thought burrowed into his mind like a splinter he couldn't dig out.

The sun was sinking fast, the last pale light ebbing away as dusk crept into night. The trees around him rustled with the whisper of a cool breeze and the musky scent of decaying organic matter rose from the forest floor. He stood in the darkening woods, staring at the remnants of yellowed DO NOT CROSS tape fluttering in the wind. The crime scene was abandoned, but the air still held a residual presence, as if the past violence had stained the very ground beneath him.

What was it that felt off about this case?

He crouched, running his fingers lightly over the hardened soil where the body had once lain. The earth had settled, and the scene had been cleaned up, but a small thought nagged at him—the slight corner of the blanket. But it was nothing obvious, just enough to suggest someone had been here before them.

Simon's gut tightened. Someone had quietly disturbed the scene, disrupting the killer's carefully controlled signature.

He flipped through the last decade of crime scenes like pages of a well-worn case file. The memories were vivid. Who had always been close? Who had slipped under the radar? Who had access—to evidence, to reports, to minor shifts that could easily go unnoticed?

The sterile feel of the task force office came alive in his thoughts—the piles of files, the quiet hum of the library, the careful, calculated moves behind the scenes.

It couldn't be...

Simon's pulse ticked faster as he stood, his breath clouding in the frigid air. He reached for his phone, fingers tightening around the device as he dialed.

The ringing cut sharply through the calm.

Then—

"Hello," a voice answered.

Simon's stomach dropped. It wasn't Rosa.

It was William.

"What's up, man? Find anything?" William's voice was casual, but something about it twisted him the wrong way.

"Nothing worth noting," Simon said carefully, eyes narrowing into the darkness. His grip on the phone tightened. "I heard Raya say Rosa has a crazy theory."

William let out a short laugh, but it was the kind that didn't reach the eyes—not that Simon could see him, but he could hear it in his tone.

"You know, she's way too smart for her own good," William mused. His voice shifted, dipping into something lower, something unreadable. Then—

"He seriously seems to take an interest in her mind. How brilliant it is. Even I'm shocked, a bit of a genius if you ask me."

Simon's breath stilled in his throat.

"Too bad," William continued, his words almost thoughtful. "His patience might grow thin just like it has before. He might go into hiding again. I can't let that happen."

Simon's world went razor-sharp.

The wind howled through the trees, but he no longer felt the cold.

He just felt something moving into place—something he should have seen long ago. The realization sent a shock through him, and before he could think twice, he was already running, tearing through the woods toward his car.

Meanwhile, Rosa's voice filtered through the other end of the line.

"Did someone call?" she asked as she opened the passenger door. "He wasn't home. We'll have to try his office—he seems like the type to work through the night."

"Here," William said, pointing to the dashboard. "Simon's on the line—he just called."

Rosa reached for it, but in a split second, William pulled it just out of reach, a smirk tugging at his lips.

"Okay, joke's over," she laughed, though the sound came out thinner than she intended.

Then she saw it.

A shift—faint but unmistakable. Something dark and unreadable appeared in his eyes. It was gone in an instant, but not before a whisper curled around her.

William's voice dropped, no longer casual but precise, each word slow and meaningful, as if savoring every moment. There was something in his demeanor that shifted—his confidence had grown, settled in like a heavy weight he'd been carrying for far too long.

"If you hadn't gotten involved…" His words hung in the air, slow, methodical. "I would have been able to keep my friends. The only family I've ever known. I could have played along… and no one, not even the badass Simon Pikes, would have ever figured it out."

Rosa paused, her hand still on the door, her mind racing to catch up, but William's eyes never wavered. They were more focused.

"But you… and your mind," he said, the words almost a whisper as he leaned back in his seat, his gaze never leaving her. A smirk curled at the corner of his lips, colder than anything she'd seen before. "You just had to interest him, didn't you? Whoever he is, he seems to think you're a threat. More than anyone else. And I can't wrap my mind around it. How did he know, exactly? What was it about you that made him want to come out of hiding?"

Without warning, William's hand quickly shifted, then—the metallic click of a gun being cocked. Rosa froze, a sudden catch in her throat as panic surged up her spine. She tried to react—but she was too slow. In one fluid motion, he pulled the pistol from his jacket and pointed the barrel at her. The movement was practiced, calm, almost casual—but the intent was unmistakable.

His finger was off the trigger, but the sight of the weapon, held so steadily in his hand, sent a chill down her spine. His voice remained steady, though there was a wild edge to it now, something that hadn't been there before.

"More than anyone else," he repeated, his eyes now fixed on her with a calculating resolve.

Rosa's heart pounded in her chest as she stood there, frozen, the passenger door still open between them. She hadn't expected this—she'd underestimated him, and now she was standing at the threshold of danger. Real danger. Something she wasn't sure she could escape.

FRACTURED COMPOSURE

RAYA LIFTED HER hand and knocked on the grand door of the mansion. When it opened, she saw a man who immediately struck her as genuine—sturdy build, kind eyes behind round glasses, and a quiet warmth that put her at ease. He had that approachable kind of charm, the kind you'd trust without hesitation.

"Hello, Mr. Franklin," Raya said softly, feeling the weight of what they were about to say.

Kershaw's voice cut in smoothly, professional but gentle. "We're with the FBI. May we come in?"

Raya noticed how Kershaw's calm demeanor steadied her, and when he gave her a quick, reassuring touch on the shoulder, it felt like a promise that they'd get through this together. Mr. Franklin nodded, stepping aside to let them in.

Inside, as they shared the news, Raya watched the man's carefully held composure begin to unravel. His voice trembled with vulnerability, raw and unguarded—a reaction she knew would linger with her long after the day ended.

Later, as they sat in the car after asking Mr. Franklin to head to Chattingsburg, Raya admired his genuine, earnest dedication to meet them there. There was no hint of guilt or deceit in his nervousness—something about him felt sincere, even in such a devastating moment.

Still, a tight knot settled in Raya's stomach. Kershaw glanced at her, brow furrowed. "I can't reach Simon. Keeps going to busy."

"He did say he wouldn't have service for a while," Raya replied, trying to steady her nerves.

But as the car wound along the road, an unease crept over her. Was this the calm before the storm?

"Hmm, feels off," Kershaw muttered, eyes narrowing as he focused on the road ahead.

***

Rosa had just stepped toward the car when she froze—the gun in William's hand lifted and pointed straight at her.

Her throat tightened. Every muscle screamed to duck, to slam the door, to run. But the weapon held steady, and the space between them was too tight, too exposed. One wrong move, and he'd pull the trigger.

She clenched her jaw, fury boiling beneath her skin. Not now. Live first. Fight later.

With simmering reluctance, Rosa slid into the passenger seat and shut the door, spine rigid.

"Gosh, it sure took a while to get you alone," William said, his voice tinged with weary frustration. He fiddled with the necklace around his neck, the movement a nervous habit. His eyes searched hers, restless and unsettled, like he was chasing a thought that kept slipping away. "I don't get why he's coming out of hiding now... playing games again, of all people—with a country bumpkin, no less. It just doesn't make any sense. And, of course, he won't give anyone a straight answer. It's all so messed up. I just want to catch Wood Riddle, end it all, and maybe... maybe find some peace."

He swallowed hard, then said aloud, voice roughening with memory, "That night... Simon's sister... she was lying there in a pool of blood. The pendant next to her, shining like some cruel afterthought. I loved her. And now she's gone. Taken by the same monster we vowed to stop."

Rosa's eyes stayed on him, watching his expression twist.

Her confusion deepened. She couldn't ignore the heavy stillness between them—the kind that made her want to scream but kept her frozen.

"Oh, Simon, you still there?" William's voice broke the silence as he connected the phone to the car's Bluetooth, setting it on the dashboard. His tone was mocking, but beneath it, there was something raw—like a child throwing a tantrum no one had dared to stop. "For once, you're quiet. I bet you're brooding, as always. The goal here is to catch the serial killer, right? Your own sister died because of you! And it was your job to protect her, wasn't it? He even sent a warning before he did that to her. Sliced her beautiful throat."

Simon's voice caught on the other end of the line, ragged and raw through the car's Bluetooth. The engine on his end roared louder as he slammed the gas pedal, urgency rising with every second.

Rosa's eyes flicked to William, who hadn't moved—still gripping the gun, still listening, every word feeding something unreadable behind his stare.

Rosa shifted in her seat, her body stiffening with discomfort. Her mind spun, trying to shake off the suffocating dread pressing down on her chest. Simon was right there, listening. But something wasn't right. His silence stretched unnaturally long, thick with unspoken tension—like he was waiting for the perfect moment to act, and every second made the air heavier. Why hadn't he said anything? Of course, he couldn't—not yet. Probably still reeling from the shock of this all. She could almost hear the blame crawling through his thoughts, the guilt he'd carried for years resurfacing. But William wasn't making it any easier. If anything, he was unraveling right in front of her.

At the back of her mind, Rosa pictured Simon—focused, likely battling his own mounting panic as he tried to track them down. She could almost feel his frustration, his fear of failing his team. Or his own twin.

William's voice dropped to a mocking whisper, as if speaking more to himself than to her. "You know, I even had a bet going that you wouldn't figure out John Willington. But that moment in the office an hour ago? I couldn't believe it. How are you just as good with riddles as Wood Riddle?"

His forced, hollow laugh cut through. He casually scratched his hand with the end of the gun, the motion so deliberate it made the hairs on the back of Rosa's neck stand up. He wasn't afraid. How had they missed his derangement?

His smile was cruel. She could see in his posture that William was desperate—manic. His shoulders were too tense, his fingers twitching around the gun. His past demons weren't just lurking; they were screaming at him, and he was listening.

But there was still his guilty conscience; Rosa could sense this wasn't what he truly wanted to do. It was like he was wrestling mentally with something deeper than he'd ever shared.

Rosa refused to comment, but her refusal stoked the fire inside him.

"Say something!" he shouted, voice rising with frustration. "Who are you?!" The gun suddenly aimed at her, finger pressing the trigger, but his grip was shaky—he wanted control, but it was slipping.

Rosa's chest tightened, voice steady despite the storm inside. "You've lost your mind," she said, words unfamiliar as they slipped out, masking the fear simmering just beneath her calm. Her hands trembled faintly, a subtle reminder of the racing heartbeat and desperate thoughts clawing for escape.

William's laugh was sharp, slicing the air like glass. "Have I?" His voice dropped to a venomous whisper. "You must know the killer. Or if you don't, he knows you. Who are you?! I need answers… I need him!"

His eyes darkened with obsession as if the lawyer Rosa uncovered—the one connected to every victim—had become the key to everything unraveling his mind. The line between ally and enemy blurred; William's grip on reality slipped as he tried to piece it all together.

Before Rosa could react, his hand shot out and grabbed the back of her hair, jerking her toward him, face inches away. His breath was hot against her skin, sweat and madness mixing. His grip was too rough, fingers digging into her scalp as if trying to pull answers straight from her brain.

"I am no one," Rosa said firmly despite the rising fear. She refused to let him see it.

He shoved her roughly against the door. "If I touch you, this whole case falls apart," he muttered, voice low and ragged. "We need you to make him show himself. We need your intelligence."

The car's Bluetooth crackled with Simon's voice on the line, listening to every word.

William's hands trembled, drumming against the gun on his lap. "I'm taking this truck. I'll catch him myself. I will." His eyes burned with feverish determination—like a man wrestling control from chaos.

The unspoken threat hung: resist, and she'd be out—maybe worse.

As William wrestled with the storm inside, Rosa made a reckless choice—a confident idiot's gamble, maybe stupid, but her only chance to turn the tide.

In one swift motion, she grabbed the gun, forcing it downward. His grip was iron, but she didn't hesitate—drove her elbow up, slamming it into his nose. A sickening crunch. Blood spattered, warm and slick against her skin.

"Damn it! Are you training for the Olympics or something? What kind of woman hits that hard?" William snarled, grip tightening on the gun, anger mounting as he struggled to regain control.

Neither noticed his foot slip off the brake.

The truck lurched forward.

"What the hell is going on?!" Simon's voice crackled through the phone, their scuffle echoing in the cab.

"She fucking broke my nose," William spat, words ripped from him on instinct. And for a fleeting second, something in his voice—an involuntary admission—hinted at guilt.

His grip tightened. So did hers. They shoved, wrestled, neither willing to let go. Then—

A sharp blow caught Rosa in the eye—a dull, blooming pain.

And then—

A gunshot ripped through the chaos.

Silence.

Through the crackling connection, Rosa heard the tires screeching, sirens wailing in the distance—growing closer.

CRACK! The truck lurched violently, metal grinding, tires skidding as the world spun out of control.

THE ROAD LESS TRAVELED, LITERALLY

AFTER WHAT FELT like hours, Simon veered off the road, following the path of destruction. A truck that size—there was no way it hadn't gone over the guardrail. His stomach twisted as he approached, forcing himself to walk slower than he wanted. Every step felt heavier, nerves knotting in his chest. His mind buzzed, thoughts scattering, the scene bearing down on him.

He finally reached the bridge and looked down. The truck lay totaled, a crumpled wreck at the underpass below. That big-ass truck wasn't going anywhere ever again. Survivors? Unlikely.

Swallowing hard, he immediately called it in, barely registering the dozen missed calls from Kershaw. They'd been worried. Hell, he was worried.

His mind raced, still trying to process the magnitude of what had just happened. The truck was gone, but something else persisted—his own rising dread. He could hardly believe he was standing there, on the edge of this bridge, looking at a mess that could have taken lives. And yet, what he felt most was the need to find answers, to make sure no one else was caught in this. To keep his team safe. To protect Rosa.

Then—

A cough.

Soft, but distinct.

He snapped his head to the side, his eyes scanning the wreckage until he spotted a figure tucked into the ditch by the bridge's barrier.

Rosa.

Beaten, battered—but alive. And despite everything, that spark of confidence still burned in her eyes.

"He ran off before I could grab ahold of him," she said, her voice weak but defiant. She sat up, wincing as she leaned against the inner part of the bridge. "And then, I swear, a damn car came out of nowhere to pick his ass up. Can you believe my luck? What the hell is going on?"

Simon let out a long, steady breath. Relief flooded through him as he rushed toward her—even as the image of her bruised and battered face made his chest tighten. His hand reached for her, but before he spoke, he cracked a faint smile. "Damn, remind me not to get in a fight with you, killer."

The smile faded when he took in her swollen eye. The bruises. The blood. The fact that she was even sitting up at all. Her face was pale, skin flushed with the aftershock of adrenaline and pain. The faint smell of dirt and blood clung to her, but it was her eyes—the way they glinted with defiance despite the bruising—that shook him the most.

He knelt down beside her, voice lowering with concern. "Your leg doesn't look too good."

She shifted her weight slightly, her leg trembling as if it might give way. "I bet my eye doesn't look any better," she shot back, coughing out a laugh. But the pain in her voice was unmistakable. She leaned into him as he gently helped her up, feeling the strain of her body against him. Her limbs were stiff, like a marionette whose strings had been pulled too tight, and every movement seemed to take more effort than it should.

He could tell she was trying to be strong, but the way she winced, the way her shoulders sagged, made his heart ache. The heat of her body radiated through the thin fabric of her clothes, and he could feel the tremors running through her, an aftershock of both fear and exhaustion.

"I've got you," he murmured, even as his own body felt tense from adrenaline. As they stood there, leaning on each other.

Rosa looked down at the wrecked truck. Her words were soft, almost mournful. "My poor truck. I'm going to pay him back if I ever see him again." She was compensating for the pain.

But it wasn't just the truck. Simon could tell the whole situation was too heavy, too confusing for her. Her pride, her purpose, was tangled in this mess. But he couldn't bring himself to say anything about it—he was too focused on making sure she was okay.

As the sound of sirens grew louder and the first ambulances arrived, Simon spotted Chadford approaching. The man's usual stoic demeanor seemed a little off—his eyes flicked between Simon and Rosa, but there was a flicker of something hidden behind them, like he was holding something back or unsettled beneath his calm exterior.

Simon's gaze lingered on Chadford for a moment before shifting back to Rosa, still leaning against his shoulder, her breathing labored but steady. Their eyes met, and something shifted—an unspoken understanding, a moment of madness he couldn't explain.

He didn't know how she was holding it together. She had to be in pain—ribs, leg, eye—he'd seen the damage, and it made something tight coil inside his chest. And yet, she leaned into him like the world hadn't just come undone. The pressure of her against him, the rise and fall of her breath, grounded him more than he cared to admit. For a brief moment, everything else—everything that had happened—seemed to melt away.

Simon still didn't know what to say. Maybe it was the absurdity of the whole thing. Maybe it was the fact that she was here, alive, still fighting. That was enough. But more than anything, just having her close, fragile though she looked, reminded him why he kept going.

She was lucky—sure, but so was he. She wasn't just resilient; she was a damn force to be reckoned with.

He leaned in slightly, glancing down at her again, his expression softening. There was something in his eyes now—something beyond the practiced calm, beyond the exhaustion of the case.

"You know… you're the luckiest newly appointed detective I've ever met. Or maybe it's not luck," he added softly, almost to himself, "Maybe it's something else entirely."

SLICED BY BETRAYAL

AFTER RUSHING BACK from Pennsylvania upon hearing about the incident from Simon, Kershaw and Raya arrived to check out the scene for themselves, both visibly shaken. The smoke had obviously cleared by the time they got there, but the air still reeked of burnt rubber and gasoline. The stench of crushed metal still in the breeze, and ash clung to the wreckage like a reflection that refused to lift. The cold wind bit at their skin. Raya watched Kershaw closely. His face was pale, jaw clenched tightly as he took in the devastation. He scanned the wreck, eyes sharp for any clue that might explain what had happened, but she could see the horror pressing in too close.

Without a word, Kershaw took off immediately, his irritation and confusion driving his every step. The crunch of his boots against the gravel was the only sound in the otherwise oppressive silence, his breath coming out in visible bursts. Raya called after him once, twice, but he barely seemed to register her. His shoulders were stiff, as if bracing for a storm brewing inside. He disappeared into the distance, the wind whipping around him, but his mind was elsewhere—tangled in the wreckage of everything that had gone wrong.

For hours, she imagined, he must have run—pounding the pavement, pushing himself harder with every step. Not searching for answers, not chasing leads. Just running to drown out the noise in his head, to keep the chaos at bay.

It wasn't until late that night when he finally returned, steps slower now, exhaustion in his features. His clothes were disheveled, the edges of his coat streaked with dirt, and his face drawn, a mixture of frustration and helplessness settling in his eyes. He breathed heavily, rubbing his face with one hand, the stubble on his chin scraping against his palm as he tried to make sense of the events, as if the truth might change if he examined it long enough.

Raya, on the other hand, went straight to the hospital after seeing the scene, her heart heavy with concern. The sterile smell of antiseptic filled the air, mixing with the burning sensation deep in her chest—a familiar ache. The constant sound of beeping monitors and the soft shuffle of nurses' feet on the linoleum floors filled her ears and made the anxious tightness squeezing her lungs worse.

What had they gotten themselves into? she wondered, pushing back against the waves of doubt that threatened to overwhelm her. The world felt fragile now—too fragile. She didn't know what was harder: seeing her best friend in this state or realizing the truth about William.

William. He had always seemed to be just a lanky, friendly fellow—someone who could make anyone feel at ease with just a smile. His unassuming nature combined with his quick wit made him someone people liked to be around. He never seemed to take anything too seriously, often cracking jokes or laughing as if the world was a much simpler place. But now, as the reality punched them, it all felt like a lie. How could someone so familiar, so harmless-looking, be part of this twisted mess?

He had his own battles, but he didn't want to share them with the world. And that was so heartbreaking. So deeply heartbreaking.

She could still see his easy smile in her mind, the way his eyes twinkled when he spoke. But now, that image seemed distant—like a fading memory of someone she barely recognized. The more she tried to piece together the truth, the more everything seemed to fracture. And she had only known him for almost two months.

When she saw Rosa, she immediately pulled her into a tight hug.

"Don't squish her too much," Mr. Ryker warned, his voice laced with concern. "Ribs are fractured, her eye's swollen like a tomato, and that leg… sixteen stitches."

He shook his head, probably now wishing she'd never joined the police force—especially now. But despite his concern, there was an undeniable pride as he watched her. Simon seemed to notice it instantly, and when Mr. Ryker caught his eye, Simon gave him a subtle nod of acknowledgment.

Raya froze for a moment, trying to hold back the tears threatening to spill. She swallowed hard, the sharp sting in her throat almost unbearable, but she didn't allow herself to break. *No one needs to see me fall apart*, she reminded herself. She had to be strong—especially now. For Rosa. For Kershaw. For all of them. Thinking about the "whys" would have to wait.

"Is it time for us to pull out of this mess?" Raya sighed, her voice uncertain. Mr. Ryker moved off to finish the remaining paperwork, while Rosa looked like she might pass out from exhaustion. Simon drifted away, likely in search of Kershaw—both of them probably needed to work off some anger, though Raya doubted that was even possible.

But it wasn't just anger in his eyes. Raya watched Kershaw closely—behind his stare. She wondered why he hadn't seen it. Why he hadn't gotten William the help he needed. Or noticed how he'd been feeling. They were supposed to be friends. At least, that's what Raya thought. But people hide things well—some more than others.

She moved to Rosa's side, steadying her when she winced, her heart clenching at the sight. Raya couldn't begin to imagine what it felt like to be in Rosa's shoes, broken both physically and emotionally. *I should've seen the signs with William*, she thought bitterly. But then again, she wasn't the one with the history—Simon and Kershaw had known him longer. She didn't share that bond. Still, the betrayal cut deeper than she wanted to admit. Deeper than she was ready to confront.

"We're too far in, literally," Rosa murmured, pushing herself up with a wince. When Raya reached out to steady her, Rosa was grateful. Every movement felt precarious, as if her body might give out beneath her at any moment.

"I guess you're right about that..." Raya began, her voice trailing off. The raw pain in Rosa's eyes almost made her flinch. But what could she say? That they were too naive to see it coming?

"But William?" Raya added. "It's hard to believe, but it all makes sense now."

Both sat there processing the truth. Raya watched as Rosa lowered her gaze, her pulse fluttering. It was hard to fathom that someone they'd trusted for two months—lived with, laughed with—could do something like this.

He fooled all of us, Raya thought, reading the pain behind Rosa's eyes. But maybe she was the easiest one.

The realization scraped at something raw inside Raya. The line between friend and foe was thinner than she imagined—and now, Rosa seemed to feel the cut of it more than most.

They kept in silence for a moment, their thoughts shrouded.

"People like us," Rosa said quietly, glancing down at her injuries, "we're supposed to be able to trust. But I guess that's the danger of being so sure of everything… We're the ones who get blindsided."

It was true. This wasn't just betrayal—it was a loss of faith.

Raya's thoughts lingered on Rosa's words, the truth about William settling in her gut like a lead weight. *How could we have been so sure about him?* she wondered. It wasn't just that he had betrayed them—it was that they had let their guard down in the worst possible way. No more trust, she promised herself, not in anyone again.

But deep down, Raya knew she couldn't shut herself off completely. Her heart still ached for the connections she'd made with people, even after all the destruction. It was hard to reconcile that part of herself with the harsh reality.

And for Simon and Kershaw, who had known William for over a decade, the pain ran even deeper. The betrayal cut sharper for them—a wound that not only shattered their trust but left them questioning everything they thought they knew. For them, it wasn't just the loss of a colleague—it was the loss of a friendship, something they'd have to reconcile with long after the dust had settled.

And the dust would settle.

***

The cabin held its breath when William finally spoke.

"Are you out of your mind?" a deep, commanding voice shouted at him, causing William to flinch back.

"To be perfectly honest, I think my mind is right where it should be," William shot back, his voice low but cold. "You, on the other hand, you're still at his beck and call. Me? I'm getting closer. My revenge against him is falling into place—just like I've been envisioning for years."

"No," the voice interrupted sharply, cold and firm. "I'm not at his beck and call. You think you're playing a game, but this is about keeping the peace—holding this town together before it all explodes in our faces. You don't see it, but your obsession is the threat. If you push too hard, everything falls apart. This isn't about revenge anymore. It's about survival."

William stared out the cabin window, his fists clenched tight. His anger wasn't just about the screw-up—it ran deeper. Angry at the world, at the police, at Simon, for things left unsaid, for betrayals never acknowledged. Was he pathetic? Maybe. Was he beyond redemption? Probably.

He could feel his own bitterness settling in, choking him. But he couldn't let go. No, he couldn't. For once, he would be the one to win. For once, he would be the one to best Simon. He would come out on top—no matter what it took, even if that meant betraying every ounce of the gullible part of him that had trusted. It was Simon's fault she died anyway.

He had come this far. And now, there was no turning back.

He couldn't forget the sight of Simon.

Blood smeared across his face and hands, kneeling beside his twin sister. Her pale body lay in his arms, her eyes wide open, unseeing. The blood had soaked through her clothes, staining the ground beneath them. Simon's face was a mask of agony, tears mixing with the blood as he clutched her tightly, rocking back and forth as if willing her to wake up.

The image of it haunted him—Simon, usually so composed, so in control, completely unraveling in that moment. The anguish was raw, unlike anything he had ever seen before. His chest tightened as the memory replayed, the echo of Simon's broken cries still wandering in his mind.

...and then, like a slap in the face, the resentment and wrath followed. Why did it have to be her? Why not him?

The unfairness of it hit him like a freight train, and in that moment, he swore to himself he would never let anyone make him feel that powerless again. He would take control. He would make sure that anyone who had ever made him feel that way would pay. His hand clenched into a fist, his jaw locking with renewed determination. No turning back. He would make the killer pay—no matter the cost. He couldn't afford to be weak anymore. Not when the world had already taken so much from him.

***

"He always let people control him," Kershaw muttered, his voice rough as he took a long gulp of whiskey. Simon watched the way the drink burned its way down Kershaw's throat, saw the flicker of relief cross his face for just a moment—a brief escape.

"He's being controlled by the same bastard who took Marybeth. The one who ripped away our lives, our happiness. Screw them all. We're getting closer. We'll catch him."

Simon said nothing. He just nodded, the muscles in his jaw clenched tight enough to feel bruised. The burn in his own throat was a pale imitation compared to the searing pain in his chest—an old, familiar fire simmering just beneath his skin. Tonight, the pain felt heavier, rawer, like it had been fed on years of the chase and endless dead ends. For once, he was sick of it all. Sick of the waiting, the lies, the losses. He wanted nothing more than to bury it deep, to forget—if only for a night.

Around them, the dim light of the bar flickered, tracing over weathered faces and cracked wood. This was the kind of town that forgot fast, where time stretched thin and hope was a scarce currency. But here, in this moment, they let themselves drown their sorrows—numbing the burden with the most expensive liquor they could find in this small fucking town.

INK AND SCARS

A SLIVER OF light slipped through the curtain, catching Rosa's eye as she sat at the kitchen table, slowly chewing her bagel. From the living room came a sudden thud—Simon hit the floor with a grunt, jolted awake by an arm smacking into his chest. Kershaw, still sprawled across the couch, groaned and shifted but didn't wake fully. The cloying, sour scent from the night before still there.

It was only six in the morning, but Simon stirred like clockwork, pushing himself up with a wince and dragging his feet toward the kitchen, shirtless and clearly nursing a headache.

"Um, wow, put on a shirt," Raya said, blinking at him as she slathered cream cheese on her bagel.

Rosa's eyes flicked toward Simon. Her gaze paused—his lean torso, defined abs, and the thorned vine tattoo that spiraled around his left bicep. But it was the scar that pulled her focus—the one across his jawline, usually hidden beneath a collar. It stretched downward, jagged and raw, disappearing beneath where a shirt would've rested.

"Not that I don't mind a show this early in the morning," Raya added with a grin.

Rosa jabbed her in the side, warmth crawling up her neck. "Shut up," she muttered.

"Come on, we all have secrets," Raya continued, gesturing with her bagel toward the tattoo. "But you've gotta tell us about that one."

Simon stood near the sink, rubbing the back of his neck. "Kinda corny," he said. "Marybeth wanted matching ones. Hers on the right side, mine on the left. Thorned vines for troublemaker twins."

"She must've been a badass," Raya said, her tone softer now. Rosa stayed quiet, chewing slowly, observing the words being said.

"Now, go put on a shirt," Raya added with a laugh. "You were wearing one when we dropped your asses on that couch."

"My head is killing me! Bring me water!" Kershaw called from the living room.

Simon filled two glasses from the tap and walked off without a word.

"That was under that shirt. Forget the scar," Raya muttered, still eyeing the doorway.

Rosa smirked and batted Raya's hand away as she reached for the other half of her bagel. "Shut up and keep your voice down."

They settled back in. Around the table, the group turned their focus to the crime scene images of Mrs. Franklin—the woman found murdered near the dumpster.

Tracking down John Willington—the lawyer tied to all the victims—had gone nowhere. Every avenue led to a dead end. Either he was purposefully unreachable, or maybe... maybe he didn't exist at all.

The memory of William's obsession with the case—and with her—still clung to Rosa's thoughts. Kershaw sat quietly across from her, his brows pinched, the betrayal still freshly sinking into his expression. No one spoke it aloud, but it was clear William's spiral had unsettled everyone.

Rosa couldn't shake the feeling that they were still missing something.

"Not that I want to revisit the clues again, but let's go back to it," Raya said, pulling up the most recent riddle.

"Who sees in the dark, with eyes wide and wise,

Catching whispers the world denies.

Patience once ruled, but age takes its toll,

Now time is the prey, not the soul.
A man will follow, his fate now sealed,
In shadows he hides, where truth is concealed."

Kershaw nodded along. Rosa noticed how he leaned in a little, every word memorized.

"Time was the soul, but now it's the prey," Rosa mumbled, mostly to herself. "Time is limited. We know there was a shift in priorities—or his fixation with time could be his way of controlling his own fate, or the world around him."

She paused, her brow furrowing. "His addiction to being wise… maybe he's losing it? Maybe someone who could be smarter is now in the puzzle? I don't know."

"You mean someone who can solve riddles better than him?" Simon said, glancing at her.

Before Rosa could answer, the front door slammed open.

All of them—except Simon, Rosa noticed—jumped in their seats as Mr. Ryker stumbled in, a side table wedged in his arms.

"My bad, my bad," he said, nearly tripping as the door slammed behind him. The noise echoed sharply, making everyone flinch.

"Shit, Dad, seriously?" Rosa groaned. "Can't you just call like a normal person next time to avoid unnecessary near-death jump scares?"

"Oh, don't be dramatic. Simon, Kershaw, please help," Mr. Ryker called.

Simon and Kershaw stood and went to help without question. Rosa watched her dad for a beat, noticing the way his energy filled the room, cutting through the tension like a warm breeze.

"I also thought you guys could use a break," he said, returning inside with takeout bags in both arms. "I went to the office first, thinking you'd be there, but Chadford said y'all were holed up here."

"He really is in a bad mood, not knowing what y'all are up to," Mr. Ryker added with a shrug.

"He'll be fine. This was much needed," Kershaw said, clapping a hand on Mr. Ryker's shoulder.

Raya wasted no time diving into the food, pulling out a hamburger and practically inhaling it.

Rosa closed the case files on the laptop and wiped the screen clean before shutting it. She followed Raya toward the food, easily spotting the hashbrowns she knew her dad had brought just for her.

"Slow down, slow down," her dad chuckled, settling beside her. "I need your help with something—actually, that's the real reason I stopped by. Can you sign me up for the vet conference next month? It's in D.C. Supposed to be a big deal. It's from y'all's neck of the woods."

"As much as I like D.C., that's not where I'm from," Kershaw muttered with a full mouth, practically inhaling his burger.

"Um, ew," Rosa said, scrunching her nose as she eyed him eating like that. She typed quickly on her personal laptop, pulled up the conference site, and entered the details.

"That's rude!" Kershaw grumbled, wiping his face. Raya held up a mirror, and when he caught sight of the ketchup and mustard smeared across his chin, he sighed and disappeared toward the bathroom.

"All done," Rosa said, tapping the laptop closed. "You're getting older—when are you going to slow down with all the traveling? Though, I feel like the real reason you came is to check on me."

Her dad gave a noncommittal shrug, ignoring the last part. "I won't stay too long, but where's the cat? I need my fill of the devil cat."

Rosa motioned toward the corner of the room, where Sir Louie lay curled in his cat tree beside one of the shelves. As Mr. Ryker approached, the cat swatted lazily at him.

"I swear, this cat is confrontational," he muttered.

"He just doesn't like people in his space," Rosa replied, chuckling. "He even swats at me from time to time. He got Simon good that one day."

"Anyways, don't stay holed up here for too long. I understand there's a lot of pressure, but get some fresh air," her dad said, concern evident in his tone. He hesitated, then added, "Oh, and I didn't want to be the bearer of bad news, or add more to everyone's plate, but—"

He cleared his throat. "At the police station I overheard something... the cops got a call and found Jacob at his place. They said... it looked like he was, uh, messing around with one of his guns and... shot himself. They found him dead on the floor. Can you believe that?"

The words dropped like stones in Rosa's gut. Her posture stiffened. She didn't move at first, but her grip on the countertop tightened.

Jacob.

She wasn't sure what she felt—shock, disbelief, or something else entirely. Her fists tightened as the news sank in, cold and strange. But as her mind swirled, one word repeated itself like a quiet whisper she didn't dare say aloud.

Karma.

BADGED AND CORNERED

"WE RULED IT an accident," Raya said. "And as much as I hated him, couldn't he have put the guns down just once?"

"Yeah, it's strange." Rosa couldn't shake the feeling that something was off. It was like an itch she couldn't scratch. But she forced it down. No point in chasing ghosts. "Gotta go—boss man's here."

She barely caught Raya's muttered "good luck" before ending the call and slipping her phone into her pocket. She knew Raya and Kershaw were heading back to the house to comb through the lawyer's files again—hoping for anything they might've missed.

Simon climbed into the passenger seat and shut the door.

"It's time to look into Chadford again," he said, his voice hoarse. "He's the only lead we have for now. I've got units and undercovers searching within a two-hour radius for William. Knowing him, he won't be too far. But we may have an advantage now that they lost their insider."

"I have a request."

Rosa's words came out sharper than intended, and Simon paused, lowering his coffee into the cup holder. He looked at her, head tilted slightly, his brow raised.

"And that is?"

The question was casual, almost dismissive, which made her hesitate—but only for a beat.

"I know we're in the middle of a case, but I cannot sit in this beauty and not ask—can I drive it? Just once."

"For someone your age, you'd think you were younger," Simon muttered, shaking his head. "You get excited over the smallest things. But I'm going to have to say no."

"Oh, come on! A man loves his car too much?"

"No. But that leg of yours is still healing, and I can't risk another accident in a seventy-two-hour span."

She held her hands up in surrender. "Fine." Rosa pulled out her phone again. "But after this case is over, you will let me." She pointed straight at him, firm.

Simon didn't answer. He shifted into gear and pulled out of the lot, heading toward the station without looking back.

When they arrived, Rosa immediately felt all eyes on them. Heads turned. Conversations paused. Suspicion hung there.

Simon met their stares with a single nod—nothing more. His face remained unreadable, but Rosa could tell he was pushing back against the way every officer seemed to size them up.

"We have a few questions for you, Chadford," Simon said, loud enough to cut through the murmurs.

Chadford turned, his smile tight. "Come to my office," he said, trying to keep his voice even.

"That's not the type of questioning we mean," Simon replied, tipping his head toward the interrogation room.

The station went still. Some officers stiffened. Others looked around in confusion. Rosa scanned their faces—puzzled, wary, defensive.

Chadford's face darkened. The shift in color was instant. She saw the slight twitch in his jaw, the way his fingers curled against his leg.

"Are you suggesting—" he began, voice rising.

"I'm not suggesting," Simon cut in, voice flat. "I'm telling. Before I call in reinforcements, you might want to do as I say, sir."

The word "sir" was a challenge. Rosa tensed, watching the ripple effect spread through the station. Shoulders squared. Eyes narrowed. Tension coiled around the room like barbed wire.

Simon glanced at her briefly. It wasn't a question—it was a direction.

Stay out of it.

Rosa didn't argue. She walked to her desk, each step slow and deliberate, under the pressure of every eye following her. She sat down, pretending to check her inbox, but her focus remained on the room. She wasn't inside that interrogation room—but maybe that was the point.

From the corner of her eye, she noticed two officers sitting near the far wall. Unlike the others, they didn't react with anger or confusion. There was no outrage in their expressions. Just something… off.

They weren't speaking, not openly—but their movements were telling.

The one closest to her tapped a pen against his notepad. Slowly. But his knee bounced with anxious energy, like he was trying to burn it off without drawing attention.

The other sat eerily still, arms crossed, but Rosa caught the exhale from his nose. Controlled. Braced.

Their eyes flicked to each other, briefly. Not long. Just enough to acknowledge something unspoken.

They weren't shocked.

She kept her expression neutral, but her focus remained sharp.

This wasn't surprise—

It was expectation.

Something inside her clicked. Her gut tightened, and she committed their faces to memory—their posture, the subtle way their body language broke from the rest of the officers there.

Whatever Simon's plan had been, it worked.

Because Rosa saw what she needed.

And now, she had faces to match the feeling that had been gnawing at her from the start.

THE GAME UNFOLDS

"YOU WANTED TO humiliate me, didn't you?" Chadford stood just inside the door, refusing to sit at the very table where he'd once interrogated countless criminals. The insult of it ran deep—that much Simon could see in his posture. But all Simon saw now was an old man desperately gripping the last shred of power. A man terrified of losing control.

Losing what, exactly? That was Simon's job to find out.

"We need answers. We need people to start talking." Simon leaned back in his chair, legs crossed at the ankle. His voice was steady, cool. The delivery didn't matter. The words did. "And Chief, we know you're somehow connected."

"And where is your evidence to prove that?" Chadford snapped, a flash of anger betraying how defensive he already was.

Simon didn't hesitate. He brought his palm down hard on the metal table. The sound cracked through the room like a whip. Chadford flinched—barely—but it was enough. Simon clocked it immediately.

"The evidence is right here." Simon slid his laptop across the table, opened it, and pressed play.

The grainy black-and-white security footage flickered onto the screen. A cloaked figure emerged from the shadows behind the community center. Then another—stumbling, dazed—Mr. Adams. The former principal of Owl Creek weaved like a marionette on tangled strings.

Simon had watched this clip too many times to count, dissected every movement with slow caution. There was something here. Something Chadford would recognize. He watched the Chief's face, looking for even the faintest shift.

"You can't possibly identify me from that video," Chadford scoffed, masking his discomfort with sarcasm.

Simon said nothing. He just stared.

And there it was.

A flicker—subtle but telling. Chadford's shoulders tightened. His eyes squinted slightly as though he'd noticed something the others wouldn't. A private recognition. Simon leaned forward, voice low.

"You saw it, didn't you?" His chin rested on his clasped hands, his expression unmoved but intense. Predatory. Calm, but not kind.

Chadford's hand tugged slightly at his collar. Sweat had started to pool along his hairline. Simon didn't blink.

"Let me replay it," he said, reaching again for the laptop.

Before he could touch it, Chadford lashed out and smacked it off the table. The laptop crashed to the floor with a loud thud, the noise loud enough that Simon heard voices stir outside the door.

He didn't react. Didn't move.

"You didn't even check if your own car was in frame?" Simon asked, his voice sharpened to a razor edge. "What kind of detective are you? Better yet, what kind of Chief are you?"

That landed. Chadford's spine slumped. His bravado cracked, then crumbled.

Simon narrowed his eyes. The man wasn't just furious—he was spiraling. Clinging to something. Thinking. That delay, that second of hesitation—it told Simon more than words ever could. Chadford was debating something. His jaw twitched, and his fingers drummed once, then curled into fists.

He was wrestling with whether it was worth pulling out his last resort.

Simon sat forward slightly, catching every subtle cue.

Chadford reached into his coat pocket with a twitch of reluctance, like he still wasn't sure if it was worth it. His fingers wrapped around something—rough. Wooden. When it hit the table, Simon immediately knew.

A jagged piece of bark, the kind that had shown up at multiple scenes before. This one was also smeared in dried, blood-red lettering.

Simon's jaw clenched. The bastard had been holding onto it.

He said nothing.

"If the police haven't caught him in over thirty years, you never will," Chadford muttered. His voice dropped low, a bitter undercurrent running through it. "You've only been chasing him for a little over ten, and even that might be too late. You might just end up like him."

The words weren't just venom—they were prophecy. A threat meant to shake him.

Simon didn't blink.

He absorbed it like stone takes in heat—quietly, without breaking.

Chadford pushed back his chair and stood. He turned, walked toward the door, then slammed it open with enough force that it rebounded and crashed against the wall. The clang rippled through the station.

Simon stayed where he was.

He didn't follow.

He didn't have to.

Because Chadford had already told him everything he needed to know.

And the evidence was already in motion.

***

Rosa walked in and softly shut the door behind her after Chadford stormed out. Simon turned the piece of bark over in his hands, his thumb grazing the jagged surface. His voice was soft as he read aloud.

She caught the unspoken question in his tone and dared to ask, "You think this bark was the one originally left with the projector?"

Both of them eyed the piece of bark.

"Who watches the night with eyes open wide?
A fool saw the truth that was meant to hide.
A cunning rose now tangled within,
As the hunt goes on and the lost fade to dim.
A secret whispered, a fate now sealed,
Buried deep where truth's revealed."

Rosa stared at the words, letting their meaning sink in slowly. The room seemed to hold its breath between them.

He's watching, she thought, the words barely more than a whisper in her mind.

Simon's jaw tightened as he glanced at her. "Yeah. And we already know by now he enjoys the game."

She bit the inside of her cheek, turning the lines over in her mind. "He added more this time—six lines instead of four. The woman that was killed… she saw something, didn't she? Something she wasn't supposed to. That's why she ended up next to that dumpster."

"She wasn't a target at first," Simon agreed.

"She just got caught in the crossfire."

Rosa exhaled slowly, feeling the implications. Her eyes settled on the line that stood out most: *"A cunning rose now tangled within."* It didn't quite fit. Maybe Louisa Franklin was the rose tangled because she was innocent? And now he's breaking his own rule—the one where he only reveals his kills every two years.

Simon's expression darkened. "You think this changed something for him?"

Rosa nodded in her mind. *Maybe. Maybe it stopped being about the kills themselves and more about the reveal. Maybe he wants to be seen for who he really is—tired of hiding behind the mask.*

But it still didn't sit right. Something had shifted. Something pushed him to act differently. The "time" reference in the other riddle—that's important.

Simon drummed his fingers on the table, his eyes narrowing in thought. "That could explain the change in frequency. He's killing faster, trying to make a statement."

Rosa hesitated, then pointed quietly to the last line. 'Buried deep where truth's revealed." *That could mean…*

Simon's jaw tightened again, already ahead of her. "Hepple's grave."

Their eyes locked.

GRAVE CONSEQUENCES

"AS MUCH AS I hate to say this, traveling to a grave doesn't sit right with me. And the thought that we might have to dig it up? Even worse." Raya grimaced at the idea. "We were taught not to defile graves back in Sunday service as kids. I remember the preacher man lost his mind when some high school boys pulled a prank in the cemetery. He went on a full-blown rampage for two weeks."

Kershaw sighed, gripping a shovel with one hand. "I'm wiped from the flight to D.C. The grave's here—remember, the clue pointed us that way. But at least we have legal permission. That should count for something."

"Yeah, yeah, you can do the grunt work." Raya exhaled, scanning the sea of tombstones stretching before them. She sometimes wondered how long it took for a grave to become just another forgotten stone—no more flowers, no more visitors, just weathered names crumbling into nothing. A depressing thought.

"He was buried over here, if I remember right," Kershaw said, scratching his head. He glanced around uneasily. "It's been a long time... Hepple died a year before Marybeth was killed. Hard to believe it's been that long since anyone visited."

As they approached the grave, something was off. The headstone gleamed, free of dust or moss, as if someone had recently scrubbed it clean. At first, they brushed it off—Hepple's family was still around, after all. But then they saw the rose petals, scattered like remnants of a ritual. A bouquet, once whole, lay ruined—stems snapped, flowers crushed, as if someone had destroyed it in a fit of rage.

Then, just beneath the disturbed soil, they spotted it—a small, ornate black box, partially buried.

Kershaw pulled on a pair of crime scene gloves and crouched down. He reached for the box, maneuvering it out around the thorns jutting from the broken roses. "I've got to say, this is some twisted shit. After we catch this son of a bitch, I'm taking a long vacation."

Raya stepped back, eyeing the box with suspicion. It was about the size of a jewelry case, delicate, yet ominous in the afternoon light. Given everything they'd been through, they braced for the worst.

"I'm gonna let you do the honors," Raya joked, backing up another step.

"Oh, gee, thanks," Kershaw muttered. He gave a small nod and hesitated, holding the lid carefully as if preparing to bag it and take it with them.

Then—the world shattered.

A thunderous blast tore through the graveyard.

A shockwave of fire and debris swallowed them whole and sent them flying. Raya's body twisted in mid-air, slammed into a headstone, then fell to the ground, sliding hard enough and far enough to tear her clothing and embed dirt in her flesh. Dirt rained down in clumps. The scent of smoke and gunpowder mingled with the sickly sweetness of crushed roses.

Everything blurred as her ears rang from the deafening explosion and her mind tried to process what happened. For a few seconds, the world was just a whirlwind of dust and fragments.

She struggled to move, every part of her body yelling in protest. The ringing in her ears slowly began to fade, and her limbs settled back into place. Her chest rose and fell in shallow gasps as she forced herself to focus, fighting through the haze. Her vision was blurry, but she pushed herself onto her elbows and peered through the fog.

Kershaw wasn't moving.

A sudden catch in her chest tightened as she tried to push herself up further, but her body refused to cooperate. Her hands scraped against the ground, searching for leverage, but the world kept spinning.

And then—it was too quiet.

She forced herself to sit up, blinking through the fog. The ground was shaking, but it was only the residual impact from the explosion. Kershaw's body lay in a distorted position, and his eyes were shut tight. His chest wasn't moving.

Panic surged through her, but she swallowed it down. She couldn't afford to fall apart now. Slowly, carefully, she dragged herself over to him, each movement slow and agonizing. She reached out, fingers brushing his shoulder, trying to steady herself against the dizziness.

Something felt wrong.

His body was limp, his body heavy and unnaturally still. A bitter knot twisted in her stomach, but she couldn't afford to waste time thinking about it now. She reached for her radio, her hand shaking as she fumbled for the device.

Raya's breath caught as she noticed movement out of the corner of her eye. A woman — tense, restless — was slipping away from the scene, her fingers twitching nervously.

Raya tried to call out, but the words caught in her throat. The black smoke devoured the figure before she could get closer.

Her vision blurred. Darkness crept in from the edges, and then everything went black.

VILE THOUGHTS

SHUFFLING THROUGH A duffle bag, he hummed a cheerful tune, his fingers grazing over cold steel and coarse rope. The scent of roses—once fresh, now sickly sweet in their state of decay—filled his nostrils, intoxicating in its own way. He relished the moment they withered, their petals curling inward, browning at the edges, before he crushed them between his fingers, turning beauty into dust. Just like his victims. The fear in their eyes—that was his favorite part.

The man in front of him couldn't see him, but he could feel him. He knew that much from the frantic way the man twisted, writhing like a hooked fish, his body jerking in wild, useless motions. It was getting annoying. Keeping control used to be effortless, a skill as natural as breathing. But now? Now, he found himself losing his grip—both literally and figuratively. Was it age? No, he refused to believe that. His precision remained sharp. It was patience that had started slipping through his fingers like fine grains of sand. He couldn't hide his face anymore.

He wanted to reveal his face to the public, to the world. No more shadows. No more masks. The game had changed, and he was done hiding. This wasn't about losing control—it was about gaining something more. The thrill had always come from the hunt, but now? He craved the spotlight. He wanted them to know who he was, to understand the genius behind it all. Let them see. Let them try to catch him.

And that Special Agent Pikes? When Agent Hepple first started leading the investigation—about twenty-five years ago—no detectives were yet assigned to the case. Hepple worked quietly, connecting clues no one else noticed. Simon wasn't even in the bureau then.

Twelve years ago, Hepple got too close to the truth and was killed. Simon was just starting his career around that time, a rookie stepping into a case that had already claimed its first lead.

Now, ten years after Hepple's death, Simon knows the old methods aren't enough anymore. The killer must be exposed—not just feared—and the plan to catch him needs to change.

But, it really wasn't supposed to happen this way. If that nosy neighbor hadn't been peering through the window at just the wrong moment, he wouldn't have had to adjust his plans. But adaptability was part of the game. And, if he was being honest, toying with those young detectives had become an unexpected source of amusement. He had been forced to stay hidden for so long, letting Simon and that other lanky boy trail behind him, letting them take the lead. It was always the same—pain, chaos—but now? He was tired of pretending. Hiding for the sake of what? Not much anymore. He couldn't feign that he cared any longer.

Especially the new girl. It was her time to make an appearance. Time to see if she could unravel what the others couldn't.

She was clever, unnervingly so. There was an acuity to her mind, a way she unraveled riddles that almost made him proud—almost. It had to be something that was nurtured since childhood, a knack for patterns and hidden meanings. A shame, really. Intelligence was such a beautiful thing.

And he couldn't wait to watch hers unravel.

The phone rang, delivering the news—two down. A sinister grin curled his lips.

THREADS OF FATE

HER MOTHER'S ARM *lay by her foot. She knew it was hers by the ring and the matching owl tattoo—the one her parents had gotten to commemorate her going to high school, just before everything changed. Why they were so obsessed with owls, she'd never quite understood. But the scene before her made bile rise in her throat.*

Then, she heard her father's screams in the distance. It was too much. The nausea surged, and before she could stop it, she threw up. Her body trembled with the aftershock, and then—she screamed too.

Rosa woke with a start, the sharp command beating in her ears. Her heart thundered in her chest as she jolted upright.

"Something happened to Kershaw and Raya," a voice said from the door. Simon's shoulders sagged with sadness she hadn't seen before.

"What do you mean?" She threw off the covers and moved quickly toward him.

"Listen." His whisper was low, but urgent.

"Just spit it out."

"There was an explosion. They were caught in it. The grave was a trap."

Her eyes widened in disbelief. *We sent them into a trap?* Panic stabbed at her mind. "Are they okay? This doesn't match the killer's usual style. What changed? Are they even alive?"

"I don't know, damn it," Simon muttered through clenched teeth. "I'm waiting for the undercover detectives heading to the hospital to keep me informed. Until then, we need to accept how serious this is and start planning our next moves."

"What does that even mean?" Exhaustion weighed on her body, but her thoughts raced. *What if they're hurt? Why would the killer do this? Maybe he wants fewer people hunting him, or he's trying to scare us off. Or maybe... he's ending the game, once and for all.*

Simon shifted uncomfortably, his eyes dark and impassive. *Things will keep getting worse,* the look in his eyes warned.

She couldn't shake the feeling something else lurked beneath his words.

"I need to know I can trust you," he said quietly, serious and low.

"You're not making any sense, Simon," she replied, pulling on a quarter-zip hoodie and wrapping her arms around herself. She struggled to steady her swirling thoughts. *Nothing's certain anymore. Raya and Kershaw—they're okay... until they're not?* No, she had to hold onto her sanity. But Simon's strange behavior only unsettled her more. *What the hell is wrong with him?*

"All this started when we came to town," he said, his voice distant as he leaned his head against the door frame.

"Yes, I'm aware," Rosa said cautiously, still baffled by his sudden secrecy.

"I was testing him. I've been withholding evidence."

Her posture stiffened. Was he sabotaging the investigation?

"You're still not making sense. Why would you—of all people—do that?" Her eyes locked on his, demanding answers.

He hesitated, the secret clear in his expression. The guilt he carried was raw and unfamiliar to her.

He looked away. "I couldn't let anyone else find the truth. Not yet. Not until I understood it myself."

Her heart hammered. Simon was wrestling with something deeper than the case—something she hadn't known about. His secret meetings with Kershaw, the pieces of the puzzle he'd kept hidden.

Trust had never been a question before. She'd always seen Simon as the steady one, the man with the answers. But now? This version of him seemed broken, fractured by hidden truths. He'd held back crucial information. How could she trust him now? What else was he hiding? The uncertainty gnawed at her, but she pushed it aside. The bigger picture still needed her focus, no matter how hard it was.

"Just shut up and listen," he said softly, voice thick with restraint. "When I found my sister… in that state, I went on a rampage. Anger swallowed me whole. It still does. But there was a riddle—different from the one Chadford gave me—that I found and hid away. Something personal I had to keep. I had to be the one to find him. But there's a line, a connection I can't crack. It kills me. Ten years later, and I still can't solve it. Maybe that's part of why William shifted… became depressed."

Simon slammed his hand against the wall. The sound shattered around them. She saw the burden of failure crush him—the loss of his sister, the fear of losing William to depression. Simon was unraveling.

"And now you think you can't hide it?" Rosa's voice was firm as she walked past him, frustration rising. She didn't understand why he was suddenly so vulnerable. Simon had always been in control, always the one with the answers. Now he was exposed—something she wasn't prepared for.

He slowly grabbed her arm, stopping her, and pulled something from his pocket.

"I need help." The words came out as though they hurt to say.

She turned to face him and caught a look she'd never seen before—a defeated man, lost for the first time. Not the Simon who tried to fix everything, but a broken one. It scared her. Made her more nervous than she already was.

"Well, I didn't have that on my bingo card this morning—Simon Pikes, asking for help?" Her voice softened, trying to ease the situation. She reached for the riddle, a half-smile tugging at her lips. "It's about time. Honestly, you all suck at riddles."

"But before I give it to you, you need to know—there was no way we could've known the location." Confusion flickered in her eyes as she tried to process his words.

She took the riddle carefully from him, feeling more than just bark in her hands. It was a piece of Simon himself.

"When flight has ended and silence takes hold,
The search must cease, for time's grasp grows bold.
A mind yet to bloom, sharp as the night,
Will rise from the shadows and set things right.
In a quiet town where secrets crawl,
The past will catch you—if you heed the call."

They had always suspected the riddle would lead them to a small town—but when, and how, remained a mystery. Every clue, every cryptic line from the killer, seemed to point toward something buried deep in the town's past—something no one wanted uncovered.

Kershaw and Simon had kept their knowledge close, pretending ignorance to throw Wood Riddle off the scent. The riddle was a game of patience, and they knew the killer's moves were calculated to the last detail. But no matter how carefully they followed, the pieces never fully aligned. The deeper they dug, the more the town's secrets unraveled—and with them, the unsettling realization that they might be chasing a new ghost.

Rosa sat at the top of the stairs, her mind spinning. The killer's plan was bigger than any of them had imagined, and this riddle was only the beginning of the mess brought to her town.

How far did the darkness stretch? How many lives had been tangled in its web?

Simon broke the silence. "Your hometown is more than just a quiet place. It's become a hub—part of something bigger, something darker. The riddle isn't just a puzzle; it's a key to a hidden world of corruption and power. Wood Riddle uses it all to fund his twisted game... and we believe he has a protégé to carry on his legacy."

Rosa spat out her disbelief. "So not only is Wood Riddle still out there, but his reach goes deeper than we thought. The riddle was never just about the killings—it was about control. We're running out of time, and the answers keep slipping further away. And now there might be two of them?!"

She clenched her fists, frustration and fear tangled tight inside her. "If the past is catching up, revealing its secrets somehow, what comes next? How do we stop a game we barely understand?"

Anger flared in her chest. She stood and paced quickly down the stairs, desperate to dull the storm in her mind. She grabbed the first bottle she saw from the cabinet and poured a shot, swallowing it in one go. The burn spread through her chest.

Before she could pour another, Sir Louie jumped on the counter, sensing her pain. She paused, setting the bottle aside, unopened.

Simon leaned against the kitchen counter, his posture soft but laden with shame.

"We didn't know how to stop him grooming another," Simon said quietly. "We just didn't have enough to go on. We had to wait two years for this riddle, then another two. A never-ending web. When the drug connections surfaced, we had to act. As soon as we could."

"William's not smart enough," Rosa muttered, confused, ignoring the regret on Simon's face. If the public or the FBI found out about the protégé, it would ruin them—and their careers. And they'd still be no closer to catching Wood Riddle.

"You seriously pulled us into some crazy shit," Rosa snapped, but deep down, she was grateful for his honesty—especially now. "I just wanted to be a detective. Maybe catch the bastard who killed my mother. And now this? My head's spinning. I need some air."

She grabbed the keys off the counter—the ones her father had lent her after her car was totaled—the keys to one of his older cars. Her movements were swift as she made her way toward the door.

As she began to open it, she heard Simon shift behind her, probably to stop her.

Before she could step outside, her breath caught in her throat at the sight of the steely, gleaming end of a gun barrel pointed right at her chest.

TRIGGERING TENSION

FROM BEHIND THE gun, Chadford's eyes burned with pure hatred. Revenge radiated from him, focused solely on the two standing before him. He forced them to step backward, his movements rough as he slammed the door shut behind them. Rosa felt a hand rest lightly on her lower back—a small, comforting touch—but it did nothing to ease the terror now inside her. Every breath was a struggle.

The irony hit her all at once: here was this older man, desperate and reckless, demanding they sit on the couch—as if the casual normalcy of a living room could contain the danger in the room.

As she studied him more closely, something struck her. His wrinkled shirt was out of place—he'd never looked so disheveled before. The deepening creases on his forehead marked the toll these last few months had taken. He had aged before her eyes, the inevitable capture pressing down on him. It was almost sad. Almost. But Rosa couldn't afford to focus on that. Not now.

"If I get rid of both of you now, my job will be safe." His voice trembled, and the gun in his hand wavered slightly. For someone as strict and strong as Chadford, it was awkward to see him so off-balance. His usual confident, imposing presence was slipping away, replaced by a man desperate to hold onto the one thing he'd built his life around.

She could hear his shallow heartbeat, see his chest rise and fall unevenly. His knuckles whitened around the gun, fingers stiff and tense.

"And what benefit would that give you?" Simon's voice was calm and unwavering. "You want the bastard caught just as much as we do. You just tried to benefit from it in a dishonorable way."

He wasn't wrong, but Rosa wished Simon wouldn't provoke the man, especially with a gun pointed at them. Chadford's desperation made him vulnerable—and that was when someone was most dangerous.

Chadford's breathing grew louder, frantic. He no longer seemed to hear Simon—or if he did, it only fed his rage. His eyes flicked between Simon and Rosa, searching for something, anything to ease the crushing moment. Then he spoke again, bitter mockery dripping from him as he sank onto the couch beside them.

"For now, the evidence is still circumstantial," Chadford spat, narrowing his eyes at Simon.

"She didn't miss it—the evidence that's not circumstantial," Simon shot back, nodding toward Rosa. "She caught your watch—the same one you're wearing now. Zoom in closer, and you'll see the initials of the wife who left you."

Rosa's chest tightened, pulse quickening. The hairs on the back of her neck rose, discomfort creeping deeper. This wasn't helping. The more Simon poked, the closer he was about to cross a line that couldn't be uncrossed.

"Shut up," she whispered, tapping Simon's leg beside her—a plea to stop before they pushed Chadford too far. But Simon either didn't hear or didn't care. Chadford sprang to his feet in outrage, chair scraping violently against the floor.

"You were always too damn observant for your own good," Chadford sneered, voice cracking with fury—and something else. Fear, maybe. His bloodshot eyes locked on Rosa, and she saw it— the glint of madness, the spiral he couldn't stop.

He started rambling, frantic now.

"I only did it because he—your serial killer—sent me a message. Said they'd pin the whole thing on me. The operation outside Atlanta, everything. I've never seen his face! So why the hell am I the one taking the fall?" He paced, agitated. "I didn't want to lose my position. I love the badge more than anything."

His grip on the gun tightened.

"And William, your friend? He was gullible. Unreliable. Obsessed with the past—still chasing revenge for that lover of his. He came here alone, stormed into my house, started throwing accusations. Said we should team up... or he'd turn me in himself." Chadford scoffed, then faltered. "He was weak—but smart. Too smart."

He was unraveling, his words falling apart faster than his thoughts.

"I don't know about the murders. Those victims didn't have to die. Ropa was just... collateral. A casualty to keep things quiet in Chattingsburg. And that was all Adams. And I don't even know who your killer is. But he knows these lands—these woods—better than anyone."

Then, as if something inside him finally snapped, he raised the gun—steady, unshaking, aimed straight between her eyes.

Rosa knew she would die. Right here, right now. It wasn't unexpected—not with the deadly game they'd been playing. Nightmares like this had haunted her for weeks, creeping in when she least expected it. Would she feel the cold barrel first? Hear the shot? Or would it all be over before she blinked?

But it wasn't just the threat of death swarming her thoughts. Chadford's face twisted with pain and regret. He hadn't wanted this—not really. Somewhere deep down, his fear of losing everything pushed him past the point of no return. He'd worked his whole life for this position, for the control, for respect. And now everything was slipping away. Clinging to the only thing left—his job, his identity—he refused to let go. But how could the old man hold on when it was all built on lies and blood?

For the first time, Chadford looked lost, struggling to face the monster he'd become chasing power. He didn't want to kill her. Not really. He just... couldn't stop himself. The game he started had turned on him.

His breath hitched as he took a step closer, fingers trembling on the trigger. "This is how it ends," he muttered, almost to himself. "I didn't want it like this. Not this way... But I can't lose everything."

Rosa's vision blurred; the world closed in.

Was this the end? Her last moment?

The shot rang out—crisp and clear—a brutal slap to her senses.

At first, she didn't hear it over the ringing in her ears and the thunder of her heart.

Everything went quiet except the ringing.

Then, time seemed to freeze for a heartbeat, nothing mattered but that sound. The sound of a gunshot.

Then—mayhem. Shouts. Scrambling feet.

The acrid stench of gunpowder filled the air, stinging her nose but failing to mask the coppery tang of fear in her mouth.

Her body stiffened, mind struggling to catch up to the shock.

A LIFE IN HIS GRIP

BLOOD. A POOL of it by her feet, dark and thick, spreading slowly across the floor. Simon's hand, slick and crimson, pressed over someone's chest—blood staining his palm, dripping down his fingers. It took a moment for him to register the figure in front of Rosa. Her father. Lying there, lifeless, in his own blood.

Rosa couldn't react. Simon saw the paralysis gripping her mind, the world spinning in her eyes, every detail blurring as shock tightened its hold on her chest.

The scene played out again in his mind: the figure lunging for the gun, his own instinctive leap into action, the violent struggle. They'd tumbled to the ground, fighting desperately, while Rosa sat frozen, unable to move. It was her father—her own flesh and blood—who had reached for the barrel, escalating everything to this terrifying point.

Simon glanced at Rosa, noticing her breathing quicken, uneven, as unease settled between them. The faint smell of worn wood and old fabric filled the space, mingling with the sour tang of panic that pressed like a vise around them both. She couldn't tear her eyes away from the sight—her father's life draining away, chest rising and falling in shallow, labored breaths.

Then Simon's bloodied hand moved slowly, gently cupping Rosa's cheek. Amid the commotion, the contact was unexpectedly tender. His eyes locked on hers—brown, darkened with urgency, but carrying an unspoken promise. He held her gaze, grounding her, offering reassurance against the storm raging inside.

"Get it together," Simon's voice cut through the haze of her panic—steady, commanding. "Call 911. Now!"

Her hands shook as she fumbled with her phone, struggling through the fog of terror clouding her mind. Her voice came out broken, barely audible. "They won't get here in time."

That crack in her voice struck Simon like a knife to his heart. She sounded vulnerable—more than he'd ever heard. She wasn't ready for this. Not this moment. Her father—the one person Rosa trusted most—dying on the floor in front of her. He had always been her rock, her anchor, the one constant in her life. And now, with every second slipping away, Simon felt her slipping with him.

He didn't hesitate. He didn't think about chasing after Chadford, who was still somewhere else in the house. His entire focus was on Rosa—and her father. He knew Rosa could handle anything else—she was capable and strong—but not this. Not her father.

Simon's gaze never wavered, locking with hers as if willing her into action. This wasn't about the job anymore, or the case. It was about saving her. Saving the woman who'd been holding everything together. The one person who mattered more than any criminal or duty.

He placed both hands firmly but gently on her shoulders. "We'll get through this. But you have to focus. Now."

Rosa nodded numbly, her breath ragged and coming in gasps. There was no time to waste. The world narrowed, leaving only the pounding in their ears and the frantic beating of their hearts.

Everything hinged on the man lying in a pool of blood beneath them.

QUIET AFTER THE STORM

A MASSIVE SEARCH ensued, stretching across the city and into the surrounding areas, eventually leading to the capture and arrest of Reese Chadford, Chief of Police in Chattingsburg. But even as they dragged him away, doubt clawed through Simon's mind. Many officers—those who hadn't witnessed the raw emotion during Simon's interrogation—remained reluctant, clinging to their trust in Chadford.

Only two officers—the ones who had sensed something was off when Simon first pressed Chadford—decided to follow up. They went back to review the footage and revisit the scene, needing to see it for themselves. What they found was exactly what they expected. Chadford had been acting strangely for a while—coming in late to work, and even before that, he'd often slipped away on his own without explanation.

After speaking to them, Simon watched from a distance as Rosa stood at the foot of her father's hospital bed. Her face was blank, her eyes glassy and unfocused, as if she were retreating from the world. The news about Raya being alive, and Kershaw still clinging to life despite his coma, should have brought relief. But Simon saw no thawing in her demeanor. Her shoulders remained hunched, her breathing shallow, like she was trying to shrink away from something too overwhelming to fight.

He reached out to her once, but she pulled back, retreating further into herself. He saw the unspoken questions flicker across her features—the what-ifs: What if they hadn't been too late? What if

Chadford had been stopped sooner? What if she hadn't missed the signs? Simon could only imagine the turmoil behind her gaze.

Her voice was gone. The woman who seemed to always carry determination now seemed drowned by defeat. Simon felt helpless. He couldn't fix this. He couldn't pull her from whatever was breaking her down. This was no longer about the case; it was about watching pieces of Rosa unravel, and feeling utterly powerless.

Then, from the bed, her father's voice cut through the quiet.

"Rosa, you look like you're the one who was shot," he joked, his tone hoarse but with a trace of humor.

The simplicity of the words seemed to slice through the fog surrounding Rosa. Simon saw a small change—a blink, a subtle shift in her posture. For a moment, she was grounded by the familiar sound of her father's voice—the warmth she had been missing.

With trembling hands, she grasped his. Simon noticed the delicate curling of her fingers around his cold ones—a plea, a fragile connection filled with desperation and love. She couldn't speak, but that contact was enough. She wasn't alone, not yet.

Time seemed to hold its breath as her father's grip tightened in response, wrapping her in a fragile comfort, a quiet reassurance that, for now, everything might be okay.

But Simon could feel the inevitable return of reality pressing in, threatening to crush that fragile moment.

Stepping back, Simon gave them space, sensing they needed time alone. His attention shifted back to the two officers who had been quietly observing the scene. Their presence felt distant, like a faint murmur beneath Rosa's grief. Simon knew they had to speak, to continue the case, but for now, something in the room kept him from moving forward.

Approaching them agian, he offered a quick, knowing glance. Their eyes met, exchanging a wordless understanding of the tense atmosphere before one finally spoke, voice low but intent.

"We didn't know about the drug trafficking ring," the first officer admitted, leaning closer to Simon. "But there were other things we noticed before he was captured—things we didn't know who to tell." He shifted nervously.

The second, arms crossed, added, "The guy's been showing up in new clothes, new shoes—he even bought himself a brand-new, high-end car recently. For a small-town chief? That doesn't add up."

The first continued, "But we think some of the other officers were involved too. Maybe taking money from him, covering for him. This town's tight-knit. They wouldn't go against each other."

Simon furrowed his brow, his mind racing through the implications. They were right—he already knew about Chadford's involvement in drugs and money laundering. But the connection to Wood Riddle... that remained a loose thread, something that still didn't quite fit.

Unless it was all part of his plan. Starting with the stolen evidence ten years ago.

And now, it had escalated this far.

COMATOSE CONFESSIONS

RAYA STARED AT Kershaw's motionless body, his chest rising and falling in a rhythm too faint for comfort. The sterile scent of antiseptic was pungent, artificial, nothing like the sweat and gunpowder that had surrounded them before this. The fluorescent lights buzzed overhead, but all she could hear was the phantom echo of his laughter, the way it seemed to cut through even the darkest of moments.

She could almost picture him now, grinning through a split lip, cracking some joke about his current state. Even half-dead, he'd find a way to lighten the mood. He was the team's humor, their reckless charm—the one who always managed to laugh when no one else could. But Kershaw was more than the class clown. He had been the one to take the hit when no one else saw the danger coming. He opened that damn box. He shoved her out of the way when he realized what it was. He took the brunt of the explosion like it was nothing, like his life was worth less than hers.

Her fingers curled into her palm as she took in the gash on his forehead, the bruising along his jaw. He'd wake up and call them battle scars, boasting that now he could finally give Simon some competition. She wanted to believe that, wanted to trust that he'd wake up at all.

She exhaled, running a shaky hand through her hair. Her fingers trembled, and she clenched them into a fist. She was exhausted—bone-deep. And unraveling—but there was no time to fall apart. Rosa was dealing with her own hell, and Simon… Simon was still chasing the past. They were all trapped in this tangled web.

She barely registered the nurse standing nearby, watching, assessing. A set of sharp eyes cataloging every twitch of her hands, the way she leaned too close to the bed, the way her body tensed like she was bracing for impact. Raya had been on edge since the explosion. None of this made sense. Wood Riddle shouldn't have been taunting them. They caught Chadford. They knew William had leaked intel. So why did it feel like they were still one step behind, still playing into the hands of something much bigger?

She took a slow breath, the harsh scent of antiseptic scraping against her throat. She never meant to let herself care. Rosa was the only one she had let in, the only one she thought she could trust. But these *idiots*—this team—they had wormed their way in without permission, without her realizing it was happening. And now? Now, Kershaw was in a coma. William had betrayed them. Simon was obsessed. Rosa was unraveling. And where did that leave her? The glue that was supposed to hold it all together? The one who picked up the pieces, stitched up the wounds, kept them moving forward?

Her fingers gripped the bed railing, her knuckles aching from the pressure. No one was coming to help her. Not her family, not anyone. She was on her own, just like she had always been. But damn it, she was tired of pretending she was fine. She bit her lip, hard enough to sting, drowning the lump rising in her throat.

She couldn't afford to break.

A FATHER'S MEASURE

ROSA HADN'T LEFT her father's side since the accident. She sat there, frozen in a trance, the kind of stillness that might have fooled anyone into thinking time had stopped. Her father's breath was slow, steady, and steadying, but not enough to pull her out of whatever place she'd retreated to. At least he was alive. That was something. Simon didn't share that luxury; he needed answers, a team, but even the thought of asking for help felt like a betrayal. He could never afford that kind of vulnerability. But there was no other choice now.

When Rosa slipped away to the bathroom, Simon couldn't help himself. He seized the opportunity to interrupt her father's dinner, his voice urgent, a voice that had learned to carry responsibility like a curse. His fingers twitched at his side, an almost involuntary response to the heaviness of the conversation he was about to start.

"Sir, you need to tell her you're okay." His words broke the calm, uneven in the still air. "She's letting this affect her work too much. With two people down, we can't afford to lose sight."

Her father didn't flinch, didn't rise to the bait. His look was intense, like he'd already seen this play out a hundred times before. His hand rested on the table, steady, unmoving. "Your obsession is one of the reasons this may have happened," he said, his voice cool but not cruel. Simon couldn't argue; he wouldn't. The truth stung too much.

The older man shifted in his bed, a low creak coming from the old mattress, his bones protesting the motion. He didn't seem to notice. Raising his hand to stop Simon from speaking, he continued, his words unfiltered, with years of knowing. "We all have our reasons. I know that all too well. She'll be fine. The trauma she's been through—losing her mother when she was fifteen… And all of a sudden, a couple of years ago, this talk of joining the force."

Simon felt the mention of Rosa's mother was a punch to the wound he already felt. His hands clenched at his sides, his nails digging into his palms. He could imagine that loss, what it had cost Rosa to keep going, to still fight for what she wanted. The burn in his chest was unbearable. It all bled into the present, into this moment where he was trying to fix things that were already beyond his grasp.

The older man took a long sip of water, his stare fixed on Simon's face. He set the glass down slowly, as if to mark the moment. He gestured for Simon to sit. Reluctantly, Simon complied, his body stiff as he lowered himself into the chair, the movement slow, as though each inch downward was a struggle.

"I didn't want her to join the police force because I didn't think she was tough enough," Rosa's father admitted, the words slow, as if each one carried a burden of its own. A shimmer of something—pride, perhaps, or fear—flashed in his eyes. It was gone as quickly as it came, replaced by the man's wince as he moved his arm. "But I see her now. She's tougher than I thought. And I don't know what you all got yourselves into, but…" He paused, the words hanging in the air. "Will you protect her? If you needed to? Can I trust you to do that?"

Simon felt the full brunt of his attention, an unspoken challenge pressing against his ribs. Mr. Ryker's eyes cut through him, searching for something Simon wasn't sure he could give. He shifted in his seat, his fingers curling against his thigh before he forced himself still, the muscles in his jaw tight with the effort. He didn't speak right away; the question stayed between them like a stone, heavy, sinking.

Simon glanced at the ink on the older man's forearm—the owl tattoo dark and worn, its lines jagged from years of life lived. He noticed the way Mr. Ryker's fingers brushed over the design, as though tracing the memory it carried.

"My wife and I had matching ones," Mr. Ryker murmured as if the memory had softened it. He stared at the tattoo for a moment, lost in something distant, something unreachable. Simon caught the brief vulnerability in the older man's eyes, and for the first time, he felt like he was seeing the man not as Rosa's father, but as a person—someone with a history, with his own grief.

Simon hesitated, unsure whether he should speak or let the silence settle between them. The air in the room felt graver—not with tension, but with something more delicate, something neither of them knew how to navigate. He ran a hand through his hair, the motion almost mechanical, as if he was trying to ground himself. He could feel his heart racing under his chest at what Mr. Ryker had requested of him.

"You're rough around the edges, but you're a good man," the older man said with a slight smile. The words were simple, but they hit deeper than Simon expected, stirring something he didn't know how to process. He exhaled sharply, his breath a little shaky. He swallowed hard as Rosa walked back in.

The shift in the room was immediate. Simon stood quickly, his movements swift and purposeful, his chair scraping back against the floor with a loud screech. He gestured for Rosa to take her seat, and without a word, she did, her eyes flicking between them both with a mix of curiosity and wariness. She seemed to sense the charged air.

"Don't even sit. You're going home to rest and figure this case out," her father said, his voice firm, the kind of command that left no room for argument. Rosa hesitated for a moment, her shoulders tense, but didn't challenge him. She gathered her things, her movements quick and purposeful, before heading for the door.

As she left, Mr. Ryker gave a small, gesture to Simon, signaling him to stay for a moment. Once the door clicked shut behind her, he spoke again. "I'm glad to hear Kershaw and Raya are okay, for now."

The sincerity in his voice caught Simon off guard. It was enough to bring a small, almost faint smile to Simon's lips—grateful for the brief moment of shared humanity.

CAUGHT IN THE CROSSFIRE

THE NURSE CHECKED her phone again, her thumb brushing across the cracked screen, each swipe quick and anxious. The long-awaited message hadn't arrived yet, but she knew it would. It had to. The seconds dragged on, stretching into minutes, as her eyes drifted to the woman with light purple braids. She was still, her gaze fixed on the coma patient, her presence impossible to ignore. The only sound was the soft beep of the machines, rhythmic and distant, mirroring the frantic thud of her heart.

She'd been given a task, and she failed the first time. How could she mess up an explosion? That failure was at the back of her mind, insistent, and a pain. She couldn't afford to mess up again. Her lover—her unworthy, broken lover—was counting on her. Each shallow inhale the coma patient took felt like a cruel reminder that time was slipping away. There was no going back now.

The instructions had come to her a week ago, slipped under the door with the precision of someone who knew exactly how to stay hidden in the shadows. A date. A time. A set of materials. She had gathered everything in secret, her every move intentional, her every breath held tight within the walls of her quiet, dark apartment. No one could know. Not a single soul. She had no one else. She thought that was why she was chosen. But now, standing in this sterile room, she wasn't sure anymore.

Her task was clear: to take the male detective's life. To end it.

And all of this was because she had wanted the wife gone. At first, that had been the only goal—eliminate the obstacle, the woman who stood between her and the man she thought loved her. She'd convinced herself it was for them—for their future. But the wife hadn't died for that reason. She'd seen something she wasn't supposed to. Something she should've never been around to witness. And now she was dead.

That had changed everything.

The nurse hadn't expected the aftermath. The guilt. The confusion. And especially not the photos—images that now burned in her mind. Her lover, tied down, bruised, humiliated. He'd been caught. Battered. She couldn't look at them without flinching.

He hadn't always been cruel, but he hadn't been kind, either. His love had been inconsistent, gruff when it should've been soft. Yelling. Silence. Distance. Nights he looked through her like she was just a body, something temporary. She remembered the coldness in his eyes when things didn't go his way, the way he pushed her aside with words that cut.

And yet… there had been moments. Fleeting ones, but powerful enough to make her stay. When he held her. When he whispered apologies. Promises. Lies, maybe—but in those seconds, she'd believed him. She had to.

Now, standing on the precipice of something irreversible, her chest ached with everything she had convinced herself to ignore.

The photos—his bruised body, tied down, battered and broken—flooded her mind again. She couldn't push them away. The fine-edged knives glinted in the dim light beside him, cruel and cold. Her hands trembled, clenching into fists, as she fought to steady herself. This was it. There was no turning back.

What else could she do?

She couldn't ask for help. She knew that. There were eyes everywhere, always watching. One wrong move, and she'd become a target herself. The fear crept beneath her skin. She could feel it crawling up her spine, the chill of it soaking into her bones. She wasn't just being watched—she was trapped in a game she couldn't win.

Her phone vibrated in her hand. She unlocked the screen. The message had arrived.

There was no time to second-guess. Her lover's fate—and hers—hung in the balance.

ALCOHOL AND VERY BAD DECISIONS

ALCOHOL AND INNER turmoil were never a good combination. Rosa knew that. So did Simon. But what else could they do at two in the morning? They had nothing and everything to lose. In the stillness of the room, their exhaustion pressed down between them, dulling the noise of everything else—just for tonight. Drowning it out didn't seem like such a terrible thing, did it?

She poured the first drink, her hand shaking just slightly as she did, and knew immediately she should stop. But some wild, reckless part of her didn't care. That part of her wanted to lose control, to forget. She'd been so careful for so long—measured, guarded. But tonight... she wanted to be free. Even just for a little while.

The amber liquid swirled as she tilted the glass in her hand, catching the dim light. She stared at it for a long moment before finally taking a deep sip. The burn hit hard, but it was welcome—familiar and numbing in just the right way. Her pulse quickened, though she couldn't tell if it was the alcohol or the man sitting beside her.

Simon was quiet. His posture stiff, unreadable. His gaze kept drifting near her but never fully landed. Something simmered beneath the surface, something restrained and heavy. She could feel it between them, in the silence that stretched too long. When their eyes did meet, it felt like he was looking straight through her—searching, maybe. For what, she didn't know.

He looked like he wanted to speak—his lips parted, only to shut again, as if the words slipped away before he could find them. The low murmur filled her ears, louder than any answer he could give.

Rosa wanted to say something, anything, to break the moment open—but nothing came. Instead, her attention snagged on the scar running along the side of his jaw. The same scar she had asked about once before. It still drew her in. Unfinished. Untold.

"Why do you have that scar, Agent Pikes?" she asked, her voice low, edged with something softer than teasing—something she couldn't name.

The words left her mouth before she could think better of it. Too playful. Too exposed. She was drunk—she knew that. But she also knew that wasn't the reason she asked. Something deeper was stirring, something that hadn't stopped since he walked into her life and started peeling back layers she didn't realize were still there.

Simon didn't answer right away. He leaned back into the couch slowly, as though trying to put distance between himself and whatever was unfolding. Rosa noted the way his shoulders tightened, his movements deliberate—defensive, like he was bracing for impact.

"Do I really need to answer that?" he finally said, his voice rough, scraped thin by exhaustion. There was something else behind it too—a flicker of vulnerability.

Rosa's lips curled into a faint smile, but not one of amusement. There was weight behind it. She wasn't just asking about a scar. She was asking about all of it—him, her, this night, the unspoken things they'd both refused to touch.

"You're not getting away that easily," she said, quieter now, not flirtatious, but something more tender. Her body moved almost instinctively, shifting closer until her thigh brushed his. Warmth radiated between them.

The world outside faded. They were here, together. The moment felt fragile, stretched thin, but not with tension—something else entirely. Something Rosa didn't want to name.

She took another gulp from the bottle, the whiskey burning down her throat.

Simon lifted his glass slowly, taking a sip. Then, after a long pause, he spoke. "After Marybeth passed... it was rough," he said, his voice quieter now, more distant. "Kershaw... he pulled me out of a dark place."

Rosa listened closely. His words were slow, pained, dragging memories to the surface.

"I was a mess," he continued. "I drank too much. Got into fights. I was just... trying to feel something that wasn't pain."

She could feel it settle in the space between them—unspoken, heavy with meaning. Her eyes softened as she watched him rub a hand over his face, like he was trying to wipe the memory away. Fatigue clung to him, along with the grief.

Without thinking, she reached out, her fingers tracing the scar on his jaw. Her touch lingered longer than it should have.

"Sad," she whispered. It wasn't a judgment. Just the truth.

The space between them wasn't space anymore.

She didn't remember who moved first. Maybe it was both of them. Maybe it was neither. But suddenly, her lips brushed his. Tentative. Testing. A question, not a demand.

And he didn't pull away.

The kiss deepened—slow, soft. It wasn't desperate. It wasn't lust. It was something else. Something real. Something raw.

Rosa's arms slid around his neck. He rose from the couch, lifting her with surprising gentleness. She felt his heartbeat against hers—fast, but steady. Her fingers curled into the fabric of his shirt as they moved, step by step, toward the bedroom down the hall.

The door closed behind them.

Whatever came next—whatever tomorrow held—it didn't matter. Not now.

CHECKMATE?

"YOU BETTER HOPE your lover succeeds," his voice sliced through the darkness, each word dripping with a cold warning. The man on the table squirmed helplessly, his body straining in a futile attempt against the ropes that bound him. His chest heaved in shallow, ragged gasps, rising and falling with erratic urgency as the ropes bit into his skin. The pounding of his pulse echoed deafeningly in his temples. Fear clawed at him, but he couldn't tear his gaze away from the merciless, calculating expression on his tormentor's face.

"I'm really getting bored," the man continued, unnervingly calm despite the terror surrounding him. "Tired of this endless game. After all these years, I thought they'd give up chasing me, but here they are—still playing a game they can't possibly win. Even after they know my face."

A hollow chuckle escaped, void of humor. "That detective, though… she's clever. Very clever for her age. I wasn't that smart, not when I started. Just an eighteen-year-old boy, wishing his parents would disappear. Took me hours, months, even a year to set the plan into motion. To get the guts to do it. Haha, guts, get it?"

He leaned over the table, face inches from the victim's, making sure his words struck with the full force of the moment. The victim's chest tightened, a startled intake of breath caught in his throat as he stared into the cold, empty eyes of the man looming over him. The ropes dug deeper into his wrists with each frantic movement, but his struggles were futile.

"…still takes me hours to come up with the right rhymes." His voice dropped to a sinister whisper as he leaned in closer. "But shhh, don't tell anyone that." The faint warmth of his breath grazed the other man's skin, sending a shiver down his spine.

A cruel grin spread across his face as he hovered the scalpel over the man's lips, the cold gleam of the blade teasing the fragile skin. "Still, she's playing in a world far darker than she realizes. Let's see just how far she's willing to go. And poor brooding Simon… he has no idea what she'll be capable of one day."

He stepped back, giving the man some space—but not enough for him to feel safe. He thumbed a message on his phone, squinting closer at the screen as if his age began to catch up with him. A slight tremor in his fingers betrayed his irritation. It almost made him show anger—something he preferred not to reveal in front of his victims. He inhaled deeply, steadying himself.

The man on the table continued to struggle, his body writhing in useless attempts to free himself. His chest heaved with every desperate breath, each movement becoming more frantic. His head jerked back and forth, eyes wide, looking for anything, any way out—but there was nothing. His throat was raw from silent screams, but even if he screamed out loud, his voice would never reach anyone.

"You should've treated your loved ones better," the man smirked, his voice cold and taunting, almost bored. "There are only a handful left who even bother with you—and even they don't stay long." He stepped forward again, running his tongue along the edge of the scalpel, savoring it. His eyes flicked to the victim's terrified expression, drinking in the moment like a predator closing in on its prey.

John Willington. The lawyer who had gotten too close. He'd been clever once—too clever. But he knew too much now, and that made him expendable. Necessary, even. His name would vanish with the rest of them.

Still, there had been a time when he was useful. Invaluable, even. He had helped clean up messes, shift suspicion, make things disappear. His legal expertise had kept the killer out of sight more than once, and his quiet over the years had been a gift. He had even helped with a few of the victims—unknowingly, of course—but that didn't change the fact that he'd played his part well.

A part that had now run its course. Gratitude only went so far. And sentiment had no place in this game.

He felt a surge of dark satisfaction as the victim trembled, shivering uncontrollably now, his mind shattered under the weight of impending doom. Images of the upcoming gruesome act flashed in his mind, and he allowed himself to picture it in perfect detail. The man's final screams, the blood splattering, the warmth of it all. He didn't eat his victims, but he relished their terror. It was a game after all, spooking them before the end. It would get bloody, no doubt. It always did. That's why he preferred it when they pissed themselves beforehand—made the whole thing easier to enjoy.

A soft cackle escaped him when the man closed his eyes, as if pretending the nightmare unfolding before him would disappear.

Too bad for him. He had seen his face. Wood Riddle would never let that slide, no matter how deluded this victim's lover might be. Even if she somehow managed to win the second time, it wouldn't matter. Not in the end.

SHOOTING BLANKS

ROSA STIRRED, THE dull throb of a hangover pulsing behind her eyes. A muscular arm cradled her head—a safety net, or just a mistake made warm? Blinking against the early morning light, she realized she'd let herself slip too far last night. The alcohol had blurred her thoughts then, but now, reality was cutting through every fiber of her being.

Her thoughts raced—Simon would eventually leave. She knew this wasn't sustainable. Weakness had never been something she allowed herself, and now she was paying the price. Embarrassment crept through her, especially knowing Kershaw was still in a damn *coma*, and Raya, who had been calling and texting nonstop, surely needed a friend right now. But here she was, consumed by her own selfish needs.

Despite the confusion, the warmth of his bare skin against hers felt both right and wrong. A deep moan escaped her lips, her head splitting from the pain. A faint scratching at the door broke through her haze—it was Sir Louie, of course. Early afternoon now, and his meal had been forgotten. The impatient feline wasn't one to wait.

She shifted away from Simon, clutching her throbbing head. The movement must have woken him—his body tensed slightly before he spoke.

"Let's get this straight."

Before she could retreat further, he spoke again, his voice clear and steady, though his words sliced through her heart. "This was a mistake, and it won't be happening again."

Rosa felt his words settle. She knew it was coming, but it still hurt, regardless of whether or not she wanted it to or not.

"Blame it on the whiskey, but yeah, you took the words right out of my mouth," she said, her tone tough, though she hoped he didn't notice the slight falter in her voice. She could easily blame it on the hangover.

She stepped out, gently closing the door behind her.

Inside, Simon remained still. Through the wooden door, he imagined her staring at the wall, thoughts turning as restlessly as his own.

Then dread set in. He realized he needed to get out of this town as soon as possible. She almost made him want to give up—too much of him had been given to this hunt, this job. He'd made it his everything. But the anchor chained to his soul—his sister—pulled him back. He needed to tear this bastard to shreds, just like he had with all the other killers he'd brought down over the years. His sister's death might've been the easiest to accept in comparison, but focusing on those haunting images—those memories—kept him from faltering. It was the only thing stopping him from turning his anger toward Rosa instead, from lashing out in despair.

Instead, he rolled over and fixed his eye on the gun resting on the nightstand.

He would kill the killer. There was no other way for this to end. His mind was resolute, the only certainty amidst whatever the hell this emotional turmoil was.

THE FINAL DOSE

THE NURSE STOOD over the hospital bed, staring down at the unconscious man. Soft light from the early sun filtered through the window above, casting a glow across his dark skin as his chest rose and fell in steady, oblivious breaths. In her trembling hands was the concoction—a dangerous mix of miscellaneous drugs, blended at his command. A request. No, a demand.

She shifted from one foot to the other, her pulse hammering against her ribs. Her mind spiraled, thoughts colliding in a frantic storm. Was she doing this out of love for her lover? If she truly loved him—did she?—would she be here, considering this? No, she had wanted him gone. She had wished for someone—anyone—to take him away after the way he led her on. And now, here she was, standing face-to-face with that very reality.

So why was she hesitating?

She shouldn't. She knew her lover wasn't a good man. But did that even matter now? Justice wasn't served on a tray like this. Not like this.

Her mind went back to the video—the inanimate objects glinting at the edges of the frame. Cold. Unfeeling. Just like the act she was about to commit. The constant replay of the video in her mind wrapped around her, squeezing her lungs.

Was this really her choice? Or was she just another instrument in someone else's design?

She looked quickly at the syringe. Did she want to go through with it? Did she want to take the life of this young man—someone who had nothing to do with her? Was she just another pawn in a psychopath's game? Had he really believed she would do it?

Would he even let her husband go if she did?

Probably not.

And yet—she shuddered—when was the last time she had felt this alive? The thought slithered through her like a drug of its own. It was madness. Methodical, creeping madness. The way this faceless stranger had wormed his way into her mind, pushing, pulling, manipulating.

And worse—how easily she had let him.

But her lover was just like him—not in such a gruesome way, but in a way that still made her stomach turn. Should she even acknowledge that? Or should she take her life back, seize control for once?

This wasn't ethical.

This was what happened when you wished for something too long—when you whispered desperate prayers into the void, only to have them answered in the cruelest way imaginable. And now that it was real, now that the choice was in her hands, she wasn't prepared.

She didn't understand why this conflict was poisoning her.

Hadn't she always wanted to be moral? Someone who protected her family? Who did the right thing?

Then why did it feel like she was teetering at the threshold of something she couldn't come back from?

She grasped the IV line, her fingers trembling as she hovered over the connection point. The syringe in her other hand felt heavy, as if the liquid inside carried chemicals with the added weight of consequence— finality.

She was seconds away from pushing the plunger, from sending whatever deadly concoction this was into the veins of the man named Kershaw.

Just a second longer and—

"What the hell are you doing?!"

The loud, commanding voice cut through the sterile air, freezing her in place. It pierced her like a blade slicing through the haze of her thoughts.

She jerked her head toward the entrance. Standing in the doorway was the woman with the purple braids—the striking one, the one who carried herself with a strength she could never quite match. Jealousy burned in her gut. Envy, too.

And now, that woman had a gun aimed straight at her.

Her grip on the IV line tightened as terror swept through her, but the adrenaline was still there, still flooding her veins, refusing to let her collapse.

She was caught… but was she out of choices?

FINGER-SNAPPING MOMENTS

THE BLOOD POOLED beneath the fat, ugly man, a dark, sticky sea that smeared the floor with each of his desperate yelps. The sound of them—guttural, raw, frantic—made him grin and sent satisfaction fluttering through his core. Only five fingers had been lopped off, and this man had already given up? Pathetic. Weak. He'd talked big, but now he folded under pain. His need to finish this quickly compelled him, but why rush it? Why give this man the choice of ending it on his terms?

Five fingers were meant to break him, to stop his endless cycle—cheating, hurting women. It should've been enough. But that hunger remained. To hurt. To harm. To feel. A psychopath didn't feel like others did—no empathy, no guilt, no remorse. Just this. The desire to bring pain. To see someone crack. To feel alive in ways that made no sense to anyone else.

Irony. How could someone so detached—so devoid of real attachment—be consumed by the need to hurt? It didn't matter. Masks were necessary. A game. Was he the friendly one today? The rude one? The wise one? Which persona would he choose now, when he stepped back into the world? He had to play the part. Make it believable. The one that a young agent would buy into.

He wanted Simon to find him. He wanted to play—a test of wills. To see how far Simon would go before losing the trail, how long could he keep up before he cracked. Watching a man break—it was almost as satisfying as the crime itself. Almost.

His eyes gleamed with that familiar predatory hunger as they bore into the man before him. The man was shaking, terror more palpable than the blood pooling beneath him. Those wide, panicked eyes—begging, but without words. His body screamed surrender. Finish it. Kill me. End this. But that would be too easy. He could feel the rush of adrenaline starting to fade. A quick kill was never enough.

There had to be more.

He paused, the blade cold and sharp in his hand, thoughts drifting back—twelve years ago. The first detective. A damn good man. He hadn't tortured him, hadn't made him beg. No. A quick shot. Clean. He'd taken a finger as a souvenir, a reminder. He'd known it would be useful later.

And it had been. Oh, it had been.

The blade flashed in the light as he cut deeper into the man's arm. He'd been in his prime then. But now? The hunger had grown, darkened, gnawing at him when he wasn't feeding it. "Duty," he muttered, the word slipping out like a foreign thing. He had responsibilities, after all—people to manipulate, plans to execute. But now? Now, there was nothing but this. This moment. This feeling. The only thing that made him feel alive.

His breath quickened, and for a moment—just a heartbeat—something almost pained him. A thought. A memory. Someone. It lingered, like a whisper lost in the storm. But it vanished. Gone in an instant. The sensation, whatever it had been, was swept away by a never ending hunger.

The bone snapped beneath the blade with a sickening crack. He didn't flinch. Didn't hesitate. The bone was always the hardest part. But it was never enough to stop him.

He pushed deeper, faster, driven by the need to feel something—anything.

BREAKING POINT

RAYA'S ANGER FLARED instantly, every thought consumed by a storm of fury and suspicion. Her feet moved with purpose, no doubt. She stormed to the side of the hospital bed, the gun in her hand steady despite the chaos in her mind. She aimed it squarely at the nurse—someone unfamiliar, someone who didn't belong here. The cold metal pressed against her palm like a lifeline.

The nurse's face curled in terror, eyes wide as if caught in the act. Something wasn't right. Why was this nurse trying to inject something into Kershaw's IV? The question burned inside her with urgency. This wasn't just routine care—this was something else. Something dangerous.

For days, Raya had been swallowed by loneliness and self-doubt, haunted by memories she hadn't dared confront. Childhood wounds that left her vulnerable, a fracture deep inside she tried to ignore. But now, the overwhelming load—the betrayal, the loss, the endless fight—had pushed her. She needed someone to pay. Not just for what was happening now, but for all the pain she'd carried for so long.

Her hands were steady, heart pounding loud in her ears. This was more than justice or revenge. It was survival. And she wouldn't let anyone harm Kershaw—not without a fight.

The woman cowered against the glass window, trembling, eyes wide with panic. *Pathetic.* Raya could almost taste the fear in the room. She kept her gun trained on the nurse, who still stood near the hospital bed, IV line clutched in shaking hands. The nurse's breaths were ragged, her body trembling uncontrollably. Raya pulled back the slide and chambered a round.

But was this really justice? The question nagged at her, cold and unwelcome. She'd spent too long chasing answers, watching people get away with worse. Now, the fight felt vulnerable—less about right or wrong and more about survival. Raya's jaw tightened. It wasn't about justice anymore. It was about making sure no one else could hurt like she had.

She looked to the nurse. The woman's face drained of color, and Raya's smirk deepened. She wanted to laugh, but didn't. She wanted to make her suffer—not because of who she was, but because of what she represented. A world full of people who turned their backs when Raya needed them most. Cruel. Indifferent. Like the nurse, pretending to care but ready to betray.

Her body surged forward, pressing the barrel of the gun into the woman's temple—unforgiving. The nurse's eyes squeezed shut, her body tensing in fear. Rosa forced herself to stay steady. This wasn't just about the nurse. It was about every hurt she'd buried—every wound no one had ever seen.

Does it feel good to make someone else feel worse? Is this my way of feeling alive again? Raya thought, but the thought barely registered before the sound of a strong, steady voice cut through her haze.

"Whoa, whoa," Kershaw's voice was low, steady, and so damn calm it made Raya's skin prickle. He stood up abruptly, his hand reaching out to grab her arm, spinning her around with the force of his strength. The gun was still clenched in her hand, but now it was aimed at Kershaw's chest. She didn't even have time to think—just react. He was so much taller than her. So much stronger. The impact reverberated, and they both stumbled—a tangle of limbs.

In the scuffle, neither of them noticed the nurse inching toward the window, her hands trembling as she slid it open. The world seemed to slow for just a moment—Raya's chest rose and fell in quick, uneven motions, her pulse roaring in her ears.

And then, in the blink of an eye, the nurse was gone.

A hitch caught in Raya's throat, and before she could react, Kershaw loosened his grip, his eyes snapping toward the window. Raya bolted across the tile floor, her heart hammering. But it was too late—the nurse was already gone.

Raya's hands instinctively gripped the window frame, her fingers scraping against the cold metal as she looked down. From the fourth-floor hospital window, the D.C. city lights shimmered like distant stars, but the view did nothing to calm the storm inside her. The cold night air rushed in, biting at her skin, seeping deep into her bones. *I should've been faster,* the thought roared through her.

She stared into the empty space below, the crushing truth settling like a stone in her gut.

The nurse was gone.

Gone.

Splattered across the pavement below, the impact gruesome enough to shatter bones and scatter blood like a cantaloupe dropped from this height.

A sick, metallic taste filled her mouth. *You got distracted,* she thought, but it didn't matter now. The bitter truth was that she had let it all slip. Just like the serial killer wanted—just like they all did. She was no better than those she hunted. Worse, maybe.

And now it was too late.

IT TAKES TWO TO TANGO

AN AWKWARD STRETCH settled over the day. Rosa found herself heading back to her childhood home, seeking refuge. Her father was still in the hospital, but the doctors had assured her he'd be well enough to leave by the end of the week. She felt a wave of relief, but it was fleeting, barely enough to ease any emotion.

It was strange, really. Despite everything, the only moment she'd felt any semblance of peace during the past couple months was last night. A haze of alcohol and bad decisions clouded her mind, but one thing was clear: sleeping with the boss was a terrible idea. How could she possibly go back to work with him? How would it look?

Still, it took two to tumble into such trouble, right? So why should she be the one to feel pathetic for running away? She regretted leaving, but she needed space. A breath of fresh air. The past few days—hell, even the last month and a half on this case—had her feeling trapped. Now that Raya was holed up at the hospital beside Kershaw, William had disappeared, there was uncertainty about Kershaw's future, and the investigation was spiraling forward with no new clues.

No clues. Not a damn thing. Just the aching certainty that the next victim was already marked. The man they had found... he wouldn't last long. She could feel it in her bones. How could they stop a killer who played with them like this? The clock was ticking, and they were running out of time to crack the riddle—even worse, was just waiting around for the next one.

Her mind drifted uninvited, pulling her back to the night three years ago when she and Jacob were still together. The night he wouldn't let her go. The night when everything almost went too far. That night had become a permanent scar in her memory. Her breath quickened, and she saw Raya again—fists flying, the rush of relief and gratitude Rosa had felt all tangled together. And the next day, when she found the strength to stand up and finally throw Jacob out in front of everyone, a strange, bitter rush of power surged through her.

That was the night she decided to become a detective, not just to seek answers for her mother, but because she knew she couldn't let anyone walk over her ever again. And yet, here she was, feeling more vulnerable than ever. How had she ended up here, so far from the woman she'd vowed to become?

She gripped the wheel tighter, pushing the thought away as she pulled into of the driveway of her childhood home. Her father's old car creaked beneath her, a reminder of everything that had been—and everything that was slipping away. For the first time in a long while, she looked at the mailbox, the small memorial resting there. A lump formed in her throat as she slowed, her eyes drawn to the intricately drawn roses on the wooden mailbox stand. Her mom's favorite—roses. So typical of her dad to keep drawing them so vividly, even now.

She put her forehead against the window, the cool glass grounding her as a memory stirred in her mind. Though she wasn't smelling anything now, she could almost imagine the scent—sweet and compelling—of rose bushes from her childhood. Her innocence had been intact then, until a thorn sliced open her finger.

"I never want to see another rose again," she had declared, holding her bleeding hand to her chest.

Her mom had laughed—soft and melodic. "Well, your name's close enough, sweetheart. You'll never escape them."

Her father had come charging out of the house, band-aid in hand, his face a mix of concern and amusement.

"How can those damn roses hurt my flesh and blood?" he had grumbled, kneeling beside her, his hands gentle despite the words.

That moment—the laughter, the warmth, the scent of roses mingling with her father's cologne—was stuck in her memory. No matter how much time passed, she could still feel that moment, how everything had felt so right, so perfect, and yet so fleeting.

But now… everything felt distant, faded, like a dream slipping away. Had it really been that long? She blinked, trying to grasp the memories, but they blurred, slipping through her fingers like smoke. It was a nagging thought, one she couldn't shake.

She forced herself to focus on the present even though she wasn't ready to let go of the past—not yet, not ever. But the distance between who she had been and who she was becoming felt unbearable. She wasn't sure how to reconcile the woman who had fought for answers, for justice, with the woman she was now—a woman caught in the tangled mess of emotions, regrets, and fears. But no matter how much it seemed to be slipping away, she wasn't ready to forget any of it.

JACKASSERY AT ITS FINEST

HE KNEW HE'D fucked up as soon as she walked out the door, keys in hand. Even her damn cat was giving him the quiet treatment, perched on the other couch, eyes narrowed in judgment. For an hour it sat there glaring at him like it could sense his terrible decisions. His sanity must have gone off the rails because, just months ago, he would never have gotten intimate with someone who worked under him.

Sure, he went out to bars sometimes, picked up women, same as Kershaw. Why not? But this was different. This wasn't a quick fling or a casual connection. This… felt real. Like something he couldn't just shrug off.

Rosa. Her damn dimple when she smiled—how it creased the corner of her mouth, like it was meant just for him. Her intelligence. The way she could analyze a scene, take in every detail and spin it all into something he couldn't quite put together himself. It was all too easy to get lost in the way she spoke, her calm precision. She was smart—smarter than him, he sometimes thought. She made him feel dangerous things. Things that made him feel exposed.

He paced the house, back and forth, back and forth, the floor creaking beneath him with every step. The silence pressed down harder with each pass, suffocating him, but even more suffocating was the thought of how easily he'd let her in. He just *let* her in.

He was here because of the case. His twin's murder. This was supposed to be about revenge. That thought, that obsession, was still his anchor, unshakable. So why did Rosa affect him like this? It wasn't just her looks—though her laugh, that dimple, the way her eyes lit up when she talked about the most random things was damn intriguing—it was something else. A fire in her. She was driven, smart, and so capable, and that terrified him. He was used to being the one with all the answers. But she? She was better at this than he ever expected. And somehow, that made everything worse.

He knew he'd grown fond of the team. But Rosa? She was different. There was a depth to her, a strength in her silence, a sharpness that cut through his thoughts. And as much as he didn't want to admit it, the self-loathing intensified—because he'd told Rosa sleeping with her was a mistake, and yet he couldn't stop himself. Worse, he was letting his distractions pull him away from the one thing that mattered: catching the killer. What the fuck had he done? He was better than this. Stronger than this. He couldn't afford to fall apart now.

When his phone rang, the name on the screen caught him off guard. He stared at it, his fingers hovering over it, his chest aching. He almost didn't want to pick up. Maybe it wouldn't be good news. Maybe it was someone else calling him from Kershaw's phone to say something he didn't want to hear. But maybe it was Kershaw himself. The feeling in his chest grew stronger. Kershaw was the one person who could pull him out of this spiraling mess.

His finger finally swiped across the screen, and the moment he did, Kershaw's booming voice blasted through the speaker, cracking the tension in the room like thunder.

"My man, my man! I feel like I've slept for sixty years, but I'm feelin' pretty damn good! You should really be put into a coma sometime—get rid of all that jackassery."

The sound of Kershaw's voice, so loud and unapologetically upbeat, filled the space around him. It was jarring, almost violent against the quiet he'd been cocooned in. Simon sank into the couch, his shoulders drooping in relief. He let out a slow breath, trying to steady himself. For a moment, he almost wanted to laugh. How did Kershaw do that? Pull him back from the precipice with nothing more than a few words? How did he still have the ability to do that, when nothing else seemed to work?

"Dude, you there?" Kershaw's voice cut through the phone once again.

"I'm here," Simon's reply was clipped, hard, and firm, the way he always responded when he didn't want to deal with unnecessary thoughts. Kershaw could read it—he always could.

"It's okay to tell me you love me," Kershaw teased, his tone light, but laced with care. "Someone tried to attack a second time, but Raya's a badass, man." Simon could hear Raya's voice in the background, muffled but stern as she told Kershaw to shut up, to not tell Simon all the details. "We'll be on the next flight back there. Doctors say I should be observed longer, but I'll be there later today. Everyone okay? You okay? Rosa? Rosa's dad?"

Too many questions. Too little time. Too much thinking.

"Just get your ass back here to work." Simon clicked the phone off, coming across as a tough boss in charge. But both of them knew the truth—Simon wasn't great with words. That abrupt, no-nonsense line was his way of sharing love, tough as it sounded.

PARANOIA PERSONA

JUST AS SOON as they seemed to catch a break, something else happened.

Local teens fooling around behind the town's only skating rink had their lives forever scarred when they stumbled upon a dismembered body out back—where they usually gathered to smoke weed. They'd been joking around as usual, using the old, cracked sidewalk behind the rink as their makeshift skatepark. No one ever bothered to come back here—too overgrown, too forgotten—but they had smoothed it down with their skateboards, carving out their own little world in the abandoned space.

They were just about to light up again when one of them noticed something.

At first, it didn't register. Then, as one of them stepped closer, his stomach churned. There, lying in pieces on a black blanket, was a body—a grotesque sight, fresh and bloody, as if the killer had only just finished the gruesome task. The area around the body reeked of iron, the sickly sweet stench of death. A piece of bark, roughly pinned through the victim's chest, stood out starkly against the scene. The precision of the dismemberment was unnerving—each limb separated with surgical care. Nothing about this was hasty; it was methodical. The killer's MO had clearly evolved: no longer draining the blood completely, but leaving the body staged with chilling attention to detail.

When the call came in, Rosa and Simon met behind the skating rink. The setting sun stretched across the body in long bands of light, but did nothing to mask the awkwardness between them.

They surveyed the scene. This time, things were different—the body hadn't been preserved. Instead, it was fresh, as if the ritual had been completed only moments before they arrived. Even though the careful placement of all the parts still spoke of his methodical precision, Rosa wondered if he was finally ready to show them a side of himself he'd kept hidden all this time.

Her thoughts drifted back to the lawyer connected to the case—John Willington—the man who never answered his door, whose silence had grown ominous. This was him. The killer had reached John before they could.

A grimness stretched between them as the night grew colder and their minds raced, trying to piece together how it all fit. Rosa sat on the hood of Simon's Bel-Air, carefully contemplating the riddle scrawled on the piece of bark.

> *"A watcher in silence, not sleeping through the night,*
> *Where wisdom dwells, hidden from sight.*
> *A gift of knowledge, sharp as the mind,*
> *Seek the old stone where answers unwind."*

Her thoughts began to click into place. The riddle held something more now. She felt it—a pull deep within—as she considered why the lines were different. A watcher... wisdom... knowledge. She knew it referred to the Wood Riddle Killer, but the mention of not sleeping through the night—insomnia? That was new. This became more personal. Why mention insomnia? Why now? He had never included intimate details before.

Her mind raced, the pieces coming together in fragmented flashes, but each new connection only seemed to deepen the mystery. She muttered to herself, trying to make sense of the words. "A watcher in silence, not sleeping through the night..." The riddle repeated in her head like a chant, turning over and over.

She frowned, trying to break it down. "Where wisdom dwells, hidden from sight..." The phrase lingered. A watcher, someone who observes, listens, perhaps? She rubbed her forehead in thought. An image flashed in her mind—no, more like a place—something cold and vast, filled with knowledge. A library, again? A place of study. Books. That made sense. But there was more.

Her mind pulled her back to the next line. "A gift of knowledge, sharp as the mind..." She whispered the words aloud, letting them sink in. She could almost picture it now. Wisdom, knowledge, a space meant for both—her thoughts drifted back to the library they were already at before. Maybe a different one that held old dusty shelves filled with untold secrets. But that didn't explain the stone.

"The old stone..." She trailed off, her fingers running through her hair in frustration. "What does that mean? A place? An object? A symbol? Why stone?" She shook her head. "It's just... it doesn't make sense." Her lips pressed together as she looked at the words again, replaying them like a broken record in her head.

She said it again, this time with more certainty. "The old stone... it could be a place, maybe—a monument or a landmark?" The pieces didn't quite align. What was the connection? "Stone," she repeated. "Could it be... something tangible? Something intimate to him again? On a deeper level?"

Then it hit her suddenly—like a lightning bolt snapping everything into place. The old stone wasn't just a place or an object. It was more. It could be the key.

But it was more than that. This wasn't just about finding answers anymore. Something close to the Woodle Riddle killer. Something tied to him, to who he was beneath the twisted, calculating exterior. She felt it—this wasn't just a case to solve. She could feel the closeness, the sense that she was about to uncover something more than she was ready for. The puzzle was closer to completion than ever before... but what was the key?

She wasn't sure yet. But the truth was waiting. She could feel it.

Before she could grasp any clearer understanding, a prickling sensation ran down her spine. A presence—unseen, but felt. It was no longer just Simon's sweet tea-colored eyes boring into her; this was different. His gaze, familiar and intense, had always been burdened, but this was something else entirely. Someone was watching her from the woods. And it didn't feel like a coincidence. Something about the way the air shifted made her feel exposed, threatened.

Her heartbeat quickened as the prickling feeling of being watched crawled over her skin. But she fought to dismiss it—no, it had to be her imagination, nothing more. She forced her focus back to the riddle. She had to figure this out.

Was the mastermind finally giving up, letting them catch him? Or was he setting up some last-minute commotion to throw them off track again? Maybe he had his protege do the dirty work now, taking a step back. It seemed possible, but unlikely. The killer had always craved the power of the kill, the pleasure of savoring it himself. His protege wouldn't be involved yet. And even if they were, he wouldn't allow them to overshadow him—not until he was finished with his decades-long game.

What did this killer really want? What was going on? What were they missing? Why Chattingsburg? Was it tied to the killer's life, his sick backstory? What was the reasoning behind all of this madness? She didn't want to think of him as a person, as a human—because how could a human do this? All of this? For over thirty years? Before she was even born, this same man had given nightmares to everyone involved. Stress, blurred lines, lives lost, all in the name of stopping him.

When would enough be enough?

Rosa's thoughts churned. She didn't want to let this case consume her the way it had consumed so many before. She had to solve it. She wasn't going to be the person who walked away broken, defeated. But at what cost? Could she stay true to herself and keep her humanity intact while chasing someone so dark? Or had the darkness already started to seep inside her, threatening to change who she was?

The thoughts circled her mind until her head was killing her. And just when it seemed like everything was about to click together, she heard it—a deafening sound, followed by a *whoosh*.

A bullet whizzed past her ear, grazing it. The sensation was so close, so real, that it took a moment for her to comprehend what had happened. Before she could react, someone grabbed the back of her hoodie, yanking her down behind the car.

The world erupted into an explosion of loud sounds. Bullets sprayed the ground, ricocheting off the pavement like hailstones. Hot panic flushed through her veins, but a second later her training kicked in.

Simon was already up, gun drawn, firing over the edge of the car, ducking behind it, his every move calculated. Rosa snapped into action with him, adrenaline spiking. She shot in the direction of the woods, her breath taut in her chest. Simon covered her, firing at a different angle, both of them working in perfect sync. Every shot felt like a heartbeat, each one pulling her in.

She fired again, the gun in her hand grounding her, but inside, she was spiraling. Was this who she was becoming? Was this the person she had to be to survive? Her fingers tightened around the trigger. She could almost feel the killer's presence out there, watching, waiting. This wasn't just about solving the case anymore—it was about her survival. And she wasn't sure how much of her was left to save.

VESTED INTEREST

IN THE MIDST of the action, Rosa moved with precision, her chest rising in quick, shallow pulls, pulse thudding like a drumbeat in her ears. She ducked behind a different car, eyes darting toward Simon, who was still crouched behind his own cover. Another shot rang out—then another. Her ribs tightened. Her lungs screamed for air.

Where was everybody? Forensics, backup—shouldn't they be here by now? The void beyond the gunfire felt wrong, like they were still on their own.

A flash of movement caught her eye—a streak of red hair shifting between the treetops. Her gut clenched. Was it real? Or just a trick of the darkness? The only reason the shooter had such a clear view of them was the harsh, artificial glow of the floodlights illuminating the crime scene. They were sitting ducks.

She squinted, trying to make out more than a silhouette, but before she could, another shot cracked through the night.

Simon jerked backward.

Time slowed.

The sound of her own gunfire was distant, drowned out by the roaring in her head. She fired again and again, barely thinking—just reacting—until she reached his side.

"Simon!" Her hands trembled as she grabbed him, shaking him. He didn't respond.

Frantic, she ripped open his leather jacket, air catching painfully in her throat—then she saw it. The bulletproof vest. The impact had knocked him out cold, but he was alive.

A broken gasp tore from her throat, her vision blurring for a split second. Her fingers curled into his jacket, gripping it tighter than necessary, as if to ground herself. Then, the tension in her muscles snapped, replaced by aching relief as he gasped loudly, his face contorting with pain.

His eyes fluttered open, dazed.

"You scared the shit out of me." Rosa's voice wavered between anger and relief as she smacked his shoulder—hard. Then, still breathless, she slumped against the car's tire, her body shaking. Her heart was still racing, a half-second behind reality, her body refusing to let go of the terror that had just gripped her.

She must have hit their shooter—had to have. And there was only one likely suspect. William. The flash of red hair she saw moments ago matched his.

But would he really pull the trigger on a friend?

She wanted to believe he wouldn't. But William was gullible, easy to manipulate. And someone was getting to him. Or emotions clouding him. Whoever it was, they knew exactly what they were doing.

The aftermath of the gunfire was almost suffocating. Rosa leaned back. The adrenaline that had kept her moving while bullets were flying was starting to ebb. She licked her dry lips and swallowed, trying to slow the erratic rise and fall of her chest as she tried to process the danger they had just survived. The intensity of those moments. Now it was just her and Simon. She could feel the stillness settling in, reminding her of how close they'd come to losing their lives.

Then, the sound of pounding footsteps broke through. Other officers were finally closing in, their weapons drawn, their voices urgent.

"Everyone okay over here?"

"A little late," Simon muttered, his voice laced with irritation.

Rosa elbowed him, a swift command to shut up.

Even after all of this, he was still a goddamn smartass.

RIDDLE ME STONE

"Y'ALL GOT ALL the fun, it seems."

Raya practically launched herself at Rosa, hugging her tightly, her energy vibrating off the walls. The room still throbbed with the aftermath of everything that had happened. Rosa caught the looks Simon and Kershaw exchanged—like they'd just crossed a finish line in a marathon none of them signed up for.

Kershaw gave Simon a small nod, a wordless acknowledgment that he was still standing, still breathing.

"Guess what you've got in your hands means we've got another riddle to solve," Kershaw said, nodding at what Simon was fiddling with. They seemed to notice the charged air between Rosa and Simon—something different.

Raya sat beside her, watching Rosa bite her nails, her thigh bouncing up and down. Rosa tried not to let her nerves show.

Kershaw and Raya exchanged a look.

"Oh. Ohhh!" Raya said suddenly.

Rosa raised an eyebrow but said nothing.

"Um, Rosa? Can we talk upstairs for a sec?" Raya grabbed Rosa's arm and pulled her up so fast Rosa had to catch herself.

Sir Louie, always the nosy one, darted toward the door just as Raya shut it. He let out a disgruntled meow and pawed at the door.

"Spill. Now."

Rosa groaned, pressing her forehead against the wall. "You don't even have to ask. You already know." Her voice was low, muffled by the close contact. "But we really don't have time to stress over my bad decisions right now."

Raya grinned like the Cheshire cat. "Way to go! The goodie two-shoes bagged the boss."

Rosa shot her a glare. "Raya."

"Don't 'Raya' me! You can't fight instincts. Anyone with half a brain could see that attraction from a mile away."

"This is literally the worst time to be talking about this." Rosa reached for the door handle, but Raya blocked her escape.

"Everyone deserves to be happy, even a tough guy like Simon. He's not a bad guy, he's just—"

"An obsessive jerk?" Rosa cut in dryly.

Raya snorted. "Exactly. But let's be real—he's a hot obsessive jerk. And girl, you scored big time." She shot Rosa a knowing wink.

Rosa rolled her eyes. "Can we please just focus on the damn riddle now?"

Raya smirked, stepping aside at last. "Fine, fine. But just know—I will be circling back to this. Let's give them a few moments downstairs, though."

After a few moments, they headed back down. When they did, Rosa caught Kershaw locking an arm around Simon's shoulders in a tight, almost brotherly grip. Simon tried to shove him off, but Kershaw held firm.

"Damn, I was gone for a millisecond, and you bagged yourself a newly appointed detective. Luck's on your side, my guy."

Simon stiffened.

Kershaw caught the reaction and gave him a knowing look. "Relax. You deserve to be happy, no matter what that messed-up brain of yours is telling you."

Simon exhaled sharply, patience wearing thin. "Not the time. Not the place. After we figure this shit out, we're getting the hell out of here."

His words landed with bitter finality.

At the foot of the stairs, Rosa froze.

She had overheard him.

Simon and Kershaw turned, their stares locking onto Rosa and Raya as they stepped back into the room. The timing couldn't have been worse.

But maybe—just maybe—it was for the better. There was no going back to normal. Not for them. Not in this life. An FBI agent's world was never stable, never still. And Rosa felt it—things would get worse. But he didn't have to be such a dick.

Better to cut the thread now before it frayed beyond repair.

Rosa slunk onto the couch, willing herself not to react to Simon's words. Instead, she refocused on the riddle, pushing the photocopy across the table toward Kershaw and Raya. She watched Simon reach for his own copy, his movements stiff. Kershaw and Raya stifled their laughter behind poorly concealed hands, but Simon's tight jaw betrayed him.

"We've already worked something out," Rosa started, tucking a loose strand of hair behind her ear. "Wood Riddle isn't sleeping—he made that part clear. He admitted to having insomnia. Maybe delirium is taking its toll on him and that's why his pattern changed. I don't think it's just old age. He got tired of the mundane life he's led for the past thirty years—he wanted—wants—something new."

All eyes were on her as she laid out her thoughts, her voice steady but laced with urgency.

"I know this is referring to another library. He seems obsessed with language, with words, with anything related to wisdom. I just don't know which one—there aren't that many. It could be in someone's house, it could be the public library. But it's definitely a place tied to knowledge. He mentions wisdom for the millionth time, and sure, he's suggesting he's smart—but where did he get his wisdom? He says it's 'hidden from sight.'"

She paused, scanning their faces, giving them a moment to process. They were trying to piece it together themselves, but the furrowed brows and exchanged glances told her they weren't quite there yet.

"A gift of knowledge is a book, I'm guessing?" Kershaw offered, shifting in his seat. He was good at fighting, good at hacking—but this kind of puzzle wasn't his strong suit.

"Yes. They're sharp as the mind and make your mind sharper the more you read." Rosa nodded, adjusting her posture, now sitting cross-legged on the couch. "But I think 'seeking the old stone' is where we'll find the answers."

"Do you think this place will also be personal to him somehow?" Raya asked.

Rosa sat up straighter, considering. "If it's a special place, then maybe this is where his obsession began. If it's tied to his past, it would have to be somewhere from his childhood… but I'm not sure. You know how much he loves to mislead us. This one just feels more intimate than the other riddles."

She glanced at the paper again, her fingers drumming absently against her knee. "'Old stone' is an old reference in history—there's the Omphalos Stone from Delphi, the Rosetta Stone from Egypt, even the Philosopher's Stone. All of them were believed to hold wisdom, or at least the key to deciphering knowledge. People sought them out to unlock hidden truths, to gain insight into things long buried."

She exhaled, realizing all of them were staring at her like students absorbing a lecture. Clearing her throat, she stood, stretching her legs before continuing.

"Okay, maybe that's a bit of a stretch," she admitted, rolling out the tenseness in her shoulders. "But if it's a building that was personal to him… maybe it's made of stone?"

She wracked her brain, trying to recall any stone buildings significant enough to fit the riddle. Nothing immediately came to mind.

"Yes!" Raya gasped suddenly, sitting forward. "Remember that old cobblestone library on the outskirts of town? Your mom actually took us there once, but you and I were too busy playing secret agents to care."

Rosa's eyes brightened. "Okay, yeah—that could work."

Kershaw grinned. "Look at you, actually using all that book smarts."

Raya laughed, elbowing Rosa. "She didn't graduate early and ace every class just to sit on her hands, you know. I told her ten years ago she should've joined the force with me."

Rosa rolled her eyes but smiled. "Yeah, yeah, keep bragging."

They gathered their things, ready to move. Rosa felt wiped out—more than ready for this nightmare to be over.

But something nagged at her—was it the riddle, or the creeping feeling they were walking straight into another trap? She couldn't tell. All she knew was she wasn't sure she had the strength left for more. How had Simon managed this for so long?

As they headed out, Rosa hesitated before shutting the car door. Her gaze drifted to her house—the one she'd built new memories in, trying to leave the past behind. But deep down, she couldn't shake the sinking feeling that when she came back, things wouldn't be the same.

She just didn't know how.

WHERE THE PAGES LEAD

THE ROAD TO the library stretched long and winding, the towering trees lining either side, their shadows stretching over the car as it sped through the encroaching dusk. The sky darkened slowly, the evening's breeze creeping in as the night began to settle.

When they finally reached the old cobblestone library, it loomed before them like a relic from another time—weathered and worn, yet stubbornly standing. Its stones, gray and cracked with age, were overtaken by creeping moss, nature slowly reclaiming what it had once given. The wind stirred the scattered leaves around them, a soft hum of rustling carried on the breeze, resounding in the quiet as the scent of damp earth drifted. The grand stone doors, now crooked on their hinges, sagged under years of neglect. The roof, bowed and crumbling in places, whispered of its history—each crack and crease telling the story of time's passage. Still, it stood strong, its resistance against time and decay a testament to its age.

The group turned on their flashlights, the beams cutting through the darkness, catching on the weathered stone. Each of them instinctively checked their guns, their senses alert as they prepared to move further. The decision to enter felt heavier with each passing second. As they stood there, the faint rustle of wind was the only sound accompanying their steady breathing. They thought it would be smarter to wait until the next morning—the light of the rising sun might offer some comfort—but none of them could stand the delay anymore.

They'd waited too long. The nurse—though not one of his direct victims—had still rattled them. Somehow, even without killing with his own hands, his reach left damage behind. They knew he wouldn't stop until they found him. But if the Wood Riddle Killer was truly that meticulous, that in control—why now? Why take risks that drew this much attention? Could someone maintain such precise control for this long without slipping? Or had every move been part of his chessboard all along?

Kershaw, ever the pragmatist, moved first. He grabbed a nearby rock and slammed it against the window of the door. It shattered with a dull thud, but thankfully, no alarm rang out. The old place seemed as neglected as the rest of the town. Rosa's eyes drifted to the cobblestones beneath her feet as she stepped forward, the texture of the stones grounding her.

For a brief moment, the evening fell away. Memories rushed in.

She could almost hear her younger self running through the field outside, chasing Raya with reckless abandon. It used to be the cutest library she'd ever seen. She had dreamed of living here one day, wrapped in the quiet solitude it offered. She had romanticized this place when they visited at that age. But now the library felt different—like a phantom of what it had once been, a place left to gather dust.

Her footfalls grew louder as she focused back on the task. This was no longer about nostalgia. She couldn't afford to linger in the past, even if the memories felt like a distant, haunting reminder of simpler days.

Inside, the smell of old books hit her first—the musty scent of worn leather and yellowed pages filling her lungs. It was a comforting scent, one she hadn't realized she missed until now. She had spent hours as a child lost in books, always ahead of the other kids, reading in corners. She smiled to herself, remembering how she used to find hidden spots anywhere to get lost in a story.

But she wasn't alone now. Raya had pulled her out of that solitary world. Together, they had spent hours exploring, laughing, and even reading side by side. She even got Raya to read more, teaching her the joy of stories and the escape they offered.

She kept looking around and noticed that the shelves weren't just made of wood—no, the architect had been fixated on stone. The shelves themselves were crafted from the same cobblestone that made up the walls and floor, giving the room a solid, almost monolithic feel. The library's bones were as old as the town, and every inch seemed built to endure. Only the books felt out of place—tattered and jammed together, some nearly falling apart with age. Silt coated everything in a layer of history. The room felt frozen in time, still clinging to its purpose but barely holding on. The library opened only once a month for travelers, though the small town rarely saw any. And whoever was in charge clearly wasn't concerned with keeping the place clean.

Now, all that remained was a relic—a place reserved for school field trips and the occasional curious wanderer. It wasn't the lively, bustling sanctuary it had once been.

As Rosa's eyes scanned the room, she couldn't shake the feeling that this place, too, was about to change forever. The mission ahead loomed as large as the building itself.

She wandered to the back of the library, drawn by something that had caught her eye—a faint glimmer in the soft light, like a hidden object just out of reach. At that moment, straying off alone didn't faze her; whatever had captured her attention held her completely, pulling her toward it with an almost magnetic force.

BRUSHED BY MADNESS

DRAGGING THE FILLED bucket wasn't easy. His age had a way of catching up with him, weighing down his body like an unseen burden. But he was fit as a fiddle—or at least that's what he told himself every day to survive the mundane, suffocating world of normal people. They couldn't see what he saw: the world as an intricate canvas, his art formed by destruction—a masterpiece painted in human suffering.

All the corpses were his art. He didn't waste his time on animals—no, they were too helpless, too innocent. Humans, on the other hand, had the choice to be weak, and that weakness disgusted him. It was their own fault, after all.

Tonight, though, tonight was different. The atmosphere around him seemed charged with something more. He felt the tightness of it. This night would be the one that marked a turning point. He would finally shed the mask that had drowned him for so long. No more hiding, no more playing the side character. Someone would eventually follow in his footsteps—he knew it. His work would live on, even after he was gone. He had his role to play in this game. Or was it his father's game? The thought of that old fool barely crossed his mind anymore, but tonight… tonight would change everything.

"No time to think about that now," he muttered, the words a thin comfort. "Everything changes after this." He dipped a brush into a tin of rusty-smelling paint, the bristles absorbing the dark liquid as if hungry for more. His mind was already lost in the next riddle—the one he'd crafted years ago. It had all been planned, from beginning to end, and the end wouldn't come until he decided. No one else had the power to decide.

He wasn't ready to give up—not yet. As much as he didn't want to wait another two years for the next kill, the hunger inside him wouldn't turn him into a maniac. Or, at least, not more of one than he already was. The detectives thought this was nearing the end, but it was just the beginning. They would soon see.

The crimson paint dripped lazily from the wall, a stark contrast to the neat tile beneath. It stained it, spreading like a slow, inevitable death. He'd spent so much time cleaning it, but now that task seemed irrelevant. It irked him, but the urgency of his escape pressed harder. He needed a dramatic exit—something to leave behind, to spice things up for the "kids" who would come after. They would remember this one.

He couldn't help but smile as the paint pooled. There was something satisfying about it. Something beautifully grotesque. His fingers tightened on the brush, and with one last musical stroke, he swiftly painted the words on the wall before him.

RED HEAD'S SILENT FURY

SIMON SCANNED THE library with narrowed eyes, every nerve on edge. They all slowly lowered their hands from their weapons once they realized no one else was there. The abandoned, cobblestoned building pulsed with a hollow calm, but the emptiness pressed against him in a way that wouldn't let go. There was something wrong about the place—not in the obvious way, but in that suffocating, crawling way that got under his skin. Stone. They were searching for something tied to stone, but how the hell were they supposed to find anything specific when the entire place was built from it?

A damn needle in a haystack.

Off to the side, Kershaw was already tearing through the shelves, books thudding to the ground with reckless intent. It was like he believed the floorboards would open up and gift them a clue. Simon didn't share the optimism. Nothing about this case had ever been that easy.

"I don't see a damn thing," Simon muttered. His voice came out meaner than intended as he kicked one of the tables, the screech of wood dragging against the floor. His body vibrated with the stress of it all. This case had consumed him. Every part of his life surrounded it, smothered by it. He'd been on a tightrope for ten years.

He caught movement from the corner of his eye—Raya shifting near the shelves, Kershaw pacing like a caged dog—but they were background noise to the fire burning in his chest. He was unraveling at a faster pace than ever before. Not just from the pressure but from the sheer length of it all. A decade of dead ends and regrets. He couldn't even remember the last time he'd slept without dreams dragging him back into this nightmare.

He didn't know how much longer he had left in him.

Simon thought of Rosa. She had walked into this storm without hesitation. Where the rest of them were frayed and faltering, she'd held steady. It was something he didn't understand and wasn't sure he deserved to admire.

A sudden shift yanked Simon's attention toward Raya. She reached for her gun, but her body stilled—too stiff, too slow. His instincts kicked in a beat too late. He saw it now. Someone was behind her.

The way she locked up, every muscle rigid—it told him everything.

"Walk. Slowly," a male voice ordered. Scratchy. Worn thin. Familiar.

William.

Simon's fingers tensed around his own gun. That voice didn't sound like the man he used to know. This version carried a chill, as if all warmth had long since drained out.

He watched William shove Raya forward, gun raised. The bastard had managed to creep up on them—again. His mind raced for options, cover, leverage.

Raya's voice carried its usual bite as she spoke to William, but Simon barely heard her. His focus remained fixed on William's weapon—the angle of his wrist, the pressure on his trigger finger.

"Come out!" William's voice cut across the space.

Simon didn't hesitate. He stepped into view, Kershaw beside him. His gun was already in hand. But then his eyes flicked past William—for a fraction of a second—to Rosa.

She wasn't responding like the others. She was… somewhere else. Her eyes locked on something the rest of them hadn't noticed. Simon tracked her hand as it moved toward a shelf. She was reaching for something.

"You better take a step back," William warned, locking his eyes on Simon. "I swear, I'll shoot first and ask questions later."

That voice. That look in his eyes. Desperation radiated from every inch of him.

Simon didn't flinch. His face gave nothing away as he slowly set his gun on the table. No sudden movements. No provocations. He wasn't here to play hero.

Beside him, Kershaw followed suit, mirroring the gesture.

He caught a flicker of motion behind William—Rosa, slipping out the front door. No one else noticed. Simon didn't call attention to it. She had a plan. She had to.

"William, come on, man, this isn't you," Kershaw said, voice laced with disbelief.

"Ten long years," William snapped. "In those ten years, we got to know each other, learned how the other thinks. But tell me, Kershaw—who's the smartest one in the room now?"

Simon didn't answer. He watched every twitch in William's fingers.

"Currently? I'd say Rosa," Raya said.

Simon's gut clenched. Bad timing. Bad move.

William's face twisted, rage breaking through whatever self-control he had left. He forced Raya to her knees, grip tightening.

"This isn't the time for jokes, Raya," Kershaw warned, his voice shaky.

But William had already shifted focus. He turned to Simon, gun pointed straight at his chest. Finger trembling.

Simon didn't move. He didn't even blink. He looked straight into William's eyes.

And that's when he saw it.

Fear.

Real fear. Not of getting shot. Not of losing. But of becoming something he couldn't undo. William wasn't just broken—he knew he was too far gone. That kind of fear... it never left a man. Simon knew that look. He'd seen it in the mirror too many times.

"Your partner Chadford was in the exact same position," Simon said.

William's shoulders jerked slightly, but the gun stayed fixed. Cocked. Ready.

"Go ahead," Simon said, calm. "Take your revenge. I don't much care if I die. But before you do, know this—I know why you're mad."

"You know nothing!" William shouted.

Simon tilted his head, refusing to back down. "You loved Marybeth. Maybe not the way I did, but you did. You were her friend before all of this, weren't you?"

There. That hit.

Simon felt the shift. He didn't need to look to know the others were staring at him. They heard it too.

"At the orphanage. And then after—you found her again, didn't you? Befriended her," Simon said, voice low, measured. "And I think she started to love you, too."

He leaned against the table. Not too close. Not a threat. Just enough to keep William locked in.

"You wanted to catch him. That much is clear. But somewhere along the way, you went rogue. Maybe it was for your own selfish reasons; maybe you thought you could outplay him. Either way—your fight isn't with me."

SWERVING DESTINY

SHE KNEW IT was reckless to go alone, but she couldn't help herself. She refused to believe it—this couldn't be happening. The evidence sat too close for comfort in the passenger seat. Papers, files, and something else... a small, stone figurine, rolling back and forth with every swerve she made. Her grip tightened on the steering wheel, knuckles white with the effort to stay steady. No. It couldn't be. She couldn't let herself think it.

She slammed her foot on the gas, the sirens roaring to life, cutting through the night like a desperate cry. She didn't even register how far past the speed limit she was going. All she knew was the rush of adrenaline pumping through her veins, pushing her faster, harder. What she had taken from the library—what was now rattling around in the passenger seat—felt all too familiar. She had to be sure. She had to see it with her own eyes.

The road blurred around her, the world outside rushing past in streaks of light and shifting shapes. The headlights cut through the night like knives, but still, a stillness settled over her. Her chest constricted with a stubborn strain, panic creeping beneath her calm. What if she was right? No—it couldn't be. She had to hold on to control.

The car was closing in on her. She reached for the stereo, fingers trembling with the need to drown out the storm in her mind. But her hand froze, hovering over the buttons. Music wouldn't calm the storm inside her. It wouldn't drown out the thoughts that were closing tight around her chest—like a vice.

It didn't make sense. The figurine, the way it felt in her hand, its strain, its familiarity. It just couldn't be what she thought. It didn't add up. And yet, the knot in her stomach twisted painfully, telling her it was true.

She glanced up, her eyes instinctively flicking to the road just in time to see headlights blinding her from the opposite lane. A car honked—long, sharp—she swerved hard to avoid it, tires screeching on the asphalt. The world tilted as she fought to regain control, her heart racing, pulse pounding in her ears.

She slammed on the brakes and the car skidded to a stop just off the road. The engine rumbled as she came to a halt, the car jolting once, twice, before the world stopped.

Her breath came in shallow gasps, stifling. She barely heard the car pass safely, the roar of its engine fading into the night like a mirror image of her panic. Her hands gripped the wheel so tightly her fingers ached, every muscle in her body tense with the effort to stay composed. Her pulse hammered in her throat, a drumbeat she couldn't escape.

She wiped the sudden sting of tears from her eyes. They wouldn't fall. Not yet. Maybe it was the adrenaline, the rush of near disaster, or maybe it was something deeper, something she couldn't name. But she refused to break. Not here. Not now.

No. She couldn't let herself think.

But the question lingered, pulsing in her mind like a faint whisper growing louder: *Was it true?*

The figurine, the way it felt in her hand, the cruel joke of it... It didn't make sense. But she couldn't shake the feeling that it was real—that the truth was just seconds away from breaking her.

FRAGILE CALM

"SERIOUSLY?" KERSHAW MUTTERED, collapsing into a nearby chair. The words rang out, harsh and ragged.

William snapped, dragging the end of the gun across his forehead. His fingers trembled, and Simon could see the man unraveling in front of him. The weapon looked fused to William's hand, as if it were the only thing keeping him grounded. He was spiraling—clearly—and Simon watched the man's breathing shift, his whole body twitching like a frayed wire about to snap. He hadn't even realized Simon knew the truth, not until now.

There was no relief in William's face. No closure. Just something empty. He looked like a man who'd run out of reasons—out of anger, out of purpose. This had been their teammate. Their friend. And now all that was left was this fractured shell, too far gone to pull back.

Simon couldn't tear his eyes away.

A pause settled between them. Something shifted behind William's eyes—something that made Simon's pulse spike. He knew that look. The moment someone chose to give up. It was all over William's face.

In the next breath, William raised the gun to his own temple.

Simon's heart kicked hard against his ribs. He didn't think—he moved.

"No!" Raya's scream shattered through, her voice cracking with panic.

Everything else went still. No one breathed. Not even the room.

Simon stared at the barrel pressed to William's head. The tremble in his hand. The tight grip. The flicker of something waiting to pull him into the dark. This man wasn't bluffing. He meant it.

And Simon couldn't let that happen.

He stepped forward. No sudden movement. No words.

Just motion.

His arms wrapped around William, the barrel still angled against his own head. He felt the cold metal brush his forearm, the tension vibrating through William's frame. Simon didn't care. He pulled him close, tighter, grounding him.

He could feel William's heartbeat against his chest, erratic and panicked. He wasn't resisting—just standing there. Frozen. Simon held on. Not like a cop. Not like an agent. Just a man holding another man who was on the edge.

The moment hit Simon hard. He couldn't say what made him do it. Maybe the years of knowing William. Maybe his sister. Maybe it was just instinct—seeing that edge, that line, and refusing to let someone cross it.

Or maybe Simon just didn't want to lose one more person.

His arms tightened. Not just to keep William grounded—but to keep himself there, too. The world around him didn't matter. Not the broken shelves, not the cases, not the team watching him. It was just this. Just now. If he let go, he wasn't sure either of them would come back.

The gun slipped from William's hand.

It hit the floor with a dull thud, metal clattering across the tile.

Simon felt that instant of relief, of burden sliding off his chest. But it didn't last.

The gun went off.

The shot rang out like a hammer. A vicious, deafening crack through the space—and Simon's head whipped toward the direction of the blast.

Toward where Rosa may have gone back amid the commotion.

He couldn't breathe.

He didn't think.

His mind screamed her name, but his body moved before the thought could finish.

They ran. He and Kershaw surged toward the back, their steps pounding like war drums. Air rushed in and out of Simon's lungs in short, panicked bursts. His heart felt like it might tear through his ribs. That shot—it had been too close. Too uncontrolled.

Too close to her.

When they rounded the corner, the space was empty.

No Rosa.

Simon froze, chest heaving. His gaze swept the floor, then the walls, and finally locked onto a section of shelving. The dust had been disturbed. A clean outline where something used to sit. Something small. Something taken.

His pulse hadn't slowed.

It had to be her. Rosa had slipped out—quiet, fast. She'd grabbed whatever they'd come here for. And vanished.

But why?

Why would she leave them behind?

Simon's thoughts spiraled. Did she figure something out before they did? Had she seen something? Did she know where to go, what to do?

Had she gone rogue?

The possibilities clawed at his brain.

She wouldn't just run. That wasn't Rosa. She was steady. She was smart. But she was also rational—always thinking a step ahead. She had found something. She must have. That look in her eyes before William came in... it had been focused. Intentional.

Did she seriously go off on her own?

His jaw clenched.

She did.

And whatever she knew—whatever she'd found—he wasn't sure they'd catch up in time.

The building itself seemed to know something had shifted. And deep down, Simon knew it too.

Rosa had moved forward to the truth.

The rest of them would just have to catch up.

ROSA, OH, ROSA

SHE COULDN'T BREATHE. The sirens wailed, their deafening scream ripping the fabric of night as she tore through the neighborhood. Panic coursed through her veins and her hands trembled as they gripped the steering wheel, the world blurring around her.

In her frantic haste, she barely noticed the mailbox she crashed into, the metal groaning as it collided with her car. It toppled, the force of the impact sending it flying—destroying the memorial. Her mother's memorial. It felt like a sin in itself. Something she would regret, but not in that moment. In that moment, regret seemed like a luxury she couldn't afford.

She slammed the car into park in front of her childhood home, the place that had been so familiar yet so foreign right now. Her hands fumbled, but she grabbed then clutched the small stone figurine tightly, lifting it to her eyes. The intricate carvings, the fine details—they matched something she thought she'd seen before. But no. No, it couldn't be. She refused to accept it.

Not yet.

Her fingers wrapped around the doorknob, but she choked. She had to let go, gasping for air as her chest constricted painfully. She steadied herself, forcing her hands to stop shaking as she gathered the courage to open the door.

The familiar creak of the hinges echoed as she stepped inside, each sound amplifying the moment. Her pulse thudded in her ears as she rushed to the clock, the same one she remembered from her childhood.

Her eyes locked on the figurine again, her fingers trailing over the carved stone owl. The eyes—blood red and lifeless—stared back at her. They mirrored the eyes of the owl clock, the same haunting look she remembered so well. The exact replica.

It couldn't be. It just couldn't be.

Her heart hammered in her chest, louder than ever. She grabbed the owl clock in a frantic rush, inspecting it as though it might hold some kind of answer, some way to make this nightmare stop. But the longer she stared at it, the worse the panic choked her. The owl, the rodent it gripped in its talons, the rusted smell of the old family relic—every detail was too real.

The figurine in her hand, the clock—it was all connected.

Ragged gasps escaped her lips, her vision swimming. She stumbled into the living room, nearly collapsing into a chair as terror slashed deeper into her chest. The walls seemed to close in. *It can't be. It can't.*

Her vision blurred as she stared at the owls, identical in every way. No, they couldn't be. But they were. The twisted, haunting likeness of the one she had grown up with, the one that had never felt right, the one her father had insisted on keeping as a "family heirloom."

Her stomach churned violently, and she doubled over, fighting the bile rising in her throat. Her hands shook as memories she could never forget surged up, flashing through her.

"Hey, Rosa," her father's voice, warm and comforting. *"Rosa, can you paint some roses for Mama?"*

She saw it so clearly—the memory of five-year-old Rosa sitting on the floor with crayons scattered around her. Her favorite color had always been red.

She could smell the paint—sour, like old pennies and iron left too long in the sun.

"Look, Daddy!" she had called, giggling. "I love the gift you brought me. It smells funny, but I painted the roses just like you said."

"Looks fantastic, Rosa! You're so creative!"

Her father's proud voice rang in her ears, the memory warping into reality.

The roses. The roses she had painted for her mother, so innocent, so trusting.

But now?

Her stomach lurched again, and her legs buckled beneath her. She staggered to the kitchen, desperate for water to wash the taste of horror out of her mouth. Her body shook so violently she could hardly stand.

Her hand shot out to grab a glass, but her fingers were too shaky. The glass slipped from her grasp, crashing to the floor with a deafening shatter, the jagged edges sparkling like broken shards of her sanity.

And there it was—scrawled in familiar lettering, the handwriting that had been stalking her dreams recently: the riddle. On her childhood kitchen wall.

The words stared at her, a cruel mockery.

"In the heart of the prey lies the predator's truth.

To catch me, you must first see yourself,

Who am I?"

The room spun, the walls seeming to close in around her. She couldn't breathe, couldn't think. Her pulse hammered in her ears as the words of the riddle seared into her mind, the truth unfurling in front of her like an inevitable revelation. The truth that had been hiding in plain sight all along.

She understood now.

Her father's voice. The roses. The figurine. The clock. All connected. The thing she had feared most—now undeniable.

Her body went cold. A violent shudder ran through her as the understanding hit.

She screamed—a raw, guttural sound that tore through every inch of the home she once knew.

The owl clock screeched in the distance.

ABOUT THE AUTHOR

A lover of books, sweet tea, and all things crime—whether it's a gripping novel, a true crime documentary, or a suspenseful TV show—T.L. Hill was born and raised in South Carolina.

When not writing thrillers, you can find her solving fictional mysteries, cuddling with her three cat babies, connecting with fellow book lovers on social media, and teaching middle school kids, where her sarcastic and funny touch shines through.

With a passion for weaving intricate plots and exploring the dark corners of suspense, T.L. Hill is the author of The Motivated Antics Series. The first book, *Tangled Splinters*, is just the beginning of a journey filled with twists, turns, and gripping mysteries.

Note from the author: "I'd love to hear from you! Feel free to drop me a message on social media or leave a review if you enjoyed the book. Your feedback means the world to me as I continue to write stories that keep you on the edge of your seat."

Website: https://tlhillauthor.com
Goodreads: https://www.goodreads.com/user/show/190831896
Instagram: https://www.instagram.com/t.l.hillauthor/
TikTok: https://www.tiktok.com/@t.l.hillauthor

Printed in Dunstable, United Kingdom